Joseph Mac Anthony was born in Dublin, and made his name as a reporter for the *Sunday Independent* and Irish television, where he uncovered the great Irish sweepstake scandal, and wrote controversial pieces on the IRA. He was then lured to CBC's current affairs department in Toronto. He is the author of *The Blood God*, published by Grafton in 1987.

By the same author

The Blood God

JOSEPH MAC ANTHONY

The Setanta Operation

Grafton Books

A Division of HarperCollins*Publishers*

GraftonBooks
A Division of HarperCollins*Publishers*
77–85 Fulham Palace Road,
Hammersmith, London W6 8JB

A Grafton Paperback Original 1991
9 8 7 6 5 4 3 2 1

ISBN 0-586-21037-7

Printed and bound in Great Britain by
Collins, Glasgow

Set in Times

Prologue

It was worst when it happened to a child.

Sean Colgan was only twelve when he rode the rumbling skateboard down Malt Street that grey Wednesday afternoon. The cul-de-sac, long abandoned, belonged to an era when the town of Glenvoy boasted a distillery. Now its granite warehouses were deserted, with doors chained and the windows crossed by timber. The street's tarmac, neglected for decades, was cracked and crumbling. There were even weeds sprouting in the gutters.

Young Colgan, still wearing his school satchel, swayed with practised ease as he guided the skateboard down the sloped street towards the entrance. His slender arms moved with an unconscious grace that an adult might envy but could never hope to emulate. In some ways, his progress was almost magical to watch.

Even Robbie Driscoll, kneeling at a boarded window with the crossed hairs of his telescopic sight zeroed on the boy's head, felt a twinge, remembering his own childhood. But he stayed intent, his grip tight on the slender barrel of the Armalite, a cool hazel eye following the boy's progress.

As he watched, young Colgan reached the end of Malt Street and slid into an elegant arc which took him on to the edge of Deegan Square. The rifle followed.

There were many people on Deegan. Women pushing prams or stopping to talk, older men resting on window sills, children skipping along the pavements, glad to be free of classes. A typical small-town scene. Except for the occasional blur of green camouflage flitting through the crowd.

Soldiers.

They were big bony men with black daubed faces and red berets displaying the winged badges of the British Army's Parachute Regiment. They held their rifles high across their chests as they advanced. Seasoned and well-trained, they moved back to back, covering each other, occasionally dropping to a knee as they sheltered in a doorway. Around them, bizarrely, the civilian population carried on as if they did not exist. The soldiers, absorbed in their exercise, continued their advance. They were moving towards Malt Street.

As Sean Colgan swept through his arc, the leading paratrooper rose from his crouch in a nearby doorway and trotted with weapon raised towards the Malt Street corner. The boy reached it ahead of him. Skilfully he leaped the kerb. Reaching a hand out, he drew a crude chalk line along the wall as he skated back up the street.

From high up at the other end of the cul-de-sac the telescopic sight of Robbie Driscoll followed the wavering white line, then halted. For a moment, the rifle sight seemed to float. Then slowly it began retracing its path along the chalk line to the corner.

With a click, the safety catch came off.

The thick walled storeroom where Driscoll knelt was still. He swallowed to moisten his throat and tightened his wrist against the rifle strap. It squeaked drily against the surgical glove he was wearing. His breathing dropped and his body became still. The sight remained balanced on the end of the chalk line.

Slowly, the dark rim of a beret appeared. Then an epaulette came into view. Robbie Driscoll saw the faded stitchmarks and knew he had an officer. Patiently, he waited. A trim sideburn emerged, followed by a ruddy cheek. Moments later, he was looking into a round young face with two clear brown eyes.

Cool and deliberate, Driscoll squeezed the trigger.

The paratrooper took it head on. The force of the bullet threw his body backwards on to the street. Robbie Driscoll watched without stirring, the smell of cordite filling his nose.

'Good shot.' The whispered voice came from across the warehouse to his left. Driscoll didn't answer. He was watching the corner for the rest of the patrol.

On Deegan Street, there was pandemonium. Women screamed, children scattered in fear. A flight of startled pigeons rose from a roof-top in a flurry of wings. On the ground, the remaining soldiers froze, stunned at the sight of their commander draped across the pavement. The first man to recover was the squad sergeant, an older man with sunken cheeks. Waving the rest of the patrol into cover, he crouched by the radio man and called back to the police compound where his unit was stationed on the outskirts of town.

'We have a casualty,' he said tightly when they made contact. 'Lieutenant Seymour. Can't approach but it looks bad from here. Shot came from the warehouse area off Deegan.' He shifted to the other knee. 'Yes, fucking Malt Street.' He eyed the entrance to the cul-de-sac. 'We need a pig. On the double. Do you read?'

Robbie Driscoll had taken his eye away from the rifle sight to keep the street under observation. He was not expecting a gun battle before the armoured car arrived. That was their pattern.

'Robbie.'

Driscoll glanced quickly across at Shay Brennan, who was crouched by the window, a radio transmitter in his hand.

'The bastard's still alive.'

Instantly, Driscoll moved his eye back into the sight. The green camouflage uniform came into vision. Carefully, he moved the crossed hairs up the chest of the para to the bloody face. It was hard to tell where the bullet had struck. Or, if indeed, he was alive.

'See that?' Shay Brennan said. 'He's trying to get to his rifle.'

Slowly Driscoll moved the sight along the lieutenant's arm to his hand. It lay outstretched, inches from the fallen rifle. Now, as he watched, the fingers stretched, the nails scraping the tarmac.

'There. See it?'

Silently, Driscoll moved the telescopic sight back along the paratrooper's body to his wounded head. Then, very expertly, he put another bullet into the fallen lieutenant.

The corrugated metal gates swung open on Forkhill Road and an ugly snouted armoured personnel carrier came crashing out, the machine gun turret revolving menacingly. The driver turned east on Forkhill and headed for the town centre. People on the pavement watched with fear and hatred. Glenvoy was a fiercely Irish Republican town which Britain retained when Ireland was divided in 1922.

Inside the armoured car, the radio crackled as the trooper driver adjusted his headset. The cramped interior smelled of oil. He was used to that. But the smell of action was something else. He felt the familiar sinking sensation that came with every call to action. He hated it, along with the reassurances that he would soon get used to it. He didn't get used to it and he was fed up with people who said he would. He wanted out, but his mother was not having much luck in getting that message across on the other side of the water.

He drove quickly down Forkhill Road and turned on to Deegan Street. The carrier clipped the kerb as he did so. He wasn't very good at that either.

'Keep your eye on the ball, Thomas!' the corporal snapped from the turret. The driver peered through the metal slit. The street had an eerie look. People were scattered in doorways, watching. Up ahead, he could see the paras. One of them raised an arm to wave him forward. He could see the prone figure, alone on the ground.

'Oh, Christ,' he said and his voice was a little shaky.

Inside the warehouse, Robbie Driscoll had moved to another window nearer to Brennan, still facing down the closed street. Without taking his eyes off the scene around the body of the lieutenant, he said: 'I can hear it, Shay.'

'Which side?' Brennan was tuning the radio transmitter in his hand.

'Right.'

Brennan set the switch. 'All right, she's ready.'

They both turned back to the windows. A minute passed. Suddenly, they saw the snout of the personnel carrier edging out from the corner beyond the dead soldier. The two men crouched lower. The full bulk appeared, its turreted machine gun turning slowly to face into Malt Street. The vehicle circled the body. The move was awkward, the gears clashing.

'Come on, baby,' Brennan breathed.

9

The driver was trying to get in front of the dead officer to cover the retrieval party. But in doing so, he was coming in over the manhole cover where they had planted the ammonium nitrate sacks, all soaked with fuel oil and primed. Robbie Driscoll watched the front wheels pass over the cover.

'Now!' he snapped. 'Do it, Shay.'

Even as he said it, an unexpected movement in the street below caught his eye. He glanced down quickly. Christ. The Colgan boy was peering from a doorway. He was not supposed to be there. Driscoll opened his mouth to shout.

Too late.

In a dazzling flash of orange, a giant force exploded into Malt Street sending a hail of metal shards, crushed rock and glass flying downwards in a vast gush of smoke. The two men hit the floor as a flurry of debris whooshed through the window and smacked into the wall behind them.

As the roar died, Driscoll caught a glimpse of Shay Brennan opposite, grinning through the dust. 'Bull's-eye, boy,' he said.

'The Colgan kid.' Driscoll scissored quickly across the floor towards him. 'He was still down there.'

The other's smile faded. In the acrid dust, the two of them edged to the window's parapet and peered down into the smoke-filled street. Driscoll winced at the sight and drew back.

'Oh Christ!' Shay Brennan had seen it too.

After that, there was nothing to stay for. Driscoll hitched the rifle on to his shoulder and they hurried quickly from the storeroom. Passing down a dank corridor they entered a former office where a heavy timber plank, varnished and shining, lay on the floor. Raising it, they

10

pushed its end through the window, guiding it awkwardly across the twelve-foot-wide alley. A man waited in the window of the house opposite. He held it as they crawled across, one at a time, twenty feet above the ground. The plank dipped dangerously but they knew it would not break. Driscoll had tested it twice the night before. He never took chances on things like that.

Inside the bedroom of the house on the other side, they helped pull in the plank and close the window. As they hurried down the stairs, the man behind them was already sawing the plank to fit the shelving brackets affixed earlier to the wall. The piled books on the bed would go on the new shelves. The shavings would go into the fire now burning in the small grate. By the time the soldiers began their inevitable house to house search, there would be a woman in the bed with a certificate of illness from the local doctor. There were no civilians in Glenvoy.

At the front door downstairs, Driscoll edged his head out into the small street. The look-outs placed at either end waved him forward. He and Brennan sprinted across the street to the opened door of the house opposite. The man inside slapped their backs as they hurried through to the rear. No one spoke. Out at the back, they began vaulting the garden fences one by one, moving away from Malt Street.

Behind them, a pillar of smoke rose into the grey sky.

Across the street from the last garden, the look-out at the Texaco station signalled all clear. This was the dangerous part. They had eight minutes before the pursuit helicopter would be airborne. Eight minutes to reach the Irish Republic's border and sanctuary. It was less than a mile away.

They ran across the last street and entered a long, five-acre field. Keeping to its hedged side they went at it,

11

Driscoll unslinging the rifle as he ran. Half-way to the woodland at the other end they pulled up by the cache spot, concealed in a small copse. Driscoll knelt and drew back the loose sod to reveal a narrow hole. Quickly, they stripped off their boiler suits.

'You go ahead, Shay,' Driscoll said quickly, as he pulled out the plastic bag from beneath the sod. 'I'll follow later.' He wrapped the clothes around the rifle, then slid both into the bag.

Shay Brennan stared astonished at Driscoll as he took the transmitter. 'What?'

'I want to see the Colgans.' Driscoll stripped off the surgical gloves and pushed them in with the rest. 'Best we tell them what happened.'

Brennan stared down at him. 'You're crazy, Robbie. They'll nail you.'

'Don't worry about me.' Driscoll pushed the plastic bundle back into the hole. 'Now get going. And tell Clanaghan to contact Belfast. There's going to be hell to pay over this.' With the sod replaced, he smoothed it flat and rose. Brennan was surprised at his pallor and the gleam of sweat on his upper lip. In all their years together, he had never seen him like this.

'Robbie, are you all right?'

'Yes.' Driscoll pushed him forward. 'Go on, Shay, move.'

'But, listen . . .'

Driscoll gestured impatiently and wheeled away. Brennan stared after him as he ran back towards Glenvoy. Muttering a curse, he turned and ran the opposite way. Towards the border.

Chapter One

'I'm sorry, but we will have to search the house.' The captain was tall, with an acne-marked face and faintly mottled skin. He spoke softly and radiated reasonableness. But he carried a rifle by his side and there was no doubt that he and his men would use force if they had to.

'You will not enter my house,' the other man said hoarsely. 'I won't have my boy's last rest desecrated by your soldiers.'

They stood before the throng of people who filled the garden of the Colgan house to overflowing. The hostility in the glowering, country-bred faces was naked and palpable. The helmeted paratroopers, marshalled under the dripping trees opposite the house, stared woodenly at the spectacle, their rifles at port, their eyes like stones.

Overhead, a lone helicopter clattered in the grey sky.

The captain said coldly, 'Mr Colgan, I don't wish to add to your family's grief. But I have my orders. We will carry out this search.'

Colgan glared, defiant in his misery. He was a stocky man, dressed in a crumpled dark suit with a white shirt and a loosened black tie. His eyes had a reddish tinge and his rough skin was creased from sleeplessness and pain.

'Damn you,' he said.

The radio on the captain's shoulder crackled. He reached up to switch it off.

'Excuse me.'

He walked back to where his company sergeant stood.

They both surveyed the crowd as he turned the radio on again.

'Philip?' It was the CO, Colonel Darnley. 'What's the situation now?'

'We have sixty to seventy people around the house, sir. The father is being difficult about entry. I'm afraid we must anticipate some trouble. All the local louts are in attendance.'

'Including our Mr Reynolds?'

Reynolds held the inflated but difficult-to-prove title of local IRA battalion commander..

'Yes sir, he's here.' The captain's eyes rested on the long-haired young man in parka and jeans who stood inside the garden with three teenagers, all similarly dressed. 'Along with his senior staff, by the looks of it.'

'We must avoid a riot, Philip.'

The captain looked at his soldiers. They seemed in good order, but he knew how they were feeling.

'We may expect a few bruised heads, sir.'

'Well, just make sure they're the right ones, there's a good chap,' the colonel said. 'Let's not provide fodder for the media people.'

'Right oh, sir.'

He signed off.

'Sir.' His sergeant touched his arm and nodded towards the IRA commander, Reynolds. As the captain stared, the young man tossed his long hair like a bloody rock singer. He was grinning brazenly at them. The bugger had something up his sleeve.

The captain heard what it was before he saw it.

A chorus of tinny voices raised in a shrill rendition of the hymn, 'Faith of Our Fathers'. As he watched, close to a hundred young school children entered the street, shepherded by two teachers. All dressed in their Sunday best, with little black mourning bands on their arms.

'Jesus,' the sergeant said.

The children, some smiling and others timorous, passed the towering camouflaged soldiers and joined the now clapping crowd. In some confusion but acting on what was obviously a pre-arranged plan they joined hands and began to form a frail cordon around the house.

His face set, the captain stared icily at the grinning IRA commander. Suddenly, Reynolds offered proof that he was not entirely unsophisticated. Just like an average man in the street, he raised a right hand and gave the captain two fingers.

The bastard.

'Hello there!'

The bereaved man, Colgan, stood in the centre of the road again. The captain crossed over to him.

'Yes, Mr Colgan?'

'I have a hearse coming. I'm taking my boy across the border to rest in Rathfaire.' He seemed close to tears. 'It will take an hour to move him. Will you leave us in peace for that time?'

Staring at the distraught man, the captain began to feel the weight of this work. The helicopter had ferried in three coffins that morning for the men killed by yesterday's bombing. Tonight, with his fellow officers, he would have to attend a depressing service in the gym before they were airlifted home.

And now, here on the street, his tired men faced a cordon of children they would almost certainly have to break through to get into the house. The thought of how that would look on television made him shudder.

'Very well, Mr Colgan,' he said finally. 'You have an hour.'

Back with the sergeant, he said. 'Keep that house under observation. Make sure nobody unauthorized moves in or out.' He gazed at the curtained window. 'I have a feeling something is going on in there. Mr Reynolds is not honouring us with his presence for nothing.'

Robbie Driscoll could hear the children singing from inside his walled-off hiding-place on the second floor of the house. He thought the lyrics sounded religious but he couldn't be sure. Still, the voices told him Glenvoy was rallying.

The dank compartment he lay in was barely two feet wide and less than six feet long. By half raising a hand he could touch the ceiling. There was no light and the sleeping bag felt like a shroud. It was as if he were in a coffin. But even that was preferable to sitting outside with the bereaved family.

He had tried to leave immediately after breaking the news to them, but the Brits proved too quick. Immediately after the explosion they had thrown a tight cordon around the village, trapping him inside. He was forced to spend the night with the distraught Colgans, sitting in their little-used parlour, listening in awkward and halting silence as armoured cars and squads of paratroops crisscrossed the damp streets in angry packs.

By morning, when they arrived to search the house, he was relieved to move into this hiding place. Although the shattered family had absolved him of blame, he still could not dispel the guilt aroused by what had happened.

In his seven years with the movement, Robbie Driscoll had killed many times. While he never thought to keep score, those who did put the figure past twenty-three. Some of the victims, he knew, were innocent. In the movement's phrase, 'tragic victims of urban guerrilla

16

warfare'. Although Driscoll considered that description self-serving, he had always accepted the deaths as part of the hazards of war. Maybe, he thought now, because he was rarely around to witness the consequences.

Introspection like that was not common in the ranks of the movement. But then, this cool and slim twenty-seven-year-old, with his distinctive blond hair and hazel eyes, did not belong in the common mould.

Robert Alan Driscoll, born in a red-bricked mansion on Belfast's exclusive Malone Road and now trapped in a labourer's house in the bleak border village of Glenvoy, had always been a man apart.

The captain outside would have been astonished to learn that his quarry did not fit the normal subversive profile in Northern Ireland. Far from it. Robbie Driscoll belonged to a powerful Protestant family whose members had held high positions in Britain's military, its colonial service and its judiciary for generations.

'Serve and Do Right' was the family motto, chosen in the time of William of Orange. And serve Driscoll's ancestors certainly did. Sir Henry Driscoll figured briefly but prominently in the cabinet of Robert Peel. Two more rose to become generals in the Indian Army. Others served as important administrators in the colonial territories.

Those in the judicial branch of the family who stayed in Ireland worked equally hard at Doing Right, as their motto demanded. By way of showing it, they hanged far more rebels than they acquitted. As their loyalty and usefulness was recognized, bench appointments rained down. By the twentieth century, the durable Driscolls perched close to the pinnacle in Northern Ireland's tightly knit ruling caste.

Robbie Driscoll's father, like many of his forebears,

had been set to join the British army, when a rugby injury incurred while playing for Ulster curtailed his career. The damage itself might not have been so serious if Alan Driscoll had not insisted on playing the game out before receiving attention. As it was, he was forced to miss a world war, and joined the Northern Ireland civil service in consequence. His dour devotion to duty and his connections brought him rapid advancement. Still, it never quite removed the feeling that he had settled for second best.

Robbie Driscoll's mother, Doris Antonia Grey, was not as highly connected as her husband, but her family did have money from their interests in the linen industry, which was the next best thing.

Taking the distinguished background and his mother's wealth into account, Robbie Driscoll might have begun any number of promising careers in the class-bound society he was born into. Unfortunately, there was trouble at home.

Robbie was eight years old before he discovered it was not normal for husbands to beat their wives. Year by year, he had watched it happen at home. When he learned through a chance remark at school that it was wrong, he began to loathe his father.

The older Driscoll's capacity for publicly concealing his true nature was phenomenal. It was matched only by the determination of his wife, Doris, to keep it that way. She knew her gaunt, lonely husband was sick. But to bring it out into the open would shatter the façade of family respectability to which she had devoted her life. As her husband pursued his double life, she gradually developed hers to match. Between them, the conspiracy grew.

The real sufferers were the children.

Robbie Driscoll's hatred for his father had crystallized

in those early years. But he held it in check. His sisters – both of them older – might cry, but Robbie had steely control. It served him well until he was twelve years old. That was when his father attacked his mother one mellow September evening and sent her sprawling before Robbie in their living-room. The grossly undignified posture of the fallen woman, the years of pain, and all the madness that stalked the house were too much. Robbie hurled himself at Alan Driscoll with every ounce of fury that had been suppressed for so long in his small body.

Afterwards, it was clear he could no longer stay in the house. He was sent as a boarder to Ravenhead High School, one of Northern Ireland's most exclusive. Nestling in the rolling green hills of County Antrim, its peaceful academic setting was a world away from the ghettos where the war that made Northern Ireland infamous had already exploded into being.

At the school, the young Robbie began the most fruitful and satisfying years of his life. Rarely given to outward emotion, helpful to those who asked for aid and unafraid of those tempted to bully him, he gathered admiration from his peers and respect from his teachers. He quickly became a prefect. The only puzzle to his teachers was that he rarely went home.

At seventeen, he was on the school's honours list and next in line to become head boy. He had his own room, his marks were good, and whenever examples were sought to impress school visitors, Robbie Driscoll was always one of those brought to the fore. His future seemed assured. But as he approached the end of the school term that year, an event occurred which shattered all his progress.

A boy called Montgomery from a class below came to see him one night. He was terrified and fearful but

19

desperate. Robbie by then was widely respected and the only one the boy felt he could talk to. Now, he unfolded a story that was as incredible as it was horrifying.

A year before, he had gone on a school outing to Coleraine with his geography class. During the outing, the teacher in charge, whose name was Masterson, made an advance. The boy, lonely and a little infatuated at an approach from so august a figure, succumbed. Red-faced and stumbling, he told Robbie that an affair had begun.

Months later, as the liaison deepened, the teacher arranged that the boy take a weekend trip with him to Belfast. There, in the Grayson Hotel, the teacher introduced him to another man and persuaded him to have relations with him too.

From there, a deadly spiral began. Almost every weekend, the boy was brought to Belfast. He was introduced to other men. He quickly gathered that these were important people. Judges, political figures, successful business men. They gave him drinks, flattered him, sometimes offered gifts. Soon Masterson suggested there might be other boys interested. Bound by the teacher's spell, young Montgomery helped gather more into the net.

'How many?' Robbie asked.

'Three besides me,' the boy said.

But now Masterson and the people in Belfast were growing more demanding. The weekends were not enough. They wanted the boy to persuade his parents to take him out of Ravenhead and transfer him to a day school in Belfast where he would be more available. Suddenly the boy had become terrified of the mess he was in.

'You've got to help me,' he said desperately.

Quietly, Robbie offered reassurance and proposals to deal with the crisis. The boy was not to see the teacher again. He was not to go to Belfast either. Meanwhile he, Robbie, would take care of it.

The next morning, he saw the headmaster, Mr Millar. Sitting across the polished mahogany desk, he watched the head's face grow pale and his lips tighten at the news. He questioned Robbie closely. Finally, as Robbie had reassured the boy Montgomery, the headmaster now reassured him.

'I will deal with this severely,' he promised, his face hard. At the door, he held out his hand.

'You're an honourable boy, Robert. You took the right course in coming to me. Rest assured that I will do the right thing.'

Robbie returned to classes, also satisfied that he had done the right thing. Through the day, he kept an eye out for the Montgomery boy and the teacher Masterson, but saw neither. By evening, with no sign of young Montgomery in the dining hall, he went to his dormitory. He was surprised to find that the boy's bed had been stripped. Disturbed, Robbie discreetly began looking for Masterson. But he too was gone.

Robbie went to see the headmaster.

'Ah, Robert. I'm glad you came. I was about to send for you.'

'The boy Montgomery,' Robbie said. 'He's gone.'

'Yes.' Mr Millar nodded.

'Mr Masterson too.'

'And the other boys,' the headmaster said grimly. 'Don't forget the other boys.'

Robbie waited. 'What happens next?' he asked finally.

'I don't think you need concern yourself with that.' Mr Millar smiled reassuringly. 'It's all being taken care of.'

'Will you be calling in the police?' Robbie asked.

The headmaster was faintly reproving. 'Now, Robert. I

know you did your duty and I'm thankful you did. But you mustn't presume to tell me how to do mine.'

'I didn't intend to, sir. I'm sorry.'

'That's quite all right.' The headmaster smiled warmly as he rose. The interview was over. He led the way to the door where he stopped. 'I realize how shocking this must have been for you,' he said. 'Thankfully, the matter is now in hand. I can assure you, Robert, that I'm going to do what's best. Not only for the boys involved. For the school, too.'

By the term's end, Robbie realized that the headmaster's method of doing his best was to do nothing. The matter was being hushed up.

Within Robbie Driscoll's limited experience, it suddenly seemed that when respectability and wrong-doing collided inside Northern Ireland's privileged society, the desire for respectability always triumphed. The seething anger he had first felt at his father's betrayal, and which had begun to lessen under his schooling, resurfaced. And this time it was directed not only at his father, but at his father's peers as well.

Weeks passed in a nightmare of anger and depression. Forced to stay at home because of a delay in holiday arrangements for France, he took to walking the streets of Belfast. One day, by a chance that would become inevitable if you walked those streets long enough, he stumbled into the tail-end of an ambush near the city centre.

Robbie Driscoll was accustomed to the blanket security of soldiers and police on the streets of Northern Ireland. But like most upper-class Protestants and Catholics he saw little of the actual violence, which was largely confined to the ghettos. His interest in it had been desultory. Mostly he let it pass him by.

Now he met it face to face.

The shooting had ended as he entered King Street. As a cordon of policemen in flak jackets held back the gathering spectators, he saw soldiers crowding into a narrow doorway alongside a shop. It was barely twenty yards away.

'What's happening?' somebody asked.

'Sniper,' a policeman said. 'They just nailed him.'

As Robbie watched, there was a bustle of activity in the doorway. Soldiers backed out and suddenly an escort appeared dragging a greasy haired, shabbily dressed youth. Behind him, a soldier held up an ancient rifle. On the far side of the road, two men clapped.

The youth, thin and scrawny and hardly out of his teens, stood hand-cuffed and sullen among the twenty or so burly soldiers and police. But then, as they crowded around him, he suddenly launched into a fury of resistance. To the watching Robbie, his actions seemed both hopeless and ridiculous. Yet he would not stop. The thin legs flailed and his head butted against the men closest to him. The press of the soldiers forced him to the ground. Finally, a senior police officer carrying a cane and with gold braid on his cap came forward. The youth, still struggling, was raised to his feet. His scratched face grey and his chest heaving, he was held as the policeman spoke to him.

Without warning, the youth tried to kick the officer between the legs. The policeman quickly struck with the cane. As the youth squirmed and still tried to kick, the officer whacked continuously at his thighs.

'You bastards, leave the wee boy alone!' a worn woman shouted from the path. A policeman moved down quickly and pushed her back. The officer finally stopped and resettled his cap on his head. The youth tried to spit.

Glaring, the officer raised his cane again but the soldiers began to drag the youth away.

'Bastards!' the youth screamed, unbowed. 'Long live the IRA!'

Robbie Driscoll stood transfixed. Scarcely aware of what he was doing, he raised a clenched fist to salute the defiance. The policeman in the cordon opposite frowned. Glancing down, he saw the Ravenhead crest on Robbie's blazer. Lifting his head, he smiled and winked.

That incident led Robbie Driscoll into a pilgrimage through Northern Ireland's gory history. The arguments and ideology he picked up did no more than harden the deep anger which already seethed in him. Barely a month after beginning his study, he turned up at the political office the IRA maintained seeking membership.

The shabby man stationed in the office stared in astonishment at this slim, elegant blond boy with the determined hazel eyes and fine clothing. He seemed like an apparition in the seedy office.

'I hope you know what you're bloody well doing,' he muttered.

Robbie Driscoll thought he did. That day, as he left the office, he believed he had exchanged his personal nightmare for a greater dream.

Now, seven years later, it looked like that once bright dream was returning to nightmare again.

As soon as the hearse arrived at the house, they released him from the tiny compartment. He emerged into the bedroom, half-blinded, finding it difficult to stand. Outside, the children were still singing. He was helped to a chair. Moments later, the door opened, and a young man in a black suit and cap entered. He stood nervously, staring at Robbie across the room.

'Come on, we haven't got all day,' the man beside Robbie snapped. 'Get to it.'

A short time later, Driscoll emerged from the bedroom. He was recovered now and neatly dressed in the black uniform and cap. As he paused on the stairs, about to descend, he heard the door across the landing creak open. His hand on the banister, he turned.

The boy's mother stood framed in the doorway. Her thin brown hair was askew around the white face. They stared at each other, not speaking. Suddenly the woman rushed forward. Robbie caught her as her arms went round him. They clung swaying on the stairs. Unable to speak, he felt acute embarrassment as her hot tears trickled down his neck.

The street was noisy with the sound of engines as cars lined up behind the hearse. The captain looked at his watch. Thirty minutes had gone by. He rather hoped the colonel would not call. He had a habit of interfering when he got too close to an operation.

The door of the house opened. He saw the milling people begin to move back. Awkwardly, funeral people and the pall-bearers began emerging. The captain counted. No more than went in earlier. As the black-suited attendants hurried to open the hearse doors, he turned his attention to the flag draped coffin and watched carefully. The scoundrels had been known to slip arms or even cram an embarrassing second body in the coffin on occasion. But the ease with which the bearers carried their burden satisfied him.

'Pass the word that they're on their way,' he said, as the attendants climbed into the hearse. It began moving out, the convoy of cars following. The captain was glad they were wasting no time. It would help defuse the situation. Already he could see people filtering away. With the border only five minutes away, they would soon be out of his territory.

'Philip?' It was Colonel Darnley on the radio. 'We've passed the news downwind. Ready to move in now, are you?'

The captain hesitated. 'I did give them an hour, sir.'

'I see.'

The captain frowned. 'There are still a good number of children in the vicinity, sir.'

There was a pause. 'Any television chaps hanging around?'

'No, sir.'

'Well, I think you should move in now,' the colonel said. 'Be gentle with the children, if you can. But I want to know what's inside that house.'

'Yes, sir.'

He gave the order and the paratroopers moved in with rifles high. There was some heaving and pushing but it was disorganized and half-hearted. The known trouble-makers had already melted away with the cortège. There was a brief hold up at the locked front door when no one answered their knock. Finally, to scattered shouts of protest from the bystanders, they forced it open.

Shortly after, a call from the party searching the bed-rooms brought the captain hurrying up the stairs. A glance at the young man sitting on the bed in singlet and shorts and at the abandoned compartment behind the closet told it all.

The colonel, knowing the circuit was open, proved decent about it.

'Not to worry.' His reassuring voice crackled over the line. 'We'll pass the word to the Garda at the border. Maybe they can nail the bugger. And Philip? Drop in to see me when you get back, will you? We must have a little talk.'

The captain, as he signed off, felt obliged now to recognize the colonel's repeated warning that in Ireland, a gentleman's agreement was not always possible.

The Garda sergeant on the Irish Republic side of the border glanced at his three men as the hearse approached the concrete barriers.

'No saluting, mind,' he said. 'We don't want to find ourselves on the front page of the *Daily Telegraph*.'

Robbie Driscoll, sitting at the front of the hearse in his black uniform and cap, finaly relaxed as they passed the boundary markers and entered the Republic. This strip of border country was familiar territory. It was almost seven years since he had done his first training here.

In those early days they were cautious and gave him a special handler. A man named Martin Harmon, a retiree with long experience. Within two weeks, to settle the issue of whether Driscoll's conversion was real or feigned, Harmon threw him in the deep end. With only a minimum of preparation, he sent him out to murder a judge. For Robbie Driscoll, he could not have made a better choice. In the historical sense, it was as if the Driscoll line had come full circle, with a scion of judges now killing them off.

The murder itself proved an ugly business. The judge, a man named Wickham who was marked for death because he was a Catholic, was trapped with his children by the door of the church as he left Mass. To save them, he gave up whatever chance he had of escaping. Almost by collusion, he and Robbie paused until the heavy black

27

door slammed safely shut on them. Then Robbie shot him in the face. The judge toppled down the hallowed steps and died almost immediately.

The killing provoked a fierce backlash against the movement. But it made Robbie Driscoll's reputation with the small group who ran it. As for the ugly sight of a man expiring at his hand, that was a shock; but Driscoll quickly recovered. Like his ancestors, he had discovered a justification for excess. Robert Alan Driscoll was a soldier now. And determined to be as hard and effective as any of his ancestors.

At his handler's insistence, he was kept separate from the normal chain of command. Under the older man's schooling, he began to accumulate skills. But Harmon was under no illusion about what he had.

'You're no patriot, Robbie,' he said once. 'You don't love Ireland or even this part of it. You just hate the bloody people who run it.'

Robbie Driscoll only smiled and went on learning Gaelic and studying Irish history as Harmon insisted. The movement might have his loyalty. His motivation would remain his own.

This Monaghan country and the little church in Rathfaire which the funeral was approaching had been part of the territory ceded by the British in 1921. But now there was war here too.

At the outset, the political leaders in the Irish Republic had watched the battle in Northern Ireland develop with quiet satisfaction. Soon, they believed, the British would tire of defending a Protestant élite they despised and would surrender the rump of the nation to its rightful landlords – themselves. But that dream quickly soured. This sleepy nation where only one policeman had died violently in the twenty-five years up to 1969, awoke to grim reality as the bacillus spread south. With their police and soldiers being cut down, and armed men kidnapping the wealthy and looting banks, the South's leaders reluctantly ordered their forces into the battle against the new subversion.

In the forefront of the fight was the Republic's Special Branch. The heavy gang. Iron-fisted, hulking plain-clothes men who favoured the Uzi submachine-gun and, on less tense occasions, a quick boot in the arse when dealing with subversives. Unlike the British in the North, they were blood brothers to their enemies. Which made them the most effective opposition the IRA faced. Within five years the Republic's prisons were bulging at the seams, two-thirds of the prisoners subversives from Northern Ireland. The Branch men were doing their work well.

Three of them now sat crammed into a small Ford, watching as the cortège arrived at the small churchyard in Rathfaire.

The radio came alive.

'You lads awake?' It was the cranky voice of the inspector, Donellan. The driver reached for the mike.

'Yes, Inspector. Grealish here. The hearse has just arrived.'

The tinny voice filled the car.

'We just got word from the Brits. One of the attendants is a suspect in last night's bombing. What's the chance of grabbing him?'

Grealish glanced out the window at the mass of people spilling from the cars. He swallowed.

'There's a fair crowd gathering, sir.'

'Can you keep them under observation then? I'll gather some uniforms and get down there as quick as I can.'

'We'll try, Inspector.'

'Peelers.'

Robbie Driscoll was standing behind the hearse with the long-haired Reynolds who had brought him into Glenvoy for the operation. They watched the three big men leave the car and cautiously approach the thick stone wall surrounding the church.

'Jesus,' Reynolds said. 'You would think they'd respect a funeral.'

Robbie glanced back to the rough land on the other side of the church.

'Can you make a diversion?'

Reynolds nodded. 'We should get you out of those clothes first. Hey, Mockler!' he called. A young man hurried over. 'We need your cap and coat.'

As the two changed, he waved in a group standing nearby.

'There's a little road on the other side of the hill,' he said quickly to Robbie. 'Wait by it and I'll get a car to pick you up.'

He turned to the gathered men.

'Get some rocks, lads, and keep those bastards busy.' He gestured to the Branch men who were moving along the wall fifty yards away.

The first stone narrowly missed the leading man, Grealish. He hissed angrily. All three began edging along the wall as missiles fell around them.

'Bastards! Turncoats!' Some broke from the crowd to throw their rocks.

'Jim.' One of the detectives pointed as Robbie darted

around the side of the church and headed for the broken hills.

'Come on.' Grealish rose and, with the others following, ran to skirt the churchyard and keep him in sight. But the crowd moved between them, keeping them back. Not even the priest who emerged from the church with his hands raised in supplication, made a difference.

The stones rained down on the detectives. One struck Grealish on the side of the head. He swayed, briefly dazed. With a roar of triumph, the crowd closed.

'To hell with this,' one of the detectives growled. Tearing open his jacket, he pulled the Uzi off its strap. Extending it with both hands, he advanced towards the mob and fired a burst in the air.

Robbie Driscoll, breasting the top of the brush-strewn hill, turned at the crackle of gunfire. He saw part of the crowd scattering, but others, wildly daring, continued to hurl stones. Suddenly, it was like a film seen too many times. The stab of emotion aroused at the sight of wildly daring resistance petering out with the realization that they had nothing else to fight with. In the first Belfast ambush he had seen, the weapon had been an ancient musket. The bomb he and Shay Brennan used was made from fuel oil and fertilizer. And now here it was again. Stones against machine-guns. He felt a familiar surge of anger.

He thought of that boy now lying in the church, killed by Shay Brennan and himself. If they had proper weapons he would still be alive. A bitter rage filled him. It could not go on like this. Something had to be done.

He turned and ran from the scene.

* * *

As with all wars, the men manning the front line were the last to know. In this case, something was being done to alter the state of play. But it was so sensitive, so fraught with consequences that very few people knew about it.

One was a select group within the movement. The other was their most knowledgeable and dangerous enemy.

The meeting was in Farradan House, an old Georgian mansion hidden deep in a state forest twenty miles from Dublin. Before 1922, it had been a private hunting lodge. After independence, the newly established Public Works Board used it as a conference centre. Now it was a safe house for the Special Branch.

The group, gathered in the spacious drawing-room watched in silence as the deputy director of C3 entered. He was a tall man in his late fifties with a pale, hawkish face and grey waved hair. The worn tweeds and the *Irish Times* under his arm gave him an academic, gentlemanly appearance. The contrast with the rough collection of undercover men assembled for the meeting was striking. But then, that was not the only contrast DDC3 provided for his colleagues.

He was the anomaly in the Irish police force. Fifteenth in line from the top, he had never held an operational command in over three decades of service. A Chief Superintendent, he chose to live in a gatekeeper's lodge inside the Police Headquarters compound in Dublin's Phoenix Park, surrounded by books and a useful collection of antiques. Mostly though, his study was filled with phone transcripts, surveillance files and situation reports that kept track of daily activities in the IRA.

With quiet self-deprecating humour, DDC3 called

himself a paper tiger. He was, in fact, the Force's leading expert on the IRA.

He stood now at the lectern, his pale eyes sweeping the room. It would have taken a trained auctioneer to see that he was not only looking at the people present, but even taking a little time to value the period furniture on which they sat. Finally he smiled softly.

'Morning, lads.'

'Morning, sir.'

'Smoke if you like,' he said. Magically, the half concealed cigarettes appeared. One rural even produced a pipe. The deputy director sighed and waited until they had their nourishment. Finally he raised a hand apologetically. 'To business,' he said.

They waited quietly.

'First of all, I want to deal with your protests at being summoned here,' he said. 'No one knows better than I do the hazards involved in a gathering like this. Unfortunately, we had no alternative.' He paused. 'The fact is, we believe something very serious is in the wind.'

That got their attention.

'As you will have seen from what happened in Glenvoy, our friends have fired another one into their own net. Which makes it the fourth time in less than two months that they've achieved this feat. In the ordinary course of events, a record like that would be a cause for rejoicing. Not, however, in guerrilla warfare. The guerrilla's most effective weapon, historically, has always been the counter punch.

'While we have examples of this from our own War of Independence earlier in the century,' he said, 'the most striking illustration of the guerrilla counter punch has to be the Tet offensive which occurred during the Vietnam War back in 1968.

'As you may recall, Washington believed then that the Vietcong had been beaten. The offensive caught them completely by surprise. The Americans did recover, of course, and even went on to defeat the Communists militarily. But their morale had been fatally impaired by what had happened. As events were to prove, they had won a battle but politically the Tet offensive cost them the war.'

The deputy director paused now, taking his time.

'We have known for some time that the IRA want to carry out a Tet offensive in Northern Ireland,' he said. 'We even know the likely targets. The Anglo-Irish directorate at Maryfield, the British Army headquarters at Lisburn and possibly the big helicopter base at Holyrood. The constraint to date has been their lack of suitable weapons.'

He stopped, then spoke quietly.

'I am afraid we have just received word that the IRA is now in negotiation for the very weapons needed for this operation. And they may be having some success.'

There was a murmur of dismay in the room. The deputy director raised a hand for silence.

'Immediately we learned of this, the Commissioner and I met with the Taoiseach and the Minister for Justice. Like you, they were shocked by the news and its implications.

'It is the Taoiseach's view that the IRA must be prevented from achieving the capability to carry out any such offensive. He made it clear that any attempt to impair the British will to remain in the North until a political solution has been arrived at, would be a serious blow to our aims in the Republic. Therefore they must be stopped. It was for that reason, and on his instructions, that you were summoned here.

'He is fully aware of the dangers you already face working under cover among subversives. But he believes the consequences would be so grave should the IRA succeed in this endeavour, that we must take any risk necessary to uncover this operation and prevent those arms from reaching Northern Ireland.'

He stopped to let that sink in. In the back of the room, a tall, black-haired young man slowly raised a hand.

'Yes?'

The young man rose.

'Fair dues to the Taoiseach and the rest of you,' he said coolly. 'But can you tell us where these weapons might be coming from?'

The deputy director smiled at the effrontery.

'We believe from the United States.'

'And what sort of weapons are we talking about?'

'Missiles,' said the deputy director. 'Of the very latest type.'

Chapter Two

The ball-room had seen better days.

Years of smoke-filled dances had turned the interior a faded brown and there were dark trailings around the walls where countless bodies had lounged. Some of the wall lights were out of action and the murky ceiling had ugly patches where the plaster had come loose. Even the crystal ball, revolving slowly above the sparsely filled dance floor, was missing some of its glass squares and glittered oddly as it turned.

Tonight, there were no more than sixty couples in the hall. Almost all were middle-aged and most sat on cheap plastic chairs around the floor. The few who were dancing were taking the exercise very seriously. Except, that is, for two younger olive-skinned men in baggy trousers and wide-shouldered jackets who were gyrating to their own private music in the centre of the floor. It had to be private music. Not in their wildest dreams would they have danced to what the accordion band was playing, which was 'Danny Boy'.

Dinny Doherty paused to watch them. He was carrying two Budweisers and stood now at the table by the entrance. Seeing the irritation provoked in the other patrons who had to manoeuvre around the two, he turned to Michael Monahan who sat with beefy forearms resting on the green baize.

'Those guys look like trouble, Mike.'

Monahan shrugged and took the offered beer without speaking.

Doherty sat down opposite.

'Why'd you let them in, anyway?'

Monahan said, 'You know another way to make money?'

Doherty shrugged.

'Didn't think we were that desperate.'

Monahan scowled. Although not inclined to admit it, he knew Doherty was right. One glance was enough to confirm what he had chosen to ignore earlier. The pair didn't belong in the Roseland. Despite the fancy dress, their faces had that cruel insolent look you saw on the characters who roamed Eighty-seventh Street – when they weren't off stealing someplace else.

Doherty glanced at his watch.

'Your man is late,' he said.

'There's time.'

Doherty gestured with his bottle.

'That pair could raise a shindy and upset things.'

Monahan looked at him. 'You'd like that, wouldn't you?'

'Come on, Mike. I thought that was settled.'

Monahan was silent.

'So what if I have doubts?' Doherty said. 'That doesn't mean I want to use a wrecking ball.'

But Monahan had turned now to watching the Hispanics. The two were giggling, laughing at the patrons' stiff-legged dancing. As Monahan stared, the smaller one raised his pug nose to sniff at the mildewed air. No doubt about it, Monahan thought. They were either on crack or sniffing on a close relative.

Shit.

The problem was they needed paying customers. Tonight, with so few attending, they would be lucky to clear $300 on the night. Things were tumbling from bad to worse. Over the years in which he had held these fund-raisers at the Roseland, Monahan had seen attendances plummet from a high of a thousand per dance to the present dregs. Bad publicity had done them in. Too many bombs with gory pictures on the nightly news. People were too finicky, Monahan thought. They could not seem to understand that it was hard to kill clean in a guerrilla war.

Doherty said: 'Watch out. They're into the beer now.'

The pair had moved to the little bar run by the building super. Monahan saw them wave off glasses and take the bottles by the neck. That was another bad sign.

Depressed as he was by the falling attendances, Monahan still didn't want to pull the plug. Although he hated to lose money, that was not the main reason. There were other, fatter, sources. It was the need for contact with the like-minded that made him hang in. When you were thousands of miles from the mainstream, it meant something.

Michael Monahan, now close to fifty, had given over twenty years to the movement. His career, which looked to the unknowing as if it might be ending here in a whimper, had started with a bang back in the seventies when he smuggled six Armalites into Belfast in the trunk of a children's dance group headed by his twelve-year-old daughter, Nan. That little coup was his own idea and his first material contribution to the cause. It was very nearly his last. The leadership, sensitive political beings, had apoplexy at the thought of how America would react to its children being used as gun runners. Their first thought was to dump him. But when he didn't get caught, they relented. Monahan was promoted to charge of drudgery. New York's Mr Flop.

That might have been it. But Monahan turned out to

be one of those work-horses endemic in revolutionary movements, the kind who hang on after the stars depart. As attrition, ambition and the FBI carried off the more gifted, Monahan started on a steady re-ascent. In the fourteen years following his first stunt, he had climbed successfully. Now he was in charge of all funds and activities in the tristate area.

His responsibilities, satisfying as they were, still had drawbacks. Those people in Belfast who aggravated him at the very beginning – they could not see then that the Brits wouldn't dare charge American children with arms smuggling – still irritated him today. But he had learned his lesson over time. He kept his mouth shut now. He knew it only needed one big score and they would fawn instead of fume.

And tonight he was working on it.

His fear now was, as Doherty had said, that this pair might spoil it. As Monahan watched, they had begun moving down towards the stage. Half-way there, the smaller one suddenly halted and pointed a bottle at the crude frieze above the band. 'Irish Prisoners Aid Benefit', it said. He made some joke and both laughed.

Monahan had put a lot of work into that sign. His hard fist tightened now around his glass.

But they were on the move again. They reached the stage where the musicians – green-shirted volunteers on accordion, fiddle, and drums – were watching uneasily. Stopping alongside, the two stared up at the leader, a thin forty-year-old who was bravely manhandling his large accordion.

Nodding approvingly, they rested against the stage.

'Give us "La Bamba", man,' the big one called. It was loud enough for Monahan to hear.

The leader shook his head wordlessly and continued playing.

'Hey! I'm making a request!'

The big one suddenly banged his bottle on the ledge. As the beer foamed over, his partner swayed back and began shimmying as if the request was already playing.

Slowly Monahan lowered his glass.

'Easy now, Mike,' Dinny Doherty said.

The Hispanics were shouting now, enjoying the disturbance they were creating. Monahan got up. Although he was only five eight, he was thick and beefy in a bartender-ish way and even formidable. He paused to glance down at Doherty now, his heavy face stern.

'You stay out of this, Dinny, you hear?' he said. Doherty had some kind of heart problem. Monahan didn't want to see his friend keel over, because of a stupid ball-room bust up.

'Just be careful, Mike.' Doherty looked pale as if his illness was kicking in on cue.

Hitching the worn trousers over his rounded stomach, Monahan walked slow and unhurried towards the stage. After twenty-seven years with the Laborers and Allied Trades of America, he was not greatly bothered by the prospect of facing two miserable dope-filled Latins.

They were engrossed in bad-mouthing the band when he arrived.

'Excuse me, fellas.' He stopped a few feet away.

The two turned. Nasty, pock-marked faces.

'You're disturbing the band,' Monahan said. 'I'll have to ask you to leave.' He smiled, amiable, but keeping on his toes.

The bigger of the two, his long dark hair smoothed back, looked at him and smiled back. But his eyes had a vacant look that spelled unpredictability.

'Hey, man, all I asked for was a song.' He gazed at Monahan. 'Anything wrong with that?'

'No,' Monahan said. 'But, truth is, you guys don't belong here. This is a private benefit for these people.' He waved a hand towards the dancers. 'You want your money back, that's OK. But I got to ask you to leave.'

The big one didn't change expression.

He said: 'Fuck off, fatso.'

Monahan stiffened. Above them, the music faltered.

'You guys here to make trouble or what?' he asked softly.

The big one nudged his partner.

'Hear that, Paco? He thinks we want to fight.' He grinned at Monahan. 'Is that it, old guy? Want to rumble, eh?'

'Watch your mouth.'

Behind them, the dancers shuffled to a stop. Some men began to move forward.

'You going to put us out?' the big one demanded loudly.

'I'm asking you to leave,' Monahan said. 'But if you refuse, sure, I'll put you out.'

The big one shook his head in wonder.

'Guy your age.' He pointed at Monahan's stomach. 'Big pot, too. Man, you must be crazy.'

Monahan's eyes glinted. He was sensitive about his girth.

'Cut the smart ass talk,' he said. 'OK?'

The big one glanced at the crowding dancers, then back at Monahan. Suddenly his smile grew more expansive. His teeth showed like in a commercial.

'All right, man. You take it easy. We just joking.' He turned. 'Right, Paco?'

The smaller one looked at him, then he smiled at Monahan too.

'Sure,' he said. 'Listen, you give us our money?'

Monahan nodded shortly.

'Well, let's go then,' the big one said.

Monahan stood aside. He had been in too many brawls to get caught with a sucker punch.

'After you,' he said.

The dancers murmured and Monahan raised a hand reassuringly.

'It's all right, folks. Just go on with what you were doing.'

Turning, he followed the two to where Dinny Doherty sat. The pair were swaying from side to side as if this were all fun. But their little display did not fool Monahan. He kept well back.

'Give them their money, Dinny,' he said. He watched as they took the crumpled bills. They put them away deep in their pockets. Seeing that, he was convinced. They didn't want it spilling out in what was to follow.

'Remember, stay out of this, Dinny.' he muttered to Doherty as he followed them to the exit.

The two had stopped by the door.

'OK,' Monahan said. 'Outside.'

Suddenly, their carefree air faded. Lithe and menacing now, they began backing out before him into the hall. The big one raised a hand, beckoning Monahan towards him, a glazed grin on his face.

'Going to throw us out, fat man? OK, let's see you try.'

His craggy face pale but hard, Monahan stepped cautiously after the retreating figures, still keeping his distance.

The old fire door was latched outwards. Beyond was the short hall, dull and dimly lit, leading on to the street.

42

As Monahan reached the edge of the door, the two stopped, poised for action. They were no more than six feet away.

Quietly, Monahan stepped beyond the door, his eyes fastened on them.

'You say you want to fight?' He grinned. 'Well, if that's the way, let's keep it private.' With a slow pull, he raised the catch off the door. Squealing loudly on its runners, the door swung closed behind him.

They stood facing each other in the dim hall. Still smiling, his eyes on them, Monahan reached down now for the baseball bat kept concealed behind the door. It was time to show them what's what.

His hand searched. Then sought again. Nothing.

Damn.

He glanced down quickly.

The space was empty.

The smaller man chuckled. Monahan looked up quickly to see him reach into the doorway beside him.

'You looking for this?'

He drew out the bat.

In that instant, Monahan charged.

His speed took them by surprise. It hardly seemed possible that a man so heavy could be so agile. He covered the six feet and was on the smaller one before he got the bat above waist level.

The small man gave a deep 'ooahh' then toppled backwards. Monahan was on top of him, grappling for the bat. The bigger one, recovering quickly, leaped on his back. In a sudden tangled mass, all three rolled over, each struggling for supremacy. Monahan got his palm around the bat. Hardly feeling the blows raining on his back, he tried to wrest it off the smaller man who held on grimly. Raising a free fist, Monahan aimed a blow at the

43

exposed chin. But the bigger one locked an arm around his forearm and blocked delivery. With a fierce heave he threw Monahan half on his side.

The small one took heart and renewed his struggle to get the bat away. Monahan, fending off the punches of the larger man, was beginning to lose his grip. Suddenly, he felt the bat being pried away. Triumphantly, the smaller one threw it back to clatter down the hall.

'Get it, José!' he shouted to the other man.

Desperately Monahan grabbed at both men. He heard the ripping of cloth as the big one fought to free himself. His head buried between the two bodies, Monahan tried to hold on to their struggling torsos. But the writhing flesh was too hard to hold. His hands began to slip.

Suddenly, he heard a startled scream. Smooth as butter, the smaller one slid from his grip. Almost at the same time, the larger one seemed to rise under some fierce invisible pressure. Within moments, Monahan found himself alone on the floor. He struggled up to his knees, raising his arms, trying to protect himself from the expected blow.

When nothing happened, he raised his head. To his astonishment, he found himself staring into the face of a huge shaven-headed man who stared down at him, unsmiling. The giant held the two Hispanics in either hand as if they were so much flotsam.

A voice spoke from the shadows.

'Get them out of here.'

Obediently, shaven head swung the two around and began propelling them towards the exit.

As Monahan stared, a small man stepped forward into the light. He was wearing an elegant linen overcoat and a sky blue scarf, as if dressed for a night out. His sallow face looked concerned as he reached down with a gloved hand.

'You OK?'

Monahan nodded, letting himself be helped to his feet. He rested briefly against the wall. 'You got great timing, Sal,' he said.

Salvatore Genta smiled, the small hard eyes glinting. He showed even white teeth. 'I work at it,' he said.

A more subtle mind than Monahan's might have wondered if that was, in fact, what happened. For it was Sal Genta who suggested that night's meet. And it was known in the right circles that Mr Salvatore Genta always liked to put customers in the right mood before he closed his deals.

Chapter Three

It was just past noon, but with the dark scudding clouds above Belfast it might have been evening. Inside Lynch's pub on Balaclava Street, the wall lights were already on. It hardly seemed worth it with just three customers. Two were overcoated pensioners sitting near the fireplace where the ashes from last night's fire still remained. The third was a younger man in a leather jacket and open-necked shirt who sat by the dusty window looking out on the narrow street. The barman, tilted back on a stool at the end of the bar, was watching the television suspended overhead. A racing commentator was outlining form for Doncaster that afternoon.

One of the battered twin doors opened. Robbie Driscoll entered. He wore a shabby grey raincoat over a neckless black sweater and his blond hair was slicked back, dark and wet. Pausing briefly, he crossed the creaking wooden floor to the counter. The barman slid forward from his perch.

'Black Bush.'

Robbie rested against the stool while waiting. The pensioners looked towards him but quickly turned away when he glanced in their direction. The man at the window continued staring moodily out at the street.

Several minutes passed. The door opened again and Shay Brennan, Robbie's partner in Glenvoy, entered. Ignoring Robbie, he went to the far end of the bar.

'Pint of stout,' he said loudly, hands resting on the varnished counter.

As the barman pulled his pint, Brennan turned to look at the man by the window, who nodded back almost imperceptibly. Robbie, who was watching, waited until the barman had finished serving Brennan then gestured him over. He inclined his head towards the two old men by the fireplace.

'They're both sound,' the barman said softly.

Robbie drained his glass and put it down.

'Make sure that's washed,' he said before turning away.

'No problem,' the barman said. Glancing at Shay Brennan, he raised his eyes. Brennan stared back coldly.

Robbie went through the small door at the rear of the bar and climbed the steep stairs to the second floor.

The upper room had high angled walls which were lined with rows of beer crates. Dull light filtered through the skylight. The place smelled of damp plaster and stale drink.

Liam Ring sat at a small formica-topped table in a cleared space at the end of the room. As Robbie came forward, he put down the newspaper he was reading and smiled.

'*Failte romhat, Roibeard.*'

'Hello, Liam.'

Ring, who was in his early forties, had a thin pinched face under the thatch of dry brown hair. A worn brown sweater hung loosely on his thin shoulders. For years, the rumour was he was dying of cancer. But he was still around.

He watched silently now as Robbie sat down.

'You know why I've come?' Robbie said.

'I can guess.' Ring's eyes flicked to the newspaper on the table. 'Jim Colgan's boy, wasn't it?'

Robbie nodded.

'Tragic.' Ring shook his head. 'Unavoidable, I suppose?'

'He wasn't supposed to be there.'

'Poor lad.'

'Twelve years old, Liam,' Robbie said. 'I couldn't believe it when I saw him.'

Liam Ring raised his eyes in concern at the tone. 'I hope you're not blaming yourself, Robert?'

'What would be the point? It's happening to others besides me.'

'Don't I know. But what can we do?'

'We might stop using fertilizer to make bombs we can't control,' Robbie said coldly. 'And give over using children as spotters.'

Ring shook his head.

'Know something? All I hear about lately are civilian casualties,' he said. 'Jesus, to hear certain people talk you would think we enjoyed killing non-combatants. But it hurts us too, damn it.'

'I can accept that some are unavoidable,' Robbie said. 'The problem here is that we seem hellbent on killing Catholics.'

Ring raised a hand.

'Not Catholics, Robbie. Nationalists.'

'Yes, of course. Liam, it's got to stop.'

Ring nodded. 'I suppose you're going to complain about weapons now?'

'And why not?' Robbie said, irritated. 'Look at Glenvoy. If we'd had an anti-tank gun or even an M60, we could have taken out that personnel carrier without blowing half the street away. And that Colgan lad would still be alive.'

'And we wouldn't have today's headlines.' Ring tapped

the paper. He paused. 'Jim Colgan took it badly, I suppose?'

'Not as bad as his wife,' Robbie said. 'I don't know if she'll recover from what's happened.'

Ring shook his head. 'That's war for you. It's not only the guilty who suffer.'

'War or not, we can't go on shooting ourselves in the foot like this.'

Ring looked at him keenly. 'This is really getting to you, isn't it? I mean, it's not just the Colgan thing.'

'Some things don't get any easier.'

Ring sat back in his chair.

'Well, we have something for you that might do just that. Make it easier.' He grinned. 'It even has to do with your precious weapons.'

'What are you talking about?'

'We have a project going in the States, a very big one, Robbie.'

Robbie looked at him.

'Oh?'

Ring nodded.

'Only trouble is, we have a half-wit in charge of it.'

'One step forward, two steps back,' Robbie said sarcastically.

'No, no. There's a lot in this one,' Ring said quickly. 'It really does look good. And to be truthful, the fellow I'm talking about is more of a hothead than a half-wit. It's just that we've had some reservations expressed from New York about the supplier and we want to check him out. But from here. There's a man in the south, an insurance investigator, who looks qualified to do the job. What would you say to setting it up and acting as his handler?'

'I don't know,' Robbie said. 'It's not really my line, is it?'

'It's a big one, Robbie. Maybe even the biggest. And besides, it would give you a rest from active service. And if you ask me, you deserve a break.'

Which was why he found himself in Dublin that evening.

As a child, Robbie Driscoll always dreaded evening time. Mornings and afternoons were warm, full of light, safe. But evenings were different. He would lie in bed then, watching the last glimmer of daylight, his stomach knotted, praying for help against the approaching darkness. But God never answered. Nothing, it seemed, not even an infant's prayer, could turn back the darkness in those days.

Now he no longer prayed.

Sitting by his hotel window, watching a last flush of yellow sunlight dapple the damp roof-tops of the city, he felt that old uneasiness returning. But it was not just shadows growing on the landscape that disturbed him now.

For months he had been having nightmares.

They were spectral things, with images and sounds merging, tearing his sleep asunder nightly. It could be the image of a prison warden grimacing on his doorstep as the bullet whacked into his white shirt. Or the bulging calf of a nurse colliding with gunfire as she ran to help a dying soldier. Or again, the rusty scraping of a wheel turning and turning on an upended Landrover. But almost always his father appeared at the finish. With those unceasing blood-red blinking eyes and the fiercely grinding teeth.

Enjoy your rest, Liam Ring said as he left. But Robbie Driscoll knew it would not turn out like that. Somewhere he had read about First World War soldiers who turned down leave and asked to stay at the front. Now he understood why. The need to remain with the action had nothing to do with courting danger. It was the natural reaction of minds that feared the consequences of having time to contemplate some very brutal memories. There were times, he was coming to realize now, when memories were even more terrible than the incidents that provoked them.

That evening, he knew he had to get away from them.

After dinner, he left the hotel. Although the air was cool, he wore only a thick grey sweater over shirt and jeans. Cars raced past as he crossed the elegantly railed Burlington Road with its tall Georgian houses. Passing a stately grey-stoned Protestant church he stopped to glance over the locked gates. Inside, the lawn was neatly trimmed, the flower beds turned. All ready to welcome a congregation that had long since gone. In 1922, when the south gained independence, Protestants made up twenty percent of the population. Now they were less than five percent. And the gates were still being closed all over.

He passed a terraced house on the opposite corner. *'Here, on July 4th, 1919, Captain Joe Malone and four volunteers held off a company of British troops . . .'*

He reached Leeson Street bridge. The ragged cloud, shot with the orange farewell of sun, reflected in the placid surface of the canal. He rested against the stonework for a moment, looking down the arrow-straight waterway with its tall, gently swaying beech trees and its edges decked with lily pads. The worn paths on the grassy banks were empty. A soft, still peace seemed to hang in the air, in spite of the cars crossing the bridge behind him.

After several minutes, he straightened and crossed to

51

the other side of the bridge. Turning right, he went down the sloping path to the road that ran parallel to the canal.

About a dozen women were strung out along the grass verge under the trees, waiting for customers. Hands in his pockets, he passed through them slowly, ignoring the invitations. Near the end, a well-shaped, big-boned woman in her late thirties, with her fair hair in tight curls, watched him approach from her resting place against a tree.

He stopped before her, silent for a moment.

He said, 'Are you available?'

She smiled and threw away her half-smoked cigarette.

'At your service, love.'

Sunday morning by Dublin Bay.

A cluster of gulls scattered screaming as the tall, solitary figure in black trunks crossed the rocky outcrop at its southern tip. The birds rose in a flurry of white and gathered in the restless breeze off the point. The man on the rocks seemed deaf to their cries. Head lowered, he moved down towards the water's edge, stepping carefully.

He's watching for bird-shit, Robbie Driscoll thought.

Driscoll was standing by the high sea wall, looking down on the bathing site, the breeze cool on his face and ruffling his hair. Rain pools dotted the crevices in the flagstones around him. The grey sky foretold more of the same. It was not a day that he would have chosen for swimming.

It did not seem to bother the man below who had reached his diving site, a worn slab of rock jutting out above the waterline. As Robbie watched, he ran a hand through his longish black hair and began wiggling his arms and legs, loosening up. Finally he took a deep breath, his lanky body poised.

In he went.

Robbie Driscoll could almost feel the icy impact as he pierced the water. The green mass swallowed him, seething briefly where he disappeared. Robbie stared, caught a thin line of bubbles, then nothing. Suddenly the water parted and the matted hair rose in a spray of foam. Shaking his head, he looked back towards the shore.

Robbie slowly raised a hand and waved. The man stared, then turned without answering and swam out to sea. His arms flayed, steadily parting the green water. Not expert, but strong. And confident, or he would not be doing this on a gloomy Sunday morning with no one around.

The sign called this place Sandycove, although there was hardly a trace of sand to match the name. Still, the view over Dublin Bay was spectacular. Only the squat tower sitting on the point to his left blocked his vision. As the swimmer disappeared into the distance, Robbie moved across to shelter under its walls and await his return.

The swimmer's name was Tom Craven.

According to Liam Ring's briefing, he was twenty-four years old and worked for an insurance brokers owned by a Republican sympathizer. He was regarded as a capable and reliable worker, with a steady but not outstanding intelligence. Robbie was surprised to learn that he was also an ex-policeman.

Craven had been peripherally involved in one of the most celebrated security scandals of the mid-eighties. An IRA sleeper named Dara Logan had been infiltrated as a recruit into the Republic's police force, the Civic Guards, at the same time as Craven joined. Although Craven was not political, during training he had become friendly with Logan.

The movement's original aim had been to slip Logan into C3 – the political intelligence branch – but he proved an impatient spy and when he found an opportunity to purloin some security documents from the Commandant's office, he took them. The loss was quickly discovered and by elimination, the investigators closed on Logan. With his options narrowing, he turned to Craven who agreed from loyalty to smuggle the documents out of the depot.

Craven's action had saved Logan from a certain fifteen-year sentence. But he did end up with three. Still, he was grateful, and when Craven, unable to shake off suspicion about his involvement, was booted off the force, Logan arranged for him to be hired as an investigator by an insurance broker sympathetic to the movement. Gradually, Craven came to return the compliment. He began doing jobs for the movement. For almost four years now, he had been carrying out clandestine background checks on aspiring members. According to Logan, his employer and the intelligence section of the movement that he reported to, his record was second to none.

Now he was to be offered the New York assignment.

Craven was out for almost half an hour. Driscoll, the collar of his black three-quarter-length jacket raised against the wind, was feeling the cold by the time Craven clambered ashore. He watched silently as Craven, his tall muscular body streaming water, hurried to where he had left his clothes. On his way he glanced up briefly, and Robbie knew that he had been spotted again. But he waited until Craven had pulled out his towel and started to dry himself before he crossed to the small iron gate and went down the stone steps.

Craven's head was covered by the white towel as he approached.

'Morning,' Robbie said.

Parting the folds, Craven looked out and nodded. Then he went back to rubbing his hair.

'I've been waiting for you,' Robbie said.

Craven stopped and slowly lowered the towel.

'For a while there, I thought you might be after my wallet.' He spoke in a rich country brogue.

His narrow face was pale and bluish from the cold, and the curled black hair still glistened with moisture. The pallor made his knitted eyebrows stand out above the slender nose. He stared at Robbie, his dark eyes curious.

'I'm supposed to call myself Setanta,' Robbie said. What an awkward bloody name.

Craven slung the towel around his neck. His lips parted in a faint smile, showing slightly uneven teeth.

'I never met a 3,000-year-old man in the flesh before.' He cocked his head in a mock examination. 'You've aged well.'

'Done with pills,' Robbie said.

Craven grinned and suddenly extended a wet hand. 'Good to meet you, Setanta. I'm Tom Craven. As you must know.'

He dried himself quickly. Robbie rested against an outcrop of rock.

'You picked a barren place for your dip.'

Craven reached for the white shirt. 'You can't be from this part of the country, saying that,' he said, pulling it on to his damp body. 'Don't you know where you are?'

'Should I?'

'You're at the Forty Foot. The most famous bathing place in Dublin.' He pointed at the tower looming above them. 'That's James Joyce's old hang-out up there. The

55

first chapter of *Ulysses* is set here.' Buckling the belt on his brown corduroys, he jerked his head towards the water. 'You can see now what he meant by the snot green sea.'

Robbie looked at the shifting water. 'He knew what he was talking about.'

Craven smiled. 'Heard a good one about him the other day, as a matter of fact. See Howth over there?' He nodded towards the dim headland on the far side of the bay. 'That's where his hero, Mr Bloom, lay down to prong his darling Molly for the first of many. Man told me the Corporation put in a tulip bed there recently. Planked a big sign in the middle of it. Know what it said?'

He paused.

'*Please Don't Step On The Blooms.*'

Robbie laughed.

Craven slipped on the grey tweed jacket. It hung loosely on his lanky frame. He rolled his trunks in the towel. 'Now what would you say to a pint?' he asked.

As he reached his car to follow Craven, Robbie paused for a last glance at the tower and Howth Head and the spired Viking city under the glowering clouds. Everywhere you looked here, he thought, there was beauty. And history, song, and love.

But still, you could never forget the blood. Like one long cataract flowing down through the centuries, drenching the people and the land alike.

He stared at the cold shifting sea.

There were times when the blood seemed to flow thicker than the water here.

'Go to America?' Craven said.

They sat in the corner of Fitzgerald's pub. The timbered

56

bar smelled of old smoke and pine disinfectant. Its stained glass dulled the outside morning light. Even the voices along the bar sounded hushed, as if affected by the church litany many had just fled from.

'Interested?' Robbie asked.

'I'd jump at it,' Craven said. 'But what about my job?'

'I've talked with them already. They said OK.'

Langans, the insurance brokers Craven worked for, knew where their interest lay. The answer to a request from the movement was a foregone conclusion.

'How long would it be for?' Craven asked.

'A week, ten days maybe.'

Disappointment flickered on his face. He's looking for a holiday, Robbie thought.

'What's the story?'

He gave him the bare minimum. Interviews with three knowledgeable sources for a character assessment of a party the movement was interested in. A written report afterwards which they would collect. Robbie was careful not to prime him in any way. He wanted anything Craven wrote to come from his own findings.

'Sounds like easy pickings,' Craven said. 'I do that kind of stuff all the time. Although I suppose talking to Americans might be different.' He raised his already half drunk pint and took a large swallow, regarding it with real appreciation before putting it down again. 'When would I go?'

'Soon as possible.'

'Fine with me,' Craven said. 'I'll be glad to get out of this kip for a while.' He looked around him sourly. 'Culchies aren't exactly appreciated here.'

Robbie looked briefly puzzled.

'A term for country people.' Craven glanced at him

keenly, then smiled. 'What your average Dubliner regards as the lowest form of animal life. Particularly the women.'

'You look presentable to me,' Robbie said.

Craven shook his head.

'It's the accent that counts.' He drained his glass. 'As a matter of fact, I've been trying to place yours.'

'Don't,' Robbie said. 'I've been all over.'

Craven shrugged. 'Another pint?' he asked.

'Not yet.'

'Think I'll have one. That bloody swim, you know. Eats up the calories.'

Robbie smiled. At least Craven had done the exercise to justify his drinking, which was not altogether common.

'We'll need to get cracking straight away, eh?' Craven said as he came back with the fresh drink. 'I'll need visa, tickets, hotel and stuff.'

'I'll help out.'

'Ten days, you say?' Craven shook his head. 'That means I'm going to miss the All Ireland final.' He grinned at Robbie. 'Cork could do with your bloody hurley if they're going to thrash Kerry, wouldn't you say?'

'Sorry?'

'Setanta, hurley,' Craven said patiently. He looked at Robbie, surprised now. 'Don't you get it?'

'Oh,' Robbie said.

Craven shrugged. 'Anyway, the trip will be worth the loss. Seeing America. That'll be something.' He paused. 'What's the name of this fellow I'll be checking on?'

'His name's Genta. Salvatore Genta,' Robbie said.

Craven raised his pint. 'Well, I look forward to making his acquaintance.'

Chapter Four

It was past midnight and Salvatore Genta sat in Midge Gallagher's bar at Fifty-first and Second Avenue, waiting for Michael Monahan to show up. Normally he reacted badly to being kept waiting, particularly in a bar he didn't know. But on this occasion he was prepared to be tolerant. Nothing persuaded like the smell of fast money.

Genta had chosen a corner table, which gave him a good view and protected his rear. He sat now with his pale linen overcoat draped on his shoulders, partly for show but also because someone had left the air-conditioning on, even though it was October. His sky-blue silk scarf lay on the back of the chair but the kid gloves stayed on the table with his pineapple juice.

Genta was just forty-two and into the mid-life fad of trying to preserve with style what he was losing through age. His clothes were the best that extortion and a small injection of cash could procure in the garment district. He wore a smoke-grey double-breasted suit, a button-down lime-coloured shirt and an ochre tie which was anchored by a diamond pin. His thin dark hair, a trial to him on windy days, was singed and blown to give it a fuller look. Even the nails were polished to reflect the gleam of his gold cuff-links and the matching pinkie ring.

Unfortunately, the expensive wrapping could not obscure what lay beneath. Genta had a roughness about him that no artifact or make-up artist could hide. The hunched shoulders and restless brown eyes belonged to a man who had travelled a hard road and still remembered every blister acquired on the journey.

There was something implicitly authoritarian about him too, which grew from a long habit of giving, rather than taking commands. Those who worked for him knew it and took care not to disturb his tranquillity. Even the hardy New York panhandler could sense it and was inclined to give him a wide berth.

To hear such a tough description of himself would have pleased Genta. He worked hard at being sour and unapproachable. The New Jersey waterfront where he held sway was unforgiving territory. It was no place for the soft touch.

Sitting at his table, waiting for Michael Monahan to appear, his mind was now on this Irish deal.

At the outset, it had seemed straightforward, if parting Monahan from his money and giving him nothing in return could be called straightforward. That had been Genta's original plan, and he had developed the scam with a confidence born of long experience.

But now unexpectedly, a complication had arisen. A gentleman named Francis Renata had begun clouding his horizon with serious problems. Genta knew he was going to need money, and lots of it, to solve them. Not only that, but the problems were also urgent. So much so, in fact, that he was now being forced into something that was previously unthinkable. It looked now as if he might have to provide the weapons Monahan wanted in order to spring the cash he needed.

He was quietly debating the issue with himself when he spotted Michael Monahan coming through the main door. Summoning up his best smile, he raised a hand in greeting.

Monahan's broad face was unsmiling as he approached. He was not in good humour.

'Sorry I'm late,' he grunted, his apology contradicted by the inflexion.

'No problem,' Genta said, not to be outdone in insincerity. He gestured to the chair opposite. 'Just glad you could make it,' he added.

Monahan nodded, unzipped his jacket, displaying a wrinkled sports shirt and part of a hairy chest. He sat down, the faded blue eyes on Genta.

'So, what's the big panic?' he asked.

'I thought we needed to talk.'

'Talk?' Monahan stared. 'You brought me down at midnight just to talk?'

Genta realized the slow build up was out of style with someone like this.

'OK, if you got to know the truth,' he said, 'I'm having a serious time problem in connection with our deal.'

The waiter approached. Monahan ordered a rye and water. They waited until he left.

'So what's this problem?'

'The stuff is being re-scheduled to leave port a week earlier than expected. We'll have to move in on it a week before we planned if we're going to get a piece.'

'For Christ's sake.'

'These things happen, Mike,' Genta said quietly. 'It can't be helped.'

'Well, it had better be helped,' Monahan said. 'Because I've been talking to the people in the old country.' He stared grimly at Genta. 'And they want to shove things back.'

Hell. Genta stared.

'For how long?'

Monahan shrugged. 'Ten days, twelve days.'

61

It was the worst possible scenario.

'They give a reason?'

'They want time to think about it.' That was all Monahan knew about what was happening in Belfast.

'You know what that's going to do?' Genta's eyes were cold. 'It's going to kill the deal, that's what.'

'I got orders.'

Genta's lips tightened. 'Things like this make me mad, Mike. Very mad.'

Monahan was not a union negotiator for nothing. Rough talk was meat and drink to him.

'Listen, I'm not in the mood either,' he snapped. 'So just shove it, OK?'

Genta scowled. 'I leaned hard on people,' he said. 'Took a lot of risks. Now I got all the stuff just sitting there. In packing cases. Waiting.'

'Well, you heard what I said. No decision until they say so.'

'You want to lose it all?' Genta asked. 'The Stingers and the rest? Is that what you want, Mike?'

'Don't bullshit me,' Monahan said. 'Your longshoremen can hold up any shipment you want on the waterfront. For as long as you like.'

Genta stared at him.

'Where have you been hiding?'

'What do you mean?'

'Don't you know the Congress has started yapping about putting an embargo on military stuff going down to Central America. The talk is that it will come in on October 18th.' The outline was true. The date was Genta's colouring.

Monahan looked at him.

'How the hell would you know about that?'

'Because they passed the word to the line captain today.

The staff must leave for Honduras by the 17th. To beat the deadline.'

'Aw, Jesus!' Monahan said.

'You got it,' Genta said. 'Not only that, but I got to tell you, it's going to be the last cargo out of there, Mike.'

'You sure of this?'

'One thousand per cent,' Genta said. He paused. 'Understand now why you've put me in a pickle with this delay of yours?'

Monahan was silent.

'What the hell are we going to do now?' Genta asked.

'Listen,' Monahan said, 'What about I see the stuff?'

'What for?'

'I could talk to them again. Once I see it and can say it's all there. Maybe I could get them to change their minds.'

Genta shrugged.

'I'm not running no free tour,' he said finally.

'Let me see it,' Monahan insisted. It seemed the only way to go. 'I got to have something to say, if I'm going to persuade them.'

Genta stared. 'You really think it might do good?'

'I don't know,' Monahan said. 'But sure as hell we won't get any change from them without it.'

'All right,' Genta said. 'You got it. Just let's hope it works.'

The truth was, it had to work for Salvatore Genta. Without the Irish money, the only problem in his life would be the date of his funeral.

Chapter Five

It had taken four days but they had done it.

Tom Craven raised his collar against the icy wind and watched tiny whorls of dust and litter which swirled along the shabby Bayonne street behind his departing cab. As an introduction to the underbelly of America, the view could not be bettered. Standing on the cracked sidewalk, he continued staring after the cab until it disappeared around the corner. Grimacing, he turned to the site of his first call.

It was a scrapyard, graffiti-scrawled and grey-walled, covering most of the block across the street. Two large metal gates hung open and awry in the centre. Crossing, Craven stopped briefly to read the sign below the rusted entrance bell. '*You better have a damned good reason for ringing this*', it said. He frowned and went through the gates.

His belted navy raincoat with white shirt and grey tie hinted at a sedate business type, matching the story line Robbie Driscoll had suggested. Unfortunately, the boyish build and longish hair conspired to create the opposite effect. In a phrase popular with his mother, he was neither fish nor flesh.

The scrap metal business being what it was, there was nothing novel in what confronted him inside the yard. Piled wrecks and abandoned parts, along with several makeshift sheds that looked like part of the inventory. While the retired cars were definitely larger and the weeds more pervasive than in Dublin, the difference was only one of degree. In the scrap metal business, it seemed, taste recognized no borders. But maybe that was because there was none.

Peering down the rows of crowded wrecks, he spotted a rare phenomenon, one of the scrap profession actually at work. The shadowy figure on bended knees was jemmying hubcaps off an aged chrome monster. Picking his way carefully along the rutted ground, Craven went down the aisle.

'Hello there. I'm looking for Zev Eisen.'

The bent figure straightened. A black man, he stood broad and muscular in a grease-stained orange windbreaker and jeans. His brown flecked eyes were cold under the tinselled red skull cap. The jemmy he had been working with hung loose in his hand.

'What you want him for?'

'Business,' Craven said. He saw the eyes rest on his dress. 'Insurance,' he added.

The black man continued staring.

'Well? Is he here?'

The other finally shrugged and gestured over his shoulder. 'Office,' he said.

It stood on crude stilts against the rear wall overlooking the waterfront area. Some men were unloading the latest cargo outside. All were black and wore decorated caps like the first one. Nodding briefly to them, Craven climbed the stairs.

There was no one in the dusty and cheaply furnished office he entered. He waited a moment and, when no one turned up, crossed to the corridor beyond.

'Hello? Mr Eisen?' he called.

He heard a chair shifting.

'Yeah?' The voice came from down the hall. As Craven stepped through, a stout, white-haired man in shirt sleeves, with glasses on his chest, appeared in a doorway half-way down.

He stared suspiciously. 'Who the hell are you?'

Tom Craven smiled, charming.

'My name is Craven, Mr Eisen. Thomas Craven. I'm in the insurance business.' He went down and handed over his card.

Eisen raised his glasses. 'Security and Mortgage Insurance. Of Dublin, Ireland?' He looked up in surprise. 'What the heck brings you to New Jersey?'

'If you'll give me a few moments, I'll be glad to explain.'

Eisen stared for a moment then shrugged. He led Craven into his office. 'Well?'

Craven touched the chair. 'Do you mind?'

'Anything else?' Eisen asked sarcastically as he sat down.

'No, sir,' Craven said quickly.

'Well, what's this about?'

Craven said: 'I'm here to do some confidential research for a client, Mr Eisen. An Irish company that's planning to expand its fleet of container ships in the transatlantic and middle eastern trade. Recently they had an approach from a potential investor, a gentleman from New Jersey. His interest appears genuine enough. Unfortunately, there seems to be a problem with the personal data he supplied. It doesn't quite tally. My clients decided to send me over here to check if he really is worth doing business with.' He paused. 'I believe you know the party I'm referring to, sir.'

'What's his name?'

Craven took a moment. 'Salvatore Genta,' he said.

Eisen peered at him intently. Then he began to laugh. It grew in volume until his face grew red.

Tom Craven stared in surprise.

'Lord Almighty.' The laughter died but Eisen's broad face stayed creased with mirth. 'Genta doing business in Ireland? I don't believe it.'

Abruptly, his mood changed. No longer smiling, he stared at Craven.

'How come you hit on me?'

'We were told of a waterfront investigation in which you were a witness. I understand Mr Genta was mentioned.'

'Mentioned?' Eisen's face became indignant. 'The whole damn investigation was into Genta.' He stared at Craven. 'You need to bone up, kid, if you're going to do any good in your business. Didn't you know?'

Craven flushed. 'I've only just arrived. And they didn't give me much to go on.'

'How much?'

The flush deepened. 'Just what I told you.'

Eisen gazed at him for a moment, then rose from his chair. 'Come over here, kid,' he said, not unkindly, as he turned to the window.

Craven, smarting, rose and joined him.

Eisen pointed down to the yard.

'Know what those guys are?'

The three black men were still unloading junk from the truck. Craven shook his head.

'They're Black Jews. The meanest bastards this side of Jerusalem. And my partners. They own fifty-one per cent of this yard.' He nudged Craven. 'Know why they're here?'

'No.'

'Because Salvatore Genta would kill me if they weren't. They keep me alive because there's no way Sal and his boys want to tangle with people like that. That's why I took them in.'

67

He turned to look at Craven. 'You're playing near the bottom of the deck with Genta, kid,' he said. 'There's only one man lower and that happens to be his boss, the ice-pick surgeon, Francis Renata. And I hear even he's a gentleman by comparison. He murders for business. Your Mr Genta does it for pleasure.'

Craven stared, shocked. 'I thought he was just a waterfront organizer.'

'Waterfront organizer?' Eisen shook his head. 'That's only a sideline. Salvatore Genta is Mafia, kid.'

'Jesus.' It slipped out.

'If I was you,' Eisen said, more gently now. 'I'd go back home straight away. Tell your guys to steer away from Mr Genta. The man's a serpent.'

He led Craven back around the desk.

'Want a coffee?' he said abruptly.

Craven nodded.

'Give me two quarters.'

Surprised, Craven fished them out. As he watched, the older man went to a coffee machine which he now saw hidden behind the door.

'A serpent all right,' Eisen said. 'Wraps himself around you nice and soft at first. Then before you know it he's squeezing you to death.' He was silent for a moment, then suddenly he chuckled. 'Maybe it could even happen to him, if we're lucky. I see from the papers that he and Renata had a falling out. The little chiseller was trying to move outside his own territory: Renata is not the kind of guy who buys that. I only hope the bastard gets what's coming to him. If anybody deserves to get hit, it's him.'

'How did you come to know him?'

'I had a trucking business.' The voice was muffled as Eisen bent and dropped the quarters in the machine. 'I was doing OK when Genta and the Renata mob arrived

68

and offered me some extra contracts. It looked like a sweetheart of a deal. They'd give me business, I'd give them kickbacks.' He brought around the coffee. 'And that's how it was in the beginning. Before they started on me in earnest. First thing they wanted was to add a couple of no-show workers to the payroll. Only two at the outset. In a couple of months it was up to six. Pretty soon, it was their wives and girlfriends as well. Before I knew it I was paying for parties and limos and even vacations in Disneyworld. And all the time, they were increasing the kickbacks I had to pay.'

Craven tasted the coffee. It was vile.

'It took nearly two years before I got to fighting back. By then it was too late.' Eisen sat down heavily behind his desk. 'They took my youngest boy and beat on him. Eighteen years old. And they put him in the hospital.'

The pain was still evident.

'That's why I turned to testifying in that inquiry,' Eisen said vehemently. 'I would never have talked if it wasn't for that. Scum, that's what they are.'

Craven was silent.

'I lost everything, thanks to Sal Genta. All I got now is a piece of this shitheap.'

'Your testifying. Didn't it make a difference?'

Eisen snorted. 'They're bigger now than they ever were. The papers call Renata the boss of all the bosses.' He laughed drily. 'And Genta is the senior vice president. The two of them are into every racket on the eastern seaboard. Unions, trucking, loan-sharking, hookers, gambling.'

'Shipping too?' Craven asked, remembering his role.

Eisen looked at him pityingly. 'Listen, they control every port between Brooklyn and Newport, Virginia. That's where Genta got his nickname. The King of the

69

Chenangos.' He grinned at Craven, enjoying the opportunity to give a lesson and maybe damage Genta's business prospects into the bargain. 'I suppose you'd like to know about that, too?'

Craven nodded.

'It goes back to when they were starting out. Renata's little group was barely a crew, never mind a family, in those days. And Genta was just another punk on the make. Back then, the big movers were the Gambino and the Genovese families. Between them, they controlled almost every union local in the International Longshoreman's Association. Trouble with them is that they got too successful. It brought attention. Ten years ago, after the media whipped up public opinion, the Waterfront Commission brought in a regulation they thought would get rid of the mobsters for good and all. They barred convicted felons from holding office in the ILA. It turned out to be one of the few regulations those bums made that worked. But only for the main locals.'

Eisen sipped his coffee. 'There happened to be other union locals in the ILA that nobody thought to cover. Minor ones that covered the chenangos. They were the unskilled guys who were used to unload cargo from barges and railheads before containers took over on the docks. As the families were thrown out of the main locals, Francis Renata saw a way to fill the gap by taking over those chenango locals. Sal Genta became point man for the operation. In three years, he took over every local in Manhattan, Brooklyn and here in Jersey. The papers started calling him The King of the Chenangos. From that, it was one jump to taking over all the territory lost by the other families. Today, they have it all. Nothing moves, nothing leaves, nothing happens in New York and Jersey ports without the Renata family OK.' He paused and put down his cup. 'Come here, I'll show you something.'

Craven rose and followed him out of the office into the corridor. 'You're getting the grand tour,' Eisen said, as he brought him into a storeroom on the far side. He crossed to the window.

'There you have it.' He pointed. 'The King's territory.'

Craven followed the pointing finger to the long, crowded New Jersey shoreline, filled with warehouses, derricks and ships. The bay beyond was a dull grey in the morning light.

'See that?' Eisen pointed to one crowded patch. 'That's the Military Ocean Terminal, Bayonne. It's called Motby for short. That's the largest transit port for arms in the world. Every weapon that our troops in foreign bases need goes through that place. Tanks, missiles, guns, you name it, they put it through. It's the biggest employer in Bayonne.' He smiled grimly. 'And two guys run it. The Secretary for Defense handles the military side. And Mr Salvatore Genta runs everything else for the mob.'

Thomas Craven stared down silently at the massive complex.

It didn't take a genius to know now why the movement had business with Salvatore Genta.

Chapter Six

I'm too trusting, Sal Genta thought, that's the reason I got in trouble.

A less subjective observer might have pinpointed greed. Either way, it did not alter the bottom line. Salvatore Genta was in the worst trouble of his life. From his record, that was a change no one could have predicted. It had usually been those he dealt with who ended up in the worst trouble of their lives.

For twenty years Genta had been Francis Renata's most trusted subordinate, working loyally as enforcer and decima captain before becoming underboss. Now it appeared that all his devoted service would count for nothing. Renata wanted him out. And even the dogs in the streets knew what that meant.

Unless he came up with a quick alternative, he was going to get bagged. Or, given the current disposal fad, barrelled.

Sitting in his plush office in the Port Elizabeth local of the International Longshoreman's Association, Genta tried to concentrate again on the most likely solution to his problem, which was Michael Monahan's money. Unfortunately, his mind kept returning to the original source of his misery and the bane of his life.

Brandon Sullivan's proposition.

That goddam son of a bitch, he thought, abandoning his earlier assessment, he's responsible for all this.

While it was indeed true that Sullivan had played a role in his fall from grace, Genta was conveniently forgetting that a certain character defect had a part too. It was, after all, his own foot that stepped on the rake. If he was now regarded as damaged goods, it was largely his own doing. And there was another turnaround.

During his long and ferocious career, Genta had enjoyed a dubious but nevertheless solid reputation as a shrewd and capable organizer. The way he ran the Renata family's New Jersey operations drew grudging admiration from his peers. Brutally efficient, was how the Newark FBI office laconically described both him and his performance.

Nevertheless, Genta always had an Achilles' heel. In some ways, it was not so odd in one so rapacious. He simply could not preserve normal judgement when confronted with the prospect of a quick profit. The larger the amount involved, the more deadly the impact was on his psyche. So striking was this flaw that a good many New Jersey crime buffs were convinced that any con man who had the balls could easily scam Genta out of his shorts to cover them. Provided, of course, the con man was prepared to risk some fearsome possibilities. Like a fifty-pound fire-extinguisher, operating at maximum pressure, in the ear.

Plump, stately little Brandon Sullivan was one who could face that prospect. Almost three years earlier he had walked into Genta's ILA office in Newark with a proposition in his monogrammed briefcase. Like all good scams, his was brilliant in conception and uncomplicated in outline.

Simply put, Sullivan offered to make Genta the gambling tsar of Haiti. 'Show me,' Genta said, who had $2½ million burning a hole in a safe deposit box in Panama City. Sullivan proceeded to do just that.

He produced a typewritten page on which it was all laid

out. It had narrow columns for expenditures and fat ones for income. To back up this impressive presentation, Sullivan produced letters of approval from leading Haitians, including one from General Namphur, who ran the country. All promised to help '*Mon Cher* Brandon' in this great enterprise.

And the figures were dazzling. Sullivan envisaged profits of $1 million on the first full year of operation, rising to $7 million annually when the project was in full swing. Sal Genta surveyed the information with bemused eyes as he listened to the glowing patter and the faint qualifications at which Sullivan was a master.

'I got to tell you, Sal, and I'm being straightforward here, it's going to cost money. You'll have to put out now if you want to rake it in later.' The voice had a nervous catch to it which was Brandon Sullivan's greatest asset. People thought a guy that edgy wouldn't have the nerve.

Casino Building, Genta read. $827,000.

'Isn't that kind of cheap for the classy premises you're talking about?'

'Hey, that's the beauty of it, Sal. The building is already there. Carpets, everything.'

'Yeah?'

'It's the Foreign Ministry. Their state department.'

Sal eyed him doubtfully. 'Come on. They'd sell their state department?'

'The country's so broke they got no need for one. These people live in shacks, Sal. The Minister, Wilson Paul, was planning to close it down anyway. This way, he gets a chance to make a little scratch.'

Sal shook his head and looked at the sheet again.

'$450,000. Licences, permissions, etc.' He looked up. 'How does that work?'

74

'We need to buy other politicians besides Paul. There's the Interior Minister who controls the cops, the Tourist Minister who issues the gambling permits, the Investment Minister who looks after all foreign capital coming into the country. I admit they're not cheap. But one thing about Haiti, Sal. When you buy politicians there, they stay bought. That's guaranteed.'

The prospect of a freewheeling gambling empire in the Caribbean was very much to Sal Genta's taste. Still, the price tag demanded caution. With uncharacteristic reserve, he decided to look over the situation in Haiti before committing himself.

The influential Sullivan arranged a meeting with General Namphur, lunch with the Foreign Minister and dinner with the Tourist Minister. (These last received $3,000 and $5,000 respectively from Sullivan just to eat their food and make the right sounds. They gracefully obliged.) By the time his social round was over, Genta was convinced he was on a winner.

Returning to New Jersey, he took the first steps towards involvement. Being naturally parsimonious, he forced his initial investment down to $500,000, which was made up of greatly reduced pay-offs and a mere $200,000 deposit on the Foreign Ministry building. Sullivan was to torture him with that later, claiming that a new Foreign Minister who took office after the deposit was paid would not recognize the deal made by his predecessor and they had to start over again. If we had bought when we had the opportunity, he told Sal, we would have been home clear. Now we need another $200,000.

And that was only the beginning.

It took time and some cloudy diplomatic explanations before the Foreign Office deal gradually faded into oblivion and an elderly hotel – 'on a prime location in down-town

Port-au-Prince' – replaced it. They got the building for what Sullivan called 'a steal', $300,000. In no time at all, Genta discovered another $200,000 was needed to tear down the surrounding slums whose aroma was guaranteed to depress the high rollers they were expecting.

Every step forward was a step deeper.

A short time after this, more bad news. Sullivan announced mournfully that the Ministers were on the bite again. Apparently there was a statute of limitations on bribes in Haiti. Sullivan softened that blow by getting Genta appointed the Haitian Commissioner for Marriages contracted by citizens from outside the state. $150,000 he had paid in bribes. The marriages brought in $3,527.50.

By then, Genta was out $1.3 million. But that was the down side. On the up side, the planned casino was actually lurching towards eventual opening, although it was going to be nowhere near as grandiose as Sullivan had outlined. Genta was prepared to accept that.

But Sullivan's fertile mind had not finished. In their original projections, based on the flimsiest of evidence, they had figured that the traffic south from the gambling fraternity would be in the tens of thousands. Sullivan thought it lunacy to give all those air fares away to Haitian Airlines.

'Why not buy our own 707?' Fortuitously, he knew someone in Miami who had one on sale for $400,000.

Genta was not so dumb that he couldn't see the drawbacks to that. Even with their best projections, the plane would be under-utilized.

It was then that Sullivan hit him with his knockout blow.

'Sal,' he said seriously, 'have you ever thought of getting into tomatoes?'

* * *

It was the tomatoes that broke his back.

The scheme should have worked, and not just because Sullivan said so. The economics made powerful sense.

First of all, the land marked out for it, prime tomato-growing territory in the west of Haiti, was dirt cheap. Ten thousand acres leased over ten years for a ridiculous fifty dollars an acre. And with a guarantee of two to three crops a year. An agronomist from New York State University whom Sal hired for a feasibility study swore by it.

The tomato pluckers, 300 of them, would cost money, of course. Ten dollars a week each, which placed them in Haiti's top bracket and effectively removed the possibility of labour trouble. The only other expense beyond that were the perennial pay-offs which came to $20,000 per year.

When all that investment was balanced against the estimated yield, the tomatoes weighed in at three cents a pound. As far as Genta could see, they would murder the local producers in the east coast markets. He and Sullivan were sitting on a fortune.

But they needed an airstrip to take their elderly 707. Sadly, good soil for bearing tomatoes was less amenable when it came to heavy payloads. As the pilot noted on an inspection trip, the Boeing was not designed to land on a sponge.

Soon, the airstrip was soaking up funds almost as fast as its soggy foundations soaked up fill. Wages, bribes, construction costs began eating up Genta's nest-egg. As time went on, and no cut-price tomatoes reached eager consumers to ease the cash drain, the very mention of the plant began to give Genta nightmares.

The most ugly moment of his life finally arrived nine months into the scheme, when he took a white knuckle flight into the mountain-locked region for a desperate on-the-spot examination.

Sullivan had done the groundwork well. Everywhere you looked were tomatoes. A vast red sea of plants filling every nook and cranny.

But they were all rotting.

By this time, Genta's bank balance was just about stripped clean. Suddenly, surveying his ruined empire, the penny dropped and he realized that he had been taken.

That night, sitting in the fly-blown shack that passed as an office, he ordered Sullivan killed. Done a little more quickly than he would have liked, because this was Haiti and not New Jersey, the little man was drilled and left to decompose among his wretched tomatoes.

Back in New Jersey, surveying his ruined financial position and desperate to rebuild his bank balance, Genta took the fateful step that led to his present plight. He began operating outside his own territory.

He knew the risks he was taking in setting up an operation across the Hudson in Brooklyn. But the way he saw it there was no choice. There was a limit to what he could unload on his home turf. And he had to rebuild.

The stuff he moved was all hijacked merchandise from Jersey ports. Electronics, frozen sea food, late model clothes. Nothing large or fanciful but all steady and profitable. As the months went by and Renata showed no sign of suspicion, Genta grew more confident. For the first time, he began to wonder if the great Francis was slipping. And that, of course, led to other thoughts. Like how to buy some of the people around Renata who would be crucial if it should ever come down to a hit.

One man he had no intention of approaching was

Renata's consigliere, Chicken Devane. A deep mutual hatred had built up between the two over the years, caused by the pistol whipping of Devane's nephew during an accounting dispute.

'Sure, I've got Frank Renata's ear,' Devane once gagged at a family roast. 'What I'd like to go with it is Sal Genta's head.'

Almost a year into the Brooklyn operation, that was exactly what Devane got.

A fat fence named Angelo Bundisi, who was handling some of the merchandise, was caught red-handed in an unexpected raid. The news did not unduly alarm Genta. As long as the origin of the goods did not come out, he believed nobody would notice. Brooklyn, after all, was full of thieves and, such is the nature of the business, large numbers got caught. One more or less would hardly be noticed.

Unfortunately, Bundisi turned out to be a special kind of thief. He was devoted to his mom, an elderly, wheel-chaired lady for whom he was the only visible support. And, when they faced him with the prospect of doing three to five, he cracked.

Again, that was annoying but still containable, although Bundisi had taken himself out of the human race with his disclosure. Retribution could wait for later.

What could not wait was what happened next.

Once Genta was named, the file went to the Organized Crime Strike Force on Police Plaza. And that place was a sieve. Within an hour of its arrival, Devane knew the contents. Within two, so did Genta.

He sent two men posthaste to grab Bundisi's mother. They marched down to the precinct with her in tow, got a bondsman and sprung her son in the mother's name. He was overjoyed when he saw her, thanked her two helpers and left with them helping him carry the old lady down the stairs.

A short time later, the elderly Mrs Bundisi was found abandoned in her wheelchair at the foot of the Brooklyn Queens Expressway. It took a while, but they eventually found her son. He had been strangled and dumped in an abandoned container yard in Red Hook.

Genta's speedy response had given him a little breathing space. But now Renata was activated. Listening to his underboss's denial, the big man nodded reassuringly, said 'Someone is out to get you,' meaning Chicken, and told him to let it drop. Soon after, every man associated with Bundisi was picked up by Renata's people and thrashed where necessary, until they confirmed what Bundisi had alleged. That the loyal underboss Sal Genta had moved out of Jersey on his own say-so and was now spreading his wings in forbidden territory.

Genta, who was working hard at keeping in step with what Renata was doing, knew then that the game was up. But he understood his man, too. Like all good Mafia dons, Renata was extremely sensitive to heat. Especially the kind that would come if his underboss were gunned down on the street.

Genta knew they would try to grab him without any shooting and then take him somewhere to finish the job. So as long as he stayed public, and kept enough people around to prevent him being grabbed, he could survive. But only for the moment.

What he had to do was set up a counter-attack. He had already taken soundings and knew that two of Renata's bodyguards were partial to the green stuff. But it would take as much as $250,000 to buy them. And thanks to Brandon Sullivan, he had nothing like that on tap.

If he did get the money, he had no problem about

setting up the hit. Unlike his boss, he wasn't picky about where it was done. He'd do it on television if that's what it took. But the question of when was growing more vital with each passing day. In the Mafia, as he well knew, time waits for no man.

The real issue now was getting that money. As far as he could see, the only one who had it in sufficient amounts was this Irish guy Monahan.

The important thing now was to prise it loose.

Chapter Seven

Tom Craven had been facing a problem. The second name on his list was of a man called Harold Malkinson who turned out to be unavailable. Luckily he found there was a stand-in, a woman friend named Norma Whitehead.

He reached her in the late afternoon at a small apartment in West Orange. A large fluffy woman, she ushered him into a cluttered sitting-room and settled him into a worn armchair. Its shabby antimacassar was soiled from some previous occupant's hair-dressing. He sat now with a cup of herbal tea balanced on his knee, watching her try to tuck legs as big as redwoods on to the sofa beneath her.

'You want to ask about my Harold?' The girlish treble sounded odd in someone of her mountainous shape.

'If you don't mind.'

She shrugged. 'Why not? Fire away.'

He plunged in. 'How long did you and Harold know each other?'

'We were together for fifteen years, day in, day out. It was a stormy relationship, Mr Craven. Up and down, but more down than up. And the reason, you ask? I'll tell you. In all the time I knew Harold, I never cared for him as a physical entity.' The beginnings of a tiny smile touched her pendulous lips. 'However, as a free spirit I have to confess that the guy was divine. I loved him passionately for that.'

Craven swallowed. 'Really?'

'Oh yes. In the spiritual Harold you had a rare creature.

A real man. Totally free.' Her eyes moistened and her veined hand strayed to a plaster bust sitting on a side table. It was of a middle-aged man with bulbous eyes and a pencil-thin moustache. Bizarrely, it was topped with a toupee. Loose strands rose as Ms Whitehead fingered it. Finally, she took her hand away.

'Frankly, he was the pits to live with,' she said briskly. 'And that's no bullshit. The little bastard stole from my purse, he drank my liqueurs like they were cheap beer and he smelled awful when he was on a gambling jag. About the only physical consolation was that he warmed the bed at nights.' She threw a quick glance at Tom Craven and smiled. 'Which is something a woman of my age is prepared to pay handsomely for.' Her eyes fluttered coyly at him. 'Even today.'

Craven stared. She was making a pass and he wasn't even old enough to be her grandson.

Norma Whitehead appeared long past sixty. And that was only the start. She might have come from a fairground exhibit, but as what was not easily discernible. She wore a chiffon dress that matched the curtains and looked like it belonged in *Swan Lake*. But her bulk suggested the fat lady's booth. As for the Adidas sneakers peeking underneath, there was no reasonable justification for including them in her ensemble.

Tom Craven cleared his throat. 'I take it your Harold is gone now?'

'Gone?' She stared then shook her head vigorously. '*Au contraire*, he's still here.' Her plump hand gestured royally towards the mantelpiece. 'That's him up there. Between the clock and the souvenirs from Atlantic City.'

Craven followed the raised hand. A small discoloured urn stood amid the bric-à-brac.

'His ashes,' she said. 'The mortal remains of Harold

83

Malkinson, gambler *extraordinaire*. His last pot, you might say.'

'I'm sorry,' Craven said politely.

She shrugged. 'We all have to cash in our chips sometime. And Harold was crying out for it. Doing what he did.'

'Testifying against Salvatore Genta, you mean?'

Ms Whitehead snorted. 'Of course.'

'What happened?'

'They took him out and drowned him.'

The brutality of the statement induced a sudden silence.

'He didn't go under without a fight.' Her rouged face appeared to redden with pride in the fading afternoon light. 'He was a tough rooster, my Harold. A real gamecock. Nothing scared him.' She looked at Craven slyly now and patted the cushion beside her. 'Want to sit here on the couch with me, dearie?'

'Thanks, but I'm fine here,' he said quickly.

She nodded without resentment and leaned over to pour herself a sherry from the decanter on the coffee table.

'I'd like to hear about what happened,' he said.

'It was all very straightforward.' She sipped from the glass. 'That Genta fellow wouldn't pay off on a point spread Harold phoned in on a Steelers Bengals game. There was only a few hundred dollars involved. Most people here in New Jersey would have let it go, knowing Genta's reputation. But not my Harold. He went down to the union hall and demanded his money. When they refused, he started screaming insults at Genta. They beat him up and threw him out. That's when he decided to testify. As soon as they heard, the phone calls started warning him not to talk. Genta himself came on once,

84

threatening to kill him if he did. But Harold shouted "up yours" and hung up on him.

'They caught him here after he testified. A local judge took away his protection on a motion from the Port Elizabeth police. Said it was an unconscionable waste of taxpayers' money. A few days later, they came for him. Harold had a hangover but he still managed to bloody them before they got him out of the bedroom. When I shouted at them, one of the brutes raised a fist to me. That mere threat to his woman was enough to revive Harold. He managed to kick the offender,' she lowered her eyes delicately, 'in the nuts.' She sighed and gazed fondly at the bust. 'It was my final memory of him.'

Craven said nothing. Words had failed him.

'Now, Mr Craven.' Suddenly her eyes were clearer as if the memory had gone. 'What is your purpose in asking me about all this?'

He shrugged. 'My clients are interested in what kind of person Salvatore Genta is to do business with.'

'Well,' she said, 'you certainly know now.'

Craven nodded.

She stared at him.

'If that's what you're after, there's another man you should talk to,' she said. 'He was president of one of the chenango locals Genta took over. He testified too. The police brought him here one day when they were collecting Harold.'

'Oh?'

She nodded. 'Harold's knowledge was piddling compared to his. I remember his name was Lascia. Juan Lascia.' She shuddered. 'He was a disgusting person. Skinny and seedy. A Columbian.'

Craven waited but she was silent.

'Do you know anything else about him?'

She shook her head. 'But I recall he was written up in the papers.' She looked at him brightly. 'Maybe you should check that?'

The night was cool and the air was filled with the smell of the river when Michael Monahan's car drew up beside the warehouse in Motby terminal. Sal Genta, waiting in the shadows with his men, scowled at seeing a second man in the car. He hurried forward to confront Monahan, who had Dinny Doherty with him.

'Hi, Sal,' Monahan said as he climbed out.

'What's this?' Genta pointed to Doherty. 'You were supposed to come on your own.'

'Take it easy,' Monahan said. 'He belongs in this thing too.'

'The hell he does,' Genta snapped. 'I told you I'm not running tours. You got no right, bringing him here.'

'And what about those?' Monahan gestured to the three men who had come out behind Genta in the gloom. 'You got your guys. Why can't I have someone too?'

'Because it wasn't part of the deal.'

Monahan glowered, controlling himself.

'I'm telling you now, Monahan. Either we run this thing my way or we don't run it at all.'

There was silence.

'Mike,' Dinny Doherty said, 'why don't I stay back here in the car?'

At the terminal door Monahan stopped, bringing the others to a halt.

'Tell those guys to back off,' he said to Genta.

Genta nodded to the others, who moved away.

'Well, what is it?'

'I don't like what happened back there,' Monahan said. 'As a matter of fact, I'm really burned.'

'We made a deal. You agreed to it.'

'I'm getting the impression,' Monahan said, 'that you think you can give orders and we're going to jump.' He looked at Genta with angry eyes. 'Thinking maybe we're suckers. Is that it?'

'That's crap,' Genta said. 'You didn't hear me say anything like that.'

'No. But I'm beginning to feel you're thinking it.'

'It's all in your mind,' Genta said.

Monahan said: 'Listen, if you've got any plans to screw around with the Irish Republican Army, Sal, forget them. Because they'll come after you.'

'Yeah, sure,' Genta said. 'Look, can we get on with this?'

'Are you hearing me?' Monahan said. 'Because I'm telling you it's been done before. And will be, if need be, again.'

'Sure,' Genta said.

'Listen, you remember that plumbing guy, John Curley, who got hit down in Philly a couple of years back? The one that was close to Angelo Bruno?'

'Is he the one who got hit by a florist kid?'

'That's him.'

'So?'

'Curley was trying to rip off the movement,' Monahan said. 'That's what got him killed.'

'You're kidding,' Genta said. 'Angelo, I thought he did that.'

'You thought wrong,' Monahan said.

A ship's siren sounded far off.

'Well, you live and learn,' Genta said.

Monahan smiled, hard and cold. 'Just so you remember the lesson, Sal.'

Salvatore Genta did not have to be taught twice.

He stood at the pier end, staring out at the murky waters of the Hudson, not bothering about the cold or even about his hair blowing in the wind, to use the only line of Bob Dylan that he liked.

He was thinking.

From inside the terminal he could hear the rumble of a fork-lift as they took Monahan around. Far out on the bay, a light winked on a passing tug. Beyond it, the Manhattan shoreline glowed in the distance. It was a scene so familiar, Genta hardly noticed. Much of his life had been spent in locations like this. Hardly any of it provided occasion for deep thinking.

But he was doing some now.

Monahan had caught him by surprise with that business about Curley. It hadn't occurred to him before that something like that could happen. Monahan's people were far away, in another country, caught up in a war. They might as well have been on another planet. That was how he thought when he was putting this thing together. Now it looked like he might have to protect his ass from the aftermath.

Or would he?

He stared at the water, hands deep in his pockets. It came, the germ of an idea, slowly growing as he concentrated. Very cautiously, containing his excitement, he nourished a possibility entirely different from what went before. The more he considered it, the more dazzling it appeared.

Jesus, he thought, it's been right in front of me all along. And I never saw it.

Turning, he looked down towards the car where Dinny Doherty sat, its chrome glistening under the caged pier light. He stared for almost a full minute at the dim outline of the man in the car, taking his time, making sure that he would present it properly.

Then he strolled down to say hello.

He was back by the terminal door when Monahan came out. One glance was enough to tell him that the burly Irishman was on the hook. His face was flecked with colour and his eyes were bright with excitement. Behind him, the capo who had taken him around, Willie Majura, grinned at Genta and winked. Well and truly hooked.

'Well, what do you think?' Genta asked, smiling. The earlier animosity between them was gone. They were different men now. But for different reasons.

Monahan shook his head, still filled with visions of what he had seen and what he imagined it could do in Ireland. He had only the vaguest idea of what Stinger missile launchers and their self-contained projectiles really looked like but from what he saw of those steely green weapons inside, all pristine and styrofoam packed, there was no doubt in his mind that he was dealing with the real thing.

Genta slapped his arm warmly. 'You see now why I was worried, eh? That's top of the line stuff in there. I got to be careful.' He grinned at Monahan. 'Liked what you saw?'

Monahan nodded. 'Listen, is there any way you can delay the shipping?' He would have eaten dung to get that.

But Genta shook his head.

'No chance, Mike,' he said. 'Unless you buy in, they all go cargo to Honduras.'

They began walking towards the car in silence.

Genta suddenly slowed and stopped. The others stood around him.

'Listen, Mike,' he said, sincerity dripping from his pores. 'I talked to Francis Renata this afternoon. You know the score, he's the man I got to answer to. I told him the situation. He was sympathetic. One hundred per cent. I don't know if you heard this but the last time he went to England, twenty years ago, they threw him in the slammer there. And Francis, he don't forget people who do things like that to him. Anyway, he told me to offer you this final deal. If you give your word to make final payment within one month, I'm to give you the full delivery for less than half down. You pay two hundred and fifty grand within the next twenty-four hours and the cargo is yours.'

Monahan stared at him.

'And that's the bottom line,' Genta said.

There was a long pause.

'How would you make the delivery?' Monahan asked suddenly.

'Easy,' Genta said. 'There's a freighter called the *Helena Castle* leaving Red Hook for Marseille next week. If you want, check the port register. We own a slice of that baby. We'll put the stuff on board and I'll get it redirected. If you're able to arrange the pick-up over there, somewhere off Ireland, you'll have it all on your home turf within seven days.'

Monahan seemed lost in deep thought.

'Jesus, Mike,' Genta said. 'The boss is ordering me to give them to you at less than half price. Possession before we get our last payment. What more can you ask than that?'

Monahan stared at him, his spiky hair rising in the

sudden breeze sweeping in off the Hudson. Still, he said nothing.

'Listen, Mike,' Genta said quietly, 'Francis Renata can be a very moody guy. Right now, he's sympathetic. But if you stall, he's just as likely to cut you out. With him, you don't get a second bite at the cherry. You move now, or in my opinion you lose it all.' He paused. 'Well, what do you say?'

'Give me a chance to think about it.'

'There's hardly any time, Mike.'

Monahan nodded. 'I know that.' He hesitated. 'I'll give you an answer tomorrow.'

As Dinny Doherty drove away, Monahan banged his fist hard against the dashboard.

'Those bastards in Belfast. I warned them this would happen. We're going to lose it all while they continue screwing around. It's all there, Dinny. You should have seen it. Those missiles. Jesus, you can almost see what they can do, just looking at them.'

'You sure you can trust these guys, Mike?'

'Damn it, didn't I see the stuff? And they're willing to hand it all over for less than half down. What else is there to trust?' He shook his head angrily. 'If we don't buy, we lose it.'

'What's the rush? Why can't they give you more time?'

Monahan looked at him impatiently. 'They don't have time. This stuff is supposed to go to Honduras in eight days.'

'So, what are you going to do?'

'I got to make up my own mind, that's what.' Monahan stared sullenly ahead.

Doherty glanced quickly at him. 'Now, Mike.'

'Mike, nothing. I got twelve hours to decide.' He gazed

sullenly through the window. 'This is American money we're talking here. Every cent raised on this side of the water.' He nodded to himself as if settling an argument. 'If it's going to be spent, then it should be a goddam American who decides.'

It was past noon when Robbie Driscoll arrived at the construction site on Black Mountain in answer to Liam Ring's summons. As the minibus which brought him moved off, Driscoll paused to gaze at the patches of smoky sunlight trailing across the city spread below. The farmland surrounding the grey mass of housing and office towers was still richly green in the October light and the water in Belfast Lough held its summer blue. But here on Black Mountain, the air was cool and filled now with the scent of autumn. The heat was ebbing from the soil. Soon there would be mist and drifting leaves. In a couple of weeks it would be Hallowe'en.

The season of short days and dark nights, he thought. That would mean more work for everybody.

The door on the trailer behind him opened. He turned. Liam Ring, a white construction hat on his head, stood in the doorway.

'You took your time,' he said.

Robbie frowned. 'I caught the first train available.'

Ring shrugged and turned to lead the way into the caravan. Inside, he took off the hat and dropped it on a table cluttered with drawings. A big JCB moved past the window.

'What's the problem?' Robbie asked as Ring sat down on one of the hard-backed chairs. He remained standing.

'Bloody Monahan over in New York is the problem,' Ring said bitterly. 'He's going off at half-cock. It looks

92

like he's going to close this deal we had going on his own say-so.'

'You're joking!'

Ring shook his head.

'That's the word we got this morning.'

Robbie was silent.

'Your fellow Craven,' Ring said suddenly, looking up. 'Can you make contact with him?'

'I suppose,' Robbie said. 'But do you think it's wise to bring him in on this?'

'He's the only chance we've got if we're to stop this bugger.' Ring rested an elbow on the table. He seemed tired. 'There's hell to pay about this, you know. The new man has just been briefed. And he's steaming.' There had been a change in the leadership. 'We can expect some fall-out.'

So that was the reason for the bad temper.

He said: 'What would you want Craven to do?'

'He's got to reach Monahan and tell him on the highest authority to cut it out. No talks, no deals, no nothing until we say it's OK to proceed. And I can tell you from here on that approval is going to be hard to come by. The new führer is bothered by the reputations of the people we've been dealing with.' He grinned wryly. 'Looks like we're back on the high moral road again.'

Robbie looked at his watch. 'It's afternoon over there. I should try his hotel straight away. Is there a safe phone I can use?'

Ring nodded.

'I've already arranged it. At the Centre Spire Hotel. Billy will take you down there.'

They rose. As they walked to the door, Ring said: 'Ever read a poet called Archibald MacLeish, Robert?'

'No. Should I?'

93

'That's up to you. But one of his poems has a marvellous line in it.'

They stopped by the door.

'*And quite unexpectedly the top blew off.*'

Ring opened the door. 'Maybe we should move our Mr Monahan into explosives. That's where his bloody talent seems to lie.'

Chapter Eight

Michael Monahan had just finished filling the briefcase when the door of his office opened.

He closed the lid quickly.

'Hi there, mister.' A young woman's face, grinning under a fedora, appeared around the door.

'Nan!' he said, surprised. 'When did you get in?'

'This morning.' She swung lightly into the doorway and stood with her hands on hips. 'How are you doing anyway?'

He rose from the chair. 'Come here.'

She came around, taking off her hat, knowing what to expect. He gave her one of his big bear hugs. Kate, his elderly secretary, stood in the doorway, smiling.

'Still Daddy's little girl,' she said.

Monahan grinned. 'Want a coffee?'

Nan shook her head.

'Nice to see you again, honey.' Kate closed the door on them.

Monahan stood back to look at her as she dropped her hat on the desk.

'How long are you down for?'

'Couple of days.' She fingered the desk slowly, remembering.

He smiled. 'Maybe it's the season, sweetheart. Or I'm biased. But you're looking beautiful.'

She smiled back. When he thought to do it, he always had the knack of making her feel good.

But it was true. She was blooming.

Nan Monahan was twenty-six, a fresh-cheeked girl with curling auburn hair worn shoulder-length and cut in a fringe. Her skin was smooth and clear in contrast to her father's freckled face, but her grey eyes seemed to mirror his direct stare. She had soft poutish lips under a nose that was straight and classical. The redness of her rounded cheeks, brought on by the cold outside, stood out now against the black turtle-neck. Even in her low-heeled calf boots she appeared tall and finely proportioned, although the grey winged coat she wore hid her figure. Only her hands seemed out of place, being large boned and noticeable now as she tugged at her coat.

'You just going to stand there?' Monahan asked.

Smiling, she sat down facing him across the desk.

'I was hoping to take you out for dinner,' she said. 'I've got some work to do in the library. But I could be free by eight.'

'I thought this down-town trip wasn't just to see me,' he said, adroitly sliding by her request. 'What's the project this time?'

She sighed. 'You don't want to hear it.'

'No, come on.'

'If you must know, it's the World Court decision on the mining of Nicaraguan harbours.' She grinned. 'There, I've said it.' She knew he was deeply proud of her role as a post-graduate student working in International Jurisprudence. But he detested the liberal slant implicit in that subject.

He snorted.

'Now, Dad.'

'I'll never understand why the administration hands out its tax dollars for studies and reports that try to wreck its policies.'

'Come on, it's not just their money. People who disagree chip in too, you know.'

'Well, that's democracy, isn't it?' he said. 'Listen, if it was me, I'd have blown those Sandinista suckers out of the water long ago.'

She shook her head. 'Can you make dinner or not?'

'Honey, I'm sorry. But I have too much to do.' He drew the briefcase off the desk. She watched him set it down.

'Dad on the go,' she said. It was not consciously intended but her voice sounded querulous. The pattern was ingrained.

'Maybe tomorrow,' he said.

'Sure,' she said, her interest gone. Her eyes strayed to the group of family pictures among the union scrolls on the wall. 'When are you going to take that down?' she said suddenly, pointing to the framed photograph of a girls' floor hockey team. Her own round childish face stared out at her.

He glanced at her. 'Still bothers you, eh?' There was an impish glint in his eye.

She shrugged quickly.

'Water under the bridge now.' Her long fingers played with the hem of her coat. 'You going to make it to the cottage for a weekend before the water's off?'

'I could try,' he said. 'If you'll come too.'

'We'll see.' She glanced up. 'You know, you ought to take Mom out more often. Maybe take her up there with you. Instead of me.'

'You know she can't stand the bugs. And there's no bingo either.'

'What bugs? It's October, for God's sake.'

'Come on, Nan. Get off my case. Work is work. I've got to put in the hours here. You know that.'

'It's not only here. It's that other stuff, too. Put you in jail, it could,' she added darkly.

'What's the matter with you? Change your tune now? I thought you agreed with all that.'

'So what if I do?' She dropped the hem of her coat. 'That's not the point. There's family too.' Abruptly, she got up. 'Listen, I've got to go.'

He got up with her.

'Tomorrow night, hon,' he said. 'Seafood. Your Mom too. How about that?'

'Yeah, sure.' She leaned across the desk and pecked his cheek. 'See you.'

He followed her to the door and waited to watch her as she disappeared. Then, almost regretfully, he closed the door and locked it. Returning to the desk, he raised the briefcase and re-opened it. It was filled with neat stacks of currency. Unlocking a desk drawer, he drew out a silver-plated .38. Silently, he hefted it in his hand for a moment before pressing it down among the bills.

After locking the briefcase in the safe, he called down to Dinny Doherty.

'Listen,' he said, 'I've got a meeting with the arbitration committee in the boardroom in fifteen minutes or so. Can you hang out here in my office, until I finish?'

At the door, he stopped to glance back at the chair where his daughter had sat.

'Tomorrow, honey,' he muttered to himself. 'We'll do it tomorrow.'

Then he went outside to wait for Doherty.

It was almost six when Tom Craven came out of the New York Public Library, a set of rolled photocopies in his hand. Fifth Avenue was crowded and glistened wetly from an earlier shower. Sniffing the damp air, which resembled his own climate, he seemed happy to walk back to the hotel.

He had spent the afternoon in the library only after using up the morning in a fruitless search for his last interviewee, the Columbian Juan Lascia. His visit had been in the nature of a breather and did not come from any faith in the original suggestion made by Norma Whitehead. Still, it paid dividends.

He had discovered several listings on the newspaper index for Lascia under the Congressional investigation into waterfront corruption done three years earlier. After locating and reading the microfiches, he found with some delight that he now had both new information on Juan Lascia and fresh insight into the working methods of Salvatore Genta.

Lascia, it seemed, had been president of one of the ILA's chenango locals targeted by Renata and Genta in their drive to dominate the union. Genta had persuaded the Columbian, with the offer of a $300-a-week no-show job in one of the family's companies, to surrender office and to sponsor the mobster in the subsequent election. Lascia's indignation at what resulted resounded through his testimony. But it was significant that he showed no hint of remorse for his own shabby behaviour in the affair.

The election itself provided a novel twist to the democratic process. There were three other candidates in the race besides Genta, one of whom was a disguised Renata man. Family insiders, gamblers all, grinningly called them a stable entry. The secret Renata man paralleled the actual campaign with a personal one of abuse and physical intimidation against the two independents which finally drove them from the race. Once that was done, a belated justice was allowed to take its course. The offending candidate was called before a union court where indisputable evidence, including his own thoughtfully provided confession, led to a guilty verdict. He was stripped of his candidacy. Which led to Genta, unopposed, taking the prize.

For exactly six weeks after the election, Lascia received his no-show pay as agreed. But then, with the appeal time expired and Genta securely in power, he was called in and told the deal was off. Before the bewildered Columbian had absorbed that shock, a cold-eyed Genta went on to rub salt in the wound. The $1,800 which Lascia had received was now described as a loan, not a pay-off, and Genta wanted it back. Spanish protests were stilled by a few meaty cuffs from the mobster's side-kicks. So the unfortunate Columbian found himself not only out of a job, but saddled with a loan annual rate of interest on which was 165 per cent. In the circumstances, it was not surprising that he agreed to blow the whistle when the feds approached him.

According to the testimony Tom Craven read, Lascia had not finished his evidence when the first hearing recessed. It was mentioned that he would be recalled, but though Craven searched, he could find no record of it. However, he now had names of people associated with Lascia who might lead him to his quarry. And that was enough to go on with.

Sitting in a tiny booth in the library third-floor corridor, he made call after call. It was only when he began spicing his enquiry with hints that an insurance windfall might be involved that he finally unearthed the Columbian's home number.

'He no here. You call tomorra,' the woman who answered told him. A little disappointed but not dispirited, he decided to call it quits.

The picture emerging of Salvatore Genta was very clear now. Duplicity seemed a way of life in his business dealings. And yet there was an important point to be noticed. At bottom, he was not really departing from the principle of 'do unto others', etc. The people he cheated were all involved in illegal activity themselves. It was not inconceivable that they would do the same to him if they got the chance.

Rambling happily now in the damp air of Sixth Avenue, he saw the tell-tale leprechaun of a Blarney Stone pub in the distance. With that unerring instinct people have in foreign countries for seeking out places that remind them of their own, he dropped in and had a few pints of Guinness.

That was how he missed Robbie Driscoll's first two calls.

The message at the desk, which did not identify the caller, said he would call again at eight.

He was waiting on the bed with a glass of home-brewed Paddy whiskey at his elbow when the call came through.

Five minutes later, with Monahan's address in his pocket, he was on his way. He had asked if he could phone, but Robbie said no. It had to be in person. Do everything you can to persuade him, he said, but he must be stopped. There was no doubting how serious the thing was.

If Craven had known New York better, he would have taken a cab to the Sixth Avenue subway, then a Flushing train to 169th Street and finally another cab to Fallingbrook Road. Novice that he was, he made the entire trip by taxi.

That cost him. And others too.

Chapter Nine

Dinny Doherty was dozing when the door opened and Michael Monahan entered and switched on the light.

'Finally finished?' Doherty asked, sitting up.

Monahan nodded and glanced at his watch. It was almost eight-thirty. They were running behind. He crossed to the safe.

'You have to wonder,' Doherty said, 'how people whose only occupation is digging holes can spend so much time discussing it.'

Monahan didn't answer. He stooped by the safe and began turning the combinations. Finally, he drew the heavy door open. Doherty watched in silence as he withdrew the briefcase.

'Where to?' he asked, as Monahan stood up.

'The Forester's hall first. We've got to settle this renting business.'

'And after?' He held the door as Monahan switched off the light and led the way out.

'After, after. Always damned questions. I'll tell you on the way.'

When Craven reached the Monahan house, he said to the cabbie, 'If you hold on, I'll let you know if we'll be making the trip back.'

The driver, a thin, bearded black man in a golfing hat, shrugged without answering.

'Thanks for the interest,' Craven said.

The house was a neat single-storey surrounded by a

smooth trimmed lawn. There was a sign, something about a grape boycott in the window. He went up the drive and knocked.

A grey-haired woman using a stick answered the door. She wore a smock and stared at him, thin and unsmiling. She did not look well.

'Yes?'

'I'm looking for Mr Monahan. Is he in?'

She frowned as she caught the accent.

'No,' she said. 'He's out tonight.'

'Is there somewhere I might find him?'

'He's probably at the Forester's hall. It's down in Sunnyside. On Almira Avenue.' She stared at him. 'You Irish?'

Craven nodded, smiling.

To his surprise, she scowled.

'That's where he'll be,' she said, and shut the door hard.

Back at the cab, Craven gave the driver the new address.

'Mister,' the cabbie said, 'you don't need a cab, you need a tour bus.'

The manager of the hall was laying out the last of the chairs for a concert the following night and working under the emergency lighting to save bills. He looked up as Monahan entered still carrying the briefcase and followed by Doherty.

'You're late,' the manager said.

'You know so much, Bob,' Monahan said.

'Well, you got your head sorted out on this?' the manager asked. 'Do you carry on or not?'

'I want to,' Monahan said. 'But I don't see why I have to pay more. Nothing's gone up in the last six months.'

'No, but your people have gone down. You see what the beer sales were the other night, eh? Five hundred bucks. The goddam Ukrainians drink that in their first hour here.'

'Maybe it's all them polkas,' Doherty said.

'Sure,' the manager said. 'Look, Mike, I know you're a good guy. But I got a committee that's set to crucify me. I mean look around you.' He gestured to the tattered furnishings. 'This place is a slum. I need more money if I'm to do anything, to keep it going.'

'The mayor called it the pride of Queens,' Monahan said.

'My ass. That was an election visit,' the manager retorted. 'Listen, the guys who run things are talking about turning it into a carpark.'

'Come on.'

'I'm serious, Mike. Sure, you've been a good customer these years. But you got to see my point. Business is business.'

'Twenty years. We've been here twenty years.'

The manager shook his head. 'I'm sorry, Mike. You got to pay more.'

'How much?'

'Two big ones.'

Monahan winced. 'That'll kill us off.'

'What can I do?'

Monahan looked around the hall. 'When do you need to know?'

The manager bit his lip. 'Inside a week.'

'Jesus.'

'If there was any other way.' His voice trailed off.

Monahan sighed. 'I'll let you know.' Straightening up, he looked at his watch. 'Shit. What's the quickest way to Lispenard?'

'That down by Canal Street?'

'Yes.'

'The Expressway, I guess.'

'I thought Queens Boulevard,' Dinny said.

'All the one,' the manager said. 'So, it's next week, eh, Mike?'

Monahan nodded. 'Yes.' He turned to Dinny. 'Let's go.'

The manager went back to finishing off the chair arrangement.

When Tom Craven arrived at the hall, he was locking the doors. Craven rolled down the window.

'Excuse me.'

The man turned. 'Yeah?'

'I'm looking for Michael Monahan.'

'You just missed him.'

'Shit,' the cabbie said.

'Any idea where I might catch him now?'

'He said he was going to Lispenard.' The manager stared at them. 'Down by Canal.'

'I know it,' the cabbie said. He gestured to the meter. 'You're hitting twenty-two bucks here. How long you going to keep this up, man?'

'I got to find this guy,' Craven said. 'It's really important.' He paused. 'But I guess this is the last shot.'

'Mister, for me it is,' the cabbie said. He swung the wheel and sent the cab into a squealing arc. 'You don't know how much money you're taking out of my pocket with all this screwing around.'

'This is it,' Craven said. 'I promise.'

But the cab driver muttered.

* * *

Dinny Doherty drove down Roosevelt headed for the Brooklyn Queens Expressway. Traffic was light on the dark, rain-slicked street. Monahan stared moodily ahead. Finally, he lifted the briefcase on his knees. With a practised hand, he turned the lock and thumbed open the catches. He raised the lid.

Doherty glanced across and caught the glimpse of steel among the piled money. But it was the money that made him catch his breath. He looked up quickly at Monahan's face, then back to the road.

'Don't say a word,' Monahan said.

Doherty shook his head. They had reached the Expressway before he spoke.

'Mike, they don't want you to do this,' he said.

Monahan stared grimly ahead.

'They've got a right to make the decision,' Doherty said.

'Not all the rights. This money was raised here. Every cent of it. That gives us some too.'

'Mike, these guys you're dealing with are bad.'

Monahan lifted the gun out and closed the briefcase with one hand. He put it in the pocket of his windbreaker. 'So am I,' he said.

'Come on. You know well what Genta is like. He's scum.'

'Listen,' Monahan said. 'I've known the guy for twenty years. Sure he's scum. When he's dealing with scum.'

Doherty was silent.

'I'm not trusting him, Dinny. Why do you think I brought this?' He tapped his pocket.

'Mike, you're not a kid. And this is not the Korean war.'

'No, but there are kids over there who need help. And that's war too.'

'But the people running it don't want the help you're offering. Doesn't that mean anything to you?'

'Sometimes, Dinny, you have to step outside the rules. Look, I know I can get this stuff. And they need it. Besides, people always break the rules in war. Look at Patton.'

'You're not Patton, Mike.'

'Why are you going on like this, Dinny?'

'Because I'm afraid you're going to screw up.' He twisted to look directly at Monahan. 'Mike, they're against this. And you ought to listen.'

'Against, against,' Monahan said. 'What are you, a know-all? How come you know so much about what they think?'

Doherty took a long time. 'Because I told them what's happening.'

The seat creaked roughly.

'You what?'

'I had to tell them, Mike. It's their decision.'

'You told them?'

'Every damned thing. They said to cut it out.'

'You bastard!'

'Who are you to talk?' Suddenly Doherty appeared angry. 'I been listening to you crapping like you were some big shot. As if it was your game we were playing. It's not your goddam game! It's theirs. It's not your goddam money. It's theirs! Calling me a bastard.' His lips worked, staring ahead.

'I'm sorry,' Monahan said. 'Let me put it another way. You're a two-faced bastard.' His bulk loomed danger-ously over the smaller man. 'I ought to smack your head off.'

Doherty shook his head.

'You can't see it, can you?'

'We're finished, Doherty. Understand that.'

They came off the Expressway.

'Make a left at the lights,' Monahan said.

'Mike,' Doherty said.

'Mike nothing. Just go to where we're going.'

Lispenard was a narrow high-buildinged street that was past its prime, if it ever had one. It was quiet and dead in the rain that spat against the windscreen of the car. Small yellow lights reflected from some of the windows on the upper levels. Monahan searched the street numbers and pointed.

'That's it. Stop here.'

Doherty drew into the kerb opposite. He turned off the engine and turned quickly.

'Please, Mike. Don't do this.'

Monahan reached for the door handle.

'Let me go with you, then,' Doherty said as he opened the door. 'Come on, Mike, don't be a fool.'

Monahan got out. He leaned down, holding the door. 'I'm never going to forget you for this, Dinny.'

Doherty stared at him, his anger drained away. 'I'll be waiting,' he said. He couldn't bring himself to say good luck.

The wind-breaker did little to protect against the rain as Monahan crossed the street, but he barely noticed. He glanced up at the second floor of the building and caught a glimpse of light behind the curtain. His grim expression did not alter.

'Twenty years,' he muttered to himself as he reached the worn side door which displayed a small hand-lettered sign that said 'The Calabrian-American Social Club'. Turning the knob, he entered the narrow high-ceilinged hall. A single bulb burned in a cheap shade. It rocked in the air drifting in from outside. Monahan shut the door, crossed the bare floor and mounted the high stairs.

He reached the first-floor landing and stopped at the door with a similar sign to the one below. Using his free hand, he unzipped the pocket of the wind-breaker containing the gun. But his movement was slow, almost careless. As if his heart was not in it.

He reached up and rang the small bell.

A good thirty seconds passed without answer. He rang again. A few moments later, the door swung open. A smiling Salvatore Genta stood in the doorway.

'Mike.' His dark eyes were bright and lively. 'Come in, come in.' He stood to one side.

Vaguely, Monahan thought he had never seen Genta in old clothes before. He nodded and stepped inside.

They were in a small vestibule with a wall rack and two side doors. The faded wallpaper was only a marginal improvement on the decor of the hall outside. Still smiling, Genta closed the door, gesturing inside as he slipped on the lock. Monahan led the way into the square carpeted room where several green baize tables were scattered about. The air smelled of fresh cigarette smoke and there were some half-filled glasses still on the tables. A slender man with silver hair and dressed in a brown leather jacket sat at one of the tables.

'This is Willie Majura,' Genta said, coming in behind. 'You met him down at the terminal. He's going to do a lot of the arranging.'

Monahan nodded. 'Hi.'

Majura leaned over without rising to shake hands.

'Nice to see you again, Mr Monahan.'

'Sit down, sit down,' Genta said, pulling a chair forward. He glanced covertly at the briefcase Monahan set between his feet as he went to sit opposite. 'I'm really glad we're doing business, Mike. All those years we've known each other and all.'

Monahan sat back, his knees apart, hands resting on his thighs.

'I thought the whole thing was going to run tight,' Genta said. 'But you coming tonight, makes it all easier. Right, Willie?'

The other man nodded.

'Sal,' Monahan said. He pulled himself together and sat forward. 'I got a lot of reasons why this thing should go right. There's a lot of people behind me with doubts. You understand?'

'Sure, sure,' Genta said. 'But don't let them worry you, Mike. Everything's going to go like clockwork.' He paused. 'You brought the money?'

Monahan waved the enquiry off.

'Let's talk about your plans before we get to that,' he said. 'Want to tell me how it's going to work?'

'That's what you want, fine,' Genta said airily. 'Willie here will fill you in. Go ahead, Willie.'

'Well, I think we got it worked out pretty good,' Majura said. 'Considering the time thing. First, we got to replace your stuff by the same weight and size in the cargo going to Honduras. Then we got to make sure that the volume in, volume out of cargo moving through the terminal is the same. Third, we got to move the stuff to this freighter of ours across the bay in Red Hook. And lastly, we got the rendezvous with your people on the other side which will be your responsibility.'

He grinned. 'Now here's how our end will work. In the next two days, I'm arranging for two truck-loads of machine parts from Philadelphia to enter the terminal. Then we pull the switch with your stuff.'

'What about people seeing that?'

110

'That's why I've been talking money, Mike,' Genta broke in. 'I mean it's going to work OK, but it's going to take a raft of money.'

Majura nodded.

'Once the switch is done, everything should be OK. Now, what we're going to do is *not* take out your stuff again by road. We're going to move it across the bay by barge. That means we only got the coastguards to contend with. And Sal is taking care of those. Right, Sal?'

Genta nodded. 'The *Helena Castle*, the freighter will be at Pier Eight over at Red Hook. All we got to do is put your stuff in a container and pop it aboard. After that, it's up to you and your guys.'

'You see?' Genta said smiling. 'Didn't I tell you? It's going to be a cakewalk.'

Monahan looked at the silver-haired Majura.

'You sure you can get all this done in time?'

'No problem.'

'Now,' Genta said. 'About the money, Mike.'

Monahan lifted the briefcase. 'It's here.'

'No offence, Mike. But I need to see it.'

Monahan twirled the small combination. He did not see Genta glance behind him. Clicking the catches back, he raised the lid of the briefcase and, turning it, laid it down on the table, the neat piles of bills facing Genta.

The sallow face lowered, the small dark eyes staring intently at the money. Slowly, Genta rifled through each of the bundles. He looked up now, a greedy smile on his face.

Then suddenly Monahan saw something else.

In a terrible flash of recognition he realized what was going to happen. With a roar of rage he reared, the chair falling away, going for his gun.

Like a silver wraith, the wiry Majura dived across the

111

table, grabbing for his arm. He tried to push him off but the scrabbling hands closed on his wrist. Then the room was filled with the sound of rushing feet and he was surrounded. Not by one or two but by a whole flurry of people. As the struggling mass pressed in on him, a thin shadow snaked down before his eyes and he felt a sudden tearing pain at his throat. Fighting desperately, his hand reached the plastic butt of the gun and he tried to pull it free. But now other steely fingers closed like vices on his arm. His eyes dilating in agony, he saw Genta, his face an ugly twisted shape. Bodies crashed against him and a sea of red pain flared inside his skull. He tried to raise his free hand to pull the cord away, but they were too strong. Choking, his mouth opened, but all that emerged was a strangled scream.

They were trying to drag him down now but he would not go. A red tide blanketed his eyes now. His head was a cauldron, every nerve fibre within it flaming with agony. Yet still some primeval instinct kept him upright. Flailing, his head rearing under the thin cord, summoning up the last strength of his powerful body, he pushed forward, dragging the clinging bodies with him, making for the window.

Dinny Doherty had left the car minutes earlier. He had tried to resist, but the bile and tension of the argument with Monahan had constricted his insides, forcing him out into the rain. He had to take a leak.

He had found an alley in the darkness twenty yards away. Standing at the wall, he had banged his fist against the brick, remembering as he leaked.

He was coming out of the alley, relieved but aware now of the rain, when he heard the sudden sound of breaking glass. He stopped on the sidewalk, his eyes darting to the building where Monahan had gone.

The shattered remains of the window glinted in the light coming from inside the room. Suddenly he saw shapes appear, embroiled in the remains of a curtain and now battling frantically. Horrified, he watched a single spike-haired head emerge from the others, straining to break free. The twin strands of a cord ran from the neck and the head was pulling fiercely like a reined stallion.

Oh Jesus.

Frozen with horror, Dinny Doherty stared hypnotized from the darkness as Michael Monahan was overcome and dragged back into the room.

In a sudden burst of panic, he turned and fled.

'Wow!' the cabbie said, as they stopped to turn into Lispenard. 'Look at that guy go.'

He pointed to the small middle-aged man who came around the corner, running like the wind. They watched him race up towards Canal Street.

'There's New York for you,' the cabbie said in disgust. 'No one takes their time anymore.'

Slowly they turned down Lispenard.

'OK, what are we looking for here?' the cabbie asked.

'Damned if I know,' Craven said. 'But this is where the man I'm looking for is supposed to be.'

Halfway down, the lights picked up the glint of broken glass on the sidewalk.

'I wonder if the little guy did that?' the driver muttered.

'Well,' Craven said, 'he had to be running from something.'

It was the only thing interesting on dead and deserted Lispenard. Not a sign of Michael Monahan or any hint of where he might be.

Well, I did my best to find him, Craven thought, and you can't do more than that.

'OK,' he said. 'Take me back to the hotel.'

As far as he was concerned, Michael Monahan was a dead letter.

Chapter Ten

The message that went to Ireland the following morning was short, succinct and shocking to the recipients:

Regret to inform you that Uncle Michael passed away last night. His demise completely unexpected. Understand last moments spent in the arms of Sally Gee and family members. Regret to report that Uncle Michael discarded best advice and did not take out insurance against hazards in latest business dealings. Asset loss accompanying fatality will be in region of $250,000.

May God grant him peace.

Cousin Seoirse

Within hours, Robbie was summoned.

'The top's blown off now,' Liam Ring said. Briefly he told him about Monahan. 'And get ready for a cross-country drive,' he added. 'The new man wants to see you.'

'When?'

'As quickly as possible.'

'Have you thought of letting Craven know about this, by the way?' Robbie asked as he was leaving.

'Forget it,' Ring said shortly. 'There's a black-out on anything going into or coming out of New York right now.'

'What's the reason?'

'I don't know,' Ring said. 'Maybe you could ask his nibs.' He was not in a good humour.

* * *

Tom Craven had by now dropped the search for Michael Monahan and returned to the hunt for Juan Lascia. And here he was more successful. After a day of calling union locals and then his home, he finally made contact with the Columbian.

Craven fed him a story about doing research on port unions. He said that Lascia's former chenango local looked like a good case for study.

Lascia grunted. 'What's so good about a local that kick me out on my head?' he asked.

'But that's exactly it,' Craven said. 'The lack of protection for the little guy. That's what I'm concerned with.'

'Sound like crap to me,' Mr Lascia said bluntly.

'No, no, Mr Lascia. My kind of research helps to create safeguards. Salvatore Genta might not have taken your job, for instance, if they were in place when he arrived on the scene.'

'Genta?' Lascia said. 'Where is he coming out of?'

'Well, that take-over of his,' Craven said. 'It interests me how it happened.'

'What are you, an agent or something?'

'No. Just a researcher.'

'You don't talk like you're from New York.'

'That's a good ear you have. I'm from the European Marine Unions Research Office, as a matter of fact. Based in Dublin, Ireland.'

'No shit,' Mr Lascia said.

'Right,' Craven said. 'Mr Lascia, I'm really interested in what Mr Genta did to you. And how he did it. Could we talk?'

'Well, it still sounds a little crazy to me. Nobody likes to spend time talking about Sal Genta around here.'

Craven hesitated.

'Well, maybe I could make it worth your while.'

'How come?'

'I could offer you a little compensation, perhaps. You know, for your time.'

There was silence.

'How much you talking about?'

'Say two hundred, two hundred fifty dollars.'

Mr Lascia was silent some more.

'That's not much,' he said finally. 'For talking about someone like Sal Genta. His guys, they spend that on toothpicks.'

'Well, it's money.'

'Maybe.' He paused. 'Look, I think about it. Give me your number. I call you back. What you say your name was again?'

'Craven, Mr Lascia. Tom Craven.'

'From Ireland, eh?'

'That's right.'

'OK, Tom. I call you back. Maybe I do it all right.'

The road ran like a grey thread through the rumpled hills of County Donegal. Even in the autumn sunlight the landscape looked awesomely desolate. The barren sweep of rock rose against the hazy sky, its surface broken by rare patches of wild grass and the occasional stunted tree. A few scattered flocks of sheep offered the only sign of life.

'If you want my opinion,' said Shay Brennan, who had been pressed into service as driver, 'our friend is playing with fire, living in a place like this.' He dodged another pothole and waved his cigarette. 'The SAS could take him out anytime. And who's to know but a lot of bloody mutton?'

The salty smell of the Atlantic gusted through the

opened window on Robbie Driscoll's side. The leather-epauletted navy sweater he wore over the white shirt and heavy grey corduroys staved off the cold.

'I mean, we all know he's smart,' Brennan said above the noise of the engine. 'But smart people get stupid by times too. And he has family to think of too. What protection does this give them?'

Driscoll slid back the white cuff and looked at his watch. Twenty minutes past three. They were making good time. Might even be a little early.

'Two little ones. And the wife.' Brennan glanced at Robbie. 'Did you hear she's English, by the way?'

Robbie shook his head. But the intermingling did not surprise him. The Provisionals' first chief of staff had been a cockney. The name, but not the accent, was later gaelicized to Sean MacStiofain. All part of a long tradition. Padraig Pearse, the man who headed the newly declared Republic in 1916 was half-English. Even more exotically, his successor and Ireland's President, Eamon de Valera, was a native-born New-Yorker. A grinning President Kennedy had pointed to him during an address to the Dail and said that with a slight change of circumstance, 'You, Mr President, could have been here talking in my position and I could have been down there listening in yours.'

But Brennan broke in on his thoughts again.

'I tell you, Robbie, if some of those bad bastards around Enniskillen decide to come calling, never mind the Brits, they've all had it.'

That made sense. Living across the border in the Irish Republic was no protection for their boss. True, the Irish Army patrolled the frontier but with 300 miles of wild territory to cover, they were thin on the ground. Nor was there incentive to protect the chief of an organization

118

committed to overthrowing the Republic's government as well as that in Northern Ireland. In fact, Paul Raymond McGovern's newness in the job was his only real security. The rumour mills had not yet started. Few knew who he was.

McGovern was the beneficiary of an IRA policy brought in during the early seventies and successfully operated since. To counter the disruptions caused when any of the movement's top leaders were captured, the movement had set up a duplicate command structure. The men in that secondary group took no active part in the campaign, but were kept fully briefed on current operations. Then, when an important commander was killed or arrested, his opposite number in the secondary structure would step in to take over.

The use of these sleepers created havoc for both British and Irish counter-intelligence organizations. Often, they were forced to leave a known IRA commander in place simply to avoid the trouble of finding out who his successor might be. Since leaders became widely known after a relatively short time in the job, the security groups were often charged with incompetence for not making arrests. In fact, they were following the most fruitful course by leaving such men at large.

McGovern's elevation had come through a bizarre twist of fate. His predecessor as chief of staff had already achieved a high profile. His relative immunity had begun creating suspicions in the Army Council that he was being deliberately left where he was. Under pressure, he agreed to run for a vacant seat in the United Kingdom Parliament in the overwhelmingly Catholic district of West Belfast. He won the seat handily. But his victory cost him his command. Ironically – and not for the first time in the twentieth century – the head of a movement committed to the violent overthrow of the British Government was elected to its highest legislative chamber.

Within days of the election, the chief of staff's sleeper, Paul Raymond McGovern, who had spent his recent years farming a smallholding in eastern Donegal, took over. One of his first acts was the terse message summoning Robbie Driscoll to this meeting.

'Mind yourself.' Brennan leaned across now and flicked the cigarette out the window where the wind whipped it away in a shower of sparks. Changing gears, he accelerated up the approaching hill. They breasted the top.

'Well, well. Look at that.'

A beautiful valley nestled under the pale grey hills. At the centre lay a small patchwork of neat green fields. The sun glinted off a small winding river running through it. On its bank was a lone white two-storey house with a grey slated roof. A barn stood close by.

'Like a bloody painting,' Brennan said.

Robbie smiled. 'I've seen one that matches. Done by a man named Paul Henry.'

'Don't know him,' Brennan said.

'He's long gone. Worked here at the turn of the century.'

'Ah.'

The car rolled down the hill, gathering speed.

Robbie gripped the dashboard as they lurched into a bend.

'Maybe the man isn't foolish,' Brennan said as he struggled for control.

They rolled on downwards to the valley bed. The narrow bumpy road straightened as they reached the bottom. Relaxing, they drove down towards the house. As they neared, both heard the loud barking of a dog above the hum of the engine.

120

A hefty German shepherd glared through the railing as they stopped. He began to bark even more ferociously when Robbie got out of the car. The door of the house opened and a woman appeared. She shouted sharply. Reluctantly, the animal backed away. She shouted again and he finally slunk back to where she stood. The woman was tall and well-built with long black hair and a pale unsmiling face. She wore a loose brown sweater and jeans in calf-high boots. As Robbie watched, she bent to take the dog's collar and drew him back to her. She was not gentle. Straightening, she looked towards him.

'Is Mr McGovern home?' Robbie called. 'He's expecting me.'

At the sound of his voice, the dog began barking again, leaping as he tried to jerk forward. The woman tugged him back fiercely. With her free hand, she gestured towards the barn. As Robbie opened the gate, she dragged the dog inside, closing the door. He heard the barking continue as he crossed the gravel to the yard.

The hum of machinery came from inside the barn. He opened the small door and bent to step through.

A dozen cows stood in stalls on either side of the long aisle. A man in grey dungarees was working over a pump at the other end. He turned as Robbie entered.

'Mr McGovern?'

The man nodded and came forward, wiping his hands slowly on a cloth. He was tall and well-built with smooth pale skin and reddish brown hair cut tight at the temples. Robbie judged him to be in his late forties.

'Robbie Driscoll, is it?' The cool light eyes flicked over Driscoll's well-clad figure.

'Yes, sir.'

A smile creased the other's face, making him seem younger. He held out a hand. 'Nice to meet you.'

'And you,' Robbie said. The grip was firm, the hand not nearly as callused as expected. 'I hope I'm not too early.'

'No, no. I'm just about finished.' McGovern wiped his hands again. 'You had no trouble finding me then?'

'No. Shay Brennan came with me. He knows the area.'

'Ah, Brennan.' McGovern nodded. 'You two have been together for a while. And doing good work.'

Robbie said nothing.

'I hear he's a good man.'

'One of the best,' Robbie said. He knew McGovern's compliment would please Shay.

McGovern glanced back to his rear. 'Look, let me connect up these last two. Then we can talk.' Together, they walked down the aisle between the humming machinery. Robbie watched as McGovern, a little awkwardly, connected up the last two cows.

'All done,' he said and turned, smiling. 'Do you want to sit?' He gestured to a bench where some equipment was stacked.

'No, I'm fine.'

McGovern nodded easily. He leaned against a battered pillar and reached into a pocket of the dungarees, drawing out an old pipe.

'Know anything about farming, Robbie?' He began prising out the ash from the bowl.

'No, sir, I don't.'

'Lucky man. It's a pain in the arse. The one business I know where any change is for the worst.' He began filling the pipe from a leather pouch. 'But of course you're a city man, aren't you? Belfast man.'

'Newtownards.'

'Of course.' McGovern nodded. 'Nice area, that. Been

122

through it a few times. Trouble-free too.' It was not a place where many Catholics lived.

The sweet aroma of the tobacco wafted by Robbie.

'You're probably wondering why I sent for you,' McGovern said finally, his back against the pillar, pipe in hand. A cow began lowing softly in the background.

Robbie nodded.

'Your little chat with Liam Ring. That one where you offered a little heat as well as light. You recall it?'

'Yes, sir.'

'Robbie, this is no reflection on you. I respect a man who speaks his mind. And your ability is unquestioned. But what you said back there raised some questions.'

Robbie said nothing.

'Are you having any difficulties with the operations we've been giving you?' McGovern looked at him directly, the cool eyes suddenly at variance with the simple farmer's image.

'No more than what I told Ring.'

McGovern nodded. 'This is the second time you've had this kind of problem, isn't it?' he said. 'I recall hearing about the Judge Wickham business. That must have been difficult for you too.'

Robbie shrugged. 'Some things aren't too easy to forget. But you learn to live with them.' The truth was he had only recently begun to think of it again. And the living was becoming harder.

McGovern drew on the pipe, saying nothing.

'I didn't think it was necessary to do the Wickham thing in front of his children,' Robbie said. 'We could have avoided that.'

McGovern lowered the pipe. 'I agree. Tell me, who arranged this recent business in Glenvoy, anyway?'

He knows, Robbie thought. But he wants to see how I say it.

'Liam Ring's people. Maybe even Ring himself.'

'Why is that, do you think?'

'I imagine he's been taking up some of the slack for the Armagh battalion.'

'If he has,' McGovern let a certain grimness creep into his voice, 'it's going to stop. We all know Liam Ring is an honest man. Not only that, he's also proved that he's unbreakable in hard conditions. But the man is a bureaucrat, pure and simple. This Colgan affair has cost us dearly.' He looked at Robbie, his eyes softening. 'To say nothing of what it must have cost you.'

'I wouldn't over-emphasize that,' Robbie said. 'I regret the circumstances, yes. But it hasn't changed my commitment.'

'Good,' McGovern said. 'That's what counts. Remember, the sacrifices made in this generation will benefit the next. That's what matters.' He gestured with the pipe. 'I don't have to tell you it would be pointless otherwise.'

Robbie nodded. That was the first article of faith. It never changed.

McGovern rested a foot against the pillar.

'When I deal with a man I respect,' he said, 'I believe in giving hostages to fortune. In letting him know where I stand.' He paused. 'I didn't want this job, Robbie. To be frank, there are things involved in it that I loathe. Executions, civilian casualties, knee-cappings. There's even the effect on my family. I can tell you honestly that I asked the Army Council to be excused. But they turned my request down. I was ordered to take this post. Well, now that I have it, I'm going to do what's required. Because I believe in the outcome. If I have to kill more, bomb more, I'll do it. Until the British leave.' He eyed Robbie. 'I have the feeling that you will, too.'

Robbie Driscoll nodded.

'This problem in the United States,' McGovern said abruptly. 'With Monahan and these Mafia people. I had no knowledge of his dealings with them and I wouldn't have approved if I had. And now, as you know, they've murdered the man.' He looked at Robbie. 'Did you know that they also stole $250,000 of our money?'

Robbie shook his head.

'They must think us fools,' McGovern said. 'And if they are allowed to get away with it, we will deserve to be looked on as such.'

He came away from the pillar. His eyes were cold now and his face had the hard look you see on men who are ready to go the distance.

'I won't have our movement held up to ridicule. Not by the British and certainly not by a gang of murdering criminals like the Mafia. I want those arms we paid for. Or that money back. And I want something else besides. I want these people taught that nobody, whoever they are and wherever they may be, trifles with the Irish Republican Army without paying the consequences.'

He looked at Robbie, his face set.

'I'm sending you to New York.'

Late that night, when Robbie got back to Belfast, he went to see Liam Ring. He was astonished at the older man's reaction. Robbie had never seen him so angry.

'Has he taken leave of his senses?' Ring snarled. The skin was tight over his cheekbones. 'It's madness! We're not talking about some boy scouts group here. These people have been around a long time. And they're as vicious as they come. How in hell are you going to take them on alone?'

'Alone? I want to take Shay. And I thought you could give me some people from the New York support group.'

'Shay, my arse!' Ring said with uncharacteristic vulgarity. 'You or nobody else is getting Shay Brennan right now. Unless they want the Lisburn Barracks job to go up the spout.'

'What are you talking about?'

Ring waved a hand and walked away. Suddenly, he turned back. 'I was going to use you, if you must know. We've got a plan going to hit their command staff. Now, with you gone, Shay is the next best. What am I saying, the next best? After him, there's nobody.'

'Come on, Liam.'

'I'm serious. We're knee deep in people with balls. But who lasts long enough to get the experience that makes them valuable? You're the longest lasting, Robbie. And Shay is the second longest, although frankly, I think that's mostly due to his being with you. Anyway, if Paul wants this operation to happen and I know he must, he can't take both of you away from me.'

Robbie shrugged.

'Well, you better tell him that yourself. He wants to see you anyway.'

'I'm sure he does,' Ring said sarcastically. He looked at Robbie. 'Was he pumping you about me, by any chance?'

'Not that I noticed.'

'He hates my guts,' Ring said. 'But the McGovern forte is not to let it show. His style is the open manner followed by the snide remark. Always pretending his views are based solely on the best interests of the movement. Like hell. As for that "let the cup pass from me" horseshit, I suppose he dropped that on you too?'

Robbie flushed.

'It may interest you to know that he's been pursuing the fucking top job for years. Taking the de Gaulle pose, sitting in his rural retreat waiting for the call. I can tell you from personal experience that the man knows as much about farming as my arse knows about snipe-shooting. Now that he's chief, it'll be goodbye country and hello city. Instead of the farmhouse in Donegal, it'll be a mansion on the Malone Road.' His eyes flickered briefly as he realized what he said. He looked down. 'Anyway, it'll be goodbye to Commandant Ring too,' he added bitterly.

'You're not serious, Liam.'

Ring looked up angrily.

'You bloody fool. Don't you realize how hare-brained this whole scheme is? It's another of the McGovern grand gestures. My God, don't you think we should beat the British before taking on the blasted Mafia? Ah no, but that's not the great McGovern's style. Extending the movement's hand to the far corners of the earth now, that appeals very nicely. I tell you, if he lasts long enough, he'll be appointing ambassadors.'

'Liam, I really don't think that's fair. The man is barely in the job.'

'Robbie, you're a good man,' Ring said impatiently. 'The best. But you're walking on eggs here. This thing doesn't make sense. All right, we lost a lot of money to some con men. So what? You and Brennan can go out, stick up a few banks, and get it back. OK, we lost a hard-working member then. Hah! That man Monahan was an idiot who went swimming with sharks without wearing a crash helmet. And now,' he waved an arm, 'we're going to risk our very best man to revenge him? It's sheer madness, I tell you.'

'Well, do you want to try and stop it?'

Ring was silent, his hands on the table.

'It would be foolish to try,' he said. 'Not with my standing and a man as stubborn as McGovern.' He looked at Robbie. 'You could do something, though.'

'Like what?'

'You could refuse to go. Nobody with any sense would blame you for it.'

Robbie was silent.

'It would be the end of your work, I admit,' Ring said. 'McGovern and his sycophants would see you drummed out for it, best or not. Like me, you'd be finished.'

They were both quiet now.

Ring shook his head. 'The bastard has us trapped.' He sat down now, slumping in the chair. 'But the greatest danger is that he might very well get you killed.'

'Can you find me any help at all?' Robbie asked.

Ring shrugged.

'What is there? At this very moment, the New York support team isn't worth a shit, given the pressure they've faced lately. None of them is less than fifty and there isn't a pisspot of talent among them. I'll try, naturally, but you'd be a fool to count on anyone there.'

He paused.

'There are excellent people in Boston but they'd have nearly as many problems working in New York as you. Maybe more since all of them are in one FBI file or another. Still, they could put together some of the hardware you're going to need. I could set that up.'

'It doesn't solve my problem, does it?' Robbie said. 'I still need people.'

'What about the Craven fellow? At least he's actually there.'

'He's no experience. And I don't really know how committed he is.'

128

Ring shrugged.

'Beggars can't be choosers. You know, Robbie, my dad used to recite a jingle that stuck in my mind over the years.

> Thanks be to God for what we have
> A little more we would be glad
> But now the times they are so bad
> We have to do with what we have.

Robbie smiled.

'It's really Craven or nothing,' Ring said. 'And I suppose the main question is, has he got what they call the right stuff?'

Chapter Eleven

A thin filmy rain was falling as the cab drew in by the fence that enclosed Small's Pier. Tom Craven paid the fare and got out on to the deserted parking lot. The air was filled with the dank smell of the nearby Hudson. The driver pocketed the tip and glanced curiously at him before pulling away. The cab's beams slid along the glinting wire. Only a faint tendril of exhaust remained as it disappeared city-ward. Craven turned to the entrance.

The high metal gate facing him was slightly ajar. A small guard hut stood inside, a light showing in the window. Craven paused. The Columbian Lascia had not mentioned this was a private site when he called to set up the meeting. Cautiously he slid through the narrow opening. Looking in the window of the hut, he saw it was empty. The rain was thicker than earlier. It had begun to wet his face.

Ahead, the grey metalled warehouse which Lascia had described stood out in the arc lighting. Craven started down the tarred roadway. The lights strung along the fence gave the compound the appearance of a prison camp. Only the distant hum of highway traffic and the murmur of wind broke the silence.

Walking steadily, Craven reached the pier, where a lonely stretch of black water glistened in the lights. The wind was blowing harder here, driving the rain into his face from the river. The traffic noise was less obtrusive. Instead he could hear the quick slap of water against the supports below. The pier itself was poorly lit and looked deserted.

Moving slowly, he searched along the warehouse wall. The arrangement was to meet at the second of the two entrances. He came to the first door. It was closed and padlocked in the gloom. He paused to examine it briefly then moved on, his pace quickening. He walked a hundred feet or so before coming to the second entrance.

This time, the doors were half open. But when he put his head in, the interior was black as pitch. He settled down to wait. Several minutes passed. Then, suddenly, he heard a car engine in the distance. Stepping out from the door, Craven moved out towards the water's edge to look back towards the main gates.

A pair of dipped lights shone on the distant wire mesh. Squinting hard in the light rain, he saw a man appear in the misty beams and begin pushing the gates apart. As he watched, the man stepped to one side. Craven's breath hissed as the car drove through. It stopped, the rear lights glinting redly as the man outside shut the gates behind him.

Craven was leaning forward now, watching intently as the car started slowly down the road. Lascia had said he would be coming alone. Something was very wrong here. The headlights reflected off the wet roadway as it came down towards the pier. Then suddenly, unexpectedly, they plunged into darkness. Only the small yellow parking showed as the car lights neared the pier.

Craven straightened. Then, after a brief hesitation, he ran for the warehouse entrance. Inside the doors, it was impossible to see. As he searched, the noise of the car engine grew stronger. Without waiting, he began moving down blindly to his right.

The interior reeked of stale grease and rusting metal

like an ancient garage. Groping forward, Craven's knee suddenly struck solid steel. He gasped, but quickly recovered. He had struck the bonnet of a truck. Breathing harder but moving more slowly, he edged around it.

The car was on the pier now, its engine louder as it came slowly down its length. A faint gleam was visible beyond the door where a steel stanchion picked up the reflection of the parking lights. Hands against the side of the truck, Craven crouched lower now. Slowly, beyond the big doors, a yellow sidelight appeared as the car crept into sight. The brakes hissed softly and it stopped just past the doors.

Moments after, the motor died.

In the sudden quiet the rain rattled on the metal roof. Craven's palms pressed against the metal as the car door opened, then closed with a soft clump. Almost immediately, the second door opened and shut. Two people were out now. Confirmation, if any was needed now, that this would not be a two-party meeting.

Craven held his position, eyes on the opened doorway.

In the gap, two figures slowly took shape against the faint glow of the parking lights outside. Moving slowly, they both crossed the threshold into the warehouse and stopped. They were no more than twenty feet off.

There was a moment of silence.

'Tom Craven?' a voice called softly. 'You there?'

Craven did not move.

'It's Lascia, Tom.'

But the Columbian had a strong Hispanic accent. This one was nasal, New Yorkish. Craven stayed.

The two kept waiting. In the faint light, one showed up as stocky. The other was much taller, less filled out. The stocky one moved forward a little, stopped, peering into the blackness.

'Come on, Tom, you in there?'

Still Craven made no move.

'He's in there all right,' the tall one said. 'I can feel it, Albie.'

'Shut your fucking mouth,' the stocky one whispered fiercely. He stood in silence. 'You got a torch in the car?' His voice was low but it carried in the hollow interior. Tom Craven shifted lower.

'Jesus,' the tall one had a whine in his voice, 'who thinks of things like that?'

Albie swore.

'Turn the heads full on and bring the car in here,' he said harshly.

As the tall one hurried out, Albie reached into his coat.

'If you're in there, pal,' he said, more threatening now, 'it would be smart to come out now.'

The moments passed as he waited. Then, as if irritated, he muttered something and went back to the half-open doors. Outside, the motor of the car started up and the headlights came on. The stocky man known as Albie now began pushing the doors apart.

Licking his lips, Craven edged sideways to glance down the warehouse away from the doors. Very dimly, a line of trucks could be seen parked flush against the side wall. The only gap was down the main aisle. Where the car manoeuvring outside would soon be pointing its headlights.

Craven began edging outwards, the noise masked by the rain rattling now against the roof. It was clear he had to make a move. Particularly as that little bastard Albie had a gun.

At that moment, the car was manoeuvring up to the entrance, its headlights piercing the gloom. Craven waited until the stocky Albie turned to direct the car in.

Then he was out and running.

His aim was to reach the end of the warehouse where he might find a door through which to escape. He ran flat out, not bothering about noise or the danger of hitting something in the darkness. That was what almost did him in. Half-way down the aisle and completely unexpectedly, his foot struck some metal object abandoned in the aisle. Tumbling, dragging the noisy screeching object with him, he sprawled by the line of parked trucks.

The fall had knocked some of the wind out of him, but luckily uninjured, he managed to scrabble along the concrete to shelter among the parked trucks.

Nevertheless Albie heard.

'Get it round!' he screamed at the driver as the car came through the entrance. 'Hurry!'

Almost immediately, the interior of the warehouse began lighting up like a stage set.

Craven scrambled to his knees, preparing to try another last desperate dash. But the car lights had begun sweeping down the interior, lighting up the grimy metal walls, the dripping girders and the twin rows of dusty trucks.

He was too late.

The beams came to rest on the squared end of the warehouse, lighting it brilliantly. And there, no more than thirty yards away, was the door Tom Craven had been hoping for. But now it was that much too far.

Back near the door, Albie was standing by the car. At waist level he held a pointed gun, waiting for Craven's move.

'Okay, pal!' The powerful voice carried above the hum of the car's motor. 'Game is over. Either you come out now and we talk. Or we come in and maybe scramble that stupid brain of yours.'

Craven gripped the cold rubber of the tyre he was

crouched behind. He began to search about. Suddenly, he shifted his knee and peered down. The object he had tripped over, half a rusty radiator, was lying where his foot had dragged it. Reaching down carefully, he took a grip. While it was light enough to lift, it looked heavy enough to hurt. Teeth clenched, a cold sweat on his forehead now, Craven drew the piece up against his chest.

'I'm coming, Tom,' Albie called. 'Last chance to come out.'

Craven shifted to a crouch and adjusted his grip on the radiator. Turning his head slightly to catch the footfalls of the approaching man, he remained tense but ready.

Albie was clever enough to mask the noise of his coming. But he could not hide his shadow. It stretched long and bulky before him. First the elongated head passed Craven, then the shoulders. As the torso passed and the approaching legs arrived by his position, he shifted softly and waited.

As Albie's body appeared, Craven sprang.

Briefly, there was an image of a fat, grey startled face and a raised gun. Then came the slamming impact as the rusting metal struck solid flesh. The force of Craven's charge knocked the shorter man backwards, but he did not fall. There was a glimpse of a bloodied face and a dirtied black cloth overcoat. Craven struck again. And this time Albie went down.

Dropping the radiator, Craven turned and sprinted towards the beckoning door at the end of the warehouse. His huge shadow, etched on the wall by the pitiless beams from the car, raced inward ahead of him.

He had underestimated his speed. It was far too fast. Skidding desperately, he slammed into the door. Metal boomed around him. Half-staggering but frantic, he clawed at the lever and pushed it down.

It was locked.

He tore at it again, a faint cry of panic on his lips. But the stubborn handle was immovable. Suddenly, as he struggled, a vicious crack exploded in his ears. Through the spraying dust, he saw a splintered hole appear by his head. Trapped in the merciless light he turned, his eyes searching desperately for shelter. Someone was shouting something at the other end of the warehouse. A second shot winged by him.

Among the shadows thrown by the parked trucks, he saw a tilted metal staircase winding upwards in the centre of the floor. The whack of a third bullet above his head sent more dirt showering. Heaving away from the wall, half blinded by the tumbling dirt, he sprinted towards the stairs.

'Albie!' a high strung voice was shouting. 'Albie!'

'Get the bastard!' the recovering Albie screamed. 'Don't let him get away!'

Tom Craven's hand closed on the metal stair. He scrambled up. Old and rusted, the steps rattled like thunder under his weight.

'There he goes!'

Flame suddenly sprouted by Craven's hand as a fresh bullet whanged off the metal. He kept going, rushing upwards, turning and turning on the rounded tier. Another shot. Again a miss. There were too many shadows confusing the shooter. By now, he had reached the top of the stairs.

His head came up through the floor in the upper storey. It was in darkness except for faint bars of outside light leaking through the shuttered windows. It was just enough to show the place was empty. And without shelter of any kind. Craven ran to get away from the stairs, his feet booming on the heavy timber floor. He reached the end wall and stopped, turning his back to the wall, trapped.

Rain rattled off the metal roof overhead. Draughty air whipped around from the grilled openings in the walls. Gasping, Craven searched the space around him. Down below, he heard them cursing, shouting. They had reached the stairs. It was time for desperate prayer but he kept looking.

Away to his left, there was a shimmering light in the wall. Different from the others, it was close to the floor. The metal staircase began creaking. With no alternative, Craven ran towards the light.

The light was coming through an oblong metal grille wide enough to pass through if he could open it. He fell to his knees and ran his fingers around the edges. The cool breeze coming from the other side gusted against his face.

Above the hiss of wind around him, the staircase groaned. They were coming.

The light coming through the mesh was from a ship moored at the next wharf. But he was more interested in what was happening at the stairs. The first faint white blur appeared at floor level when his fingers found the two protruding wing nuts. Still watching the stairs, he began forcing them apart. The metal squeaked in protest.

The first figure was rising like an apparition from the gloomy stairs. Craven heaved in opposite directions with all his strength. The grips held for what seemed an eternity, then slowly yielded. The dim image of the second man had begun to rise from the stairwell when the metal guard sagged inwards.

As the two men who had previously been in the light stared about uncertainly, Craven pulled the screen and it came away. But he had miscalculated the weight. With a sudden heart-stopping action of its own, it slipped from his hands and crashed to the floor.

The two at the stairtop straightened instantly.

'There he is!' one shouted.

The first shot zipped across the floor as Craven dived for the opening. As he went through, his raincoat caught briefly, pulling him to one side. Then it ripped wildly and he was through. He fell, tumbling over down to the water below.

The icy impact tore the air from his lungs. He went down into the blackness, his arms flailing, fighting the panic brought on by the massive roaring in his ears. Twisting wildly, he started fighting his way up but inward now towards the shelter of the pier.

The cold air against his face and the slap of the water in the blackness greeted his arrival on the surface. Shaking water out of his eyes, he stared up and found himself under the pier. Breathing deeply, bobbing in the tide, he turned quickly in a circle, searching around him.

In the distance, beyond the end of the pier, he could see the beaded lights of the flat New Jersey shoreline. To his right lay the ship at the next wharf, its lighted superstructure brightening the surrounding water. He trod water, taking deep breaths. Then, wasting no time, he swam down beneath the pier towards the outer end.

Once he reached it, he rested again. Taking the trouble now to discard his coat and shoes. After more deep breathing, he moved away from the pillar, filled his lungs with air and dived under. Striking out this time for the midwater darkness of the Hudson. Some distance out, at the last possible moment, he surfaced for more air, then went down again, repeating the exercise several times until he was more than a hundred and fifty yards out.

Once there, he allowed himself to drift slowly downstream, only stopping when he had a clear view of the pier he had so quickly vacated.

After what seemed an age with the chill growing, the headlights of the car slowly appeared through the doors of the warehouse. As Craven trod water, the car turned on to the pier and headed slowly down towards the gate. The bastards didn't even close the doors after them.

Still upright in the water, Craven watched as they reached the main gate where they stopped. Again the lights went out. Smiling now, Craven slapped his hand on the water in exultation. Then he turned and began swimming powerfully downstream.

He had difficulty staying upright when he came ashore ten minutes later at a bared lot downstream. Stumbling across the rubble-strewn ground, he was barely aware of the pounding his stockinged feet was taking. Pushing forward, he reached the vandalized fence which separated the lot from the highway. Keeping a perilous balance, he managed to get through the broken mesh. Reaching the verge of the road, he waited until a lighted cab approached then stepped out and waved. The taxi slowed. Craven stepped into the light and, as he did so, it suddenly shot away again, narrowly missing him. It took a second experience before it became clear that no one would pick him up in his present condition. Shivering and close to collapse, he dodged traffic to cross the highway to a warren of streets on the other side. He had come down one of these on the way from the hotel. So he knew it was up there somewhere.

'Hey you!'

The sound jarred Craven as he stood with his legs apart

above the warm grille. Slowly, he opened his eyes and turned.

A police car stood at the kerb.

'Over here!'

Tentatively, Craven approached. An uncapped policeman, hand draped on the steering wheel, stared at him from the opened window. He was a stout, beefy man with grey-tinged black hair. His partner, a young man, was writing on a pad.

'What you doing?'

Craven pointed back at the grating.

'I was feeling cold. I stopped a minute to get a little heat, that's all.'

'You wouldn't be the first,' the policeman said drily. He squinted. 'You new around here?'

Craven nodded.

'Where's home?'

After a moment's hesitation, Craven said: 'The Chelsea Hotel.'

The policeman chuckled. He turned to his partner. 'Hear that, Ray?'

The partner bowed his head down to look across at Craven and smiled. 'That has to be a first,' he said.

'Got a suite at the Chelsea, eh?' the older cop said.

'No,' Craven said, low-voiced, 'just a room.'

'Ah.' The policeman nodded slowly. 'How much they charge now for a room? Hundred bucks a night?'

'Something like that.'

The policeman nodded sympathetically. 'It's a bitch, eh? Having to pay out that kind of money for a bed.' He looked down, taking in Craven's shoeless feet, running his eyes up over the rumpled wet clothing to the dank hair. 'Still, I guess if you have it, you might as well flaunt it.' He paused. 'Although to tell the truth, you don't look to me like you have it.'

Craven said nothing.

'All right,' the policeman said finally, 'in the car.'

'Wait a minute, sir. I'm only a few blocks from the hotel. I'll make it there all right.'

'Don't give me no more of that hotel shit,' the policeman growled. He stabbed a thumb over his shoulder. 'I said get in the car.'

Craven looked around briefly. Then he shrugged and climbed into the back seat.

The patrol car rolled away from the kerb. Rain spat against the windscreen as they drove down Ninth Avenue. Craven slumped in the seat, water still seeping out from under him. To some degree he had been acclimatized as well as being traumatized by his experience and was not aware of the Hudson's unique smell.

In front, they suddenly began talking earnestly. As if to make some point, one of them even opened his window wide. The other began to shake his head. Abruptly, they pulled in to the kerb. The younger policeman got out and walked round to the side door. He pulled it open.

'Out.'

Hurriedly, Craven slid across the seat.

'Jesus.' The policeman swung the door several times as he stood on the street. Then he slammed it closed. He looked at Craven viciously. 'Listen, you.' He leaned forward to make his point. Then his nose wrinkled and he recoiled. 'Get the hell out of here,' he shouted suddenly. 'Go on, beat it. And I'm warning you. Next time we catch you in this district, you get the shit kicked out of you. Stick to the Bowery in future. Understand?'

Craven nodded quickly then turned and hurried away.

141

'Get yourself a goddam bath!' the policeman yelled after him.

Craven grinned.

Twenty minutes later, he shuffled down the sidewalk to the Chelsea's door. He stopped by the double glass doors and took out his wallet first before ringing the bell. There were certain rules to grease a difficult passage in New York and Craven was already beginning to learn them.

When the desk clerk arrived at the door, the first thing he saw was a five held flat against the window. He opened the door on the chain.

'I'm Thomas Craven. Room 1105. Some people tried to mug me. Let me in.'

Being offered money by a bum threw the clerk's brain into overload. He stood staring.

'Come on, open up,' Craven shouted. 'The bastards threw me into the river. I need to get out of these clothes.'

Glancing at the five again and reassured by the noisy impatience which came as naturally as breathing to troubled New Yorkers, the clerk opened the door.

Craven pushed the money at him and brushed past.

'I need my key.'

The clerk, a thin young man with a worried air, blanched at Craven's wake.

'God, you smell,' he said, relocking the door and hurrying to follow.

'To hell with you,' Craven said. But strangely he was smiling. 'Just get me that bloody key.'

When he stepped into the elevator, there was already a tall pale man standing statue-like with arms folded in the corner. He was dressed in black leather and his long hair was pulled back in a pony tail. Craven nodded to him and pulled the crossed bars shut.

As the elevator rose, the man sniffed loudly behind him.

'Don't tell me.' The voice had a deep highly pleasant southern drawl. 'You just got a shipment in from Paris. I'd know it anywhere. Canal Number Five, right?'

Craven turned.

'What the hell are you doing, riding the elevator?'

'My lady and I have been humping since midday,' the man said calmly. 'Let's just say I'm in need of a time out.'

Craven turned away, grinning again.

'I have to say,' he said over his shoulder, 'that I'm beginning to take a liking to this city.'

'Do something about that smell,' the man said, 'if you want it to reciprocate.'

Chapter Twelve

Certain people travel a lot without leaving home mentally. Robbie Driscoll had not done much travelling but he had that characteristic. His eye constantly sought the familiar.

In the field, he often turned that habit to advantage by mixing common things in unusual combinations to achieve disarming and sometimes devastating effects. As, for instance, when he dressed a very old man in a familiar Major's uniform and sent him shuffling past a British Army post in Upper Belfast. As the chuckling sentries watched, Robbie walking behind, released the bomb suspended under his coat and left it primed against the sandbags.

Again, disguising two women as drunken prostitutes, he put them down the road from an emplacement where they could become known. For a week, he had them go through the motions, making sure they were picked up night after night by his own men. Then he had them stroll past the emplacement, stopping briefly for a few steamy words with the soldiers hidden behind the gauze. When the girls left, two white markers remained, pin-pointing the exact positions of the concealed soldiers for Driscoll's Armalite. It was all magician's stuff. But deadly too. And always seasoned with the familiar.

Now here, in a hotel corridor three thousand miles from home, his eye was doing it again. But this time he was the one being surprised. This place had none of the antiseptic cleanliness normally associated with American hotels. The faded ivory-coloured walls and the brown sisal were only too familiar. He even thought he smelled damp. Still, it was all quite pleasant. And friendly too. A stout woman in mannish tweeds and string tie, carrying a pipe, had just smiled warmly as she tramped past. The unusual seemed normal here, he noticed. Which was probably why the New York support group recommended it. (An added incentive might have been that the hotel had erected a bronze plaque to a former member above the entrance. Brendan Behan had stayed too.)

Walking down the corridor, Robbie found the number 1105. The door looked as if that might have been the year of manufacture. He rapped several times before it finally swung open with some violence.

Tom Craven, his face puffed from sleep, stared out. The room behind him was in darkness.

'Christ Almighty,' he said.

Robbie grinned.

'When did you get in?' Craven stood aside, tucking his shirt in.

'Couple of hours ago. Woke you, did I?'

'What do you think?' Craven closed the door and followed Robbie into the darkened bedroom. 'What time is it, anyway?'

'One o'clock,' Robbie said. 'In the afternoon.' He stopped suddenly.

'Good God, Tom. This place smells.'

Craven grinned. 'Gives you a start, eh?' He crossed to raise the blinds. 'You can blame the bloody Hudson. I took a fair share of it home with me last night.'

The room, brightening now, was in chaos. Craven swept a pile of clothes off the armchair and tossed them on the bed where he went to lie back against a raised pillow. He stifled a yawn.

'What were you doing in the Hudson, if that's not a rude question?' Robbie sat down.

Craven told him.

'You're a lucky man, Tom.'

Craven shrugged and reached for a cigarette. 'I would have been a little happier with some advance warning.' He lit his cigarette. 'What the hell is going on, Robbie?'

Robbie paused. 'Monahan was trying to make a deal for arms on our behalf. It went sour.'

'With Salvatore Genta, eh?'

'That's what we thought at first. But no. With his boss.'

'The great Francis Renata?'

Robbie looked at him in surprise.

'He kept turning up in Genta's dossier,' Craven explained.

'Ah. Well anyway, we were trying to take things carefully. To check credentials first. But Monahan was impatient. He decided to forge ahead on his own. Which was why we asked you to stop him. Unfortunately, that wasn't to be. He got murdered, Tom. Strangled, I believe.' Dinny Doherty had passed a full report to Ring. ('I'm the new Minister for Foreign Affairs,' he said tartly when informing Robbie.)

'Jesus,' Craven said. 'That's terrible news.'

'I'm guessing,' Robbie said, 'but when you turned up from Ireland two days later, asking questions, they must have thought you were a hit man.'

Craven drew on the cigarette.

'Right conclusion, wrong identity, eh?' He looked at Robbie. 'That's why you're here, isn't it?'

'No,' Robbie said. 'I didn't mention it but they took

146

our money too. I've simply come to take possession of the goods paid for.'

'That's telling them,' Craven said. 'You think they'll hand stuff over, just like that? Having already murdered the first man in the door?'

'Using the front door is not the only way to do business,' Robbie said calmly. 'A little indirect pressure can help too.'

Craven snorted.

'You're going to lean on the Mafia? Come on, Robbie, I don't doubt you're good. But I smell pie in the sky here.'

'You could try being a little more positive,' Robbie said. 'They did try to kill you, after all. Where's the old thirst for revenge?'

But Craven was not so gullible.

'What is this? You trying to get me onside or something?'

'Tom, I'll be frank,' he said. 'I need help. I'm not talking about shoot-out stuff. I know that's not your game. And I don't want to play it that way, either. Not against the odds here. What I need is some of your practical experience.'

'In what way?'

'I need every piece of information I can get on Francis Renata. But without your getting into the trouble you had with Genta. I can no more afford that than you can.'

'Well, I'll tell you something,' Craven said. 'It would be a lot easier to dig up stuff on Renata than it was on Genta.'

'Why?'

'There's masses of stuff on him in the New York Public Library. The computers are stuffed with references.'

'So what would you think of gathering it for me?'

'I don't know. There's the job at home to think about.'

'You needn't worry there. They've already told us we can have you for as long as we like.'

'Really?'

Robbie nodded.

'Well, I suppose it might be all right to do a little then.' Craven smiled. 'As you said, they did try to put me through the wringer. They deserve something for that.'

'Good man,' Robbie said.

'I still think you're crazy though.'

'I know,' Robbie said. 'And I appreciate that.'

Craven laughed.

'You're a hell of a fellow, Robbie. Let's just hope you're not biting off more than you can chew. These lads are tough.'

'Well, they use real bullets in the North too, Tom. And they have twenty thousand soldiers and police out on the street there, armed to the teeth, looking for us every day.' He paused. 'How many troops has Mr Renata, would you say?'

Craven shrugged.

'Seven, eight hundred, I suppose.'

Robbie smiled.

'I haven't seen odds like that in years.'

But that was really morale boosting. He still knew this was not going to be an easy one.

On the way out, he stopped by the door.

'Incidentally, did you mention where you were staying to anyone?'

Craven shook his head.

'And your name? Did you give that out at all?'

A little crestfallen, Craven nodded.

'To Lascia?'

'Yes.'

148

'Well, I don't imagine that's likely to create a problem,' Robbie said quickly. 'There's hundreds, even thousands of hotels in this city. Still, I think it might be wise to swop rooms.'

'That would put you in the firing line.'

Robbie grinned as he opened the door. 'But that's what I signed on for, isn't it?'

Returning to his own room, he felt pleased. That Hudson experience had blooded Craven and he had come through. Although he had no plans so far to involve him further (he had barely a plan at all) it was good to know Craven had the ability to take pressure and come through unscathed. He might not be as valuable as an experienced man like Shay Brennan. But it would be good to have him nevertheless.

After they changed rooms – without informing the desk which would defeat the purpose – Robbie left the hotel to call the Boston support team.

These teams formed the bedrock on which the movement was built. They were made up of sympathizers who came from all walks of life and across every age group. Their commitment extended to helping the movement but not going so far as to risk getting killed or copping long jail terms in return.

In a conventional army, the proportion of support personnel to combatants was usually three-to-one. In an underground army, with the peculiar problems involved in clandestine supply and communications, the proportion had to be at least twenty-to-one to be viable. In Northern Ireland where the latest atrocity by any of the contending parties dictated the zeal of support among the others, the figures generally fluctuated wildly. With the IRA, it ran between twenty- and fifty-to-one.

In the States, the support teams provided safe houses for fleeing IRA men, intelligence for arms-buying crews, and local back-up for the political lobbyists whom the movement sent out regularly to counteract the British information services in the United States.

Robbie had no idea how many there were in the Boston support team. But he knew their reputation. In guarded conversation now he told the contact what was needed. He was surprised but happy to hear that it would be ready in three days. Not for nothing were they considered the best outside of Ireland.

Even so, there was a long way to go.

'I've been thinking,' Tom Craven said as they sat down to dinner that evening, 'of what pressure you might apply to get your stuff from Renata.'

'Oh?'

'I assume you might have to kill or kidnap somebody in order to threaten him.'

'And what would you think about that?'

'It would scare shit out of me,' Craven said. 'Although I can see from reading about them that they're not nearly as all-powerful as people imagine. As a matter of fact, when you study it, you find that they're really anarchical and even a little weak. Their skill seems to lie in their ability to marshal people of proven ability in certain fields when they need them. Also, they know how to frighten opponents by using violence.'

He stopped suddenly.

Robbie grinned.

'Well,' Craven said, 'I'm glad to see you have a sense of humour.'

'Getting back to this other business,' Robbie said. 'It might be that I will have to move in on one of these people. It's important to know how you would feel about it.'

Craven was quiet.

'You're actually talking about Renata himself, aren't you?'

Robbie nodded.

'Well, that really scares me, Robbie. Not so much the doing of it. From what I've read and as I've said you have a much better chance of pulling it off than people think. Nobody believes more in their own image than the Mafia. And that makes them vulnerable. But if you fail, or they catch you, the consequences don't bear thinking about. They'll cut you into little pieces.'

'I'm aware of that.'

'I don't know if I'd want to go along with it,' Craven said. 'The lead-up, now that would probably be OK. Although for that I suppose you could get three hundred years over here.'

'Come on,' Robbie said, 'how could they convict you of kidnapping a Mafioso when none of them would testify? You can discount the law. There are only two people with hands in this game. Them and us. Everyone else is spectator.'

'Well, I'll tell you what I'll do,' Craven said. 'I'll gather all you need and stay helping through the lead-in even though I know now what you're doing. But you can't count on me after that. I'm not saying that I won't help, but I draw the line at giving any more commitment than you have right now. I just don't know enough.' He looked at Robbie. 'How does that sound?'

'I'm happy with it,' Robbie said.

'Good,' Craven said. 'Then maybe now we can have dinner.'

* * *

In fact, Craven was more interested in drink than food. Robbie watched that. It was always the crucial test. If the movement ever enforced breathalyser tests before operations, they would be unbeatable. As it was, they had to rely on the four stages of Irish drunkenness as a guide.

These were: *Jocose, Bellicose, Morose and Comatose.*

Men in the first category didn't want to kill anybody, those in the second wanted to do in everybody, those in the third did it with malice while those in the fourth usually ended up prisoners, where they were usually made comatose again, but without the benefit of alcohol.

Drink made Craven chatty. If he had bellicosity, it was of the intellectual kind. He seemed proud of his deductions. Robbie noticed that as his drinking increased, so did his judgements. As they were not greatly off, it did not bother him. But then Craven said something which seemed amusing at first, but soon was not.

'You don't look like a member, Robbie,' he said suddenly, pausing with Jack Daniels in hand. 'Anyone ever tell you that?'

Robbie smiled.

'A few,' he said. 'But maybe you should tell me again. How is a member supposed to look?'

'Oh, you know.' Craven gestured with his glass. 'Designer-stubble and rundown clothes. Looking a bit half-starved. Fond of a pint but usually short of the wherewithal. Struggling between boasting and confessing. And never very far from flying off the handle.'

It was a good description of Robbie's partner, Shay Brennan. 'And you're not the other type either,' Craven went on. 'The spoiled priest with the holy joe eyes, always spouting Gaelic. Going on about the next generation. Treating nationality like it was a religion. Wearing Irish-made materials down to the jockstrap.'

That was Liam Ring.

'So what do I look like?' Robbie asked.

Craven was silent for a moment. Then he grinned suddenly. 'SAS.'

Robbie said: 'Thank you.'

'I could see you weren't a Dubliner from the start,' Craven said. 'You didn't know about the Forty Foot. Or James Joyce's tower. And you didn't know what culchie meant, so you definitely weren't from the country either. That left the North.'

'Tom,' Robbie said, a little disturbed now.

But Craven was grinning, the bit in his teeth. 'And then there was that Setanta thing. Unusual that. Everyone who went through primary school in Ireland knows about him and his famous hurley.' He paused. 'Except for one group. The group in Northern Ireland who are never taught anything about Irish history.'

Robbie was watching him carefully now.

Craven leaned forward, a triumphant smile on his narrow face.

'You're a Protestant, Robbie, aren't you?'

If it hadn't been for that conversation, he might have waited longer before taking his next step. But Craven jarred him. Robbie had admired his deductive ability. Now, suddenly, he was uneasily aware that Craven was marching level with him although he had not started out with the same information. That not only bothered him. It was a warning. Craven's references might appear impeccable, but Robbie Driscoll had not survived for seven years by believing in angels of mercy who appeared on short acquaintance. He realized now that although he needed Craven, he would have to watch him.

153

Which still left him needing someone he could trust.

That night, after seeing Craven off, Robbie went back on the street and found a phone booth to call the man whom Ring indicated might provide some local help.

The soft, hesitant voice of Dinny Doherty came on the line. From the careful conversation it quickly transpired that Ring had made contact. And suddenly the news appeared good.

'I've been talking with a party who is very interested in participating,' Doherty said and paused. 'It's somebody who knows the city well, which is what you're going to need. And it's also someone who has worked for the movement, although it's been a while since.'

'You're sure they can be trusted?'

'No question about that,' Doherty said. 'When you hear who it is, you'll understand why.'

'Sounds good,' Robbie said. 'Who is it?'

He knew he had no choice. He told Doherty to go ahead anyway and make the appointment.

Chapter Thirteen

Tall and elegant, she came through the glass doors a few minutes after noon. She paused, framed by the light, to glance about. Even shadowed, her pallor was evident. Yet it enhanced the medieval quality of her face under the soft auburn hair, Robbie, admiring the blend of grace and beauty she presented, raised a hand in greeting.

She came towards him quickly, the soft leather purse bobbing on her shoulder. He took in the dark squared jacket, the white blouse and the fashionable baggy greys and thought she was nicely dressed, considering the circumstances.

'Nan Monahan?'

She nodded, her face softening briefly.

'You must be Robbie.' The voice was low but firm. She extended a hand.

'I'm sorry it has to be like this,' he said. Her touch was cold.

'Dinny Doherty said you came over specially,' she said.

He nodded.

'As soon as we heard.'

She hesitated. 'Have you anything new?'

He realized with surprise that she was still hoping.

He shook his head.

She gazed at him, her grey eyes luminous.

'They still haven't found him,' she said.

'I realize that,' he said. 'But from what we already know, it would be wrong to expect anything.'

She looked down.

'That's what Dinny said.' The pain in her voice was palpable. 'He wants me to accept it.'

Robbie said gently: 'I think he's right.'

For a moment, he thought she might cry. A little awkwardly, he took her arm.

'Poor Dad,' she said softly as they walked to the restaurant. Her voice caught. 'He had a good heart, you know.'

Certain memories anchor people to their parents. Some are happy, others not. Nan Monahan's strongest memory of her parents centred on her seventh birthday. That was when her mother told her the most intimate secret in their family.

She recalled sitting on the bed then, surrounded by gifts, being baffled by what her mother said. It was only later, when she asked Michael Monahan to explain what adoption was and saw his fierce reaction, that she realized something awful was involved.

Michael Monahan knew his wife's depressive illness was responsible for the disclosure. But that did not stop him deserting the sick bed from which she made it. Nan, tiny and bewildered, got to sleep in his large comforting arms in the family spare room for the first of many nights. It was the start of an attachment that came to dominate her life.

Years later, when discussing it on an analyst's couch, she was at pains to emphasize that no sex was involved. At first, it was the warmth. Then the whispered words of tenderness. Finally, and most powerfully, it was the sense of security which her father's massive presence gave her. Her mother, immersed in her own guilt-ridden world, could not compete.

To please her father and where possible to imitate him

became the guiding ambitions of Nan Monahan's child-hood. She pursued both with an intensity that rarely faltered.

Her passion for Ireland was kindled by this devotion. When she saw that her father never tired of talking about what was happening over there, she began using the country to hold his attention. Inevitably, it became an obsession for her too.

She was delirious with joy when he finally took her there with a dance troupe to participate in a pageant called *The Homecoming*. She did not know then that her father used the trip to smuggle arms across the Atlantic. But if she had she would have approved wholeheartedly.

The country itself was a revelation to her. Away from the violence, the lush green land with its meandering by-ways and historic ruins seemed made for fairy tales. And the people were overwhelming in their hospitality. She had the eerie sensation, common to many diverse people who see the place for the first time, that she had come home.

She returned to New York after that visit, tear-filled but brimming with happiness. The wildest dreams she had espoused for the love of her father, had finally become her own. She was then just twelve years old.

What happened next, she suspected, was a judgement from God. Her mother, excluded from the coterie of father and daughter, slid into a breakdown and had to be hospitalized. With that, everything changed. Michael Monahan tried hard to cope with caring for a motherless daughter, taking time away from his job, even babysitting her in his office. But finally, it proved impossible to continue.

Nothing equalled Nan Monahan's anguish when her father told her he was sending her away to the Convent of the Little Flower in upstate Rochester. She begged and pleaded desperately. She would stay at home and even look after her mother there. When that was rejected, she swore to look after him herself. I won't be afraid, she said, even when you go out of town. I'll do the groceries, I'll cook, I'll wash and clean for you. We'll be happy, you'll see. Finally, she collapsed in tears. Please, Daddy, don't send me away.

But it was a losing battle. Only when she saw the agony it was causing Michael Monahan did she finally give way.

When the day finally came for her to leave, she was pale and dry-eyed. It was her father who was in tears.

'Do you know the people who did this?' she asked suddenly.

They had a corner table in the restaurant. The waiter had offered to take her jacket, but she waved him away and slipped it on the back of the chair. That small practical act might have helped, for she was outwardly calm now. Elbows resting on the table, a gold bracelet dangling from her freckled wrist, she ignored the casually admiring glances coming from other tables. Her eyes were on Robbie.

'Yes,' he said.

'I'd like to know who they are,' she said grimly. 'And why this all happened.'

He told her then of her father's negotiations for the movement and of their efforts to stop him. She knew about that, she said. Dinny Doherty had told her. Feeling he owed her more, Robbie gave the details she wanted.

Her eyes widened in disbelief. '*The* Francis Renata? He's involved?'

Robbie nodded.

'You know who he is?'

'I understand that he's a well-known criminal.'

'More than that,' she said. 'He's the most dangerous crook in New York. If not the United States.'

'I've heard that too.'

'So he's the reason you came?'

'Well, he broke an agreement, killed your father and took our money. He really left us no choice.'

She nodded. For a moment, she fingered the table cutlery. Finally she looked up. 'You're experienced in this kind of business, are you?'

He frowned slightly.

'I'm sorry,' she said. 'Maybe I shouldn't have said that.'

'It's all right,' he said. They both fell silent. This is hard going, Robbie thought.

'I'm told you worked for the movement in the past,' he said finally.

She nodded.

'That was some years back.'

He looked now at the firm, youthful face.

You must have been very young, he thought.

Eight years.

That was how long it was since she had sat in an analyst's office and heard him tell her that either she broke the link with the movement or it would end up breaking her. She was seventeen years old at the time and she didn't need to be told that she was going under.

The early years at the Little Flower convent had been miserable. There were constant disputes and clashes of will with the nuns who ran the school. These conflicts baffled the sisters who recognized that she was both personable and intelligent. They did not realize that being told by your mother that you were not her natural daughter at an age as sensitive as seven was likely to produce catastrophic consequences.

A firebrand, the Mother Superior called her. The best team scorer and the worst team player in the school, the floor hockey coach said. Neither thought to wonder what she would have been like if the authority figures had not been the same sex as her mother.

Somehow, though, she managed to survive the first four years. By the time she was sixteen, the prognosis was that she might, just might, make it. Then sexuality hit her.

The tide of events that almost swept her away began when she and another girl slipped out one night to attend an Irish gala in a Rochester tavern called Salty Daly's. By then, Nan had developed the willowy beauty of which she was hardly aware and from which she drew no satisfaction.

That night, the two girls changed and made up in the downtown bus station toilet before heading for Daly's. Nan passed muster at the door. Her companion did not. Stubbornly, Nan fought for her. The manager, a handsome thirty-year-old Irishman named Mattie Murtagh, was called. A glance told him all he needed to know. He confirmed the refusal. But as they trudged away, he called Nan back and slipped her his card. Let me know if you decide to come back on your own, he said.

A week later, she called him. Soon after that, an affair began. At first, Nan thought she loved him and Murtagh certainly displayed the qualities that encouraged it. He was a warmhearted, generous man whose major fault was a lack of imagination. His gifts always came in predictable shapes and quantities. Roses in dozens, chocolates by the pound, jewellery from display counters. Even the poems he sent her were on Hallmark cards. Still, he was anxious to please and Nan was touched.

But soon her attention began to drift. It irritated her that this should happen, because he was so solicitous. But she could not help it. Whatever it was she craved, Murtagh could not supply it.

Two months after their first meeting, he produced a surprise. By then he was familiar with her passion for Ireland, which he largely shared. The surprise was a real-life refugee, a vagabond singer out from Northern Ireland. His name was Jackie Smith.

Nan was hardly impressed. He had a narrow sardonic face, pocked cheeks, and long, carelessly combed hair. He looked like a starveling. The brown turtle-neck hung loose on his slight figure and the stove-pipe corduroys were a joke. Even with the high heels on his scuffed cowboy boots he was still shorter than she was.

But Smith was an artist with the virtues and the disabilities of his breed. That is to say he had the perception of a saint trapped inside the personality of a devil. People of his type are best admired from a distance. Sitting ten feet from the stage when he performed was too close for Nan Monahan.

On the first night they met he sang:

> 'Armoured cars and tanks and guns
> Came to take away our sons'

and that unhinged her. Listening to him, she could actually hear the rumble of the tanks and see the visored soldiers dragging teenagers from the mean Belfast houses. And when he sang 'She Moves Through the Fair', she felt the overpowering conviction that it was her he was singing about.

Driven by need rather than encouragement, she manoeuvred herself into his arms. And when he accepted her submission with easy self-confidence, she was lost.

A single incident, within two weeks of the first consummation, summed up the relationship. She had arrived on a Saturday afternoon to find him alone in Mattie Murtagh's office. The sight of him and the newness of her passion, held her breathless and childishly shy as he drew her to him. Without a thought for the hazards involved, he began to undress her by Mattie Murtagh's desk.

Her agitation, heightened by the danger in the situation, made her tremble as she fumbled for him. But he brushed her hands away, forcing her to submit to his calmly continued undressing. When she finally stood naked before his fully dressed figure, she never felt so exposed or so erotically excited in her life.

Cool and unhurried, he laid her back on the desk and gazed down at her. They might have been the only two people on the planet. She was staring up at him, her body on fire, when the phone, only inches from her head, pealed in her ear. She jerked in fright but almost instantly he pushed her firmly back down. Then, smiling, he picked up the phone.

It was Mattie.

She could feel the blotting pad against her naked back, and the sharp edge of the desk biting into her bared thighs as he chatted. All the while, his hand, soft but immovable, held her in place. She felt utterly captive and totally miserable. But if it had taken a thousand years, she would not have moved from where she was.

The conversation could not have taken more than a few minutes. But it was the casual ease with which he conducted it that transfixed her. It proclaimed an ascendancy over her so total that, when he took his hand away, she remained lying where she was, waiting.

Later, when she thought of how it would have looked to anyone coming through the unlocked door, she almost died. Still, in the years that followed, whenever a phone rang suddenly in the night, she would recall that other time and flush at the feeling it provoked.

Mattie found out, of course.

She never knew if it was revenge or concern that motivated him, but he called her father. Then he called her and told her what he had done. After that he went looking for Jackie Smith.

They fled across the Canadian border, to Toronto.

It was then that she found Jackie Smith belonged to the movement. But to a fringe section, originally financed by bank robberies, who now traded drugs for arms. Largely addicted to the product they were trading, these men were disowned whenever they were caught. But the IRA's threats to punish them were a façade. By the late seventies they were indispensable to the movement's operations. Activists like Robbie Driscoll could only suspect at their existence.

Nan Monahan had no time to be shocked by what she discovered about Jackie Smith. For by then, he had started her on drugs too. At first it was fun. There was the thrill of clandestine activity in another country, the heady excitement of smuggling guns across the Atlantic and the wild camaraderie of sex and drug-taking as well. But then, as they went from cocaine to pills and she found herself trading forged prescriptions for Jackie, the lights began to dim.

And perhaps more than anything, she desperately missed her father.

One night in Montreal, when percodan and a powerful

hit of acid sent her out into the night to seek the purest of white milk made on earth, she had the ultimate experience.

As she walked down the silvery, snow-packed street, she felt a presence leave her body. She stopped, feeling the iciness, watching as the ghostly shape formed in the moonlight. Without hesitation, she knew it was the spirit of the foundling who had been living inside the body of Nan Monahan all these years.

Although it had no recognizable human form, she knew it was aware. And that it wanted to get away from her.

'Please, don't go,' she called softly.

But it began moving away. Not fast, but very decidedly. Knowing the danger that would develop if it got away, she started after it. But it glided on, staying ahead of her. She began to hurry, stumbling in the snow, her panic rising. Then she was running, shouting, with houses, street lights, cars flashing past in a dazzling kaleidoscope.

The chase ended among the late-night crowds of St Catherine's when the police finally tackled her screaming figure and brought her down.

Michael Monahan came up from New York to take her home. He did not rant or shout when he saw her for the first time in a year. He put his big arms around her and cried.

The union's analyst had seen it all before. Although he was on the pay-roll to help the officials, he knew that they were skilled in riding the swell. It was families who drowned in the wash. He was extraordinarily careful with Nan, not just because of her beauty, but because the damaged layers were so fascinating. Like a skilled surgeon, he drew each one away. Together they worked at making repairs.

It took a year.

By the time she was ready for university, her personality was in frail alignment. She did not forget Jackie Smith or the drugs but she knew that she could not go back to them. Her passion for Ireland remained strong. But on the psychiatrist's advice, she put it on the back burner.

Now here it was front and centre again.

'What do you want me to do?' she asked.

She had refused a drink and ordered a salad. Robbie joined her.

'I haven't laid out anything firm yet,' he said. 'But there are a few things we could talk about.'

She said: 'Do you intend to kill Renata?'

He looked at her calmly. 'Is that what you want?'

'I don't know,' she said. She hesitated. 'Dad is really gone, is he?'

'It's almost certain.'

She bit her lip. Then, with an effort, she pulled herself back.

'I want to do what's right by the movement. That's what he would have wanted.'

'I'm glad you said that,' he said, 'because I have to tell you, Nan, killing is not my first priority. My immediate aim is to get those weapons your father was trying for.' He paused. 'I know how angry you must feel about what happened. Is that likely to bother you later?'

'No,' she said. 'I don't think so. As I said, it was what he would have wanted.'

'He must have been a very fine man,' Robbie said. 'Being so committed. Working so hard. It's really tragic what happened.'

'He loved Ireland,' Nan said. 'That always came first. Ever since I was a child. We talked about it often.'

'It was important what he was doing. It could have made a big difference.'

She nodded. 'He took me over there when I was twelve. I understood why he loved it when I saw it,' she said.

'People like your father were always crucial. No matter how far away they were.'

'We drove all round the country,' she said. 'Everywhere we went, there was history. And he knew every detail.'

'What happened needn't be in vain,' Robbie said. 'We can . . .' He stopped.

She was crying. 'I'm sorry,' she said. 'I shouldn't be doing this.'

He stared at her.

'Let me go to the washroom,' she said. She was starting to rise when he caught her wrist.

'Nan.'

She stopped in mid rise.

'I can't have you working for us if this happens,' he said.

Slowly, but firmly, he pressed her down. She sat in her chair, making no effort to disengage, staring at the fingers around her wrist. Waiting. After a moment, she raised her head, her cheeks tear-stained.

'I'll be all right,' she said slowly. 'You can count on that. Once I know exactly what you want.'

Later, when she was calmer, he brought her up to his room to introduce her to Tom Craven. He told her he would be doing research for the operation.

'I'd prefer if you said nothing about your family background to Tom,' he said, before calling him in. 'For the moment, anyway.'

Composed now, she was even curious. 'Is that need to know or something?'

He smiled. 'Not really.' But he did not explain.

Tom Craven arrived, knowing he was to meet somebody, but not a somebody like Nan. He gazed at her astonished.

'Well,' he said, finally recovering his balance, 'this makes a nice change from looking at his mug all day.' He grinned at Robbie as he took her hand. 'I like your taste, fella.'

Robbie glanced at Nan whose eyes widened in reply. Then she looked at Craven and forced a smile. Robbie thought briefly that she looked very attractive when she wasn't being solemn.

'Maybe we should all sit down,' he said. Tom Craven finally let her hand go. But he sat on the end of the bed close to her chair and grinned at her. Robbie felt a little schoolmasterish as he tapped for attention.

He took Tom Craven's situation first. With his agreement to start digging, the important question now was how long it would take.

'The references won't be difficult to find,' Craven said. 'They're right on tap. But tracing the individual microfilms is another matter. They're scattered through so many newspapers and magazines, that will take a while. And making photocopies will be time-consuming too.' He paused. 'I'd say the whole job will require two or three days to complete.'

'That seems OK,' Robbie said. He looked at Nan. 'Now, there's something quite important you could do while Tom is working at that, Nan.'

She looked at him expectantly, hands wrapped around a crossed knee. 'Yes?'

'We need a safe house. This hotel is too public. And it's awkward to communicate.'

'What kind of house do you want?'

He had been thinking about that. 'It should be detached for a start. But I'd like it to be in a built-up area so we can mix in easily and don't attract too much attention. Also, it should be near a main artery and perhaps the subway to let us move about easily and quickly if we want to.'

'Queens might be a good idea,' she said thoughtfully.

'Is it close to downtown?'

'Fifteen, twenty minutes.'

'That's good,' he said. 'By the way, another important point about the house. We should be able to get in and out without leaving a car or van.'

'You mean a garage with an automatic door?'

He nodded. 'Connected to the house.'

'That shouldn't be a problem. They're very common.'

'Fine,' he said.

'Does that mean you're planning to hold Renata there?' Tom Craven asked suddenly. Nan looked at him quickly, then at Robbie.

He frowned. 'If it comes to that, yes.'

But Nan was smiling now.

'Son of a gun,' she said.

They settled the details quickly. Nan would start on the rental ads next morning, using Robbie's room. At her suggestion, they set $2,500 a month as a reasonable rent. She was much brighter now, as if happy to be doing something connected, however distantly, with her father. When he asked her if she was happy with what they were doing, she nodded vigorously.

When they finished, Tom Craven was the first to rise.

'Well,' he said, 'I think a drink is in order to celebrate the beginning.' He looked at Nan. 'What do you say, Nan? Care for a jar?'

She looked quickly at Robbie. Almost imperceptibly, he shook his head.

'I'm sorry, Tom,' she said. 'But I have some things to do. Another time, perhaps.'

'Pity,' he said. He looked at Robbie. 'By the way, Robbie. You never said what you'd be doing, while we're toiling away.'

Robbie smiled. 'I have some calls to make. I may even have to go away for a short while.'

'Oh? Do we get to know where?'

'Sorry, Tom.' He smiled again. 'We're on a need to know basis from here on.'

Nan smiled.

'Well,' Tom Craven said. 'That's it, I suppose. Can I walk you down, Nan?'

'Not right now, Tom. I'd like to have a word with Robbie, if you don't mind?'

'No problem,' he said. But he looked disappointed. 'Well, I should move along. I'll be in my room, if you're looking for me, Robbie. Or downstairs.' He turned to smile at Nan. 'It was nice meeting you, Nan.'

Nan chuckled as the door closed.

'He came on a bit strong, didn't he?' Robbie said.

'He seems nice enough, though,' she said. 'Just needs a little seasoning, that's all.'

Robbie nodded.

'Has he a drink problem?' she asked.

'I don't think so. But I don't see much point to sitting around drinking right now, do you?'

'No,' she said. 'But look, I wasn't making an excuse to

avoid that, saying I wanted a word with you. There is a small problem.'

'What is it?'

'This moving into the safe house.'

'Oh?'

'I have an apartment up in Rochester where I'm studying that I'll have to make arrangements about. But that's not the real difficulty. It's my mother here in New York. She's not well. I think I can get her sister to come up from Philadelphia to take care of her. But the problem is, for how long?'

'Unfortunately, I can't say right now.'

'Well, just so long as you know the problem is there.' She smiled now. 'I'm sure you'll think of something.'

'I'll try,' he said.

Her perfume stayed on after she left.

He hadn't noticed before going down to dinner with Tom Craven. It was when he returned, after making a weak excuse about work to avoid another loose interrogation, that he noticed.

It was there as soon as he re-entered the room. Although it wasn't strong, he felt its presence as he sat back on the bed and tried watching television. After a while, he turned on the fan. But it was no use. The fragrance had entered his mind by now and there was no way he could evict it. Strangely, it wasn't Nan Monahan that the scent evoked but other darker images from the past. After an hour of it, he turned off the television, lay on his side and tried to sleep.

It was after one when he finally gave up and got up off the bed. He dressed without showering. Slipping out his wallet, he extracted a hundred dollar bill and some

170

smaller ones. He paused, looking about, then went and put the wallet behind the radiator.

Turning on the television, he took his coat and headed down to the street.

Chapter Fourteen

The phone rang as he finished his shower. Towel in hand, he returned to the sunlit bedroom to take it.

'Good morning.' It was Nan Monahan. 'I'm not too early, am I?'

He glanced at the bedside clock.

8.25 A.M.

'No,' he said. 'You're fine.'

'Are you decent?'

He frowned. 'Come on up.'

He was in a string vest and trousers with shaving cream in his hand when she knocked. She carried a thick set of newspapers.

'Oh.' Her smile faded. 'This is what comes of being an early bird. I'm sorry.'

'No, it's OK.' He stood aside. 'I won't be long.'

She wore a grey leather jacket with matching corduroys and a speckled wide-neck jumper. Her black ankle boots were low-heeled. Otherwise, she would have been taller than he was. He noticed she was wearing make-up.

She laid the newspapers on the coffee table as he went back to the bathroom. He did not see her glance around. There was little to see. The room had profited from losing Tom Craven. Even the bed was roughly made.

'How did you sleep?' she called. 'Jet lag bother you?'

'No, it was all right.'

As he spread the cream on his face, he caught a sudden movement in the mirror. 'I hate shouted conversations,' she said from the doorway.

He nodded and reached for the razor. 'You look as if you had a good night too,' he said.

'Well, having something to think about makes a difference.' She stood, watching as he shaved. 'Don't you get tired of doing that every day?'

He smiled. 'You find other things to think about.' He worked quickly and expertly. 'I imagine it's the same for you with lipstick.'

She flushed faintly.

'You noticed,' she said. 'I don't usually wear it, you know. I just thought I needed a little colour right now.'

He nodded absently, bending to splash water on his face. As he straightened, she reached forward and passed him the towel.

'Thanks.'

'I can't wait to get started,' she said, as they returned to the bedroom.

He slid back the closet door without replying and looked at the handful of shirts hanging inside. He took down a beige-coloured buttoned-down shirt. 'Nice cut,' she said.

He smiled vaguely and slipped it on. As he was buttoning it, there was a knock on the door. He went quickly to answer.

It was Tom Craven.

'Not dressed yet?' He came in before Robbie could speak. 'Lazy bugger.'

He entered the bedroom and stopped.

'Well, this is a surprise,' he said. 'Good morning, Nan.'

'Hi, Tom,' she said. 'You're out early too, aren't you?'

'Ah, but you still beat me to it,' he said. He turned to Robbie. 'I dropped by to tell you that I planned to go straight to the library.'

'Not joining us for breakfast?'

Craven shook his head.

'Work before play,' he said. It sounded faintly mocking.

'See you later then?'

'Yes. I'll probably finish around five or six.' He looked down at Nan. 'I expect I'll see you then, Nan?'

'Sure.' She gestured to the newspapers. 'I'll be working here today.'

'Well, you're certainly off to a quick start.' He grinned. 'You don't believe in letting the grass grow under your feet, do you?'

'I try not to,' she said, pleased.

Outside, Robbie said: 'I hope you're not getting the wrong impression, Tom. Nan really is here to work. And she really did arrive only minutes before you.'

Craven looked at him, the picture of innocence. 'Of course.'

Robbie shook his head. 'You're a cheeky bugger, Craven.'

'Go on with you. I'll see you later.'

Inside, Robbie looked at her, amused.

'Tom thinks we have something going,' he said. 'Even suspects you spent the night here.'

'What an imagination,' she said. But she looked faintly embarrassed.

He finished dressing. As Nan rose and he slipped on the brown tweed sports jacket, he suddenly remembered.

'Just a minute,' he said and went to retrieve his wallet from behind the radiator.

She looked at him and shook her head in admiration. 'You don't leave anything to chance, do you?'

'You know, I'm almost afraid to talk to you,' she said.

'Why?' He stopped eating.

'In case I step over the line again.'

174

'Oh.' He went back to his food.

'It's maddening because I have to admit I'm curious,' she said. 'I mean, you're so different from Tom. And not at all like the people I knew in the movement.'

I'm getting tired of this, he thought.

'You don't look Irish,' she said. 'You even dress like,' she hesitated, 'a Yuppie.'

He looked at her coldly.

'Don't be like that,' she said, then paused. 'Look, just answer me one question. How old are you, anyway?'

He lowered his fork. 'Twenty-seven,' he said. 'Now, can we get on with breakfast?'

Chastened, she nodded.

He led her back to the room and went to call Boston. When he returned she was sitting cross-legged on the bed, her jacket discarded, talking briskly on the phone. Marked newspapers were spread out on the counterpane. He waited until she had finished.

'A dud,' she said, putting the receiver down.

He nodded. 'Listen, I've got to go away for a while.'

'Oh. Not for long, I hope?'

'Just overnight. I'll leave you the key. You'll be OK to carry on?'

'Sure.'

'If you do find something good, save it for me. I'll want to look after the closing myself.'

'Fine.'

'And tell Tom, will you?'

She nodded.

In the New York Public Library, Tom Craven was already finding Francis Renata a rich subject for research. The references to Salvatore Genta he had seen earlier paled

175

beside what existed on his boss. The *New York Times*, the *Washington Post*, *Time*, *Newsweek*, *New York*, *Esquire*, even *Fortune* had picked over Francis Renata. It was bizarre that a man could direct a lawless empire under the glare of such publicity and still keep out of jail. But, as one leading article showed, they had a phrase for it.

Only in America.

The details Robbie sought about Renata's habits were all there, even down to precise descriptions of his daily schedule. Every morning, flanked by bodyguards, the Mafia boss left his modest home in Brooklyn by 10.30 A.M. for work downtown. The front used was a small cheese-importing company in Little Italy's Grandof Street. From Monday through Friday, in a cramped office on the second floor, Renata received a procession of fellow mobsters, acquisitive businessmen, labour officials, hangers-on, and, if things were particularly bad, lawyers. He ate lunch almost every day at Pontes Restaurant on the west side and usually visited his mistress in the afternoon. By seven in the evening, he was home again to the bosom of his family for dinner. (Menus, usually pasta-based, were on a seven-day rota in the Renata household.)

Every Sunday, he accompanied his wife to eleven o'clock Mass at the Church of the Precious Blood, five blocks from their home. At two-week intervals, he visited his grandchildren in Yonkers, and, when he had time, called on sick and infirm gangsters from his early days. Occasionally, he went to the opera at Lincoln Center. Apart from his activities at the cheese company, Renata appeared to lead a blameless life. There were times, surprisingly, when it was even praiseworthy.

The man actually did charity work. Each October, for almost twenty years, he sponsored a benefit for an Italian orphanage. Reportedly, it netted several hundred thousand dollars per year. It was amusing to think that the man could be as talented at warming hearts as he was notorious for stopping them.

By the time Craven's work ended late in the afternoon, he had much of what Robbie would need for planning his operation.

That evening, the photocopies under his arm, he went to Robbie's room to tell him the news. He showed surprise rather than disappointment when he found Nan there alone. She explained Robbie's absence and then turned to her day, which had been fruitful too.

'I think I've found a place.' She flopped back on the bed which was still littered with newspapers. 'Robbie will love it, I'm sure. It's just off Queens Boulevard, near the subway and only fifteen minutes from downtown. The owner's wintering in Florida. It looks perfect, Tom. Detached. With a drive-in garage. And close to a main artery, as Robbie wanted.'

'Great,' he said, smiling. He raised the photocopies. 'I've made progress too.'

'Marvellous. He has to be pleased.' She began pulling the newspapers together on the bed. As she piled them neatly, she glanced at the documents he held. 'I wouldn't mind looking through those while we have the opportunity, Tom. What do you say to eating here rather than going downstairs?'

'You know, it's odd when you think about it,' she said, sandwich in hand. 'Here we are, sitting in a hotel room, preparing an operation that could turn this entire city on its ear in the next few weeks. And we hardly know each other.'

177

He smiled.

'Well, how it goes really depends on Robbie,' he said. 'He's the one who has to pull it off.'

'I'm optimistic about that. He looks to me like someone who can do it.' She smiled. 'I think he's quite a character.'

'I suppose he is,' Craven said.

'Have you worked with him often?'

'No. This is the first time. But you're right. He is impressive.'

'I can't help wondering about his background,' she said, then caught herself. 'But that's out of order, isn't it?'

'I'm afraid so.'

'Well, it's still exciting. Even just thinking about it.'

He looked at her. 'You're not bothered by the danger at all?'

'Well, I've thought about it, of course. It was on my mind just before you arrived, as a matter of fact.'

'Find it a little scary?'

'Some. But no more than natural, I think.'

He shook his head.

'What's the matter?' she asked quickly. 'Is there something I should know about?'

'No, no. It's just that a job like this does need seasoned people.'

'Well, we have Robbie, don't we?'

'Yes. But he's only one, remember.'

She looked at him, her eyes cool. 'You're bothered about me, are you?'

'Well, it would be easy for you to get in over your head,' he said.

She looked at him silently. 'How old are you, Tom?'

He frowned. 'Twenty-four.'

She gazed at him, then said deliberately. 'When I was

178

half your age, I took a consignment of Armalites into Belfast.'

'Eh?' His mouth opened.

Nan nodded, a cold smile on her lips now.

'Don't worry about me,' she said. 'I'll be OK.'

The atmosphere was strained after that. When they finished eating, she began reading the cuttings. Finally, she glanced at her watch.

'Shit. I've just remembered I need to make a call upstate.' She paused. 'Do you think Robbie would mind if I used his phone?'

'Here, you mean?'

She nodded.

'No problem,' he said. 'This room is actually in my name. Go ahead.'

'I'll fix up with you later.' She gestured to the tray. 'For the food as well.'

'Don't be silly.' He waited for a few moments and, when she made no move, he said, 'Oh, I'm sorry,' and rose.

He stopped by the door, and said with forced amiability: 'Care for a drink when you're finished?'

'I don't think so, Tom,' she said. 'I have to leave immediately after I finish.'

He nodded shortly. 'See you then,' he said, and left.

Robbie arrived back from Boston the following evening. The support team had done its work well. The truck they had supplied was a plain black GMC model with false Massachusetts plates. The fake identity papers including a social security card, a driving licence with an altered picture and credit cards for a Joseph E. Sleator. Along with the papers went a pair of dull-metalled .357 Magnums

179

with the serial numbers filed off and ample clips of ammunition.

He was surprised at the warmth Tom Craven showed when he called to his room. But he made no reference to it.

'Where's Nan?' he asked. The newspapers were all piled neatly on his coffee table together with some notes but there was no sign of her.

'She has to go home for a while. But she said she'd be back later. How did your trip go?'

'Very well. I've got about everything we need now for the job.' He cleared the armchair himself this time.

'Good. Here's your photocopies.'

Robbie eyed the thick bundle. 'You've really been at it, Tom.'

'Wore out at least one machine,' he said. 'And it looks like Nan has had some luck, too. She's found a house.'

'Great.'

'So it's on to the next stage now, eh?'

'That's what I want to talk about, Tom.' He rested the bundle of papers on his lap. 'I realize you're probably thinking it's time to bail out. But you can see my situation. Shorthanded isn't the word for it.'

'I don't envy you,' Craven said. 'But we did agree.'

'Tom, you have no idea how important this project is. We need those arms Renata is holding back. Desperately.'

Craven shrugged.

'I don't pretend to know about these things, Robbie,' he said. 'But has it ever been otherwise?'

'This time it's exceptional, Tom.' He looked at Craven. 'We're planning a big one. There are people standing by, all ready, to use what we get here. I'm breaking security by telling you this but there are all kinds of very sophisticated weapons involved.'

'What's the blitz against?'

'We're going after a group of major bases.'

'What is it, a kind of Tet offensive?'

Robbie nodded. He was not used to lying but there was reason here. 'It's going to be a make or break operation. With everybody who can taking part. If we pull off this thing here, the results could settle matters with the Brits for once and for all. You've got to hang on for a little longer, Tom, and give me a chance to pull it off.'

Craven made difficulties, of course. He expected that. But finally, very reluctantly, he agreed to stay on.

'But no more being kept in the dark,' he said as they prepared to go back to Robbie's room to see if Nan had returned. 'From now on, I expect to be told what's going on. I'm not about to take risks like this for nothing.'

'You have a deal,' Robbie told him. Naturally, he had to say that in the circumstances.

When Nan returned, they drove north through Manhattan and across the Queensboro Bridge to inspect the house she had found. She directed him off Queens Boulevard on to Thirty-ninth Street, a dark and poorly lit thoroughfare. They passed through the intersection at Forty-seventh Avenue where some young kids hung out by the run-down convenience stores. It was a depressing area. But quiet.

'There it is,' Nan said.

An anonymous redbrick two storey over a garage with a small drive. Differing only slightly from its neighbours in that it was detached. Robbie drove around the block for a second look.

'How much are they looking for?'

'$3,200 a month. I spoke to the lawyer. We can have immediate occupancy.'

'I like it,' Robbie said. He turned. 'What do you think, Tom?'

'Looks fine to me.'

'All right,' Robbie said. 'We'll take it.'

'It's a two month minimum,' Nan said.

'That's OK.'

'What about the agreement?' she asked. 'How do we work that?'

He smiled. 'We'll leave it to Joseph E. Sleator. That's what he's here for.'

Tom Craven took the wheel for the return journey. The experience would do no harm, Robbie said.

'Tomorrow morning,' he said, as they drove through the darkened streets, 'we start the last preparations. That includes getting rid of everything that might identify us before moving into the house.' He glanced across at Craven. 'Every stitch of clothing, Tom. Toilet bag, tooth-brush, shaving cream, watch, anything that can link you with back home.'

'I've already ruined my watch,' Tom said.

'That's right.' Robbie grinned. 'Get yourself a new one.' He turned to Nan in the rear. 'You too, Nan. Buy yourself whatever clothes you need.'

'What about passports and that? What do we do with them?' Craven asked.

Nan said: 'We could use a deposit box at Grand Central Station.'

'Good,' Robbie said. 'Can you take care of it tomorrow morning? While I contact the lawyer about the house?'

'Sure.' She smiled at him.

'One final thing,' he said. 'The moment we move into the house, we cut off contact with everybody. That includes family, I'm afraid, Nan.'

182

'Oh,' she said.

'I'm sorry,' he said, 'but that's how it has to be.'

'Not even phone calls?'

He thought for a moment. 'Well, perhaps an occasional one. But only from a public box and even then it has to be kept short. It's essential that we avoid anything that could lead back to us.'

Tom Craven looked at her in the mirror, remembering the call she had made from his room. Nan saw his glance. She frowned but said nothing.

Soon after that, things began to move.

The renting went smoothly. A day later, Robbie and Tom checked out of the hotel and Nan left her mother's home to move into the house.

The interior was as nondescript as the outside. Three bedrooms with moderately clean floral wallpaper and well-worn furniture. A roomy living-room and a bright, yellow painted kitchen. The basement was almost tailor-made. It had barred windows, a separate bathroom and a corridor leading to the garage. Between them, they moved a bed down from the top floor with Robbie installing the necessary fittings.

By the end of that day, with cold blustery weather settling in on New York, everything was comfortably in order on Thirty-ninth Street.

As Tom Craven remarked drily, all it needed now was the unsuspecting guest.

Next morning, their first in the house, they sat at the living-room table, passing the photocopies round, reading, hardly talking. When they finished, Robbie stretched.

'Well, Tom, what do you think?'

'I don't know. This fellow Renata has more security than the bloody President.'

'Come on,' Robbie said. 'I see gaps. One in particular.'

Craven looked down at the documents again, his brow wrinkled. Nan sat silent, watching.

'The only time he leaves his bodyguards is when he goes to Mass,' Craven said. 'There's just family then. Is that what you're thinking of?'

Robbie frowned. 'No,' he said. 'We don't go near the church.' There was an odd finality in his voice that made Craven look up curiously.

'Well, where then?'

Robbie smiled. 'What about that orphans' benefit?'

Craven looked at him, astonished.

'You can't be serious. You saw what the articles on it said. Every crook on the eastern seaboard will be there. Six hundred turned up last year.'

'Yes,' Robbie said. 'But isn't that an advantage? Nobody, Renata included, could possibly expect trouble in that kind of setting.' He held up the copies. 'Besides, weapons of any kind are barred at those gatherings. Which means we would be the only people armed. And finally, it happens to be conveniently timed. I don't know if you noticed but it's coming up next week.'

'Jesus,' Craven said. 'You're mad.'

Nan was looking at Robbie with awe.

'Mad as may be,' Robbie said, 'but I believe I might be right on this one.' He looked down at his papers. 'If we go by what happened last year, I think I see a way. But it all depends on the hall.'

And there was the problem. For Robbie to reveal himself on a reconnaissance visit might result in his being recognized on the night of the banquet. To avoid that, he was inclined towards breaking in, despite the dangers involved. Then Nan spoke up.

'Let me do it.'

Robbie looked at her in astonishment.

'This St Dominick's Hall probably runs banquets, weddings, even office parties,' she said. 'There would be nothing unusual in my calling to make enquiries. Different from you guys,' she grinned. 'With those weird accents. Nobody would pay much attention to a woman who dropped by to enquire about holding an office party. Or even a wedding.'

When he thought about it, she seemed right. There would hardly be any danger to her in a quick visit.

'You sure?'

'Absolutely,' she said.

Two hours later, looking cool and assured, she left on the trip to St Dominick's Hall.

It was only on her return that Robbie Driscoll finally realized how closely she resembled her father. He had noticed a certain pushiness. Now she revealed a second family trait and the one that had brought such disastrous consequences to her father. Like Michael Monahan, she showed a tendency to move things in the direction she personally wanted them to go.

It came out in the first sentence on her return.

'You're either going to hug me or kill me,' she said when she came in, 'but I changed your plan when I saw how it was over there.'

As Tom Craven stared open-mouthed, she told Robbie what she had done.

For a well-ordered mind like Robbie Driscoll's there was something innately aggravating in having a subordinate doing the right thing for the wrong reason. But he had to accept it. What she had done completely changed his game plan. But it opened up a prospect that even he had not imagined. It took a second visit to confirm that she was right.

After that, they were ready to roll.

Chapter Fifteen

Cold weather had arrived from Canada for the night of the orphans' benefit. It did not affect the turn-out. The parking lot at St Dominick's Hall was crowded when Robbie and Nan arrived by cab shortly after nine. Rows of cars gleamed under the ringed moon. Most were large and almost all were black. Inside the glass-walled lobby, groups of formally dressed men stood scattered around the grey broad-loomed area. Most were short and all were white.

The voice of a crooner battling through 'Love is a Many Splendoured Thing' could be heard coming from the banquet hall. Some of the loungers, faces rough above the tuxedos, glanced briefly at them as they passed.

A middle-aged woman with jet black hair and tipped glasses sat at a baize table by the hall entrance. She sat up, drawing her cardigan around her shoulders as they approached.

Robbie smiled. 'Hello. My name is Raymond Case. And this is Miss Ballardo. The manager said he would put tickets aside for us.'

The woman looked down at her cards, then smiled suddenly, remembering.

'Oh, you're the engaged couple, right?'

Robbie nodded as Nan took his arm shyly. 'I hope it's no trouble having us like this?' he said.

'No problem. My husband, he already told me you were coming.' She wanted them to know who she was. 'We thought to give you a nice table where you could see everything. I got you one on the far side of the hall. Number forty-eight. Just for two.'

'That's very nice of you,' Robbie said.

'My pleasure.' She smiled at Nan. 'I'm sure you're going to like it here. We make a special effort to please our brides.'

'I like it already,' Nan said brightly, looking around. 'That singer, he sounds so nice and all.'

'Talk to me if you want to book him,' the woman said briskly. She drew out two cards and handed them to Robbie. 'Although I have to tell you Fred don't come cheap. Nice man, though. Flew in from Florida for tonight. Sort of a favour to the folks who are running the affair.' She smiled at Nan. 'I think it's nice to see that, don't you? Putting out to help those poor kids back in the old country.'

'That's very thoughtful of him,' Nan said. 'I would like to have a person like that singing at my wedding. Does he do hymns and that?'

'Fred? Sure. He does it all,' the woman said. 'But you're looking at two grand minimum.'

'Oh, my,' Nan said.

'Not everybody wants to go that deep,' the woman agreed sympathetically.

'We would have to think about it,' Robbie said.

'Your privilege,' the woman said genially. 'Frankly, if it was me, I'd put the money into a bedroom suite. I wouldn't pay that kind of money for Pavarotti.'

Led by a waiter, they entered the hall.

'My God,' Nan whispered, as they crossed the crowded floor. 'Pity poor Fred.'

The gathering resembled a packed union convention rather than a charity dance. At least half of the attendance were on their feet and most of those were on the move.

Scores of men, mostly thick-bodied and overdressed, roamed freely between tables, their faces flushed, joking, waving glasses, sometimes entwining. The restless mass paid no attention to the burgundy-jacketed singer who had flown two thousand miles to help. Fred's face was red as he sought the elusive note that might command attention from the throng. It was wasted effort.

The waiter, a thin, elderly man who found time to pull out Nan's chair, took Robbie's two dollars and slipped away without giving them time to order.

'Love it.' Nan rested her elbows on the table and stared fascinated. Robbie saw the sparkle in her eyes and felt reassured. He leaned back and looked about at the rounded tables laid out in a horseshoe pattern running back from the dance floor. He was looking for Renata.

'Robbie. There in the middle,' Nan whispered suddenly. 'I think it's him.'

Robbie followed her gaze to a large table, crowded with over a dozen men and women, on the edge of the dance floor. The place of honour was occupied by a silent man who sat directly facing the stage. His shadowed eyes stared impassively at the singing Fred, now hustling towards the end of his set.

'Am I right?' Nan asked softly.

Robbie nodded. Discreetly, he examined the boss of all the bosses.

Francis 'Chills' Renata was a low-sized man in his mid-fifties with a broad chest and a pale, almost grey face under the thick black hair combed back from the temples. He wore the waistcoat of a grey business suit over an opened white shirt and a loose blue silk tie. His jacket hung on the chair behind.

'Doesn't look too healthy, does he?' Nan whispered.

Robbie didn't answer. He was examining the other

189

people at the table. To Renata's left was a woman of similar age, dressed modestly in black, who listened patiently to the younger, glamorous woman sitting beside her. Her eyes kept glancing at Renata, who paid her no attention. On his other side, a stout bald man sat looking isolated and deeply uncomfortable. Beyond him, a young man in a full three-piece, dark blue and expensively cut. Occasionally, he would lean across the stout man and Renata to talk to the two women beyond. But with Renata himself there was no exchange. Family, Robbie decided.

Directly opposite Renata, a tall thin man sat, talking with animation, a glass in his hand. Two hulking men flanked him, both silent, nursing their drinks. They had to be what the old detective magazines called 'the torpedos'.

'Talk about casting,' Nan said. 'We could be in Hollywood.'

She was right. This was fact imitating fantasy. The silent brooding boss, the Italian family, the menacing tough guys there to protect him. All the ingredients that made up the pizza. Except . . . Robbie looked around the table. Where was the underboss, the man who had clipped Michael Monahan?

He leaned across to Nan. 'Can you see Salvatore Genta anywhere?'

They both scoured the main tables.

'Not here,' Nan said.

'He has to be,' Robbie said. 'You read the articles. Renata doesn't allow no-shows when it comes to this affair.'

'Well, there's no sign of him.'

'He has to be here, Nan.'

Finally, they found him. And not surprising that they

190

had missed him. Genta's table was in an alcove just under the entrance stairs. His isolation, taken with his prominence in the family, emphasized the dispute with Renata.

'Looks like he's out of favour,' Nan whispered.

Robbie nodded.

They both watched Genta's table. The six guests who sat there, two women and four men, paid little attention to what was going on around them. It was almost as if they were isolating themselves by choice. The only conversation appeared to be between Genta and the huge, bald-headed man on his right. Robbie noticed that Genta's table had few visitors. Those who came said little and left quickly.

By contrast, a steady tide stopped by Renata's. Almost all climaxed their visit with the discreet offer of an envelope. At first, Renata accepted the offerings himself, returning no more than a brusque nod as he slipped them into his jacket pocket on the chair. Soon, the tide of contributions proved too much. He began passing them to his wife who stuffed them into the capacious purse she held on her lap.

'My God,' Nan said in awe. 'He's outdoing Brando.'

A waiter bustled forward. Robbie ordered a Scotch on the rocks and Nan a glass of white wine.

The waiter looked at them pityingly. 'What are youse, from another planet? This blast is all bottles, no glasses. Scotch, thirty-five. Wine, thirty. Sides are on the house.'

'Thirty dollars for wine? What is it? Château-bottled?' Nan asked.

'Come on, lady, it's for the kids. For crying out loud, that's what we're all here for.'

They watched him hurry away.

'Even when it's for charity the bastards gouge,' Nan said.

191

'Look, Nan,' Robbie said. 'Genta's on the move.'

They watched the small sallow figure rising, brushing back his thinning hair, the others around the table attentive. He pushed in his chair and straightened his shoulders with a small defiant shrug for his audience. Then he turned and started between the tables, offering a nod of recognition to those who said hello. Robbie and Nan saw he was headed for Renata's table. By the time he got there, he was smiling. Greeting the others at the table, he moved alongside Renata and bent to speak.

His boss, the thick forearms resting on the table, inclined his thickly thatched head slightly but did not move otherwise as Genta whispered. Finally, the under-boss drew out an envelope and slid it on to the table. Renata's eyes fell on it. He looked up and spoke. Genta nodded quickly and, taking the envelope, passed it to the woman who appeared to be Renata's wife. They each smiled. Now Renata turned to say something to him. They saw a protest form on his face. Then he turned away to return to his own table, a scowl on his sallow face.

Over an hour passed with Robbie taking just one drink from the unmarked whiskey bottle. Nan had finished a single glass of wine. Her face appeared slightly flushed but it was from the heat and smoke rather than from the alcohol. Robbie had continued to survey the flow of contributors to Renata's table. He saw now that it was tailing off.

On stage, the band had come to the end of another romantic set. As they watched, the singer Fred and another man consulted briefly and went to the wings, returning with a small table which they placed carefully in the centre of the stage. Robbie looked at Nan.

Speech time.

'Is this it?' she asked softly.

He nodded.

She drew a long breath.

'Nervous?'

'Some.' She looked at the tough faces around them, the thought apparent but unspoken. If anything went wrong, they were as good as dead.

Silently, Robbie leaned across and laid his hand on hers. She caught the flicker of concern in his eyes.

'Don't worry,' she said quickly. 'I'll be OK.'

He smiled, reassuring. 'I know you will.'

She was silent. Then, very hesitantly, her fingers turned and closed on his hand. He felt the warmth of her touch but sensed the questing too. Gently, he squeezed. They sat, hands joined, the picture of a couple headed for marriage. Finally, Nan took a deep breath and disengaged.

'I'm ready,' she said.

'That's my girl.'

She looked quickly at him, her eyes clouding. It's only a phrase, he thought. Then he saw her chin rise and a quick, almost defiant look passed across her face. She looked at him. 'Well? Are we moving or not?'

Robbie grinned, drawing back. He knew now she was going to be OK. Nan took her bag and they rose.

They edged through the noisy crowd, passing the pugnacious and the mean faces, the drunk, the animated and the cold. Robbie ahead, glancing back occasionally, smiling encouragement though he knew it wasn't needed. Nan tried to keep her eyes on the blond head in front, holding off the fears invited by the faces around her. They passed close to Renata's table, but neither looked in his direction.

The manager's wife was still at her station, quietly

smoking a cigarette. She smiled as they stopped and laid it down in an ashtray.

'Not leaving, I hope?'

'Oh no,' Robbie said. 'We've decided to make our booking.'

'Good for you,' she said. 'I know you won't be disappointed.'

'Is Mr Crenna around?'

'He's in the office. Want me to take you there?'

'No need,' Robbie said. 'I already know where it is. At the back, right?'

'You got it.'

They crossed the lobby and entered the corridor leading backstage. It was empty. Half-way down, Nan began unzipping her bag. The gleam of metal showing through the opening. Robbie glanced about quickly, then took the gun and slipped it into his waistband, covering it with his jacket. They turned the corner, Robbie heading for the manager's office, Nan for the exit door.

Tom Craven was sitting low in the driving seat of the van when he saw the heavy door open. Nan's head appeared. She beckoned. His face pale in the gloom, he slipped out of the truck and crossed the gravel quickly to join her in the corridor. A thin round of applause floated down from the hall.

'This way,' she said.

In the office, the manager lay slumped as if sleeping in the chair behind his desk. Robbie had taken off his tie and was tying his wrists. His gun lay on the desk. He glanced up as they entered. 'Help me get him into the closet.'

Tom came forward quickly. While Nan held the narrow door open, they laid the unconscious man inside.

Robbie locked the door and looked at Tom. 'Bring the torch?'

'Yes.' Craven's voice was cracked and dry.

Robbie glanced quickly at him then smiled. 'Good.' He picked up the Magnum and put it back under his coat. Outside, a voice was speaking over the microphone on stage. Robbie smiled briefly at Nan. 'OK, let's go. And remember, Tom, stay close.'

They entered the empty corridor and stole quietly to the door leading backstage. Robbie led the way through.

The area behind the huge curtains was in semi-darkness. Abandoned props lay scattered across the floor space. Robbie gripped Nan's arm. She nodded and hurried to her place by the fusebox. With Tom close behind, Robbie moved cautiously forward.

A man on stage was speaking in Italian.

They reached the flies that hid them from the audience. Robbie and Tom moved around them until they reached the narrow space parallel to the stage.

They were looking directly on to the stage. The tall man who had been sitting at Francis Renata's table was speaking into a hand-held mike. Renata, hands clasped in front, stood alongside. He turned to glance briefly at them as the tall man finished his speech. The scattering of applause suddenly grew as he handed the mike to Renata. It became deafening as the audience began to slap their tables. Some began to whistle.

Renata stood without any sign of emotion, waiting for the applause to end.

Robbie tugged at Tom Craven's shoulder, drawing him close.

'Make sure Nan sees you,' he hissed. Craven nodded and leaned back around the curtain. Nan stared at him, gripping the lever on the fusebox. Craven raised his hand.

'I want to thank you people,' Renata's deep powerful voice filled the hall, 'for coming here tonight to help out a lot of poor kids who don't get any of the breaks we have here in the United States.'

'Now!' Robbie snapped. As Craven brought his hand down, Robbie started out on to the stage.

'These kids didn't ask for what they been getting . . .' Suddenly catching sight of Robbie Driscoll bearing down on him, Renata turned. At the same instant, the hall was plunged into darkness.

Robbie, the Magnum in his right hand, had a clear picture of Renata's head. He whacked the barrel down and heard a strangled gasp. The mike clattered to the floor in a crackle of sound. Grabbing quickly, Robbie caught the sagging shoulders. The microphone, still live, blared loudly at his feet. Holding Renata's body against his chest, shoving the gun back into his belt, Robbie shouted.

'*Beir greim air!*'

There was a pause.

'*Ce'n ait?*' Tom Craven called in the darkness.

'*A cosa, a cosa. Brostig! Brostig!*'

Uproar filled the hall.

Tom Craven found Renata's limp feet. The two of them began backing towards the curtain.

'Here!'

They saw the brief flash of torchlight as Nan raised the curtain. Ducking, they pulled the limp Renata underneath. Nan dropped the curtain. They heard screaming and wild cursing from the hall as she guided them to the rear door. She pulled it open, the torchlight darting across the floor. Robbie and Tom dragged the unconscious man through into the corridor.

Nan slammed the door and ran to open the emergency

exit. They could hear the noise of people scrambling and colliding with props back in the stage area.

They spilled out into the night.

'Get the rear open, Nan,' Robbie shouted as the outer door swung closed behind them. Her feet crunched on the gravel as she ran ahead.

At the rear, Renata's coat snagged as Robbie heaved him into the van. Tom Craven got the legs in and then pushed hard at the slumped body. There was a long tearing sound and he was in.

Robbie scrambled in after the limp figure.

'Get going!' he snapped.

Craven and Nan ran to the front as he pulled the rear doors shut. Craven scrambled into the driving seat. The engine sprang to life. Squirting gravel from under the burning tyres, the truck shot forward across the gravelled lot.

Robbie, kneeling by the unconscious Renata, stared through the rear window at the dim outline of St Dominick's Hall receding behind them. They had crossed the lot and entered the feeder road before he saw the building's lights go on. There was no pursuit. Exultation growing in him, he turned.

Nan grinned down at him.

'You son of a gun,' she said.

Suddenly, the blaze of headlights filled the truck. A horn blared madly, Nan turned.

'Tom!' she screamed. 'You're driving on the wrong side!'

The truck rocked crazily as Craven spun the wheel and sent it skidding across the road. Somehow, he evaded the other car and got the van under control. They hurtled away from the hall towards the city.

* * *

Back inside the lighted hall, pandemonium reigned. Mobsters, union men, construction guys, stood shouting, questioning, still not sure what was going on. Some of the women were in tears.

Salvatore Genta grabbed a passing capo from a Renata decima.

'What the hell is going on, Jimmy?'

'Don't know, Sal. But right now, it looks as though something's happened to Chills.'

'What do you mean?'

The capo gestured towards the stage. 'You saw him up there. Well, he ain't around no more.' He leaned close. 'Albie talked to one of the band guys. Saw it up close. The guy said it was a snatch.' He wiped his reddened forehead. 'Jesus, if it's true, those guys have got some nerve. In front of all these wise guys. All I can say, Sal, is I just hope it ain't the start of something nasty.'

Genta sat down slowly.

'That stuff that come over the mike,' he said. 'You make out what they were shouting?'

'Search me.' The capo was anxious to be gone. 'I don't hear too well.'

'The guys looking out back?'

Jimmy nodded.

'Majura's doing it.'

'Tell him to come see me. We don't want nothing to happen to Chills.'

'You got it, Sal.' Jimmy hurried away.

Genta turned to look at the other men at the table with the sorrow of a professional mourner.

'Poor Chills,' he said.

Chapter Sixteen

Back inside the garage at Thirty-ninth Street, they lifted the still comatose Renata from the truck and carried him into the basement. As they laid him on the mattress, Robbie snapped on the manacles which were already attached to the bed frame by slim but strong chains.

There was no elation, only tiredness now. In the dim light cast by the lamp above Renata's bed, Nan looked exhausted. When Robbie suggested she lie down upstairs, she went without protest. Tom Craven, who was freshest, elected to keep watch. Robbie stretched out gratefully on the sofa. His eyes had barely closed when Craven called out.

'Robbie. He's coming round.'

Pulling himself up, Robbie crossed to join him. They stood watching as Renata groaned, his limbs twitching in some half-conscious nightmare.

'You'd wonder how Mrs R gets any sleep with him,' Craven whispered. Whether it was the reference or the sound, Renata's eyes opened. He stared at them now, uncomprehending.

Robbie bent closer. 'Mr Renata. Can you hear me?'

Renata raised a manacled hand and rubbed his forehead.

'Feeling bad, eh?'

Renata grimaced. Slowly, becoming aware, he looked at the trailing chains and then up into the staring faces.

'What's going on?' he asked thickly.

'We'll get to that,' Robbie said. 'Anything you need right now?'

'Water.'

While Tom Craven went, Robbie sat on the edge of the bed. When Craven returned, Renata raised himself on an elbow and drank thirstily. Robbie took the emptied glass as he lay back on the pillow. For a few moments there was silence. Suddenly, Renata jerked upright. Eyes wide, he stared again at the cuffs on his wrists, then at Robbie.

'What the hell is going on here?' he snapped.

Tom Craven grinned. 'That's what I call a quick recovery.'

The angry eyes swept the dimly lit basement, returning to Robbie again. 'What is this? Who are you guys?'

'I said that can wait. Do you want more water?'

'Forget the goddam water.' The voice was stronger now. 'I want to know what's happening here.'

'In good time,' Robbie said. He took out the cigarette packet he had found in the mobster's pocket and held it out. 'Here, have a cigarette.'

Renata looked at him contemptuously.

'No answers until we're all calm,' Robbie said. 'Better get that into your head first.'

'I don't need no cigarettes to calm me,' Renata said. Silently, he stretched out his chained hands. They were rock steady. 'See?'

Tom Craven grinned.

'OK,' Renata said. 'Start talking. What's this all about?'

Robbie shrugged. 'If that's what you want.' He turned to Tom Craven. 'Would you mind leaving us alone for a few minutes, Tom?'

Craven's smile faded. He looked briefly as if he might protest. Finally he rose abruptly and left without speaking.

200

'Well?' Renata said.

Robbie listened to the footsteps fading on the stairs. He turned.

'We brought you here to discuss a certain deal you made with my people,' he said. 'A deal that went sour.'

'Deal? What deal?' Renata looked puzzled. 'And what people are you talking about?'

'You gave an undertaking to supply my organization with weapons,' Robbie said, 'for which you received $250,000. I'm here to see that they're delivered. Without delay.'

Renata stared at him. He seemed genuinely astonished.

'Weapons?'

'You heard me,' Robbie said.

'Are you crazy?' Renata said. 'I don't know anything about weapons. Or your goddam money.'

'Stop faking, Mr Renata. You know what I'm talking about.'

'Hey, are you deaf? I just told you otherwise.'

'Oh, sure,' Robbie said.

'Look, why don't you just cut the crap?' Renata said. 'Why don't you come right out and tell me who you're fronting for?'

'As if you didn't know.'

'Jesus,' Renata said. 'How long does this go on?'

'All right,' Robbie said. 'Let me refresh your memory. We're from the IRA.'

'The what?'

'You heard me. We're from the Irish Republican Army.'

Renata shook his head.

'I don't believe this.' He lay back on the pillow and stared up at the ceiling. 'Maybe you can tell me. Is he crazy, God? Or am I?'

* * *

201

If he was acting, it was Oscar quality.

'I'm telling you for the last time.' Renata banged his fist against the mattress. 'I made no deals for weapons and I don't know anything about your money.'

He was animated now and remarkably changed. The dark eyes glowed with energy, making them stand out against the unnaturally white-skinned face. His thick body seemed harder, more charged. Robbie had even caught him slyly testing the chains. Some chance, he thought. He and Tom Craven had tried their combined strength against them to no avail.

'The deal had your OK,' Robbie said aloud. 'Salvatore Genta himself said so. Are you telling me that your own underboss would say that, make a $250,000 deal and then kill, all without letting you know about it?'

'You heard me,' Renata said stubbornly. 'I didn't know any of this.'

Robbie sat back.

'We're going in circles,' he said.

'Listen, I don't care where you're going. I'm just telling you what I know. And what I don't know. And one thing I don't know is anything about your goddam money or those weapons. OK?' The chains rattled as Renata lay back on the bed.

'You know Mr Genta?'

'Sure I know him.'

'He works for you?'

Renata shrugged.

'There's no fifth amendment here, Mr Renata,' Robbie said harshly. 'You better get that into your head right now.'

'All right, so what?' Renata said impatiently. 'Me and Sal are business acquaintances. What's the big deal?'

'Business acquaintances, my foot,' Robbie said.

'According to every newspaper and magazine in the country, he's your second in command.'

'Well, I ain't responsible for everything he does,' Renata said.

'In this case,' Robbie said. 'You are.'

'What's that supposed to mean?'

'We're going to trade you for those arms,' Robbie said. 'And this time, your Mr Genta had better play ball.'

Renata stared down at the bed, his lips tight, silent.

'We're in a war, Mr Renata,' Robbie said. 'We need that firepower and we'll do whatever is necessary to get it.' He paused. 'And if it doesn't come through, I have my orders.'

There was silence in the room.

'You want to know what they are?'

Renata shrugged.

'I'm to shoot you, Mr Renata,' Robbie said.

'Bullshit,' Renata said.

Robbie smiled a hard smile. 'Don't make me enjoy it.'

He waited but there was no reaction. Suddenly tired of it all, he rose and glanced at the time. He would have to arrange watch duties with Tom Craven.

Renata said: 'You got that cigarette?'

'Sorry,' Robbie said. 'You lost your chance. There's no smoking unless there's someone here with you.'

Renata glowered after him as he walked to the door. Robbie stopped and turned.

'You better do some serious thinking about what I just said, Renata,' he said. 'But remember this. You don't have a lot of time.'

'What the fuck were you doing down there?' Tom Craven said angrily when he entered the kitchen.

Robbie looked at him, surprised.

203

'Sorry, Tom. I didn't mean to offend you. I just thought a one to one thing would be better.'

'Don't give me that,' Craven said. 'You didn't want me to hear what was being said. Isn't that it?'

'For Christ's sake, Tom!' This was really the last straw. 'Look, I've had enough of the prima donna stuff downstairs. There was nothing going on. If you want, ask Renata yourself. He'll tell you. Just like he told me. He knows nothing about anything.'

Craven stared at him. 'You're telling the truth?'

'Yes. About him and about me. So just keep your imagination in check, will you?'

'Well, it seemed very strange to me,' Craven muttered.

'Listen, we need to set first watch. Do you want to do it like we agreed?'

Craven nodded grudgingly.

'Just make sure you keep your distance. He's getting stronger by the minute.' He tossed the cigarette pack across. 'He's looking for one of these. Better take them down.'

'Robbie,' Craven said as he reached the door.

'Yes?' He turned.

'Sorry about the outburst.'

Robbie nodded. But he was too tired to smile.

'That's OK, Tom.'

It was close to dawn when Craven came up to wake him. By then, Francis Renata was entering his sixth hour of captivity.

He was lying on the bed with his face to the wall when Robbie entered the basement. Craven had put a small reading lamp by the sofa. The rest of the room was in shadow. Robbie took up the paperback he had been reading. *The Big Sleep* by Raymond Chandler. He stretched out on the sofa and drew the reading lamp closer.

He had been reading for five minutes or so when Renata suddenly spoke.

'You want to know something?' he said. His voice sounded muffled for he was still facing the wall.

Robbie lowered the book. 'What?'

'You've got the wrong guy.'

Robbie said nothing.

'Those arms you're talking about,' Renata's voice carried above the humming furnace. 'You're not going to get them. No matter what you do to me.'

Robbie stared at the large, unmoving back.

'That would be too bad,' he said.

Renata shifted and slowly turned. His face was pale in the gloom. 'You believe me when I say I didn't know?'

'No.'

'It's a fact,' Renata said. He was silent for what seemed like a long time. Then he reached for his cigarettes. Silently, Robbie rose and crossed to light it.

Renata gestured to the bed. 'Sit down,' he said.

Robbie rested at the end, safely out of his reach. The Mafia leader lay back on the pillow and stared at the ceiling, the smoke curling up from the cigarette in his hand. The furnace cut out and the room was silent.

'Sal Genta is no pal of mine,' Renata said. 'Not right now. He'll do nothing to spring me loose. That I'm sure of. You say you're going to kill me. He'll say go ahead.' He drew on his cigarette. 'He thinks I've been raining on his parade long enough.'

They were both silent.

'You're pretty smart, you know that?' Renata said suddenly. 'The way you did this thing. All those guys.

205

Supposed to look out for me. You went through them like butter.'

Robbie shrugged.

'Only a kid too. How old are you, anyway?'

'Twenty-seven.'

Renata sighed. 'Your age, I wouldn't have been caught like this. Front or back.'

Robbie felt a certain compassion for a man who had fallen so low, so quickly. And some respect too for the way he was taking it.

'If we don't get those arms . . .' he said and paused. 'Some things I don't enjoy. But if there's no choice, I do them.'

Renata drew on his cigarette. 'From seeing you work, you got me convinced.' He smiled wryly now, growing more human.

Robbie was silent.

The chains rattled as Renata shifted.

'These handcuffs. They're a bastard when you're trying to sleep.' He paused. 'Want to help me out?'

'Sorry, Mr Renata. No chance.'

Renata shrugged. 'Listen,' he said. 'Since we're going to be together here, we better get on first names. Try calling me Frank, OK?'

Robbie smiled. 'OK, Frank.'

Renata nodded. 'Tell you something, kid. I believe what you've been telling me about what Sal did to you guys. That's his style all right. Thing is, he not only screwed you guys.' He nodded. 'Looks like the little scumbag did it pretty good to me too.'

Chapter Seventeen

For many New Yorkers, the first news of Francis Renata's disappearance came from veteran columnist and inveterate overwriter, Emmet Grogan.

The Iceman . . . Goeth

He is the most watched man in New York. And without question the most feared. Some say he is the most powerful of all our citizens.

His name is Francis 'Chills' Renata.

And last night he disappeared.

It was a vanishing act worthy of Houdini. Performed at St Dominick's Hall in Brooklyn before an audience of 800 of his fellow mobsters. And before the undercover representatives of such powerful institutions as the Federal Bureau of Investigation, the Drug Enforcement Agency and the Treasury Department. Not to mention the crack Special Investigation Unit of the New York Police Department.

Renata disappeared from under the collective snouts of what might be described as the cream of our crime prevention apparatus. Officers trained to detect and forestall, among other crimes, that most heinous and detestable of offences.

Kidnapping.

Which is what is alleged to have happened to our mobster friend. Yes, the word on the street is that Chills Renata, the boss of all the bosses, has been kidnapped.

I say eyewash.

Ask me, I'll tell you.

I believe this blue-blooded bully of the criminal world who got his nickname through his loathsome facility with the ice pick, has gone on the lam.

The reason?

Why, to avoid the RICO indictment pending on the desk of

Manhattan DA Marvin Goldstein. An indictment that Captain Brent Halligan and his armchair sleuths at the SIU have conspicuously failed to serve. For reasons known only to themselves.

RICO has done a great deal to break up the bloody network of high-flying criminals who have dominated much of our city life to date. As Renata's disappearance shows, they are on the run.

I say keep up the pressure.

How?

Let Halligan and his men throw off their *laissez-faire* attitude and pull out all the stops in the hunt for the scoundrelly Chills Renata. Let them search remorselessly until they find his luxurious bolthole, pull him out and then throw him behind bars where he belongs.

It is time to reject the old standards, time to prise our criminals loose from the veins of commerce – shipping, trucking, the airlines – through which the life blood of New York flows. Let us begin that crusade with unearthing Renata.

If we should do so, then perhaps the day will dawn when some future police brat can look up at his dad and say: What did you do in the war against crime, dad? And the answer will be: I was there, son, when Chills Renata went down.

Should that time arrive then we, the people and the media (excluding the performing fleas of television), will rest satisfied, knowing at last that justice has been done.

The grey Ford LTD pulled into the kerb on Fifty-seventh. It was just after 11 A.M. and the morning was cold. A big soft man in a grey jacket and check trousers got out. Although he was middle-aged, the lank greying locks framing his sagging face suggested he wasn't going down without a fight. He stopped by the meter, glancing about casually as he fed it. Tugging his belt up, he walked slowly north.

Jerry Grayson, or The Doughboy as he was called behind his back, was making a rare visit to his Special Investigation Division command post.

* * *

'Jerry, Jerry!' Captain Brent Halligan bounced up from the sofa in the equipment-packed suite and hustled forward when he entered. 'Good to see you.' He shook hands.

Jerry almost believed he meant it.

'Everything OK?' Halligan gripped his elbow and looked at him critically. 'You're looking good, you know.'

Smiling cynically, Jerry Grayson allowed the captain to lead him to the sofa.

'I've been planning to confer,' Halligan said as they sat down. 'I mean you've been doing great. Not a man upstairs doesn't know about your work. It's just that we never seem to hit the right moment to talk.'

'Do I have to ask the reason for this summit?' Jerry asked abruptly.

Halligan took a moment, wanting to make it sound unimportant. It didn't do to put yourself in the debt of the hired help.

'Well, it's this Renata business,' he said finally. 'They tell me you planned to attend that dinner last night. Did you make it?'

Grayson nodded. 'The damnedest thing happened,' he said. 'Still can't believe it. The place was packed with bad guys. Wall to wall. And somebody snatches Chills from under their noses.'

'Did you see it?'

'Close to. They hit the lights just as it happened. There was a guy came on the stage at the time. Where Renata was.'

'Get a make on him?'

'Only a glimpse. Young guy, blond-haired. Somebody said he'd been in the place earlier with a dame. He sure moved fast. They took maybe a minute to get the lights on again. By that time, the guy was gone. Chills too. A real Houdini act.' He smiled wickedly. 'Like Grogan said.'

'What were they saying in the hall?'

Grayson grinned. 'Mostly it was how the hell do I get out of here? Everybody was scared shitless, thinking they were going to get hit.'

'Whoever did it showed some moxie,' Halligan said. 'Any ideas on that?'

Grayson shrugged. 'Could have been any of the other families. Maybe even his own. Genta, the underboss, is a possibility. He's a mean bastard. And he's got the nerve. Ambitious too.' He looked dead-pan at Halligan. 'That's always a factor, isn't it?'

'What about Renata himself?' Halligan ignored the implication. 'Think he could have staged it? He's got a grand jury on the way.'

'If he did, he's got an Academy Award winner in his wife. She just went crazy. Screaming, crying. They were going to call an ambulance to get her out of there.'

'Did you see the story in the *News* this morning?'

Grayson nodded.

'They said the FBI and the DEA had body-packs in the hall. Picked up what the guy shouted from the stage.'

Grayson grinned. This was one of the nice parts of the job. He took out the cassette and tossed it into Halligan's lap. 'Snap.'

Halligan's hand closed on the tape. 'Beautiful.' He looked up at Jerry and smiled. 'What did I say about nobody doing a better job?'

'I'll take money any day,' Grayson said. But he still felt good.

'They say the guy was shouting in some kind of dialect.' Halligan turned the tape over in his hand.

Grayson nodded. 'It figures to be the only mistake he

210

made. The mike, it was one of those hand-held battery things, carried his voice all over the place. Showed there was a second guy in on it too.'

'Any of the wise guys there know what he was saying?'

'I heard a few suggestions. Somebody said it was German. But they were reaching.'

'Are we likely to get anyone for eye-witness stuff?'

Grayson laughed. 'No way.' He sat up on the edge of the sofa and looked at Halligan. 'It's kind of funny, eh? Over 800 witnesses and three body-packs taking it all in there last night. And still nothing to tell us what the hell it's all about.'

Halligan hefted the tape. 'Don't worry,' he said. 'I got a feeling this voice thing is going to break it. Good thing we're knee deep in wop dialect guys. Now they get to earn their pay.' He smiled. 'You did a good job last night, Jerry. And I'm grateful. From here on in, I'll be looking out for you. And I'll make sure we get to talk more.'

He rose and looked at his watch. 'Time to meet the big guys.'

As Grayson rose, the captain put an arm around his shoulder, discreetly ushering him towards the door. 'You know how they hate to go begging to the feds down there. Well, I have a feeling this tape of ours is going to make their day.'

'You got any other leads?' Grayson asked as they reached the door.

'Just a report of a black panel truck leaving the scene at high speed. We figure that was the one. Shows they weren't all that perfect, by the way. The wheelman was so freaked he drove down the wrong side of the street.'

'Good morning.'

Nan lowered her cup and looked up smiling as Robbie

entered the kitchen. He saw she had no need for make-up this morning. Her face looked radiant. Grinning, he glanced at Tom Craven who sat across from her with a newspaper in front of him. By contrast he looked gloomy.

'Morning, Tom.'

Craven nodded without speaking. Robbie slipped into a chair.

'Want some coffee?' Nan asked, already rising. 'It's fresh.'

'Thanks.'

He watched her cross to the counter. 'You're in fine form,' he said.

She laughed, pleased. 'Thanks to you,' she said, bringing his cup. She stood over him. 'Like my sweat-shirt?'

He looked up. The emblem of the Dublin rock band U2 was emblazoned on the white sweat-shirt. He grinned.

She pulled out the chair beside him.

'I still can't believe it,' she said. 'I just can't.' Her white teeth glowed. So American, he thought.

Craven interrupted suddenly. 'See this?' He held up the newspaper.

Robbie stared and suddenly realized it was that morning's paper. 'Where did you get that, Tom?' he said sharply.

'Kid left it.'

Oh, shit.

'We'll have to do something about that,' he said.

'No problem,' Nan said. 'I'll call and cancel.'

Craven passed over the paper. 'Take a look. They're screaming for a police investigation.'

Nan leaned across. 'Oh, that's only Grogan,' she said. 'I wouldn't pay any attention to what he says. He's just a clown.'

212

Craven glanced briefly at her; then looked at Robbie. 'You said we didn't have to worry about police.'

Silently Robbie read the article. Finally he put it down and shrugged.

'I don't see anything to worry about. He's just sounding off.'

'Absolutely,' Nan said. She looked at Craven. 'I really wouldn't worry about him, Tom. He writes that sort of stuff every day. Nobody pays the slightest attention.'

Craven ignored her.

'If they come after us, we're looking at serious trouble,' he said to Robbie. 'It means we'll have the police on our tail as well as the mob.'

Robbie shrugged.

'So what? They've nothing to go on.'

'You hope,' Craven said. 'Personally, I don't fancy the prospect of time in Sing Sing.'

'Come on, Tom,' Nan said, irritated now. 'You came here to do a job. I hardly think you should start crying about it now.'

Craven flushed. He opened his mouth, but Robbie raised a hand. 'Hold it,' he said. 'Let's not get into an argument here. There's more important things to worry about.' He paused. 'Renata claims he doesn't know anything about the arms deal.'

'Like hell,' Craven muttered.

'He sounds serious,' Robbie said. 'Claims Genta is responsible. Not only that, he says also that we'll never get a swap. He's convinced Genta wants him dead.'

Nan watched him, absorbed.

'And you believe him?' Craven asked.

'I don't know.'

'I think he's lying,' Nan interjected. 'He's probably trying to save his own skin.'

'What are you going to do?' Craven asked Robbie.

'I'm not sure,' he said. 'Work on him again, maybe.'

Craven sighed. 'And how long is that going to take?'

'I can't say.'

'This watch business. We're going to keep it up?' Their scheme was never to leave Renata alone for more than half an hour. They both knew it was going to be draining.

'We have to.'

'Robbie.' Nan leaned forward now to ensure she would get his attention. 'Let me take some of the watch.'

'He's dangerous, Nan.'

'I can handle it.' There was a stubborn pout to her lips. She no longer looked radiant. 'Or have you forgotten?'

More trouble, he thought.

Renata was awake, his face grey above the rumpled bedclothes when Robbie carried in the breakfast tray.

'How are you feeling?' He set the tray down on the small bedside table. Renata regarded it with distaste. 'You got some aspirin?'

'You better eat first.'

Reluctantly, Renata took some toast as Robbie sat on the edge of the bed. He seemed absorbed. 'How long do you expect to hold me like this?' he said at last.

Robbie shrugged. 'We need a couple of days to let things cool down. The papers have it, you know.'

'Yeah?' Renata looked vaguely interested. 'What they say?'

Robbie grinned. 'The columnist in the *Post* claims you did it to avoid indictment. But their crime reporters, who seem to know their job better, are claiming that your Mr Genta had a hand in what happened.'

'They ain't far wrong,' Renata said.

'They said you've been feuding with him.'

Renata looked coldly at him. 'I don't feud with people who work for me.'

'Still, they claim that relations between you aren't good.'

'Look at what's happened,' Renata said. 'You think that came about because we were pals?'

'You really believe he pulled this to get you in trouble?'

'He has that kind of twisted mind.' Renata did not mention what really angered him. He had been working up to taking Genta. And now he had been beaten to the punch.

He looked at Robbie now and shook his head. 'Look,' he said. 'It's no secret that Sal and me were having problems. I admit it. That's the reason he stuck it to me. It bugs me that he got away with it. But I got to face facts.' He looked at Robbie. 'Maybe you ought to face some too. I told you, he's screwed you as well.'

'We'll see about that,' Robbie said.

'It's the truth,' Renata said, taking his toast. He chewed on it, glancing occasionally at Robbie.

He's working up to something, Robbie thought. He's just taking his time before he springs it.

It didn't happen until he finished eating and had reached for a cigarette. Robbie lit it.

Slowly Renata took a deep pull. 'Listen,' he said. 'I think it's time to have a straight and honest talk here.'

Chapter Eighteen

'Let me lay it out for you,' Renata repeated. 'Salvatore Genta will do nothing to get me out of here. He knows that if I get back in harness, his days are numbered. On the other hand, if you keep holding me or even kill me, he gets to take over everything.' He looked at Robbie. 'He's probably taking over right now. And I'm warning you, if he does get control, one thing you can be sure of. You'll never see your arms.'

'Well, what's the alternative?'

'I'm prepared to do a deal with you,' Renata said. 'Get you those weapons you want. But the thing in the way of my doing that is still Genta. He'll stamp on any orders I give if he thinks they might get me out of here.'

'So what do you suggest?'

'Don't play dumb,' Renata said. 'To settle this thing, you've got to do something.'

'Like what?'

'You want me to spell it out? You're going to have to hit Genta.'

Robbie stared at him. 'You must be joking.'

Renata stretched out his wrists angrily. 'What are these, a joke?' he said. 'For Christ's sake, I want to find a way out of this mess. Can't you see that?'

'Let me tell you what I see,' Robbie said coldly. 'Frank Renata trying to reshuffle his board of directors. And getting his kidnappers to carry out the dirty work.' He looked at Renata. 'You've got some nerve.'

'Nerve nothing. I'm serious,' Renata said sharply.

'Come on,' Robbie said. 'There's a lot here I don't accept.'

'Like what?'

'I don't believe Genta would defy you if you ordered him to hand over those weapons.'

'You really don't understand, do you?' Renata held up his cuffed wrists again. 'What is this, power? With these, I'm nothing. I'm telling you now that if Sal gets to know you're holding me and threatening to kill me, that's it. And to hell with your plans.'

'Why haven't you taken care of him already if he's as power-hungry as you say?'

Renata scowled. 'This is the first time he gave me reason,' he said. 'Look, I know it would be tough. Sal's a smart son of a bitch. But if we put our heads together, we could come up with something. I mean, it isn't as if he was an innocent party here. He already clipped one of your guys, right? And that alone gives you the right to take him out, deal or no deal. I mean, if somebody took out one of my guys, I'd do it.'

Robbie was not taken with the comparison.

'Just for interest's sake, how would you do it?' he asked.

'The set up would be difficult. No question there. But after what you done, I think you'd be up to it. What you really need, though, is someone on the inside to help you. Someone who knows Sal's habits and how he operates. But a guy who's also with me one hundred per cent.'

Robbie smiled. 'I take it you have a candidate in mind?'

Renata nodded. 'There's a man who's been with me for close to thirty years who knows Sal better than he knows his own family. And better still, he hates Sal like nobody else on this earth. Even including me.'

'And who is this paragon?'

'I don't know what you mean, paragon,' Renata said. 'But his name is Chicken Devane.'

He wanted to sit down and think. That was why he went to the darkened living-room. He slipped inside and closed the door quietly.

'Hi.'

He turned quickly.

Nan was sitting on the sofa by the window.

'I'm sorry.' He turned to leave. 'I didn't think anyone was here.'

'No,' she said quickly, swinging her legs off the sofa to sit up. 'It's all right. Come on in.'

He paused for a moment, then crossed to sit in an armchair opposite her.

She watched him.

'Do you want the light on?' she asked at last.

'No.'

They sat in silence.

'Problem?' she asked softly.

He did not answer.

'I can sense it,' she said.

He looked at her, surprised. In the gloom, he did not notice she had flushed. She was becoming acutely sensitive now about appearing foolish before him. But she remained determined.

'Well, what is it?' she asked.

Why does she have to press, he thought. It wasn't that what she wanted was wrong. It was how she went about it. He looked out of the window at the darkening evening, forced to weigh what he hadn't intended. Finally, he said, 'Renata wants me to kill Salvatore Genta.'

He thought he heard her gasp. Silent, he waited for her to speak. To his surprise, she said nothing.

He went on: 'He believes that Genta has been plotting against him and wants to take over the family. And that he will never hand over those arms.' He looked again at her dim face but saw no reaction. 'He claims that my killing Genta will restore his power. And let him honour the deal we made for the weapons.'

There was a pause.

'And that's it?' she asked finally.

'No.' He leaned forward. 'I didn't tell you this before, Nan, but I have orders to kill Renata if we don't get our arms. So the issue really comes down to which one to kill.'

'Let me hear that again,' she said.

'If I approach Genta and he refuses to give us the weapons, I'm supposed to kill Renata as an example to them. But if I adopt Renata's proposal, it will be Genta that goes first.' He did not say that the prospect of killing either was beginning to disturb him greatly.

Outside, a car drove and a flash of headlights passed the window. They listened to it rumble into the distance.

She said suddenly: 'Why not combine both things you were talking about?'

'What do you mean?'

'Why don't you make the approach to Genta anyway? If he does hand over the weapons in exchange for Renata, everything is fine. But if he refuses, then you'll know that Renata is telling the truth. In that case, you can adopt his plan.'

He was silent for a moment. 'Stupid of me not to think of it,' he said.

'You've a lot on your mind,' she said quickly.

He shook his head. 'I've been missing the obvious

lately.' He grimaced. 'Now I'm even beginning to talk about it.'

'It's no big thing, Robbie,' she said softly. 'You're bigger than that. Don't let it bother you.'

He shook his head. 'I know Genta deserves to be punished for what he did to your father, Nan,' he said. 'But that's not what I joined the movement for. I know these people are criminals and I know what they do is bestial, but this is not their war. They don't belong in it.'

She was quiet for a moment. And then she said something that put him in his place. 'Have you forgotten why you came here, Robbie?'

He sat very still.

'Those weapons. You know they could change everything in Ireland. They're paid for, they belong to the movement now.' She paused and said firmly: 'Your first and only duty is to get them back.'

She was not sure why she said that, but she knew it was for his own good. He had to be reminded. But just in case, she sat absolutely still now too.

He rose from the chair. A twisted bar of light crossed his chest from the window as he stood for a moment. Then he walked over and stopped before her. She looked up, seeing his pallor even in the darkness.

'Thanks, Nan.' He leaned down quickly and kissed her on the forehead.

The touch of his lips sent an eerie feeling running through her body. She froze for several moments then began to raise her hands, to reach for him. But he was gone. Outside, she heard the soft drum of his feet on the stairs.

A hot glow rose from her chest to spread across her shoulders. Slowly, she lifted her fingers to touch her forehead where he had kissed it. Without understanding why, her eyes began to fill with tears.

When Robbie said he was going to contact Genta first, Renata's pale face showed no emotion.

'You do what you have to do,' he said. 'But don't get close. Something happens to you, something happens to me. I don't want that.'

Robbie had already decided there would be no face-to-face meeting. But now Renata decided to co-operate.

'Look,' he said, 'every straight phone within a mile of Genta is bugged by somebody. FBI, Jersey State Police, DEA, Treasury, you name it, they got a piece.' A sly smile came over his face. 'But we got one on them.'

'Where is it?'

Renata laughed hoarsely.

'On his goddam desk.' It was so simple, it was amazing no one had thought of it before. They simply tapped into the line of an innocent neighbour. Renata gave him the number. 'Answers on the fifth ring, it's him.'

Robbie drove well east on Queens Boulevard before he stopped at a vacant phone booth. It was four-fifteen in the afternoon, a time when Renata said Genta was almost bound to be there.

Sure enough, at the fifth ring, the phone was lifted.

'Yeah?'

'Salvatore Genta?'

'Who is this?'

'I'm calling for Mr Renata.'

'Eh?' There was a long pause. 'What do you want?'

'I'm calling about an agreement, Mr Genta. About a cargo to go to Europe. You remember a Mr Monahan?'

'So?'

'We have Mr Renata.'

'I see.'

'And we want our goods.'

'Do you now?' Genta said amiably. 'And what do I get if I give you these goods I know nothing about?'

'You get Mr Renata back.'

'I get Mr Renata back?' He chuckled. 'And that's your bargain?'

'That's my bargain.'

'Ha ha ha.' It was the awkward laughter of a man who was not familiar with the experience. 'So that's what I get, is it?'

'Yes. Now what's your answer?'

'Hey now, don't get mad. Don't spoil things. Just tell me what you'll do with Mr Renata, if I say no?'

'You know what will happen.'

'Don't be like that. Tempt me, tell me what you're going to do.'

'We'll do what you did to Mr Monahan.'

There was silence.

'Listen,' Genta said, 'that whole thing was Renata's idea. Everything you got to blame, blame on him. He did it, nobody else.'

Robbie said: 'Then how come you still have the money?'

It was unrehearsed. And inspired.

Genta paused. But it was too long.

'To hell with you,' he said and hung up.

Renata listened with grim enjoyment to what Robbie had to say.

'I should have made you talk to him the day you brought me here,' he said. He looked at Robbie. 'You believe me now?'

Robbie nodded.

Renata grinned.

'What's done is done,' he said. 'Time for business now. We got to put you in touch with Chicken Devane.'

Chapter Nineteen

If there was one thing Captain Brent Halligan hated more than being left out in the cold, it was being exposed to heat. In his time at Special Investigations, he had managed to avoid both. But now enter Chills Renata. Or rather exit Chills Renata. And all hell had broken loose.

Producing Jerry Grayson's tape at the brass meeting immediately after the kidnapping had earned him points. But the gain proved ephemeral. With the investigation stalled and the media in full cry after three days without progress, certain people upstairs were showing impatience. From their vantage point, the glitter surrounding the Boy Wonder – as his wife called him behind his back – had begun to look dangerously like tinsel. Halligan realized that he was in the kind of trouble for which there was no quick fix.

He had already responded to his difficulties with a mounting work programme that drew in more investigators. Now he was in the position of a poker player whose rising commitment to the pot had reduced his other options. Still, he knew that if he won this one, it would add to his empire. But if he lost . . . well, the consequences were unthinkable.

He pressed the intercom. 'Darlene, can you come in here?'

The pert blonde-haired secretary who was Mrs Halligan's *bête noire* scurried in. A forty-year-old whirlwind, maintained in equal parts by diet and Estée Lauder potions, Darlene had been with Halligan for four years. He had been into her for two.

'Yes, Captain?'

That powerful designation was what fuelled this neat little secretary's life. She kept a picture of the Captain in full dress uniform lit by a night-lamp over her bed. The picture had been a present from him to tide her over the lonely nights. The light was her idea, although he approved.

'Captain?' she repeated, studiously correct.

He waved a white cuffed hand to a seat.

She perched on the edge of the mock leather chair. No pad, no pencil. All she had on offer was her brain, an organ the captain admired, although somewhat less than her other moving parts. He stared at her.

'Darlene,' he said solemnly. 'We're in deep trouble here.'

She gazed at him, her mouth forming a small 'o'.

He nodded, offering a hardy grin, his spine straightening under her gaze.

'That's the only way to describe it.' He looked at her. 'You've seen the *Post*?'

'Yes, Captain.'

'That bastard Grogan is having a field day. Nothing his kind likes more than crucifying policemen. Still, when the going gets tough, the tough get going. Nixon said that. And that's just what I'm going to do.'

'Right, Captain.' She nodded quickly. No doubt about it, he thought. She's with me all the way.

'We're going to give it the works, Darlene,' he said suddenly. 'Everything we've got.'

She smiled, delighted.

'Now, here's what I need you to do. Over the next few

225

days, I want every scrap of paper, every report, every detail of this Renata business here on my desk.'

She looked at him, her eyes glowing with excitement. 'You got it, Captain.'

'Work nights, if you have to. But make sure that nothing is left out. I'm going to break this thing, Darlene, if it's the last thing I do.'

She rose, her little face working under the tight blonde hair. He could see the chest heaving.

'Come here, sugar,' he said. She came around the desk.

He placed a manicured hand on her tightly harnessed buttocks, letting it rest for a moment by way of encouragement.

'Give it your best shot,' he said, a catch in his voice, as he propelled her towards the door.

While much of what Captain Brent Halligan said and a lot of what he did smacked of burlesque, he was not a senior policeman for nothing. His subordinates might feast on the comic diet his vanity and lusty passions provided. But his superiors were far more interested in the results he achieved. And, as the record showed, they were right and the subordinates were wrong. More often than not, Halligan delivered the goods.

Even now, with little to go on, his confidence was not impaired. Given time, he believed he would break this case. All he needed now was the first opening.

It was Renata's idea to use a tape to make the first connection with Chicken Devane. He recorded a message setting up the rendezvous, and Robbie delivered it to the little bar called Patrones which Chicken frequented on Canal Street.

'When he hears it, he'll come running,' Renata assured him.

The meeting was to be outside Ponte's restaurant off the Henry Hudson Highway. That afternoon, as Robbie got ready to leave, he was startled by a sudden shout from the basement. He rushed down to the basement, gun in hand.

Renata was sitting up on the bed, a huge grin on his face. It was the first time Robbie had seen him looking so human. He lowered the gun, relieved.

'What was that about?' he asked.

'I got the way to do it!' Renata pointed to the television screen. 'Look, there it is!'

It was lucky he left early. Finding Ponte's was a problem with the one-way streets. It was with relief that he finally reached it and saw the thin figure standing outside, reading a newspaper. He had planned to circle twice but, no longer confident that he could do it successfully, he drew in to the kerb.

Devane lowered the paper and watched as Robbie opened the door.

'Hello there.'

Nervously, as befitted a man with his nickname, Devane approached. Up close, his wrinkled face looked wary under the worn fedora.

'Yeah?'

'I've come from Chills. You want to get in?'

Devane craned to look in the back. Satisfied, he climbed in.

Robbie glanced around. The area was deserted. It seemed safe. He pulled away from the kerb.

'Any place you'd like to go?' he asked. Traffic was light on the parkway as he pulled out. The crisp October sun gave the scene a whitish glint.

'Makes no difference. Francis wants we should talk, anywhere is fine with me. Why not just drive around?'

'OK. But I don't know this area. You'll have to guide me.'

'From out of town, eh?' Chicken glanced at him curiously.

Robbie nodded.

'That figures. There's no big line-up waiting to ice Sally Genta in this town.' He stared ahead. 'A lot willing to add an extra bullet maybe. But sure as hell not the first one.'

Robbie concentrated on joining the traffic.

'You know much about Sal Genta?' Devane asked finally.

'Some.'

'He's the meanest son of a bitch in the entire United States,' Devane said, shaking his head. 'Things he's done make me sick to the stomach just thinking about them. But what keeps the bastard alive is that he's careful as well as mean.'

Robbie nodded.

'What Chills wants ain't going to be easy. This guy never eases up. He's always on the move, changing routes, switching bodyguards. Even changes houses. Never less than three guys around him, day and night. He uses two cars but you never know which one he's in. It's like a game with him. Switch and change all the time.'

'Sounds a little discouraging.'

'Not a little,' Chicken Devane said grimly. 'Make that a lot.'

'Well,' Robbie said, 'Chills has an idea that might make a difference.'

* * *

228

'Jesus,' Devane said, amazed, when Robbie described Renata's plan. 'Chills has got to be crazy. Doing it with all those people around? He's nuts.'

'That's how he thinks it should be done,' Robbie said.

Chicken shook his head. 'Wild,' he said. 'Really wild. I think we're going to need the Zumacher for this one.'

Chapter Twenty

Finally, Captain Brent Halligan had the break he had been waiting for. If it hadn't been for the dignity thing, he would have run down the hall to the squad room.

'Haney!'

'Captain?'

'In my office. On the double.'

The detective scurried up the corridor after his boss, his heart thumping. But he need not have worried. A grin wreathed Halligan's face.

'This Renata case,' he said happily. 'The word is in. The snatch team that grabbed him. We broke what they were saying. It was Gaelic. What do you think of that?'

'Gaelic?' Haney looked at him blankly. 'That Scotch, Captain?'

'Bone up, Haney,' Halligan said impatiently. 'They speak it in Ireland, too. Our people say that's where the snatch team came from.'

'Jesus. That's one for the books, eh?'

'Listen, Haney.' Halligan had small respect for his subordinate's intellect. When the time came and that relative of his in personnel retired, Haney's head would certainly roll. 'Darlene tells me you did that computer course the Commissioner's office was blowing about. That right?'

'Yes, Captain.'

It was a safe bet that nobody else wanted to do it.

'Got into all those programs, systems and software stuff, eh?'

'I got some idea,' Haney said doubtfully.

'Haney, I'm giving you a chance to put it on display.' Halligan held up the sheet in his hand. 'Here's a list of all major organized crime figures in the city. Run them through one of your programs and see if there's a mick connection to any of them.'

It took an hour.

Halligan was writing one of his self-serving reports to the Commissioner's office when Haney reappeared. He clutched reams of computer paper.

'What the hell is that?' Halligan asked amazed, lowering his pen.

'All the connections between Irish guys and the mob since 1923,' Haney said proudly.

'1923? You dumb bastard. What do you think I'm running here? A museum?' Halligan shouted. 'It's recent stuff I want. Going back a year, maybe two, no more.'

'Hold on, Captain. I got something recent,' Haney stammered. He poked through the paper and pulled out a few sheets. 'Here. Listen to this. We got a missing person, possible homicide, down in Little Italy just two weeks ago. Guy by the name of Michael Monahan. He had lots of connections with that stuff going on over in Northern Ireland. He turned up as a suspect in a number of arms-smuggling operations by the IRA.'

'And?'

'His union logged three calls to his office in the week before he disappeared. All from Salvatore Genta, Francis Renata's underboss.' He paused. 'That the kind of connection you're looking for?'

'You got it,' Halligan said. Even though he wasn't quite sure what it meant, it could be the start of something. He leaned forward.

'Listen, Haney,' he said. 'You've done a good job here.

Don't let up. I want you to get a copy of the investigator's report on the Monahan case. Start checking on the people around him. We might be talking about a union power struggle here. Whatever it is, give it your best.'

'OK, Captain.'

'You did good, mister. Just make sure you have your report on my desk by Friday night.'

Haney swore inwardly. That meant long hours. Ever since he did that goddam computer course, life had been nothing but trouble.

'You got it, Captain,' he said.

Robbie and Chicken Devane crossed the parking lot under the towering north wall of the stadium. The man they were to meet stood by the entrance to Gate twenty-seven.

'Hi, Cosimo.' Devane gestured to Robbie. 'Meet my friend.'

Cosimo, a small sallow-faced man in his mid-thirties who held a fast food concession there through the mob, nodded curtly. He did not remove his hands from the wind-breaker.

'You're late, Chicken,' he said.

Devane frowned. 'Traffic,' he said.

Cosimo came away from the wall. 'Let's make this quick,' he said, as he led them past the security guard into the cavernous interior. 'I got things to do.'

'Sure,' Devane said, as they reached the first ramp. He glanced at Robbie and raised his eyes as they began to climb.

'There's a couple of new offices they're putting in over the stand here. One of them should fit what you're looking for.'

'Fine,' Devane said, beginning to pant now from the

232

climb up the circular ramp. 'Chills is going to be happy with your help, Cosimo.' They passed the first level.

'Yeah. Sure,' Cosimo said. He did not seem impressed. 'What's the scam anyway, Chicken?'

Devane paused to hold the rail. 'That ain't your business, Cosimo,' he said shortly.

The younger man shrugged. But quietly his pace increased. By the time they reached the top of the stands, Devane was in trouble.

'Up here,' Cosimo said. He pointed to a flight of stone steps that rose off the wide hallway.

'Let's give it a moment,' Robbie said.

Cosimo looked at him and then at Devane. He grinned. 'Sure. Why not?' Robbie was beginning to dislike this young man. Purposely now, he took the lead himself to slow the climb. On the last landing, they went through a fire door and entered a long corridor where reconstruction work was going on.

'Any one of those.' Cosimo pointed to the row of doors to their right.

Robbie chose the second one. It was a half stripped room with building materials piled in the corner. A long window sloping inward looked down on the empty ballpark.

Devane, still out of breath, managed to grin at Robbie. 'Perfect,' he said.

As they approached the window, Cosimo remained in the corner, arms folded, watching curiously.

They stared down at the vacant green arena. The baseball diamond was a faded brown against the grass. Behind it, a sea of blue seats rose to an overhanging ledge of glassed boxes.

Robbie unclipped the catch and slid the window open.

233

The faint echo of morning sounds floated in from the outside.

'Ten rows up. Directly behind home base there,' Devane said softly. He pointed. 'Fourth in from the right. That's his seat.'

Robbie glanced back. Cosimo was watching them silently.

'Anybody on this floor during a game?' Robbie asked.

Cosimo shook his head. He dropped his arms and came forward. 'Nobody allowed up here at game time.' He gazed down on the field. 'You got it all to yourself.'

'The one tomorrow afternoon. What's the starting time?'

'Three fifteen. It's NBC's Game of the Week.'

'We figure on arriving around the seventh innings,' Devane said. Robbie wanted to leave it as late as possible so they could melt into the departing crowd. 'Can you meet us downstairs then?'

Cosimo shrugged. 'No problem.'

'Chills don't want anybody to know about this,' Devane said quietly. 'You understand that?'

Cosimo nodded. 'Sure,' he said.

'We'll be bringing in something with us.'

'What kind of something?'

Devane extended both hands silently.

Cosimo's eyes widened.

'OK,' he said at last. 'That's what Chills wants, he's got it.' He looked at the rows of seats behind the baseball diamond for a moment, then turned and smiled. 'Anything you need, Chicken, just ask Cosimo.'

Afterwards, they crossed Manhattan in Devane's aged Monte Carlo and went through the Holland Tunnel to New Jersey. The interior of the car smelled of dogs even

234

with Robbie's window open. The wind had risen under a thin grey sky when they finally reached the sloblands. The damp air whipped by Robbie's forehead causing his fine blond hair to rise.

'You really good with rifles?' Devane asked. He drove hunched over the wheel and with care for the speed limit. Chicken was no tearaway.

'I've worked with them,' Robbie said.

Devane grunted. The cigarette was burning low between his thin browned fingers.

'Just remember, the first couple has got to count.'

They turned on to a dirt road that wound through the soft waving grass. The old car bounced on the broken trail. They stopped finally by a disused railway line. The lonely silence and the hissing wind reminded Robbie of the lowlands around Lough Neagh.

The gun Devane produced was a beauty. An assembly job, the barrel concealed in the stock. The craftsman showed his love in the polished flowing lines and careful finish. This was the Zumacher.

'A Zumacher?' Robbie hefted the assembled weapon in his hand. The name was new to him. 'What is it, Chicken? Czechoslovak?'

'Naw, homemade. The name's a joke.' Devane took the square of chipboard from the trunk. 'How far you want this away?'

'Make it 500 feet.' Resting the gun on the passenger seat, Robbie unfolded the handkerchief containing the brass plated bullets. He unclipped the breech and slid each in. Straightening, he brought the rifle to his shoulder and sighted on a distant water tower. It felt well balanced, the barrel steady.

'OK?' It was Devane calling back to him from his

distant spot. The chipboard target rested against a thicket of reeds.

'Fine. Move off to your right.'

Devane waved acknowledgement. Robbie's knee sank in the thick grass as he went down. But the ground below was firm. He took aim, taking his time, readjusting. He noticed that Devane, away to the right, was almost cringing. Robbie grinned, thinking that his mind must be on the numerous betrayals that took place in this territory.

Slowly, he raised the rifle, took final aim and fired.

The report was surprisingly quiet. The rifle itself hardly shifted.

Beautiful.

Devane came forward at a shamble. Robbie watched as he indicated the hit. He smiled in satisfaction. The ordnance chap, whoever he was, had done his work well. It was within an ace of where he wanted it.

'Another,' he called.

Devane nodded vigorously and retreated.

It was just as good the second time around.

'Holy shit!' Devane shouted. He waved happily.

Only the fifth was off but Robbie could account for that. When Devane brought the board back, it was clear he was proud of his man. Robbie was gathering the empty cartridge cases.

'You're some shooter, you know that? Take a gander.'

A tight clutch of holes. Even the single misfire was a bare three inches away from the rest.

'It's a marvellous job,' Robbie said, as he dismantled the Zumacher. 'I just wish I could take it away with me.'

'We ought to go to Coney Island,' Devane said on their way back into town. 'With that eye of yours, we could clean up there.'

* * *

That evening, Brent Halligan was having his weekly discreet outing with secretary Darlene. The dinner conversation, as was the pattern, centred on the Captain's past conquests. Where circumstances thwarted passion, Halligan was always prepared to settle for nostalgia.

On this occasion he was discussing an Egyptian woman called Wazira, who was less an old flame than a fiery blowtorch. Wazira occupied a pedestal in the Captain's steamy psyche that was at least eight storeys taller than that occupied by Mrs Halligan, who would not have lost a wink of sleep at the news (and which contributed to her low rating).

Wazira's major defect, according to the Captain, was a learning disability which prevented her from understanding the desperately shouted word, 'Stop!' when a guy's trousers were on the dresser and the bit was in her teeth.

What fascinated the Captain about Wazira, on those rare occasions when they untangled, was her devotion to wacky religions.

'Of course, I wasn't looking for religion when I went to my first church meeting with her.' Halligan chuckled in his worldly way. 'I was after something else.' He leered with an effect which his secretary found pleasing and which was not at all diminished by the spare-ribs in garlic sauce he was chewing.

Her eyes heavy under the weight of false lashes, Darlene watched the Captain crack the spare-ribs, even finding it vaguely displeasing to see those masterful sausage-shaped fingers tearing into flesh other than her own.

'That's a funny name, Wazira,' she said brightly, keeping her end up.

'Crazy she was.' Halligan smiled fondly now, ignoring the boned meat waiting to be ground under his crowns. 'Know what she liked to do?' He leaned forward and whispered.

'Sweet God!'

'Hey, it's a free society. Don't knock it until you've tried it.'

She shook her head. 'I hate yogurt. Please, go on with your story.' Darlene always got points for thoughtfulness.

'Well, she took me to this place called the Charismatic Unitarian Church,' he said. 'The minister was a smirky little guy with only one arm. He claimed the baggage handlers lost the other one in Vietnam. What a freak! At one point he raised the stump and said, "Whenever I hit Vegas, this proves to be an infallible guide at the black-jack table. It tells me never to split a pair against the dealer's ace." That brought the house down although I didn't quite get it myself. No surprise there. I mean, it's twenty years since I got out of morality and vice.' He paused and winked slyly. 'Professionally, that is.'

Darlene giggled. He seemed to have an endless supply of anecdotes.

'Anyway, telling you this story. The preacher guy stands up in this plywood pulpit and says: "We will now start with hymn number one. You will find the sheet music, courtesy of CBS records, in the front of your pew." And get this. He puts on an old seventy-eight of Julius La Rosa. Guess what it was?'

She thought quickly. ' "Amore"?'

'Naw. That's Dean Martin. It was "Anything Goes".'

'Gee.'

'How about that? I mean a church and religion and all, and here's La Rosa warbling,' he tried it, ' "In olden days a glimpse of stocking is looked on as something shocking,

238

now Heaven knows, anything goes."' He trailed off. 'That heaven is the only religious thing in the whole stupid song.'

'You sing nice,' she said. 'I didn't know that about you.'

'Lots of things you don't know about me, hon.' He winked. 'Say nothing. We'll get to them.'

'I like that "Anything Goes",' she said. 'The lyrics are very catchy.'

'Catchy nothing. You know what happened when we finished singing it? Someone shouted: "Play the B side." Sweet Jesus, I'm thinking, this is a congregation of fruitcakes. But this minister, he smiles and says, "Wise choice." He flips the record like he's been in the business all his life. And what does he come up with? "The Sunny Side of the Street"!'

'I know that,' she said. '. . ."*Just direct your feet to the sunny side of the street.*"' She sang it softly although not as well, just to keep up with him.

He nodded. 'Where's the religion in that? I ask you. Just direct your feet to the sunny side of the street.' He stopped suddenly. His eyes widened. He gave a sudden gasp and his face went brick red.

'Jesus Christ!' The words escaped in a choked gurgle.

Darlene stared at him, frightened.

'What's the matter, Captain?' she cried. She thought he was having a heart attack.

He stared into space, then banged the table.

'Why didn't I think of it before?' Realizing he could be overheard, he leaned towards her. 'Darlene, the Renata kidnapping.' He always used her real name when it was business. 'Listen,' he whispered urgently, 'we have two clues, right? One, the guys spoke this Gaelic stuff. Two, a witness phones in a complaint about this black panel

239

truck leaving the scene. *On the wrong side of the street!* Don't you get it?'

She wanted to desperately. Miserably, she shook her head.

'They're foreigners! New to the country! Jesus, why didn't I see it before? They weren't trying to escape. They just forgot and drove European style! Lordy, Lordy. They must be just out of Ireland. Maybe over specially for the job.'

To be privileged to watch the workings of a great forensic mind was almost too much to bear. Her chest heaving, Darlene had to close her eyes for a moment.

'Get the lead out of your drawers, Darlene,' the Captain said crudely. 'We got work to do.'

She opened two shining eyes. 'Yes, sir!'

Detective Second Class Christy Haney was anchored to his sofa with a beer in his hand and Wheel of Fortune on the screen, when he got the call.

'Haney, I want you to get on to Immigration at Kennedy,' Halligan barked. 'I want New York domiciles for every male between the ages of twenty-four and thirty-two who arrived in the city from Ireland in the past month. Also a woman in the same age group. You got that?'

'Yes, Captain.'

'Look for addresses that pair people up. Man with man. Man with woman. Any you get, pass on to Darlene. If you need help, let me know.'

Outside, as they waited on the pavement for a cab, Darlene longed to cross the regulation two feet that always divided them on public thoroughfares, but she knew that was out. Still, she could feel the warming aura. The Captain was on a roll.

Despite his weakness for playing to the gallery, the confidence Halligan exuded was not all show. Momentum, he knew, was at least as important as individual clues in any investigation.

And now, for the first time, he knew he had it.

Chapter Twenty-one

Robbie spent most of the morning with Renata. The bond between them had grown stronger. Now, as Robbie rose to leave for the rendezvous with Chicken Devane, Renata waved him over.

'Listen,' he said. 'I got a lot of faith in you and I know you can do this. But you still got to be careful. Remember, don't ease up while Sal is still on his feet.' He reached out and squeezed Robbie's hand. 'Good luck. And keep an eye on Chicken. This is going to take a lot out of him.'

Nan gave Robbie a quick hug. Tom Craven was lying down in his bedroom. Robbie was glad not to wake him. He was becoming increasingly uncooperative.

Devane was on time. Robbie parked the van in the lot on Forty-first and went to join him in the car. He noticed that the signs of anxiety that earned Devane his nickname were the strongest yet. Devane barely spoke and smoked incessantly as they drove up to the Bronx. Robbie felt fresh admiration for this frail but stubborn man, knowing the stress he was under.

The parking lot was crowded when they arrived but they found one of the last spots far from the stadium and just inside the entrance. The late afternoon sun slowly dipped as they waited, barely speaking, listening to the game on the radio. The commentary, with its interminable statistics and bizarrely titled technicalities, was incomprehensible to Robbie. He found it hard to maintain interest. The cloud-spattered sky was starting to be tinged with orange when he heard them announce the end of the sixth innings. The Yankees were leading the Toronto Blue Jays by a score of three to one.

He sat up. 'Looks like it's time.' He smiled at Devane. 'Ready?'

Devane punched out his last cigarette in the overflowing ashtray. 'Now or never.'

Turning back, he took the long flower box off the rear seat. Together, they climbed out on to the chilly lot. The hum of the crowd rose from the towering stadium before them. Hefting the box under his arm, Devane led the way towards the entrance gates. It was as if he wanted to get it over with.

Except for a few attendants, the car-filled lot was lifeless. Overhead, a silver airship carrying the Goodyear name glistened in the last rays of sunshine.

Robbie touched the older man's elbow.

'Going to be all right, Chicken?'

Devane nodded without speaking.

'Don't worry. We'll do it all right,' Robbie said. 'I guarantee it.'

'Sure.' But Devane did not take his eyes off the entrance ahead.

The small figure of the concession operator, Cosimo, was visible by the gate. As they neared, he straightened and stepped out to greet them. Robbie saw him glance nervously at the box Devane was carrying. With a nod to the ticket collector, he hustled them through the side gate. The ticket collector gave no sign of noticing them.

'We use the elevator this time,' Cosimo muttered and led them to an alcove in the entrance way. The little bastard, Robbie thought. He put Chicken through all that climbing needlessly. Robbie gazed coldly at him as the elevator climbed. But Cosimo had developed a strong interest in the floor and didn't notice. They emerged on the narrow corridor where they had been the day before. As Cosimo had promised it was empty. They crossed the hall and entered the lounge overlooking the stadium grounds.

The transformation outside the window was startling. The packed seats teemed now with movement and colour. Music boomed from loudspeakers. The grounds were filled with a carnival atmosphere.

Cosimo hesitated. 'Listen,' he said, 'I know you guys don't want to be disturbed. I better wait outside and make sure you ain't bothered. OK?'

'Go ahead,' Robbie said.

As Cosimo slipped out, Devane knelt and began unpacking the rifle. Expertly, he assembled the parts and clipped on the separate telescopic sight. Robbie crossed to slip the catch off the window. He slid it open. A hum of noise rose from below.

'There you go.' Devane rose awkwardly and handed him the rifle. 'All primed.'

Standing well back from the window, Robbie balanced the rifle in his left hand and brought it to his shoulder. With the barrel pointing across the stadium, he moved his eye down to the sight and began making adjustments. The crowded seats across the ball-park sprang into view. He brought them into focus.

His eye was filled with myriad colours. Sweaters, jackets, shirts stood out in a rainbow etched sea. He saw faces, white, black, tanned, pale, old and young. His lips tightened. The sight of many children in the crowd bothered him. He would need to be very careful.

Slowly, he dipped the scope to the bottom of the seat rows and began counting up. Reaching the tenth, he moved in four.

Damn.

A black man sat in the seat supposed to be occupied by Genta. Sure he had made a mistake, Robbie repeated the process.

After a moment, he lowered the rifle.

'Something's wrong, Chicken. It's not Genta in that seat.'

Devane glanced quickly at him. 'You sure you got it right? Ten up and four across, like I said?'

Robbie nodded. 'I did it twice. There's a black guy in the seat.'

'No way that could happen,' Devane said. 'Here, give me a look.'

He took the rifle and brought the scope to his eye. Robbie waited.

'How the hell did that happen?' Devane lifted his head from the rifle and stared at Robbie.

'You're sure he still uses that seat?' Robbie asked. He took the rifle and rested it sideways against the wall.

'No question.'

'Couldn't he have given it up?'

'Not with the Yankees chasing the pennant. And no way to a black guy. That's not Sal.'

Robbie frowned. 'Maybe we better ask Cosimo about this.'

'If we do and Genta survives, he's going to get told. That little scumbag will pass the word.'

Robbie shrugged. 'Get him in here.'

Devane went to the door and leaned out.

'Cosimo,' he called. He put his head out further. 'Cosimo!'

There was no answer.

Devane turned. His face was grey. 'He's not there.'

Robbie went quickly to the door, looking out into the corridor. It was deserted.

'Jesus.' Devane's voice was low and strained. 'Sal skips a pennant game. There's a black guy in his seat. And now Cosimo's gone.' He swallowed. 'We're in trouble, fella.'

Robbie turned quickly. 'Get that elevator up here!' he snapped.

As Devane brushed by him, he hurried back to where the rifle rested. He took it to the flower box and knelt to unclip the sight. Suddenly, from the hallway, he heard Devane scream in fright. With lightning speed, Robbie slid a bullet into the breech, rose and sprinted to the door.

He burst into the corridor. The scene etched on his mind like a framed picture.

Devane was backing up on the far side of the elevator, moving away from Robbie, his hands above his head. Cosimo and a towering bald man were coming out of the opened doors, guns pointing at his thin body. Devane's movement had turned them momentarily away from where Robbie was.

'Hey!' he shouted.

Cosimo whirled first, the pistol raised. Robbie fired from the hip. The bullet took the smaller man in the chest and sent him slamming against the wall. The big man, reacting slower, half raised his gun. Robbie took a step forward, the rifle raised.

'Go ahead. Try it!' he shouted. His eyes blazed fiercely. But his heart was empty. So was the breech.

As the hulking man hesitated, Devane suddenly sprang forward and clawed at the gun. It was enough. Robbie made a rush, swinging the Zumacher. The stock slammed into the bald head. With a groan, the big man buckled. Devane followed him down, still grappling for the gun.

Robbie dropped the splintered rifle and dived in to help pull it away. Devane came up on his knees, trembling. The big man clutched his bleeding head, half sitting against the wall.

'It's Coppola,' Devane's voice was shaking. 'Genta's bodyguard.'

'Get Cosimo's gun, Chicken!' Robbie kept the sitting man covered.

Devane scrambled across and pulled the gun from the dead man's hand. He rose unsteadily. The two of them rested against the opposite wall.

'The little bastard, Cosimo,' Devane said, as they watched the burly Coppola who was shaking his head, trying to clear it. 'He must have passed the word.'

Robbie said nothing.

'What now?' Devane asked.

'We better get ourselves out of here.'

Devane looked down at Coppola. He turned to look at Robbie.

'Listen,' he said. 'Maybe this game ain't over yet.'

Robbie kept his eyes on Coppola. 'What do you mean?'

'Genta is around here somewhere,' Devane said.

'What makes you say that?'

Devane pointed his gun at Coppola. 'This guy's his driver as well as his bodyguard. Genta never leaves him behind. Ever.'

Coppola's eyes were clearing. He ignored Robbie and glared at Devane with hatred.

'You're dead, Devane,' he snarled. 'Sal's going to finish you for this.'

Devane stared at him. 'If he's got the keys,' he said softly. 'Genta will be down there in the car. On the lot.'

Robbie saw Coppola's eyes flicker.

'Empty your pockets.' He levelled the gun.

Coppola glared defiantly at him.

Robbie stepped forward and whacked him hard on the side of the head.

'One more time,' he said.

Blood streaming from his head, Coppola emptied his pockets. A wallet, ammunition clips, bric-à-brac. And a set of car keys. Robbie scooped them up. He backed alongside Devane.

'Where do I find it?'

'It's a dark blue Caddy. The licence plate is Sal Gee. You can't mistake it. He parks three, maybe four rows in from the North Gate.'

Robbie gestured to Coppola. 'What about him? We can't leave him here.'

Devane was silent. Finally he grimaced. 'You go. I'll stay to watch him. I'll follow in five minutes.'

Robbie looked at him doubtfully. 'Sure you'll be all right?'

Devane nodded impatiently now. 'Go on. You're wasting time.'

As Robbie pressed the elevator button, Devane suddenly shouted 'Hey!'

Robbie looked back.

Devane grinned and tossed him two extra ammunition clips from the pile on the ground.

'Give Sal my regards,' he said.

The limousine had darkened windows making it hard to see if anyone was inside. Robbie came up on the driver's side and rapped the bunch of keys he held against the window.

'Somebody drop their keys?' he called.

There was a long silence. Then, slowly, the rear window slid down.

Salvatore Genta, mean and dark, looked out. 'What do you want?'

'Found this bunch of keys,' Robbie said. He held them up. 'Got your licence number on them.'

Genta's hand reached out. 'Give them here.'

'Wait a minute.' Robbie stepped back. 'How about a reward?'

'Reward?' Genta's face took on a scowl. Robbie remembered his legendary meanness. 'You want your chops busted? Hand them over, punk.'

'Not a chance.' Robbie stepped even further back. 'I want something for my trouble.'

The door burst open. Genta came scrambling out, a sap in his hand. Always prepared for emergencies, Robbie thought. He was faintly amused but very careful.

Genta began slowly circling, his arm raised. Robbie glanced about quickly. There were some attendants in the distance. He edged around to put himself between them and Genta.

'Hand over those keys,' Genta growled. 'Now!'

Robbie flicked back his coat and brought out the gun.

Genta's face fell like a landslide. He stared at it in shock. Slowly he raised his eyes, the aggression fading. 'Hey, now.' His voice quavered.

Robbie glanced past him towards some sheds clustered at the end of the parking lot a few hundred feet away. They offered some cover.

He gestured. 'Over there.'

Genta hesitated. Robbie took a step forward, the gun raised, Genta quickly began backing. They reached the guardrail.

'Step over,' Robbie snapped.

Awkwardly, Genta straddled the metal runner. 'Look,'

he said, his eyes on the gun. 'Take it easy with that thing, OK?'

'Move!'

Unwillingly, Genta swung the other leg over. Robbie followed, pointing towards the sheds.

'Down there.'

'Look,' Genta said hurriedly, facing him. 'You want money? Go ahead and take my wallet.'

'Turn around,' Robbie said. 'And start walking.'

They began moving across the shadowed tarmac. Suddenly Genta stopped and turned, his face pale.

'Oh no.'

The penny had finally dropped. A gusting breeze whipped his thin black hair high. He stared at Robbie. 'You're the guy that was on the phone.'

Robbie closed on him. The nose of the gun stuck into his ribs. 'Move.'

Genta stumbled backwards. As Robbie came on again, he backed away, but towards the sheds now.

'Christ, man, there's no need for this. You want to talk, we can talk.' A note of desperation crept into his voice at Robbie's lack of response. 'You got to listen to me.'

'Keep walking.'

'Jesus, guy.' Genta turned again, his face tight with strain, moving backwards. 'Don't you want to talk about this? I mean, if there's a problem, we can sort it out.'

'Shut up and turn around.' They were half-way to the sheds.

Unwillingly, Genta faced forward. 'Look, I understand why you're mad. I don't blame you.' He kept glancing nervously over his shoulder. 'But this could be a big mistake.'

'We'll talk about that when we get to those sheds. Just keep walking.'

'Look, if it's those arms that are worrying you, we could still fix up something. It's not over yet. There's still time to do something.'

They left the hard grey concrete of the parking lot and stepped onto the wide swathe of gravel surrounding the sheds. Their feet crunched on the stones.

'To your right.'

Weeds lined the grassed space between the buildings. Some abandoned machinery lay against one of the walls. The wind died away. The clouds were darkening as the sun sank low.

Genta stopped and turned.

He tried to grin, his thin lips trembling. 'All right. You want to talk, let's talk. OK?' He hesitated. 'Is it the money that's bothering you?'

'What did your people do with Michael Monahan's body?' Robbie asked coldly, deliberately phrasing it to let Genta himself off the hook.

He saw the flicker of hope.

'That was all a mistake,' Genta said quickly. 'I was sick when I heard what happened. The guys got out of hand.'

'Where's the body?' Robbie asked abruptly.

Genta looked at him, desperately trying to weigh his answer.

'On Jimmy Coppola's farm,' he said finally. 'Outside Roselle.' He swallowed. 'Behind the barn there.'

So they had done it.

Robbie felt his palm grow clammy against the butt of the gun now. His throat was dry. The dark smell of the wild undergrowth filled his nostrils. For the first time since he had known action, his heart began to pound.

Genta was suddenly aware. His eyes fell to the gun in Robbie's hand. He looked up and an expression of abject terror came over his face. His dark eyes began to blink

251

rapidly. His mouth jerked open as he watched the barrel of the gun rise.

'Ah, Jesus, no.' It was like the pitiable, begging cry of a terrified child. 'No, oh no!'

In the stadium, the bodyguard Coppola glared at Devane.

'You just wait, Chicken!' he hissed. 'What Sal's going to do to you shouldn't happen to a dog.'

Devane tried to control the shiver that shook his thin frame. But Coppola saw it. He leaned back against the concrete wall and grinned.

'Go ahead. Be scared. Any time now, the rest of the guys are going to get here. And nobody's going to save you after what you done.'

Devane's padded wind-breaker no longer kept out the draughts sweeping the corridor. Trembling, he lifted his left hand to support the gun which was growing heavy.

'What are you going to do?' Coppola asked. 'Stay here and get killed? Or beat it, maybe, while you have the chance?' He leaned back against the wall, folding his arms. 'Go ahead, work it out.'

Devane swallowed. 'Lie down,' he said suddenly.

'What?' Coppola unfolded his arms and stared into the white face.

'I said lie down.' Devane's voice rose higher.

Coppola looked at him contemptuously, not moving.

Devane raised the gun, his two hands stretched out awkwardly.

Coppola grinned and refolded his arms. 'Make me.'

Devane fired.

Coppola's head banged back into the wall as the bullet smashed into the wall above him. The corridor echoed

252

with the thunderous explosion. Devane staggered under the recoil.

A cloud of white dust settled around Coppola's head. He stared in shock.

'I said get down!' Devane screamed.

Coppola quickly dropped to the floor. He stared up at Devane, his powdered white face disbelieving.

Devane watched for a moment. Then he began to back around to hit the elevator button.

Suddenly, they both heard a door slamming way down the corridor. A voice was shouting.

'It came from that end! Jimmy! You down there?'

Coppola raised his head from the floor, his mouth open. Devane leaned over him and pointed the gun. Coppola closed his mouth and lowered his head.

The loud echo of running feet came from the corridor.

'Jimmy! Where are you?' The voice shouted again.

Knowing now that it was too late for the elevator and without the reserves to face another fight, Devane suddenly turned and ran for the exit.

He had barely hit the door when Coppola scrambled up. 'Here!' he screamed. 'He's down here!'

Devane raced down the concrete stairs, two at a time, his arms flailing. He burst out on to the wide hallway with its long line of brightly lit concessions and scattered fans. The roar of the crowd rose from the park outside. People were turning now, staring in astonishment at this thin, elderly man who turned back into the ramp and ran on down, skidding into the first rounded turn.

He got by it and kept going, running down the grey slope with gathering speed. He banged off the wall as he reached the next turn. Down and down the spiralling ramp he went, hardly conscious of what he was doing, unaware even of the feet booming above as Coppola and the others came hurtling after him.

He ran on and on, scrambling and skidding, until all his sensations blurred. The last turn, twisting sharply to the left, proved too much. He slammed into the wall, his body whirling. Out of control, he tumbled down, rolling over and over. The gun spun ahead as he came to a stop at the bottom under the gaze of an astonished gate attendant.

Somehow, he dragged himself to his feet. Now he could hear the shouting of his pursuers. In front of him, through the archway, was the darkening car park. His chest heaving in agony, he ran out.

Robbie Driscoll emerged from between the sheds, the gun loose in his hand. He turned to glance back and felt a wave of nausea sweep up from his stomach. He bent, coughing, the gun resting between his legs. Straightening, his forehead damp with perspiration, he put it in his pocket and tried to steady himself.

For the first time since he had taken up a gun to fight for the movement, he had the horrifying feeling that he had committed murder. All the other deaths, many of them brutal and every one cruel, had been insulated because he could label them as acts of war.

But not this one.

He realized now, in this dismal grey lot thousands of miles from home, that something terrible and irrevocable had happened. He could not describe the feeling exactly. All he knew was that a deep, fathomless vacuum had opened up inside him.

Slowly, his body still unsteady, he began walking towards the stadium. He had been concerned about what killing Genta might cost ever since Renata suggested it.

254

Even so, he had not expected the impact he was experiencing now.

He was half-way across the parking lot, still agonizing, when he heard the shouts. He looked up in time to see a figure dash out from one of the stadium entrances. The thin shape and the black wind-breaker told him all he needed to know.

'Chicken!'

He had completely forgotten. Breaking into a run, Robbie waved frantically. The older man, 300 yards away, saw him and turned in his direction. He had gone a fraction of the distance when three men burst out of the entrance behind him. Robbie saw one of them raise something in his hand.

'Chicken!' he screamed. 'Behind you!'

The ungainly head turned to look back. Robbie heard a popping sound. But the shot was wide. Even from his distance, he could see that Devane's weedy legs were beginning to buckle. He looked to be at the end of his strength.

Robbie raced towards him, pulling the gun from his pocket, waving to draw attention to himself. He had closed to within 150 yards of Chicken when he saw them fire another shot.

They had a hit.

Devane's body arched as he staggered. He grabbed his back in sudden pain, his elbows sticking wide. The three men kept running towards him, still firing. Like a ragged doll Devane slowly slumped to his knees. Robbie skidded to a halt, dropped to one knee and loosed off a desperate shot. He missed.

They had reached Devane. He couldn't fire now for fear of hitting Chicken. But suddenly it didn't matter. For one of the men leaned down and fired at point blank range.

They clustered briefly at the fallen figure till one pointed at Robbie and shouted. The three quickly spread apart, facing him.

There was no question of taking all three at that distance. Hearing a bullet whine off the tarmac, he backed up and loosed off a shot. Glancing back, he saw Genta's abandoned limousine on the apron, the door still open. He ran towards it now, pulling the keys from his pocket, without hearing another shot. Sheltering behind the opened rear door, he unlocked the driver's door and slid in behind the wheel.

The three were barely 100 yards away and closing cautiously.

Robbie leaned out, pointing the Magnum.

'Back!' he shouted. He loosed off a quick shot and turned the ignition. As they dived for cover, he slammed his foot down on the accelerator. The Cadillac went into a skidding turn and roared down the wide lane towards the exit. Behind him, they fired off a fusillade.

The car hurtled towards the barrier. Throwing the gun on the seat, he clutched the wheel and ducked as the bonnet struck the wooden pole and sent its smashed ends flying in the air. The rear bumper crashed off the pavement in a shower of sparks as he hit the street.

He turned down Grand Concourse as other cars skidded to avoid him. Remembering the map he had glanced at, he knew there was a bridge ahead that he would have to cross. With sudden anger, he realized that he had been depending on Chicken to get him home. Now he could not be sure of how he would do it.

He glanced in the rearview mirror and for the first time saw the bullet holes. They had made some hits. He leaned across and took the gun from the passenger seat. Steering with one hand, he wedged it between his chest and chin and replaced the used clip.

Ahead he saw the green sign, locating the bridge he was looking for. He found the entrance and entered the ramp in the centre lane, doing around forty-five, taking protection from the clutch of cars surrounding him. They swung on to the bridge.

Suddenly, just as relief spread through him, the Cadillac began to slow. Damn! He glanced down. The speedometer needle had dropped sharply. He pumped hard on the accelerator. But the car began to lurch. Now he caught the smell of petrol. He shot a glance at the fuel gauge. It showed below empty. The bastards must have hit the tank.

Flipping the indicator, he crossed lanes. The motor cut and at that instant, the transmission locked. Cars screeched to a halt behind in a deafening din of blaring horns.

Ignoring them, Robbie threw on the hazard lights and jumped out. With a gesture of apology, he pointed to the Manhattan side of the bridge and began to walk away quickly ignoring a chorus of angry shouts coming from behind him. A hundred yards on, he began to jog and then to run. The glow of the city stood out in the distance beyond the darkened river.

He didn't know where he was, except for that rough glance at a map when he had been with Chicken. But now Chicken was dead and he was on his own. As he reached the far side of the bridge, the raised pavement he was on suddenly petered out. He halted to stare at the ramp that curved away under arc lamps. It had no walkways. The route he knew vaguely back to the city, in fact the only one he knew, was out. He looked about and suddenly saw a small stairway that ran down to the darkened streets forty feet below.

He stared down, knowing that Genta's men were somewhere out there behind him. But now, walking the streets offered a fresh menace. He was entering Harlem.

Chapter Twenty-two

He had read about the place in those superior stories that European papers favoured when comparing New York living with their own. Tales of poverty, racism, drugs and murder. Always murder. Despite his bias against such stories, Robbie Driscoll realized he was on the edge of a ghetto where white flesh was prime cut. But there was no alternative. He had to go through to get home.

Cars rumbled across the brightly lit bridge above him as he reached the darkened riverside street beneath. He stopped to stare ahead. Way into the distance, he saw only dim circles of light splashed on the cracked pavements. The shadowy boarded-up buildings lining the street appeared deserted.

He began moving forward, his footsteps echoing on the broken trash-strewn concrete. The smell of the river hung heavy and dank in the air. Off to his left, he heard metal scraping as some empty barge rode up on its moorings.

A burned-out diner loomed, the lettering barely visible on the blackened wood. Next to it, high weeds filled a vacant lot, the stalks rustling secretly as he passed. Reaching down into his coat he closed his palm around the smooth butt of the gun.

Behind him, the hum of traffic on the bridge had slackened. The wind took over, hissing mournfully between the wrecked buildings.

He reached the first intersection and paused under the dull lamp. 143rd Street. A hundred and one blocks from the comforting noise and life of Forty-second Street where the van was. He had no idea what length a block was or what distance he would have to cover. But one way or another, he guessed it would be too far.

He walked on, covering several more blocks before he saw the first signs of life. A small shopping mall with lighted store fronts up an intersection to his right. He barely hesitated. Finding a phone to call a cab was his only chance.

As he neared the mall, he suddenly saw three young black men lounging outside what looked like a pizza outlet. Lips tight, he came on, maintaining a smooth, business-like pace. They stopped talking and stared as he came closer. He nodded without breaking step and made for the lighted door.

'Hey, honky, what you doing here?' one of the men said sharply. Robbie ignored the call and entered the fluorescent lit outlet. He heard them approaching the door as he went up to the high counter. A stout black woman, who seemed to be eating her own product, looked up from behind it. Her jaw dropped.

'I need to call a cab,' Robbie said. 'Do you have a phone?'

She stared without answering.

'A phone, ma'am,' he repeated. 'Do you have one?' He heard the men entering now. His fingers tightened around the gun. Resting his arm on the counter he half turned to keep the three in sight. 'My car broke down. I need a cab.'

The woman rose with difficulty and stared at him, hands on her hips.

'No phone here,' she said suddenly. 'So you just take yourself off and go look someplace else.' She shuffled to the back, muttering.

'What's the matter, man, you lost or something?' a mocking voice drawled behind him.

Robbie turned. 'I had a breakdown. I need a cab.'

'Don't he speak nice?' the smallest of the three said. He had sunglasses raised on his forehead and there was a mean glint in his eye.

'Where you going?' This one, tall with silky curled hair, appeared to be the leader.

'Forty-second and Sixth.' The car park was close by.

'You're going to have trouble getting a cab up here, man.' He smiled easily. 'Why don't we take you down there? We got a car outside.'

'No chance. I want a cab,' Robbie said.

Silky hair looked at him. 'How much you pay?'

'Twenty bucks.'

'Let's see it.'

But he was learning fast. 'Trust me,' he said.

Silky hair stared for a moment. Then he shrugged and turned to the small man.

'Call Alexander. He'll do it.'

The red flashers twirled as the policeman redirected traffic around the stalled Cadillac on the bridge. It was backed up for several hundred yards.

'So this is it, eh?' The burly man in the pale brown raincoat leaned down to peer in the window.

'Yeah. Looks like he took a shot through the gas tank,' his companion said.

The big man straightened. 'He get hit?'

'No sign.'

'Lab boys on their way?'

The other nodded.

The big man stared down at the car.

'The word is he went down that way.' The other pointed

261

to the end of the bridge. 'Took the stairway down to the street.'

The big man shook his head, smiling. 'Sounds like a tourist.'

'Well, he's down there somewhere.' The other man waved a hand out towards the black shapeless mass of Harlem. 'On foot.'

The big one crossed and gazed down, his hands on the cold girder. 'Blond and white,' he said, musing. 'Don't give much for his prospects.' He turned. 'Throw in everything you can,' he said abruptly. 'Let's see if we can reach him first.'

Alexander was a long-faced man with thinning hair and a bent nose that looked as if it was no stranger to opposition. He appeared in the lighted doorway, his hands thrust in the pockets of the leather jacket. His hooded eyes surveyed the group briefly as he leaned against the door. Then he smiled.

'This the man?'

'You got it, dude,' the tall one said.

'Cab's outside,' Alexander said to Robbie.

His hand resting on the gun, Robbie followed him into the open. With his growing fatigue now, he was conscious of the sudden blast of cold. He raised his collar with his free hand.

Alexander led the way to the beat-up yellow cab.

'Forty-second and Sixth, right?' He held the rear door open.

Robbie nodded. Alexander watched him get in and slapped the door shut.

The interior was stale and oily. The upholstery felt hard and brittle. He sat back, watching through the milky plastic divider as Alexander went around the hood to talk

262

with the others. They stood, outlined against the lighted window, their heads close.

It didn't take a crystal ball to forecast what was going on. Robbie watched for a few moments then reached to wind down the window, to break it up. But the lever spun hopelessly in his hand. He searched for the door handle. There wasn't any. Shit. They had him locked up. Angrily, he rapped sharply on the glass. The group looked towards him. Robbie gestured impatiently.

Alexander finally nodded and after a last few words came across and climbed in behind the wheel.

'No sweat,' he said. His voice was muffled behind the screen.

'Look, let's get going, OK?' Robbie snapped.

Alexander shrugged and started the motor. They pulled out of the parking lot, the cab rattling like an old crone. As they turned south Robbie saw Alexander's eyes staring in the rearview mirror, then turn away. Robbie twisted and looked back.

The other car, its uneven headlights giving it a lop-sided appearance, had fallen in behind.

He sat back, his face grim. At home they had a phrase for a situation like this. Out of the frying pan, into the fire.

They had travelled a dozen blocks, moving back towards the river, when they suddenly left the built-up area and entered a sparsely lit abandoned roadway. To the left, a huge lot opened up where scattered hulks of stripped-down cars lay like discarded sculptures from a some long dead civilization. In the distance, he could see figures moving by a mound of burning tyres. The glow of Manhattan with its tall spires and neon, edged the horizon.

263

With a sudden twist of the wheel, the cab swung abruptly off the road and on to the lot. The aged shock absorbers groaned as they bounced across the hard earth. Robbie turned and saw the lop-sided headlamps still following. Quietly, he drew the gun and rested it on his lap.

They had gone a bare hundred yards when the cab jerked to a sudden halt as Alexander stood on the brakes. The move, so sudden and unexpected, caught Robbie by surprise. Before he could stop himself, his head shot forward and slammed against the plastic screen.

He jerked back, momentarily blinded by the lash of pain. He shook his head quickly, his hand against the divider. Vaguely, he heard the motor die. There was a sudden violent banging on the screen in front of him. Half dazed, he squinted, trying to clear his vision.

Alexander's face, shimmering in the light, danced on the other side of the screen.

'Journey's end, man.'

A wide grin split his face. A set of keys dangled in the hand.

Robbie blinked hard.

'What?'

He saw the bent nose almost touching the milky screen. The grin widened further, showing uneven teeth. 'Game over, honky.'

Vaguely, he heard the squeal of brakes as the other car drew up. With all the strength he could muster, Robbie raised the gun and rapped the glass barely an inch from Alexander's nose.

'Fuck you,' he said.

Alexander was thunderstruck. His eyes crossed as they zeroed in on the pointed nozzle. The grin vanished.

The doors of the car behind squealed open. Robbie

glanced back quickly. The movement only took an instant but it was enough to unfreeze Alexander. With a sudden motion, he hit the door and was out.

'Gun!' he screamed. Robbie swung the revolver to the side window as he saw the dim shape scrabbling past. 'The fucker's got a gun!'

He heard people running. He tried to search beyond the blaze of headlights lighting the rear window, but he could see nothing. Suddenly, he heard the motor of the other car spring to life. It shot back violently. The bouncing headlights swept across the lot as it screeched into a turn. His heart pumping with relief, Robbie watched it speed off towards the road.

His face close to the window, he searched the darkness to see if anyone had stayed behind. He saw nothing. As his head cleared, he became aware of the dull ache. He lowered the gun and touched his forehead gingerly. There was a small swelling. Well, he had been through the wringer today.

And the trouble was, he wasn't home yet.

He had to shatter the window to get at the door handle. He searched the front seat and the ground around, hoping he might find the keys to the cab but they were not there.

He leaned against the side of the cab, breathing deeply. Then, reluctantly, he started off across the broken ground. His head really aching now, he reached the dimly lit street.

Wearily, he started walking south again.

A tavern.

The yellow plastic sign was broken and half lit. Webster's, it said. Two shuttered windows stood on either side of a heavy wooden door. It was built like a blockhouse.

God only knew what was inside. But ahead, the street

was dark and menacing. And there were many more beyond. Maybe up to seventy before there was any hope of sanctuary. And perhaps not even then.

To hell with it, he thought.

Clenching his teeth, he pulled the door open. A blast of hot air and heavy reggae music hit him as he entered the dimly lit interior. Small groups of people were scattered among the rough timber tables in the smoky room. More lined the bar. The place smelled from long use, and probably from the clientele as well.

Committed now, Robbie walked quickly to the bar. Ignoring the swivelling black faces, he picked a spot at the end and stopped by the waist-high counter, his back to the wall.

The bartender, a burly man with a round coffee-coloured face, scowled as he came down the bar.

'Jack Daniels, please,' Robbie said.

'Get the hell out of here, mister,' the barman growled. 'Before you get your ass kicked.'

Robbie smiled as if he had not heard. 'Have you got a phone?'

'I'll give you phone.' The barman leaned forward and whispered urgently. 'You're looking at serious trouble here, man. Beat it quick, before it happens.'

'Give me the drink. Then I'll go.'

'I'll throw you out before I give you one,' the barman said loudly as he straightened. 'This place is off limits to white boys.'

Robbie looked at the black faces, staring down the counter at him. He could see the open hostility. He turned back to the barman.

'I don't want any trouble,' he said. 'Just one shot.'

The barman shook his head angrily.

Robbie drew the gun. 'And make that with water,' he said.

Robbie heard the collective intake of breath along the bar.

'Jack Daniels coming up,' the barman said. 'Water on the side.'

Robbie smiled now at the faces staring wide-eyed from down the bar. 'Nice evening,' he said.

Nobody spoke as the barman silently poured the drink. He brought it over and laid it on the counter, the liquid rocking in the glass.

Robbie raised it, noticing for the first time that his hand was dirt streaked and trembling. He drank half.

'Hey!' a voice suddenly shouted from the end of the bar. 'I know you.'

Robbie looked up as the other heads turned. A small elderly man was pointing at him from the far end of the bar. He was nodding his head, grinning wildly in excitement.

'Don't you guys recognize him?' he said. 'It's the hitman!'

'Jesus!' somebody said.

They stared at Robbie, who had been about to finish his shot.

'What?' he said.

'You the guy hit that Mafia mother?' the little man called. 'At the basketball game, right?'

Robbie lowered the glass.

'We saw you.' The elderly man shoved out a finger like a gun. 'Bam bam. Then you took off in that car.'

Robbie stared, astonished. Heads were beginning to nod along the bar.

'Didn't you know?' the little man asked.

'Know what?'

267

'Millions of people watched you, man. YOU WERE ON TV!'

Robbie felt a sickening wrench in his stomach.

Oh, Jesus.

It was the damned Goodyear airship. The field producer had it sitting on a wide shot when the shooting broke out in the parking lot. The operator in the network control truck on the lot had picked up on it as Chicken Devane came running out of the stadium. All it took was a quick zoom to make television history.

The barman reached up and switched off the stereo. The rush of silence magnified the small sounds of feet scraping, elbows shifting.

'You're famous, man.' The barman was suddenly grinning, pouring another Jack Daniels. There was a rumble of approval.

'Like the gunfight in the OK Corral,' a voice said. All at once, the spell was broken. Everybody was talking.

'Can't kill too many of them bastards for me, man.'

'Three to one. Dumb fuckers still couldn't take you out.'

'Guy called hisself The Extinguisher. You sure put his lights out, hitman.'

It was as if television, master of the remote and unattainable, had suddenly dropped into their bar. They were animated, grinning, even overawed. Here was a celebrity. The gun, earlier a source of fear, was now part of the props.

In a state of shock, Robbie Driscoll drank his second shot. He stared at the watching faces.

'I need to get downtown,' he said.

Nobody seemed to hear.

'That Dan Rather. He said that this Genta was a top number. Most dangerous guy in the whole of New York.'

'He killed people like a mad dog. There weren't nobody that weren't afraid of him.'

The barman raised his hand. 'I got a question.'

The noisy talk died.

The coffee-coloured face turned towards Robbie.

'This Renata guy that disappeared. You kill him too?'

The bar was hushed, everybody hanging on the answer.

Robbie ignored the question. 'I need to get downtown.' He felt the thickness in his voice, the words exaggerated. 'Anybody give me a ride?'

No one spoke.

'Come on,' Robbie said. He was beginning to feel dizzy. He gripped the counter. 'I need some help.'

'He looks beat,' a voice said.

'See that bump on his head?'

'Give the man some coffee, Herbie.'

The barman brought a mug of coffee. Robbie took it gratefully and drank. The warm liquid began to revive him.

'Look,' he said. 'This drive downtown. I'm willing to pay.'

Suddenly, he realized they didn't want him to go. The unbelievable magic aroused by his appearance would vanish with his going.

With an effort, he raised the gun and banged it on the counter. That got their attention.

'Somebody is going to take me downtown,' he said harshly.

There was a long pause.

The barman, Herbie, was staring at him. With a sigh, he reached behind to untie his apron.

'I'll take you, mister.'

Suddenly, there were two, three offers. But Herbie was adamant. Now he had the prize he wasn't going to give it up. The entire bar crowded forward as he left. Some slapped his shoulder. One man even asked for an autograph.

Herbie's car was a battered relic of Detroit's affluent days. Robbie sank thankfully into the crumbling front seat.

'Where are we going?' Herbie asked as he started the motor.

The attention he had drawn in the bar suddenly hit Robbie. Anyone could recognize him now.

Herbie must have been thinking the same thing. He put the car in neutral. 'Here,' he said. He reached back over the seat and thrust a cap at Robbie.

'That blond hair of yours. Camera came right in on it. Cover it and you're going to be all right.' He grinned.

'Thanks.' It was much too large, but the thought counted.

'Well, where to?'

Robbie hesitated. He would be fair game on the streets now. The parking lot attendant he would have to pay had probably been watching the game on a portable. There could be others too.

'Queens Boulevard,' he said. Tom Craven would have to collect the van tomorrow.

Herbie dropped him at Lowery, promising silence. Still, Robbie went into the subway entrance under the viaduct as if he were headed out to Flushing. He waited until the barman left, then came out and hurried back to Thirty-ninth Street.

The relief he experienced at getting home was tempered by the alarm he felt at being exposed. He went over every place he had been since coming to New York. The hotel was the biggest problem. They might recognize him there. But even if they did, he still believed he had covered his tracks. There was nothing to connect him with the kidnap house.

The precautions he had insisted on were paying off now. He ticked them off as he had done since beginning Setanta. Never leaving the house, except inside the van. Never eating out in Sunnyside. Buying food at odd locations outside Queens. The only thing he was sorry about was not dyeing his hair after the kidnapping. But he could do that tomorrow.

By the time he crossed Forty-seventh Avenue, he felt a resurgence of confidence. Even the moral issue was fading under the impact of his escape. Besides, with Genta dead and Renata back in control, the way was open for getting the arms cargo together. All he need to do now was lie low.

As he let himself into the house for the first time through the front door, he felt very, very tired.

They had been sitting up, waiting.

Nan led the way from the kitchen as he closed the door. He turned and she was on him, her hair brushing his face as she hugged him. Tom Craven stood behind her.

Robbie grinned now and disengaged.

She held him at arm's length, her eyes still glowing with feeling. 'You're all right?'

'Fine,' he said. He looked at Tom who was still staring. 'Everything OK here?'

'Yes,' Craven said. He hesitated. 'So you shot Genta?'

'It was necessary, Tom.' He looked at Nan. 'Is Renata awake?'

She nodded. 'I just brought him coffee,' she said. 'He wanted to wait up for you.'

Robbie unbuttoned his coat.

'I should see him,' he said, as Nan took the coat.

By the basement stairs he stopped to look back at Craven.

'You're not upset about this, are you, Tom?'

Craven shrugged. He said nothing.

'Nobody likes casualties,' Robbie said abruptly, and went down the stairs.

Nan stared after him, then went to the closet and hung up his coat. Tom Craven stood silent, rubbing his chin.

Renata lay on the bed, his manacled hands across his stomach. He opened his eyes as Robbie entered and sat up.

'What a hit.' His grey face split into a grin. 'It was beautiful. I knew you could do it, fella.'

Robbie flopped on the sofa across from the bed.

'You saw what happened to Chicken?' he asked.

Pain flickered in Renata's dark eyes. He waved a hand as if to dispel it. 'Bastards. They didn't give him a chance. Shot him down like a dog.'

'I tried to stop it.'

'I saw that.' Renata leaned on an elbow. 'What about Genta? Did he say anything before you clipped him?'

'No. Just asking me not to.'

Renata grinned. 'I figured he was yellow.'

'Well, he's gone anyway. Now we can get on with what I came for.' He rubbed a hand across his eyes.

'Beat, huh?'

Robbie tried to smile but his head ached. 'Yes.'

'You did a great job, Robbie. Even with what happened

to Chicken. And tomorrow, I'll do mine. But right now, if you ask me, you need some sleep.'

'You're right.'

At the door, he stopped.

'Chicken wasn't really like you thought,' he said. 'He was a real fighter. Those were real guts he showed at the end.'

'Thirty years we were together,' Renata said. He stared in front of him. 'Maybe I knew there was something in there all along. But he had to die to show it. In front of all those people.' The bed creaked under him. 'Get some sleep, fella. We both got a lot of work to do tomorrow.'

Chapter Twenty-three

He was sitting by the window in the living-room with schoolbooks scattered on the table. They did not interest him. He wanted to be away, to seek out freedom.

Beyond the opened window, the garden bloomed. Bright flowers rising in profusion along the thick stone walls. Fuchsia, dahlias, chrysanthemums. On the trim lawn, sparrows glided in and hopped to feed. Above the walls, the landscape climbed toward Black Mountain which was not black now, but golden in the afternoon sunshine. Above its squatness, a small but dainty patch of cloud floated in the blue sky. He knew without being told that he was small and dainty too. Brother to the cloud.

And yet afraid. Still afraid.

The sweet mother, with the sad smiling face, was smiling now from the flowered sofa. Pale and broad-cheeked, with china blue eyes and tight grey curls against the temples. The blue and white summer dress sticking to her large knees. She had soft, beautifully soft hands, but with nails that clicked and went on clicking as she read her book. She glanced up absently to smile at him, not seeing him, the nails clicking, the eyes vague behind the smile.

The pendulum on the grandfather clock drummed louder now. He's coming, it said, he's coming.

A whiff of cold wind swept into the room. The exercise book ruffled, a page rising to touch the raised pen. Magically, a broad head appeared beneath the furry tip. With slitted eyes and massive teeth, thick rows of uneven, grinding teeth. Two giant hair-backed hands waved their iron palms. But there was no body. Not a sign.

The nice mother's flat brogues began tapping with the pendulum. Everything grew louder, thumping, thumping. He's coming, he's coming.

The pen fell to the paper as it flapped in the icy wind. He stared horror-struck as ink poured across the page. He saw the beady slitted eyes blinking rapidly through the spreading black.

The clock chimed.

The nice mother leaped upright and the glass door imploded in a milky white cloud. He saw him now, his hairy hands swimming through the murk. Smoke and heat swirling. The nice mother swayed like a pendulum as the giant hands began whacking, smacking. The teeth ground, the wide nostrils flared. He saw blood pumping through the muscles. And those eyes. Seething, seething.

The exercise book was waving wildly, the ink flooding the small dark eyes which went on blinking, blinking.

Suddenly the black liquid gathered in a menacing cloud. He raised a small hand to protect himself. But it was too late. The ink rose from the page like a black bird of prey. Malevolent, gruesome, it swamped him, splashing, hot like oil, burning, burning . . .

Aghhh.

'Robbie!'

He shot up in the bed, eyes wide, lips tight across his teeth, his torso rigid.

'Robbie!' Her hands were on his shoulders. 'Wake up!'

He heard the voice as if she were calling from a great distance. Then he crossed the dividing line, saw her dim shape in the white cloth robe above him and knew that he was back. He felt immeasurable relief.

275

Nan stared at him, her eyes wide. 'My God, you scared me. I thought something terrible was happening. What was it, a nightmare?'

He tried to speak, to tell her.

'It's all right.' Gently she pressed him down. 'Just lie back. Let it go.'

Slowly, he lay on the pillow. She came down on the edge of the bed, her eyes luminous in the faint light.

'You poor man,' she said. She reached forward to touch his forehead and suddenly felt the clamminess. 'Robbie,' she said, alarmed. 'You're freezing.'

As if in answer, he began to shiver.

'Oh, God,' she said. Reaching out awkwardly, she took his hand. His fingers too were like ice. Anguished, she gripped them tightly.

A fresh bout of shivering swept over him.

Impelled by an emotion she could not control, she leaned forward and touched her lips to his cheek. He lay still and cold as a corpse. Her heart filled with his pain. With her free hand she drew back the coverlet. The bed creaked softly as she slipped in beside him.

There was a long silence as she turned and put her arms around him, drawing his cold body to hers. The rough cloth of her robe slipped away as her bared leg crossed his thighs. She was enveloping him. Like a soft cloud, her scented hair brushed his face. Gently, she kissed him.

He lay passive, feeling the silky bareness of her thighs warming him, driving off the cold. Her fingers gently touched his cheek. A tremor ran through her and she kissed him again.

Her body began to move slowly against him. He felt her shuddering, her thighs undulating as she moved above him. She reached down gently and he felt himself responding to the slowly enveloping softness.

But it was happening too fast.

The alarm began to sound within him. A nameless fear was spreading like a dark torrent through his body. He was trembling but no longer from the cold. A cry was surfacing in his throat, a protest that emerged as a moan.

She quickened at the sound. Her head rose above him as her body arched. Her hands gripped his shoulders, her breath coming in quick gasps.

No, he thought, no.

Her thighs were scissoring over him, closing, gripping. He felt a terrible panic, as if he were being swallowed. His hands pressed against her. She was staring down at him, the grey eyes wide, not seeing. A yawning terror filled him. His palms pressed harder against her damp flesh.

She was saying things, loving things. His mind screamed. Desperately, he writhed under her. She redoubled her efforts. In a sudden rush of power, he pushed to get her off. She jerked back, unable to grasp what was happening. With a powerful heave, he thrust her away.

There was an awful silence, broken only by their breathing.

'Robbie?' Her voice was trembling, uncertain.

'Get away from me!' His voice was high, at breaking point. 'Get away!'

She stared at him, horrified, then burst into tears.

For long after she had fled, he lay as if dead. It was hours before he slept.

It was just after 10 A.M. when the two beefy men entered the lobby of the hotel and walked down its length to the cramped alcove at the end.

The taller of the two men tapped on the plexiglass covering the reception desk.

'Yes?' The clerk's head popped into the opening.

'NYPD.' He flashed his badge. 'Let me talk to the manager.'

'You'll want Stanley. He's back there.' The clerk pointed to a tall door back down the lobby. 'Just knock and holler.'

'Informal, eh?' the tall one said as they crossed the hall.

'Arty,' the other one said. 'Lot of writers and painters lived here over the years.'

'Anybody I know?'

'How about Arthur Miller and Arthur C. Clarke?'

The tall one thought for a moment and then said: 'That why they call it arty?'

They both chuckled over that.

The manager, a slight nervous man, took the names and went off to check. He came back ten minutes later with a small sheaf of bills in his hand.

'Yes, we had those two.' He consulted the papers. 'Craven, he stayed ten days, and Driscoll, he stayed five. They both checked out on the 2nd of this month.'

'They leave any forwarding address?'

'We don't often have things like that.'

'Mind if we have at look at their bills?'

'Go ahead.'

There wasn't much. Just three additions for Craven's room. One was a dry cleaning bill for a complete set of clothes. One was a meal charge.

The third was a three dollar charge for a long distance phone call to Rochester, New York.

The sun filled the yellow kitchen with a pristine light that recalled the glow of summer. The radio was playing a

Mozart concerto he recognized. She sat at the table with her head bowed, eating from a small bowl of cereal.

'Morning,' he said absently, without looking at her as he crossed to the counter. He poured the coffee and turned back to the table. She was looking at him, her face pale above the orange sweater.

'There's toast here,' she said.

'Thanks.' He came across and sat down. He smiled at her as he took a slice.

'Where's Tom?'

'Down with Renata. They're watching the news.'

He nodded.

She watched him butter the toast.

'Robbie, that was a terrible thing you did last night,' she said abruptly.

He looked at her, the piece to his mouth. 'Eh?'

'You heard me.' She spoke more strongly, with passion. 'That was the cruellest thing anyone ever did to me.' Her voice trembled. 'You made me feel terrible.'

He bit into the toast.

She frowned now. 'Well? Aren't you going to say something?'

'I'd rather not.'

'Robbie, we have to talk about it.'

'Please, Nan,' he said. 'There's no point.'

Her face flushed as she put down her spoon hard.

'For God's sake! You were breaking down. What did you want me to do?' She slapped her chest. 'Walk away and leave you like that?'

He laid down the toast.

'I told you I don't want to talk about it.'

'Robbie, listen to me,' she said. 'All I wanted was to help you.'

He looked away from her. 'I'm sorry,' he said.

Her face reddened. 'And that's all? Just that you're sorry?'

'It was a mistake.'

'A mistake?' Her fists clenched in frustration.

'Yes,' he said. 'And it's over.'

'So that's it, is it? You humiliate me and you expect me to forget it?' She stared furiously at him and banged the table. 'What's wrong with you, anyway?' Her voice was high. 'What kind of a person do you think I am?'

'Nan,' he said. 'Don't shout.'

'You think I'm some kind of slut who does that with any man I meet?'

'I didn't say that.'

Her lips were trembling, her eyes swimming in tears. Suddenly she lowered her head into her hands. Her shoulders heaved.

'You don't know what you've done to me, Robbie.' Her voice was breaking. As he stared at her, she pushed her chair back and scrambled up. The tears were streaming down her face. 'Damn you!' she shouted suddenly, and rushed from the room.

He sat still, staring at the untouched cup of coffee in front of him. Finally, he rose and poured it down the sink. Not seeing, he washed the cup and put it away. Then he went downstairs to join the other two.

Back in the squad room later, one of the detectives put in a call to the number on the hotel bill. He had a story ready.

When a young woman answered he identified himself and gave her the spiel.

'I'm with a special detail investigating obscene phone calls here in New York City, Miss.' He paused. 'I suppose you get that kind of stuff up there in Rochester too, eh?'

'Sure we do. It's everywhere nowadays.'

'Ain't it just?' He lit the second half of his breakfast cigar. 'Reason I'm calling is because we got a big one going on here at the moment.'

'That right?'

'Yep. And it's got a special wrinkle. Guy has been calling up numbers all over the country from a down-town hotel. Made fifty, maybe sixty of these calls. Disgusting stuff. Know the type?'

'I can guess.'

'Anyway, Miss, I got the job of checking out all the long distance calls made from the hotel in the last week of September. Your number is about the twenty-seventh.' This was pure inspiration.

'From New York City?'

'Yeah.'

'I don't recall getting a call from down there. Not for a while . . . Oh, wait a minute, I did have one. But it wasn't obscene.' She laughed. 'Nan Monahan, that's a pal of mine, she called me. She wanted me to look after her apartment for the couple of weeks she'd be away.'

The lady turned out to be a chatty number. It took a while to get her off the line. The end of the cigar was moulting as he wrote up the notes of what she said. But he managed to finish both it and the report at the same time.

The cigar end he stubbed out in the ashtray. The report he tossed in the out basket to go upstairs to Halligan's secretary and secret pleasure, the titty little Darlene, along with all the others done earlier in the week.

He looked at his watch. Almost noon.

Beer-time.

* * *

'No bullshitting,' Renata said, 'but you are something else.'

Robbie smiled.

'Don't be too sure. It was a close run thing.'

'I'm serious. Give you a crew, you could make a million dollars.'

'Wellington said that,' Tom Craven said.

'What?' Renata looked at him.

'A close run thing. The Duke of Wellington said that about the Battle of Waterloo.'

'Nice.' Renata turned back to Robbie. 'I'm not kidding about making money, guy. You've got real potential.'

'Be serious, Chills,' Robbie said.

'I'm just telling you. Don't turn your back on it. And don't call me Chills.'

They looked up as Nan entered quietly and went to sit on the sofa. Robbie turned quickly back to Renata.

'Look,' he said. 'We have business to get on with.'

'All right, all right,' Renata said. 'Just keep in mind what I said.'

Reluctantly, he returned to the matter in hand. The key to releasing the arms, he explained, was a capo in Newark, a man named Willie Majura. He was business agent of the Genta union local that ran the Jersey shoreline. Motby belonged in his fiefdom.

Getting them to turn over part of their supplies was not a problem in Renata's mind. They'll play ball, he said. If not, we'll take the fucking stuff. Either way though, it had to go through Willie.

Making contact, they agreed, would be the most delicate part of the operation.

'No way you can do it,' Renata said to Robbie. 'You're hotter than a firecracker now.'

Robbie found himself agreeing.

'How about you?' Renata glanced at Tom.

'Forget it,' Tom said.

Renata looked at Robbie sympathetically.

'Some partner, this boy.'

Tom's face coloured. 'I've gone as far as I'm going.'

Renata shrugged. 'You got to reach Majura,' he said to Robbie. 'Otherwise, the whole thing's a bust.'

'I'll go,' Nan said suddenly. She had been listening from the sofa, saying nothing.

They all stared at her in surprise. Robbie shook his head quickly. 'No, Nan. I can't let you do it,' he said.

She looked at him coldly. 'Don't be a fool. You have no choice.'

Renata glanced quickly from one to the other, saying nothing.

'It's too dangerous,' Robbie said.

Nan's eyes sparked and it looked for a moment as if she were going to retort. But instead she turned to Renata. 'If I brought this Majura a tape, like with Devane, would he accept it as orders from you?'

Renata paused.

'I think so.'

'Wait a minute,' Robbie said.

Nan ignored him. 'How would I make contact?'

'Easy. He eats breakfast at a small diner on Nelson over there in Newark every morning about nine. Never misses.'

'Is he watched?'

'He might be. But if you appear out of the blue to talk to him, they won't know who the hell you are. And they're not going to put a tail on someone turning up like that. You'd be safe.' He looked at Robbie. 'You're worrying too much. A restaurant, broad daylight, nine in the morning. What's to happen? She'd be all right.'

* * *

That afternoon, Robbie went to Nan's room. She was sitting by the window, staring out at the row of houses to the rear. She looked up as he entered, but didn't speak as he handed her the recorder and tape.

'Nan?'

She seemed to drag her thoughts back. 'Yes?'

'There's something I have to tell you,' he said. 'It's about your father.'

Chapter Twenty-four

The morning seemed to stretch interminably as they waited for Nan to return. Tom and Renata played gin rummy. Craven had improved greatly since the mob boss taught him. But now he was careless and was down thirty points.

'For Christ's sake, keep your mind on what you're doing!' Renata growled as he shuffled. Tom had expressed surprise that the mob boss was such a stickler for honesty in these contests. Renata professed offence at this slur on his character. 'Put down some money and then we'll see,' he told Craven.

Now Craven had lost interest.

'Let's take a break.'

'One more.'

'No, I've had it.'

Annoyed, Renata tossed the cards on the table. He glanced at Robbie, who was compiling the list of weapons they had agreed on. It was made up from Monahan's earlier report. 'You done there?'

Robbie looked up to smile briefly. 'Just about.'

Tom glanced at his watch. 'Want to watch "Wheel of Fortune", Chills?'

'No!' Renata said. 'And I'm telling you for the last time, stop calling me Chills.' He listened. 'Someone's coming.'

Tom Craven met her on the stairs, her coat still on. 'How was it?'

'Fine, Tom.'

They came downstairs. Robbie was out of his chair as they entered. He stood with papers in hand. 'Hello, Nan.'

She nodded briefly and slipped off her coat. Tom took it and hung it behind the door. Robbie watched her as she sat down.

She had taken the news about her father's death with a tired almost exhausted resignation. He had been disturbed by that, knowing he was responsible for much of it. Still, he was aware of a kind of gritty determination surfacing in her too. As if she realized that the only valid resistance to the blows raining down on her had to come from within herself. Unlike him, Robbie vaguely recognized, she was rebuilding. That he had to admire.

'Well?' Renata said to her now. 'You going to keep us in suspense?'

A slow smile crossed Nan's pale face. 'Your Mr Majura turned out to be a very nice man,' she said.

Renata snorted. 'Willie's always had a soft spot for broads,' he said. 'Just tell us what happened.'

Nan frowned. 'He's prepared to come.'

'On his own?' Robbie asked.

She nodded without looking at him. 'We talked for a while. I feel we can trust him.' She looked at Renata. 'I can't think why, but mentioning your name seemed to have a very strong effect on him.'

Renata grunted.

'Any sign of surveillance?' Robbie asked.

'Not that I noticed. But there were a lot of people moving in and out. I couldn't be sure. Anyway, nothing out of the ordinary happened on the way back.'

Renata might have told her that that could be a bad sign, but he didn't bother.

'I'm to see him on Number Four platform at Grand Central,' Nan said. She smiled. 'He was worried that he

286

might have to go to the Bronx. But I told him no. I said I'd tell him exactly where on the platform tonight.'

Robbie nodded. 'We should drive down to the Hunter's Point station this afternoon. And look it over.'

'Fine,' she said.

Later, Renata saw Robbie alone. 'Listen, I need a favour.'

'What is it?'

Renata raised his manacled hands. 'I don't want Willie to see me in these.'

Robbie was silent.

'I've been his boss for twenty years,' Renata said. 'He holds me in respect. Something like this, it could change things. You understand?'

Robbie said: 'No funny business?'

'Listen,' Renata said. 'I've been learning. Anybody tries fun and games with you is crazy. You're a brutal guy.'

It was strange but of all the hours of talk they had, that was the phrase that stuck most in Robbie's mind afterwards.

'All right,' he said. 'We'll do it like you say.'

Nan came out of Hunter's Point station, the tall man with her holding an elbow as they stepped into the darkened street. He bent to say something and she laughed. Robbie, watching from the van, thought they made a nice couple.

The man glanced about as they crossed the small parking lot under the street lights. He was wearing a grey overcoat and gloves, a little like a stockbroker. Robbie turned his attention to the subway entrance behind them. No one emerged. He waited until they came close, then switched on the headlights. Up close, he could see that

Majura was nervous now and trying to hide it. As they approached, he moved closer to Nan. Robbie leaned over to open the door. 'Hello there.' He pulled down the passenger seat. 'Hop in.'

Reluctantly, Majura clambered in. Nan followed and pulled the door shut.

Majura watched uneasily as Robbie came into the rear with them.

'It's all right, Willie,' Nan said. 'We just need to check for a weapon.'

Robbie began running his hands over the crouching man. Nan smiled reassuringly.

Majura had a small derringer strapped to his ankle.

'That's not very bright,' Robbie said harshly. He pulled hard. Majura winced as the strip holding the gun came away. Robbie handed the weapon to Nan who looked shocked.

Quickly Robbie blindfolded him. He was not gentle.

'OK,' he said. 'Now sit tight.'

He took thirty minutes to make the five-minute journey back to the house. Inside the garage, he left Nan with the still blindfolded capo while he let himself into the basement.

Renata looked up expectantly. 'He's come?'

Robbie nodded. He took out the keys and tossed them across.

'Francis,' he touched his holster, 'don't make me bring this out.'

'Do I have to repeat myself?'

'Your friend was carrying a gun,' Robbie said. 'I took it away from him.'

'You can't blame me for that,' Renata said. He rubbed his wrists free from the manacles. 'Don't worry. It's going to be OK.'

'Well, you better make sure of that.'

'Christ, what's wrong with you tonight?' Renata said. 'I told you. Just let me handle this my way and everything will be OK. And listen, leave the talking to me. Don't say anything unless I ask. OK?'

Robbie smiled, amused at the charade.

'All right. Now give me those keys.'

They brought in Majura. He blinked under the fluorescent as the tape came off.

'Frank.' He stared at the grinning Renata before him.

'Hello, Willie.'

'Jeez, boss, it's good to see you.' He rubbed a hand through his silvery locks. He seemed a little dazed and nervous as he gazed at his boss. 'The word was out that you took a hit.'

'Like hell I did,' Renata said. He led the way to the sofa. 'So what's happening out there?'

'Lots of heat. What with Genta and all. Everybody's on edge.'

'Sit down, Willie. We got to talk.'

'Sure.' Majura was slowly regaining his composure. 'Boy, I'm glad to see you, Frank. These last few days have been crazy.'

Renata glanced at Robbie and nodded towards Nan. But she took the cue without waiting.

'I've got to be going,' she said, and smiled. 'Nice meeting you, Willie.' He glanced up.

'You too, doll.' He half rose, watching her leave. 'Good-looker,' he said as the door closed. He saw no answering smile from Renata and promptly forgot her.

'You met my friend?' Renata nodded to Robbie, who sat in the corner.

'Yeah.'

Robbie, his arms folded, nodded unsmiling. He was

coming to realize how much store these people set on appearance.

'He's the guy who snatched me from St Dominick's Hall.'

Majura's eyes widened.

Renata smiled. 'I told him to do it.'

'Jesus.'

'Willie, I'm going to tell you what's going on. You ever speak of this to anyone, I'll knock you on the head.'

'Hey, Frank. You know me better than that. I'm with you all the way.'

'OK. Now listen up. I went on the lam for a very good reason. Sal Genta was getting set to clip me.'

Majura shook his head. 'That sonofabitch. I always knew he was no good. How many times did I tell you that, Frank? The man was no good.'

'Going to strangle me, he was,' Renata said. 'With piano wire.' He gestured to Robbie, who was trying to restrain his enjoyment. 'He found out about it and came to me.'

Majura looked at Robbie and smiled gratefully.

'He not only warned me, Willie,' Renata said. 'He's the one who chilled the bastard too.'

Willie shook his head, sated. 'So that's what it's all about, huh?'

Renata nodded.

'Now, Willie, as you say, we owe this man.'

'I'm with you there.' Majura looked at Robbie. 'Just give the word, friend.'

Robbie wondered briefly what would have happened if the boot was on the other foot and Genta had displaced Renata.

'Here's the picture,' Renata said. 'This man cut a deal with Genta to get a pack of arms out of Motby.'

'My turf,' Majura said. He looked at Renata and said quickly: 'He never said nothing to me.'

Renata nodded.

'Genta never came up with the stuff he promised,' he said. 'Instead he and his guys waltzed away with our friend's money.'

'That figures.' Majura nodded.

'The money has to be in Genta's decima, Willie. And we're going to get it back.' Renata indicated Robbie. 'Our friend says we can hold on to it if we get him his arms.'

Majura glanced quickly at Robbie.

'What stuff is he looking for?'

'This'll give you a laugh. He wants a piece of those Honduran shipments that everybody is trying to keep under wraps. The stuff that's going through your terminals.'

'My terminals,' Willie echoed.

'Know how much money those bastards were holding out on us? Two hundred and fifty g's, Willie. Well, we're going to get it back. And you're in for a cut.'

Willie smiled.

'Our friend will give you the list. I want you to line up those arms. Deal or steal, it's up to you. After that, I want you to grab those guys in Genta's decima. And hold them for me. Because I'm going to do some whacking before this is over.'

Willie looked at Robbie and grinned. 'Don't you love it when the man talks dirty?'

Chapter Twenty-five

It was just past seven o'clock on Saturday morning and the offices of the Special Investigation Unit at old City Hall were quiet. Captain Brent Halligan found that congenial. He did not subscribe to the theory that when the king was off his ass, everybody had to move. Like his great mentor in the sky, he preferred to work in more mysterious ways.

Even at that early hour, Halligan was bright and alert in crisp white shirt and maroon cords. And in his element. Darlene had done her work well. The desk before him was piled high with files on the Renata case. Every report, interview, transcript and theory was there. He rubbed his jowl as he regarded the mound of paper. For a man cut in the Captain's mould, this was the breakfast of champions.

Beyond him, her little frame coiled in the mock-leather chair, Darlene slept. To Halligan's mind, it made a scene that belonged up there with that famous painting of three dogs playing cards (of which he had a limited edition print). He eyed the petite secretary with an affection that Mrs Halligan had been spared for some years now and for which she no longer cared two cents. It took an effort to turn away.

The slanted yellow rays glinted on the windows lining Canal Street opposite his office. The sound of traffic below was muted. As the city snored and snuffled through its last hours of slumber, its guardian bent to work.

Begin at the beginning, he murmured to himself. A

little rule he learned at the academy. His devotion to it showed that, despite his grandiose and sometimes dangerously apocalyptic visions, Brent Halligan on a certain level was still a severely practical man.

Robbie Driscoll came into the kitchen where Nan and Tom Craven were eating breakfast.

Craven looked up, much brighter now. 'Looks like we're in the home stretch, eh?' he said.

Nan, silent, fingered her cup.

'Seems so.' Robbie sat down.

'What's the plan?'

'Depends on Majura. I call him at noon.'

'I meant about getting back to Ireland.'

Robbie glanced at him, amused. 'Anxious, are you?'

'Well, there are flights and things to arrange.'

Robbie shook his head. 'No flights, Tom. We go on the ship with the cargo.'

Craven's eyes widened in surprise.

Nan said suddenly: 'What about me? Do I get to go with you too?'

He wasn't expecting that. But now he smiled. 'If you like. You've earned your place.'

She looked at him, hesitating. 'There's something I need to talk to you about.' She glanced at Tom. 'Alone, if you don't mind, Tom.'

Craven shrugged and rose. They both watched him leave.

Nan said: 'Robbie, I'll have to tell my mother about what happened to Dad. I couldn't leave without seeing her first.'

He stared at her. Then he shook his head slowly. 'Nan, I'm sorry. But I can't let you do that. There's too much at stake now.'

'For God's sake,' she said. 'My father is dead. I have to let her know what's happened. And where he is.'

Damn, he thought.

'Look,' he said. 'I know this sounds terrible. But could you just phone? I mean, if it were quick and made from somewhere other than here, that would be fine. What do you think?'

She stared at him, an ugly glint in her eyes. 'You bastard,' she said. 'You're doing this deliberately.'

'Hold on there,' he said.

'You know there's no risk. You just want to spite me.'

'Oh, for God's sake,' he said, his voice filled with irritation. 'Don't talk rubbish.'

'What's wrong with you?' There were tears of outrage in her eyes now. 'Can't you understand how a family feels about something like this? Haven't you parents of your own? Or have you lost your feelings altogether?'

'Listen,' he said, his voice hard. 'You can phone her. Or you can stay behind. But you can't go to see her. And that's final.'

'You swine!' she said.

Suddenly, he no longer cared. About her or anything else. All that mattered now was to get the job done.

'Take your choice,' he said.

Immediately after, he went out to call Majura. On his return, he went down to see Renata. The mob boss looked up from the football game he was watching and smiled amiably. Nothing like light at the end of the tunnel to change a man's mood.

'I talked to Willie,' Robbie said. 'He's certainly on the ball. He wants me over at Motby tonight.'

'Good.' Renata did not seem surprised.

'Apparently the stuff was there all along. If Monahan had held out, Genta would have delivered.' He paused.

294

'The poor bugger was too hasty. That's what got him killed.'

Renata was silent for a moment. 'You think by any chance that Willie knew about this?'

Robbie looked at him. 'Don't create problems for yourself, Frank. Wherever Willie stood before, he's on your side now.'

Renata shrugged. 'Maybe you're right. Still, I'd like to know. You heard me ask him to round up the guys who were in on this with Genta?'

Robbie nodded.

'Do me a favour. Ask him what's happened on that.'

Robbie stared at him. 'You're thinking if they're likely to implicate him that he'll hide them rather than bring them to you?'

'Nice try, but no cigar,' Renata said. 'Willie wouldn't hide them. If they're likely to finger him, he'd clip them.'

'Nice family you have there,' Robbie said.

'Look, just ask him, all right?'

The warehouse, lit by a long line of fluorescent lights, felt chilly as Robbie and Willie Majura entered through the big entrance doors. The smell of the river flowed in behind them.

'Down the end there,' Willie said, pointing. His voice echoed hollowly among the piled packing cases. 'It's all ready.'

The arrangements with the Honduras liaison man to purloin part of their cargo had followed the standard mob pattern. 'We put ten grand in his hand and a foot on his neck,' Majura said. 'He made the right decision.'

'How do we move it out?' Robbie asked now.

'By barge.' Willie grinned. 'Hope you're a good sailor.'

As they stood, watching the loading, Robbie suddenly remembered Renata's request.

'Those guys in Genta's group, Willie,' he said. 'Renata wants to know what's been happening with them. He told me to ask you.'

Majura looked a little unhappy.

'We got the money back, no problem,' he said, 'but that other thing Chills wanted, bringing them together for him? Well, some of my guys were really burned about what happened.'

'Don't tell me.'

Majura nodded. 'They took things into their own hands. They clipped the bastards.'

You poor bugger, Robbie thought. But his pity was not strong enough to tempt him to intervene. He had his own problems to deal with.

Unknown to him, the most serious one was about to erupt across the river in Manhattan.

Brent Halligan had gone through most of the files on his desk. To drive off his growing tiredness, Darlene had dragged in her typing chair and was kneeling on it, massaging her Captain's reddened neck. It did not conform to regulations but since it kept him going that extra mile, it had its place.

Darlene had been regarding her lover's thinning crown with that fond resignation women retain for the laden nappy of their firstborn, when she suddenly felt the neck muscles contract like hardened steel. No longer worried about heart attacks, she realized instantly that it was the Captain's brain summoning up the blood necessary to making another earthshaking conclusion.

And it was.

Halligan held up a folder from the hotel in his bunched fist.

'That union guy Monahan who disappeared. Find me his file,' he shouted. Darlene scrambled off her chair.

When she finally pulled it out, he was waiting. She stood watching as he went through it and found the summary he was looking for. He laid it down beside the report he had already extracted.

He looked up, his eyes glowing. 'We got the connection, babe. It's his goddam daughter.'

After a rapid call to Safe and Loft for personnel, he dialled a second number. As he waited for an answer, he winked at Darlene. 'Now we pull the plug and smoke them out.'

With that, celebration was inevitable. To use the local patois, Captain Halligan and his secretary had a quick diddle on the couch. The Commissioner's portrait looked down approvingly.

It was well into the night when they finally crossed the bay. None of those aboard the barge was worried about the cargo being intercepted by the authorities. These wide waters flowing down to the Statue of Liberty were, in Willie Majura's grinning phrase, the last area of collective bargaining in the world. Only the pay-offs, not the contents, created disputes here.

They crossed without incident and slid past Governor's Island into Red Hook where the fork-lifts were waiting. It was past dawn by the time the cargo was taken ashore. They loaded it into a container and drove it down to the nearby freight yard where Robbie made his final inspection.

As he examined the contents of the opened crates, he felt a growing exultation. Everything they dreamed of

297

back home was here. And especially the hard cast Stinger missiles. With these coned charges, he knew now that the movement was not just better off than before. For the first time in two decades of the campaign, they were about to change the rules of the game.

The doubts that he had felt earlier seemed stilled now. He felt nearer to his original beliefs than he had for some time.

He did not realize was that the frantic activity and planning which followed Genta's killing had only sidelined the problem. It had not eliminated it.

It was past 7 A.M. when he got back to Thirty-ninth Street. He woke Nan and called Tom Craven from the basement.

'It's all done,' he said when they assembled in the kitchen. 'The stuff is in Red Hook. It goes aboard the freighter this afternoon.'

'My God, that's fast work,' Tom Craven said.

Robbie grinned and poured a coffee. He was tired. But this time it left a pleasant glow.

'When do we leave?'

Robbie's grin broadened. 'Tonight.'

'Wow.'

Robbie took a deep draught of the hot coffee. 'The sooner we get out of here, the better for everybody.'

'How long will the trip take?'

'Four days.'

'That's really pushing it. Are you sure you'll have time to arrange things on the other side?'

'I talked to them this morning. On my way here. It's all set up. We're set to rendezvous off the Donegal coast. A trawler will take us into Gweedore.'

'What about Renata? Do we let him go now?' Tom asked.

Robbie shook his head. 'He doesn't know it yet. But he's coming with us. I'm not taking any chances with a loose cannon back here in New York.'

Craven shook his head. 'He's going to be mad as hell when he hears that.'

'Too bad.' Robbie shrugged. 'Now, listen. I have to get back there to supervise the loading later this morning. But I expect to return around two. I want you two to be ready then for a clean-up operation here. We remove everything from this place. Including garbage and finger prints. But especially prints. After that, we're on our way.'

Tom Craven stood up. 'How soon before you leave?'

'Just as soon as I shower. Why?'

'Chills has been asking for cigarettes. I need to use the truck.' He grinned. 'With what you have in mind, I better get him a carton.'

'Make it fast,' Robbie said.

'Robbie,' Nan said as Tom left.

'What is it, Nan?' he said impatiently.

She hesitated. He noticed now she was pale.

'What's wrong?' he asked more gently.

'My mother.' There was no fight in her, only worry. 'I can't get through to her. The phone seems to be dead.' She looked at him, her face concerned. 'I'm afraid something might have happened to her.'

He bit his lip.

'Robbie, please.' She was pleading. 'Let me go see her.'

He stared at her for a long time, then slowly shook his head.

'I can't tell you how sorry I am to say this, Nan. But I can't let you go.'

Chapter Twenty-six

'Tom?'

Craven looked up. Nan stood in the basement door. 'Can I see you a moment?'

'Sure.'

Renata watched them go outside and shook his head. In the hall, Nan leaned against the banisters. Her face looked drawn. 'Robbie is late,' she said.

Craven glanced at his watch. 'So he is.'

She hesitated, plucking vaguely at her skirt, avoiding his eyes.

'What's the matter, Nan?'

'It's my mother,' she said. 'I've been trying to contact her. But her phone seems to be out. I'm worried something might have happened to her.' She paused. 'She's only about forty minutes away on Fairmount. I'm wondering if I could make a quick trip out there. To check on her.' She looked at him. 'What do you think?'

'Well, I'm not the one to ask,' he said. 'It's Robbie that counts.'

'Tom, she's not well. And since Dad's disappearance she's been very depressed. Now, with his death, it's going to get much worse.'

'I'm sorry,' he said, puzzled. 'Something's happened to your father?'

She nodded.

'I didn't tell you this before, Tom. Robbie asked me not to. Michael Monahan was my father.'

He stared at her, shocked.

300

'So far, Mom only knows that he's disappeared,' she went on. 'But Genta confessed to Robbie that they killed him. I have to tell her, Tom.'

'You've talked to Robbie?'

'Yes. But we had a fight. He hasn't been very understanding since.'

He stared at her intently.

'Was it because of your father that you got involved in this?'

She flushed, then nodded. 'I know I misled you,' she said. 'I'm sorry.'

He shook his head. 'Listen, you asked for advice,' he said. 'Now, I'll give it to you. Go home to your mother. And stay there. You've done enough, Nan. Don't get involved any further. This is not your battle.'

She looked at him, then she shook her head firmly. 'My father died trying to get those arms to Ireland,' she said. 'I'm going to see it through.'

He reached and took her hand. 'Nan, Nan,' he said. 'If anything goes wrong, you could go to jail for years. Or even get killed. Don't do it.'

'I have to, Tom.'

Slowly, he let go of her hand.

'All right,' he said. 'Do what you have to do. But you better hurry. If you make it back in time, I won't bother telling Robbie.'

She leaned forward quickly and kissed him on the cheek. 'Thank you, Tom.'

He watched her silently as she ran up the stairs. Then he shook his head and went back to rejoin Renata.

Down at Red Hook, the sky was overcast, with a cool wind sweeping up from the ocean. Across the channel, the clustered office towers of Manhattan stood out sharply in the clear air.

Willie Majura was watching the longshoremen levering the doors closed on the big blue container. He turned to Robbie Driscoll who stood with gloved hands resting on the fence.

'Well, that's it,' he said.

Finally, Robbie thought, watching the men finish locking up. They were running well behind. The delay had been caused by Majura's insistence on using a picked crew of his own men to handle the job. Although he grudged the time lost, Robbie found himself admiring the capo's caution.

'You've done a good job, Willie.' He straightened.

Majura smiled. 'Went well, didn't it?' He gestured towards the tramp steamer tied up at the pier in the distance. 'By dark you'll have it aboard and be at sea.' He glanced at the sky. 'Although it looks like it might be soupy out there.'

'The soupier the better,' Robbie said.

They walked to the panel truck and stopped by the door.

'You'll tell Frank?' Majura asked.

Robbie nodded. 'He's going to be pleased,' he said.

Two men from the work crew passed, nodding to Majura. Robbie had counted eleven men handling the one container. With that overmanning, he was beginning to understand now why mobsters made popular union officials.

'What time will you get back here?' Majura asked.

Robbie looked at his watch. It was almost half past two.

'Say around four.'

'The boss coming too?'

Robbie nodded.

Majura looked at him shrewdly. 'I don't know what's been going on between Chills and you. And it's none of my business. But if you want some advice, I'd clear out for good when you finish here.'

Robbie thought that Majura would have benefited from his own advice. But outwardly he smiled. 'I've no plans to return. Thanks all the same.'

Majura held the door as he got into the truck and then pushed it closed.

'You've been a good partner,' he said. 'Here's to smooth sailing for the rest of the way.'

To Robbie Driscoll, as he started the engine to drive back to Queens, that looked like a fairly apt description of how things were unfolding.

Jimmy Sullivan was eating a pastrami off his knee in the rear of the surveillance truck when he saw her.

'Dick! Looks like the pigeon has arrived.'

The man lying on the cot across from him opened his eyes and peered up sleepily. Although the afternoon was bright outside, the interior of the panel truck was dusk-like and gloomy.

'Come on. Get your ass over here. She's going up the drive.'

Dick Gallagher came off the cot. They both watched Nan Monahan walk up the drive to her mother's house.

'Sure it's her?'

'She fits the description.'

Nan stopped at the door, fumbling for a key. They watched her glance quickly about. Some hope. The van they were in was mirrored to appear empty.

'You're right.' Gallagher's face broke into a grin. Halligan's brainwave on disconnecting the phone line had paid off. The rush of adrenalin that came so rarely in surveillance work now hit them both.

'Love it!' Each raised a palm and smacked it off the other.

'How's she travelling?' Gallagher asked as Nan disappeared into the house.

'Hoofing it, I think. No car around. Bus stop is just around the corner.'

Gallagher grimaced.

'We better call in,' Sullivan said. Safe and Loft liked to get the good news as soon as you had it.

When Nan got back to the bus stop on Hillside Drive fifteen minutes later, Gallagher was already there. He thought she looked a little tense, eyeing him uneasily despite his unassuming get-up of baseball cap and red mackinaw. He responded with the old working man's leer. As he expected, that turned her away.

They took a 20 bus, with Sullivan trailing in the truck, down to the 179th Street subway station. By that stage Gallagher had her tagged as a mule who would hopefully lead them to the principals, whoever they might be.

'How was it?' Sullivan asked as they joined up inside the station.

'Clean so far.'

They followed her down the steel stairs to the downtown platform.

'Want to make the next call?' Gallagher asked. They stood barely twenty yards from Nan, screened by a loose group of commuters in between.

'Naw,' Sullivan said. 'Let's wait until she gets off.'

Robbie waited until the garage door closed behind him, then climbed out and let himself into the basement.

Renata looked up from the scattered cards on the bedside table.

'About time,' he said. 'How did it go?'

'Like clockwork. That Majura deserves a medal.' He noticed Tom Craven didn't look up. 'We should be away by eight,' he said.

'Good,' Renata said. He slid his pad across the table to Craven. 'That makes twenty-five grand you owe me. Not including interest.' He grinned. 'I got some advice for you, young fella. Stick to scrabble. And stay out of casinos.'

Robbie glanced around. 'Where's Nan?'

Tom Craven seemed intent now on Renata's calculations.

'She went to see her mother,' he said absently. Reluctantly, he looked up. 'Said it was urgent.'

'That a joke, Tom?'

Craven shook his head.

It was unbelievable. 'And you let her go?'

Craven shrugged and crumbled Renata's calculations. 'What could I do? She had her mind made up.'

'When did this happen?' Robbie snapped.

Craven looked at his watch. 'An hour or so ago.'

'For Christ's sake!' He felt a surge of anger now. 'How could you, Tom?'

'Take it easy,' Craven said. 'She'll be back soon.'

Robbie looked at him, struggling for control. 'Damn you, her father's connection to us is well known. If anyone links his disappearance to Salvatore Genta, they'll be waiting for her.'

Renata shook his head, sympathizing. 'That was dumb, kid.'

Craven flushed.

But Robbie was already moving to the door.

'Come on, Tom,' he snapped. 'We've got work to do. We're getting out of here.'

When the train arrived, they slipped into the car next to Nan's. They watched her through the glass door as the old coaches rumbled downtown. Gallagher stood silent, chewing gum, hanging on a strap. Sullivan sat, a favourite posture. As they approached Roosevelt station, she moved to the door.

'I'll take her,' Sullivan muttered as they got off. 'You phone.'

Gallagher nodded. They both followed until she entered the Number Seven platform, still headed downtown. Then Gallagher slipped away.

When he returned, the two of them were still there. He grinned. Even a decrepit subway system like New York's had its advantages. They stood, their backs to her until the train arrived. Then it was the same procedure as before. Four stops later, at Lowery, she rose.

She got off with hardly a glance behind. They followed as she hurried down the platform to the grubby metal stairs.

'What do you think?' Sullivan said as they crossed the dank station lobby. 'Phone or wait?'

'Let's just see where she goes.'

They emerged on the street under the viaduct. The rumble of the outgoing train echoed overhead. Nan crossed Queens Boulevard now and headed west.

'Let's stay with her,' Gallagher said. 'You take this side.' He crossed and fell in a block behind her. Sullivan kept parallel under the viaduct. She was walking quickly, still heading west. Passing a Texaco station on the corner, she turned into Thirty-ninth Street. There were only a handful of people on the street. Gallagher fell back a little.

She was about sixty yards into Thirty-ninth when he turned the corner. Sullivan, behind him, was waiting to cross Queens Boulevard. As Gallagher moved down the cracked pavement to follow, he was startled to see her stop. He quickly moved towards shelter thinking she might turn around. But she was staring ahead. He saw what had her attention.

A black panel truck, coming towards them from the intersection. As it neared, she suddenly crossed to the kerb and waved.

Whoever was driving the truck had to see her. In fact, it seemed to slow. But only for a moment. Almost immediately, the engine raced and it accelerated. Gallagher watched it coming towards him now, the driver gunning the motor. Through the window, he saw a smooth pale-skinned face and blond hair. The driver looked directly at him and then at Sullivan across the street. Oh boy, Gallagher thought, this one knows the score. It was too late for him to get the number but he thought Sullivan might. He turned quickly to see what the girl would do.

She wasn't moving. Just standing on the pavement, her arms limp by her sides, staring past him, watching the truck as it turned on to Queens Boulevard and disappeared. As he watched, she raised her hands in annoyance and turned away. She began walking on down Thirty-ninth Street. Then he saw her increase her pace. To his irritation, she suddenly broke into a run.

Damn these kids, he thought, don't they have any consideration? He hurried to follow.

* * *

'Tom?' Nan Monahan called from the top of the stairs. The eerie silence in the darkened basement deepened her alarm. 'Anybody down there?'

Getting no answer, she turned on the lights and started down. The basement door hung barely ajar with the key in the lock. She stared at it, then pushed the door wider and turned on the lights.

Except for the bed where Renata had been held prisoner and the sofa and chairs, the room was bare. Not a single sign that it had once been occupied. She stared, hardly able to comprehend what had happened.

Oh, no.

Turning, she hurried back up the stairs. The living-room was clean and neat. Just as when they first entered the house. The bedrooms had been gone over too. Closets, drawers, even the wastebaskets were empty. With a sudden shock, she realized that her clothes, even the most personal things, were gone. She slumped on the bed, suddenly unable to choke back the tears.

'Here she comes,' Gallagher said.

They watched her from the unmarked car the precinct had rushed over.

'Boy, that's one upset lady,' Sullivan said. Nan's face was pale and angry-looking now as she closed the door and hurried down the steps.

'I love them when they're like that,' Gallagher said. 'Ride the storm.'

Sullivan raised his eyes. He had heard it many times. The man was an animal when it came to talking sex.

'Look there. She's got a car,' Gallagher said. 'Wonder why she didn't use it before?'

They watched her stop by a Chevette and bend beneath to extract something. Hurrying, she got in and made a quick U-turn. They both ducked quickly as she came back past them. Sullivan started his motor. She had reached the corner by the time they fell in on her tail. They watched her turn right on to Queens Boulevard. Just as the truck had done earlier.

'I'd say she's out to run down her pals,' Sullivan said. 'Better call Halligan. If we're going to make a killing here, that man will want to be in on it.'

Chapter Twenty-seven

Once, when she was a teenager, Nan Monahan remembered fleeing along a white painted corridor from the Parker arena with a storm of booing in her ears. Recalling it still brought an ache to her stomach.

Her coach – an emotional Slav woman – had screamed at her to get to the dressing room, she had disgraced the team. And so she had. Not for the first time, she had disobeyed an order and got involved in a dispute with the refereeing staff. It had been an ugly incident, so ugly she did not want to remember the details. Still, she could not escape the awful feeling of *déjà-vu* which it brought to today's events.

For the second time in her life, Nan Monahan felt she had let her side down. It did no good to feel that she had not put the operation in danger. What mattered was how Robbie judged it. And his flight showed that he had abandoned her.

The tears welled up again in answer to her misery. More than anything, she wanted to find him now, to forget everything that went before, to tell him she was sorry. But where would she find him?

All she knew was that they were to leave from Red Hook.

Robbie pointed through the windscreen of the truck.

'Down there, Tom. By that blue container.'

Craven drove down the freight yard between the stacked containers and drew in by the one Robbie had indicated. As he switched off the engine, Robbie turned to look at Renata in the back.

'We're going to see a lot of your people here, Frank. But let's not get too excited.' He tapped the gun under his coat.

Renata said shortly: 'I got enough to think about.' The news that Majura had betrayed him was not making his day.

Through the window, they saw four men approaching. Willie Majura, his grey longcoat buttoned to the neck, was at their head.

'Look at that skinny bastard,' Renata said bitterly. 'You heard him the other night? I'd like to whack him right now.'

'Simmer down, Frank,' Robbie said. 'We've work to do. Come on, let's go.'

Before they got out, Renata touched Robbie's arm. 'Listen. That little rat ain't above pulling a double cross. So watch him for me, OK?'

Robbie nodded.

Renata shivered at his first contact with the cold but he quickly pulled himself together and stood immobile as Majura reached them. Majura offered a quick embrace. As he drew back, Renata mussed his hair, knowing he wouldn't like it.

'Everything go right?' he asked.

'Just like you ordered, Frank,' Majura said heartily. 'Done one million per cent.'

'I expect no less,' Renata said. 'From Willie Majura.' He stared at the capo, a bland smile on his face.

'Frank,' Robbie asked. 'Can we get on with this?'

'Eh?' Renata turned. 'Yeah, why not?'

'We need to get rid of the truck,' Robbie said to Majura.

The capo nodded. 'Ron,' he said. The smallest of his three men stepped forward smartly.

'There's garbage in it to be dumped too,' Robbie said. 'I'd like it done first. And separately.'

The little man looked at Majura. 'Maybe Damo could take that in his car? There's an incinerator by Forkland's.'

'Right,' Majura said. 'Do it.' The two men hurried off.

'I'd like a final look at the cargo before it goes aboard,' Robbie said.

'No problem.'

They moved to the rear of the container.

'Listen,' Majura said, 'don't be worried by this. But I'm planning to put you on board inside the container.' The doors swung back. The packed crates were piled high on either side. 'It's the customs guy on the pier-head. He's OK to let the stuff go through. But no way does he want you guys seen.' He saw Robbie's frown. 'It's the only way to do it.'

Robbie glanced at Renata.

'Closed space bother you, Frank?'

Renata stared back. 'Not if it don't bother Willie,' he said.

Majura blanched. 'Christ, Frank, I'm supposed to organize things on the outside.' But he caught Renata's cold stare. 'I guess Georgie can do that.' he ended lamely.

'How long is all this going to take?' Robbie asked.

'Ride and all, twenty minutes.'

Renata peered into the gloomy interior. 'How about the air in there?'

'No problem,' Majura said. 'There's a conditioning unit.'

They were silent.

'Well,' Robbie said finally. 'Let's do it.'

* * *

Although they had been joined by a second car from Safe and Loft and still classed the lady as a rank amateur, Sullivan and Gallagher were careful. They alternated between two and six cars back from the Chevette, taking shelter when they could – Sullivan even lay down on the back seat for a time to change the occupant appearance. In every way, they treated their quarry as if she were the most skilled anti-surveillance pro in the city.

Not surprisingly really, since the beastmaster himself, Brent Halligan, had shoe-horned in on the operation after they called him.

'How we doing, guys?' The fruity voice that could as easily spew gall boomed from the radio set.

'Fine, Captain.' Sullivan, who fancied himself as the disc jockey of the team, clicked in. 'Subject's still headed downtown on BQE. Traffic is light. We have easy sighting. Expect to maintain it without difficulty.'

'Make sure you do,' Halligan said. 'This is a biggie. A big biggie. We're pulling in some help from Plaza One. They expect to join you off the ramp. But it's your beat until then.'

Sullivan swallowed at the revelation. 'Right, Captain. We'll give it our best.'

The small convoy, led by Nan, sped onwards. By now they were overlooking Red Hook.

Robbie, Renata and Craven sat together on the packing cases as they waited for the rig to start. Majura, perched across from them, held a shimmering flashlight in his hand.

'It ain't your regular first class,' he said above the humming noise of the air conditioner. 'But it'll get us there just the same.'

Robbie tapped Renata, who was staring silently now at Majura.

'I've got something to tell you, Frank,' he said.

'Yeah?' Tom Craven leaned in to listen.

'I'm afraid we have to take you with us. On the trip.'

Renata jerked back.

'No way!'

'I can't leave you here, Frank. Not while we're still out there in the Atlantic.'

Renata's face hardened.

'Forget it,' he snapped. 'I'm not going.'

'Sorry, Frank, but you are,' Robbie said calmly.

Craven felt the muscles bunching in Renata's arm. He shifted away to prepare for the worst.

'You bastards!' Renata spat the words. 'I delivered on everything I promised. Now you want to rat on the deal.'

'It'll only be for a couple of days.' Robbie's voice was soothing but Tom Craven saw his hand slip to the opening in his jacket. Craven transferred his attention to Majura who was watching intently.

Renata stared at Robbie. 'I won't forget this.' His voice grated.

'Yes, you will,' Robbie said. 'Because you know by now that I don't do things without a reason.'

Renata glared in front of him. His eyes suddenly caught Willie Majura.

'You!' he shouted. 'You and that Sal! See what you got me into?'

Majura recoiled as if struck.

'I ought to twist your goddam neck!' He started to rise.

The gun appeared by magic in Robbie's hand.

'Hold it, Frank.' A movement caught his eye from across the aisle. 'Tom!' he shouted.

Craven was already rising. He threw himself forward

and caught Majura's wrist as his hand reached for his pocket. With a fierce jerk, he pulled the hand away. Robbie had risen too. He stood in the aisle, covering both men. Craven reached in.

'Got it.' He held up a pistol for Robbie to see.

Robbie nodded, backing down on to the packing case. Majura, shaking and white-faced, stared across at them.

'So!' Renata leered gleefully at him. His anger with Robbie seemed to have disappeared. 'Planning to finish the great Sal's work, eh?'

Majura shook his head quickly. 'I was trying to help you, Frank. I swear it. I wouldn't do nothing against you.'

'Where did I hear that before?' Renata said. He stared at his capo. 'Had it all planned, didn't you?'

'I swear to God, no!' Majura's voice was shaking. 'You got it wrong, Frank.'

Renata's eyes glinted vividly in the white face. 'You wiped out Jimmy Coppola and the others so they couldn't finger you. You wanted to see me killed.'

Majura raised his hands, thin, shaking.

'It was Sal, Frank, he forced me into this. Just at the beginning, that's all. I didn't have anything to do with it after that. I asked, but he told me to shut my face. What could I do, Frank? He would have killed me.'

Renata stared silently at his capo. He turned to Robbie. 'You really serious about taking me with you?'

'Yes.'

Renata raised a thick finger and pointed. 'Then he comes too.'

Suddenly, unaccountably, Gallagher saw Nan Monahan's car accelerate.

'Jimmy! She's taking off.'

Sullivan, resting on the back seat, sat up quickly. They

315

both stared as the small red Chevette flew along the inner lane of the expressway close to the rail. Gallagher pulled out from behind the sheltering cars in pursuit.

'Think she spotted us?'

'Can't see how with all this shit between us.'

'Look at her go. But what's she doing in there?' She was hugging the rail.

'Crazy broad.' They pushed forward. As they came within range, they saw that she was glancing out of the side window every few seconds.

'She's looking at something down below,' Sullivan said quickly. Gallagher angled the car, crossing lanes, and reached the shoulder. Raising his head, Sullivan looked down over the guardrail. Underneath was the feeder road that serviced the Red Hook district or what was left of it. There was some traffic but nothing unusual to see.

'Can't figure it,' Sullivan said, drawing back.

'It's got to be something there.'

They passed under the Red Hook exit sign. The ramp was coming up.

'It won't be long before we find out,' Gallagher said. 'She's turning off.' He lifted the mike to warn the other car.

From the moment the Red Hook shore came into sight, Nan had been searching. The devastated wasteland with its freight yards and dumpy pier buildings was spread to the left of the elevated expressway. There were some ships at anchor but there was no way of telling which was theirs. She had a clear view of the avenue which paralleled it. She had been staring down along it when she saw the tell-tale white bar on the back of the black panel truck below her and ahead.

From then on it was a race. She had closed and was

316

almost level when she was forced into the ramp and lost sight of it. There was still no way to tell now if she would catch up. As she came down off the expressway, she was searching both ways. But there was no sign.

Panic-stricken, she turned right, hoping that the truck had already passed. By now, she had dropped her conscientious checking in the rearview mirror for anyone following. Since leaving Queens she had checked every several minutes. But there had been nothing but a steady stream of changing cars behind her. Never any one there long enough to arouse suspicion. Now it seemed pointless.

Accelerating between lanes, she pushed forward. Suddenly, she saw it. About 300 yards ahead, caught in the ramp lane. It was going on to the expressway back towards Queens. Overjoyed, she fell into the narrowing traffic lane. The thought struck her that Robbie was regretting what he had done and was going back for her. Ignoring the blaring horns, she pushed through the traffic, closing the gap. They surged up the expressway ramp. Once on it, she pulled out, increasing her speed. The truck loomed larger. Any possibility of confusion was removed now when she saw the Boston plates.

She was behind it now.

A quick glance in the mirror and she pulled out to draw level with the driver's window. Bending low, she sounded the horn and waved.

Willie Majura's man, Ron, glanced down curiously.

Nan stared back in surprise.

That was the moment when the peal of the sirens split the air.

All things considered, it was the right thing to do. Captain Halligan, the man on the bridge, had listened to the story of the black truck and the lady and their encounter on

Thirty-ninth Street. A quick, warrantless search of the house back there had shown it to be empty. Now here was a rendezvous between the parties involved. To Halligan, it looked like he was getting a second chance.

'Move in,' he said briskly, then sat back with fingers crossed to await the results.

A white-faced Nan Monahan and the more experienced Ron stood with their hands on the side of the truck.

'Clean,' Sullivan said.

'Turn around,' Gallagher said. Men from the back-up car, its signal light flashing, directed traffic past.

'What the hell is all this about?' Little Ron demanded pugnaciously.

'Shut up, asshole,' Gallagher said.

'You,' Nan said suddenly. 'You were at the bus stop. Over at my mother's.'

Gallagher grinned. 'Ain't you observant?' he said mockingly.

A faint flush spread over her face, lessening the pallor.

'Don't say nothing, lady,' Ron cut in quickly. 'I don't know who the hell you are, but these guys are out to make trouble. Just keep quiet.'

Gallagher glared at him.

'Am I being arrested?' Nan asked quietly.

'We have some questions we'd like to ask you,' Gallagher said. He hadn't the faintest idea what they were.

'I want to see a lawyer,' Nan said.

'That's tellin' them,' Ron said. He winked at her.

Sullivan sighed. 'Take them downtown.'

As they climbed into the back of the unmarked car, the late afternoon sun suddenly swept across the flat Red Hook shoreline below the expressway. The rays caught a tiny sky-blue container as it lifted off Pier Eight and swung gently over on to the deck of the small freighter tied alongside.

The Setanta mission was entering its end run.

Chapter Twenty-eight

They left port just after seven. With the night hours slipping by, they lost the lights of New York and ploughed deeper into the Atlantic, fighting the swell. The shuddering of metal and the drum of water against the sides echoed inside the cabin where Robbie and Tom Craven were quartered. Behind the locked connecting door, Renata appeared to be asleep.

Robbie lay on his bunk, fully dressed, trying to divert his mind from what his stomach was telling him. His body felt clammy and his insides nauseous. Although he hadn't thrown up, it remained a threat. He remembered this had happened before, on a ferry to France. He cursed himself for not bringing Gravol.

Craven, who sat at the small table between their bunks, looked like he was enjoying the experience. He was actually chewing on something as he thumbed through a worn magazine he had found. Catching Robbie looking at him now, he raised the magazine in disgust, showing the obscure script which was also posted on notices around the ship.

'Bloody gibberish.'

The freighter was crewed by Asians. Only the skipper, a small saturnine Filipino, seemed to know English, and he was slow to use it. Still he had been amenable, quietly surrendering his quarters when Robbie outlined their needs. He was now camped out on the bridge. The accommodation he left them was cramped but adequate.

Struggling to escape from the thought of sickness,

Robbie turned to one of his major problems. Willie Majura. The New Jersey capo was distraught. Willie had been around long enough to know that when Chills Renata put the evil eye on you, the smart course was to make your will and party with what was left in your wallet. But Majura did not want to die. And he was feverishly, almost hysterically, grappling with ways to prevent it.

That worried Robbie. Willie resembled an untethered cannon, roaming loose between decks and likely to do damage if unchecked. But with only Craven and himself to watch Renata, keeping a separate eye on Majura was out. They could not even move him closer to the Mafia boss for convenience. Renata was implacable on the subject of Willie.

'He's going to kill him,' Robbie told Craven earlier after another futile attempt to gain clemency. 'The only question left is when.'

'The poor bugger.'

'I wouldn't go overboard on the compassion. Remember, he was happy to snuff out three or four lives to save his own skin.'

'When do you think Renata will do it?'

'I imagine after we've gone.'

Craven looked at him. 'What would you say to slipping him ashore with us? I know he doesn't deserve much. But at least it would give him a chance.'

'Forget it,' Robbie said, knowing how cruel that sounded but not much caring. 'Remember the radio,' he said. 'If we tried something like that, Renata could turn us all in.'

Window-dressing, Craven called the radio thing. But Robbie shrugged it off. As far as he was concerned, Willie was doomed. Just as long as he didn't cause trouble before it happened.

The grey light of dawn was filtering through the porthole when they both heard a soft tapping on the door. Craven sat up, but Robbie's feet were already on the floor, the gun out from under his pillow. Craven frowned. Robbie, unaware of the irritation his quick response had aroused, crossed quickly to unlock the door.

Willie Majura, his face ashen under the night's stubble, stood in the companionway.

His formerly elegant longcoat was creased and dirt-stained. The collar of his expensive lemon shirt was crumpled and his silk tie hung loose. His eyes, pale and watery, regarded Robbie Driscoll's pointed gun, then moved up to his face.

'We've got to talk,' he said, his voice low.

Robbie was silent.

Majura raised a hand that shook. 'Come on, give me a break. At least listen to what I got to say.'

'Tom,' Robbie said finally. 'Can you come here a minute?'

Craven rose and crossed in his stockinged feet.

Robbie handed him the gun. Quickly and expertly, he ran his hands over the still Majura. He straightened.

'What do you want to talk about?' he asked.

Majura glanced quickly over their shoulders into the cabin. 'Not here,' he said. 'On deck.'

Robbie sighed. 'All right. Let me get dressed.'

The murky water reared and slapped against the ship's hull in the grey light as they came on deck. White caps tossed on the wide sea, made restless by the freshening wind. Massive clouds towered above the horizon, suffused now with pink and silver. The air around them smelled of brine. They stopped by the rusting rail, dripping now with spray.

'Well, what is it?' Robbie asked.

Majura gripped the metal, oblivious to its icy wetness. His swaying body faced Robbie.

'We both know Chills is going to kill me.' The words spilled out. 'It's wrong, but he don't care. He's going to do it anyway.' The wind scattered his once immaculate grey hair.

Robbie said nothing.

'You're the only one who can stop it,' Majura said. The dumb, almost animal plea in his eyes was embarrassing. 'You could do it if you want.'

'Sorry, Willie, I can't.'

'I helped you.' Majura's voice rose, protesting. 'I got you what you wanted, didn't I?'

'That was your boss's doing, Willie, not yours.'

'I gave you advice. Told you to get away from him. I didn't have to do that.'

Robbie was silent.

Majura looked at him, desperate. 'Jesus, you can't let me die.' He gestured to the rising sea. 'Not here. Not like this.'

Robbie said nothing.

'Look,' Majura said. He leaned close. 'I'm going to say something here that'll get me killed for sure if Chills wasn't already going to do it, which I know he is.'

The swaying deck was affecting Robbie now. He gripped the rail. 'What is it?'

'I'm offering a deal.'

'Come on, Willie.' It was hard to imagine what a man in his situation could offer.

'I'm serious. Look.' He twisted to point towards the

coverings on the ship's holds. 'That stuff you got down there. It's all out of Motby, right?'

Robbie nodded.

'And Sal. He ran Motby.' Majura paused. 'But who stands next in line to take over?' He stared at Robbie, then tapped his chest. 'Me, that's who.'

'What are you getting at, Willie?'

'Motby. I can still run it. All the stuff you got here. I can get it for you. Again and again.'

'Not with Chills Renata around, you can't.'

Majura slapped the rail. 'That's the point. Without him, there ain't nobody can stop me running Motby. I got it all. The union, the muscle, the connections. And I'm willing to put it on the line, to set up supplies for you, if you'll help me on this one.'

Robbie stared at him.

'Kill Chills,' Majura said, 'and we could be in business like you never dreamed. That's my offer.'

Tom Craven was sitting up when Robbie returned.

'Jesus, you look like death,' he said. It was true. Robbie's stomach churned as he stripped off his coat and sought the bunk.

'What did Willie want?' Craven asked.

Robbie hesitated. 'Nothing,' he said.

'You were out there for twenty minutes.'

'So?'

'Come on, Robbie, what's going on?'

Robbie turned away, facing the bulkhead. 'Just drop it, Tom. All right?'

'Sorry I asked,' Craven snapped. Robbie felt his stomach suddenly starting to heave. The riveted metal facing him began to spin. He blinked hard, trying to stop it.

324

'Tom.'

'I'm going for breakfast,' Craven said. Robbie heard him moving to the door. Then he stopped. 'What is it?' he asked.

Robbie gripped the side of the bunk, trying to stave off his growing dizziness.

'See if the captain has some Gravol, will you?'

In New York, it was breakfast time. For Brent Halligan, it was make or break time.

'Face it, Halligan. We'll have to release them,' the district attorney said. He smiled cruelly at the forlorn figure opposite. 'Sorry, fella, but you crapped out.'

Halligan winced at the judgement. But there was no doubt about its validity.

The legal search of the house on Thirty-ninth Street had proved fruitless. The birds, whoever they were, had flown. True, the rental of the house had turned out to be fraudulent. But there was no direct link to this woman Monahan they were holding. And yes, she had been driving the car rented by a fraudulent credit card. But again, any simpleton could produce a myriad of justifications to explain that. As the DA said, they had nothing strong enough to hold her.

The driver of the panel truck faced a little more trouble, but even he knew it was not much. Brimming with honesty, he claimed he had found the vehicle abandoned – he could not remember where – and was doing his duty as a citizen by bringing it to the pound in Queens.

'Oh yeah?' the interrogator sneered.

'Word of honour,' was the calm reply.

None of the law enforcement people doubted that they were on the money. The blond-haired gizmo who rented the house had been placed at five different locations relating directly or indirectly to the Renata disappearance. The Monahan woman was tentatively placed at three of those, including the snatch itself. Even the driver of the truck, Ron, was connected to the Renata family. All this provided marvellous grounds for speculation. But it didn't make a case worth shit, as the deputy commissioner – a burly, iron-grey-haired woman – remarked when making her contribution.

She sat alongside the dispirited Halligan across the desk from the DA. She had been assigned to run interference at any suggestion of department incompetence, but even she could not deny the facts as presented. And there was no doubt they were overwhelmingly against the Captain.

Still, she felt a creeping sympathy for her associate. By way of showing it, she let a broad knee brush against his under the desk. But he showed no reaction. From the stooped shoulders and the loosening paunch, it was clear that the Captain had struck bottom.

The DA eyed the tweed-suited woman opposite. He wondered briefly if she still puffed on her big Meerschaum at meetings downtown as rumoured.

'I vote we let them go,' he said finally. He shuffled his files in the standard manner prosecutors use when closing shop. He smiled at her. 'Sarah?'

The deputy commissioner chose a compromise. She nodded affirmation to the DA. Beneath the desk she laid a horny hand on Halligan's thigh and squeezed it warmly.

It was well intended. But it failed to get a rise of any kind out of the demoralized Halligan.

The lawyer from her father's union, whom Nan Monahan had called the night before, arrived to give battle for her release. His name was Rumbuck. The union guys called him Lazy Wally because he never worked a case without sleeping on it first. But this one was so easy, he would have been embarrassed with a nap. Still he put in an effort.

'In all my days as a lawyer,' he shouted in a high, excitable voice at the prosecuting attorney when he finally came down. 'I have never seen such naked abuse of due process. A bereaved woman, forced into detention with the dregs of New York City and subjected to crude and overbearing interrogation – and for what?' His voice dropped to a sepulchral level. 'For waving hello to someone she wrongly identified as a friend on the highway.'

'Now, Mr Rumbuck . . .'

'Are we descending to the level of the Russians, Harold, is that it? Throw up gulags, put us all out of business? Is that where we're headed?'

'Come on, Rumbuck . . .'

'Spring her, mister,' Rumbuck said coldly, 'before I set the media on your tush.' He glanced at his Rolex. 'You got an hour.'

'I've been trying to tell you,' the prosecuting attorney said in exasperation. 'Your client is already on the street.'

The roller-coaster ride was over.

From the awful horror of her father's disappearance through the stomach churning events of the kidnapping; from that dazzling triumph to the bitter alienation after her failed lovemaking with Robbie; and then on to being told of her father's death and her cruel abandonment. And finally, those last terrifying hours in prison when she thought she would never see freedom again. It had been a dizzying ride. A lifetime of emotion in a few short days.

And now it was over.

Nan Monahan felt numb.

'What's on your mind?' Renata gnawed on the chicken, watching Robbie who sat silent across the table.

'Nothing.'

'Don't give me that.' Renata put the piece down. 'Something's going on in that head of yours. What is it?'

'Anything's going on, it's in here.' Robbie touched his stomach.

Renata stared, 'You've been talking to that prick Majura, haven't you?'

'Eat your meal.'

'I heard you go outside with him.'

'Frank, I'm warning you, I'm not in the mood. Keep this up and I'm going to leave.'

Renata leaned forward. 'In case you forget, we're still in this game together. You want to keep it that way, you better start telling me what's going on here.'

Robbie stood up abruptly.

'Take it easy,' Renata said, 'I didn't mean nothing. Come on, sit down.'

He stared surprised as Robbie walked out.

'What the hell is the matter with your boss?' he asked Tom Craven when he came in later. He had borrowed a greasy card deck from the captain. It was almost like old times. Except for the question.

'He's not my boss,' Craven said shortly.

'Jesus, you guys have a fight or something?'

'No.' He began to deal.

'He talked with Willie, didn't he?'

'Play cards.'

Renata picked up his hand. 'He went out with him early this morning. I heard.'

Craven grunted.

'What did he say about it?'

'Nothing.'

'They were out there for a while.'

Craven nodded, surveying his cards. 'Twenty minutes.' He caught himself and looked up sharply. 'Knock it off, Frank, and play your bloody hand, will you?'

Renata grinned. 'My, aren't we pissed off this morning?'

That evening, when Robbie came in to watch as the steward brought the evening meal, Renata was amiable. But he seemed to take a perverse pleasure now in reminding Robbie of his sickness. The pills which the captain provided had helped lessen the nausea. They had even made him drowsy. But not enough to smother the irritation he felt at this persistent needling.

Renata kept pressing on his illness, enquiring about his stomach, asking for details. As if emphasizing the difference between them, he attacked the chicken on his plate with gusto, holding each morsel up with sauce-stained fingers before downing it.

'Boy, this tastes good.' He grinned at Robbie. 'You ought to try it. This chow mein stuff, it's supposed to settle the stomach. Here, give me that soya sauce there.' He plastered it liberally over the piled food.

The noisy chewing and the constant belching proved too much. For the second time that day, Robbie walked out.

* * *

He was to blame the pills for what happened that night.

Since early childhood, he was accustomed to nightmares during sleep. Just as he was accustomed to his mind working clearly when awake. He tried to reconcile this sharp division of his life into light and shade, but he failed and eventually he grew to tolerate it. It never occurred to him that those two opposing aspects of his character might blend.

The nightmare began in an almost familiar way. He was running through grubby, overlapping streets, with thin figures in cloth caps screaming at him as he passed. Suddenly, he came up against a mass of soldiers blocking his passage. They wore visors, steel helmets, berets. Some had wavy hair. They stared at him, laughing, drumming their rifles on the concrete, preventing him from getting through. People were gathering around him. Rain began to fall in thick heavy sheets. Suddenly, the rifles were up, floating, the noses pointing. Then, without warning, they boomed. People began tumbling like skittles. Horrified, he saw hands rising from the seething mass of bodies. White scraping hands, hundreds of them, drawing towards him on raised nails. He felt an unspeakable terror as they began tearing at his trousers, moving up his legs, rocking him from side to side.

Suddenly, above the scene, a martyred, suffering face appeared. It was huge and grey and glowing with a heavenly light. He knew, without thinking, that this was a saint. The eyes swam luminously as they looked down on him, pleading but filled with compassion. They were giving him a message. There were no words but he knew what was being asked of him.

The people had begun screaming now, deafening him, forcing him to act. He rose slowly in the darkness, the real and unreal mingled, drawing the gun from beneath his pillow. His feet seemed to move above the steel floor as he glided across the cabin to Renata's door. He stopped, waiting, nòt sure of what to do next.

Tom Craven woke at the soft sounds in the darkness. Lying still, staring, he saw Robbie rise like a ghost in the darkness and then the gun in his hand. Holding his breath, he watched him move to Renata's door. Robbie stood there now, not moving, the gun raised, his fist touching the door. For a long time, nothing happened.

In a quick motion, Craven sat up. The sound seemed to startle Robbie. He turned instantly, dropping the gun to his side.

Craven leaned forward in the gloom. 'What the hell are you doing?'

The pale face peered at him. It seemed awake now, no longer dreamlike. 'I thought I heard something,' Robbie whispered. 'Must have been a false alarm. Go back to sleep.'

Craven stared at him. 'There's something going on between you and Majura, isn't there?'

But Robbie, without speaking, had moved back to his bunk. Craven, his eyes adjusting to the gloom, saw him slip the gun under the pillow. Suddenly, it hit him.

'Jesus,' he said.

Robbie lay back full length on the bunk.

'You were planning to kill him, weren't you?' Craven whispered.

'No,' Robbie said. 'I wasn't planning anything. It was just a nightmare. Go back to sleep, Tom.'

'My God!' Craven was wide awake now. He swung his legs off the bunk and sat staring across. 'Robbie, what's happening to you?'

He heard the slow intake of breath.

'I told you. It was a nightmare.'

'Robbie, this thing is destroying you,' Craven said softly. 'You've got to stop.'

'Look, just forget what happened, will you.' His voice was thick. 'I'll be all right now.'

Suddenly and unexpectedly, they both heard the distant cry. A terrible wailing scream that sounded far off but which both knew had to be on the ship.

Robbie, alert now, scrambled off the bunk. Craven followed.

They both listened again. But there was silence. Now they heard Renata moving about. He must have heard it too.

'Hey, open up.' He was banging on the door. Robbie reached across and switched on the light. The hazel eyes glittered in his pale face as he pulled the gun out from under the pillow.

'No, Robbie,' Craven said.

Robbie looked at him impatiently. 'Forget it. Unlock that damned door.'

Renata faced them in a white T-shirt and shorts. They saw he was grinning widely.

'You hear that?' He chuckled loudly. 'It means your pal Willie Majura is out of the ballgame.' He pointed at Robbie. 'You were making a deal with him, weren't you?'

Robbie shook his head.

'Don't give me that.' Renata was in high good humour. 'I don't hold it against you. It's what we do.' He grinned. 'We're the same meat. Just different gravy, that's all.'

Robbie Driscoll slowly sagged to the bunk, the gun loose in his hand.

'You're a real bastard, you know that, Renata?' Craven burst out in sudden fury.

Renata looked at him sourly and then at Robbie. 'You ain't the only smart one around here,' he said.

Robbie gazed at him, haggard. 'How did you do it?'

'Through the steward.'

They were silent.

'Listen, it's no big deal,' Renata said quickly. 'It just removes a complication. Now it's settled, we can get on with the business we came for.'

Looking at Robbie Driscoll afterwards, Tom Craven didn't know whether to be sorry or glad that they were entering the last act.

Back in New York, Captain Brent Halligan was facing a new day in a familiar posture. Recumbent on his bed of sin. The petite Darlene perched astride his substantial thighs listening to him moan. Contrary to what might have been imagined, the mottle-faced Captain was not responding to sexual passion. He was, in fact, bewailing the collapse of the Renata investigation. Darlene, charged up, felt let down. For the first time since these congressional sessions, as he called them, began two years before, she was being denied the opportunity to yield to the member for New York. Junior partner or not, she felt that wasn't right. She tried again but it was a wasted effort. The member was in recess.

'Can you believe it?' Halligan was wailing. 'They let that little bitch go.' The reddened eyes stared up at his loyal assistant. 'One more day, honeybun, and I'd have bagged them all.'

Darlene gazed down into the flushed physiognomy, seeing the tiny hairs sprouting from his nose for the first time. A tremor shook her little body. A spiritual revelation, not unlike that of St Paul astride his horse on the Damascus road, swept through her.

Her god, the centre of her universe, was becoming man. Before her very eyes.

Feeling desperately religious, she raised her head to look at the red-lit picture above the bed. The glowing image of the strong, super-confident figure stared down, the epaulettes laden with silver, the cap at just the right snappy angle. She tried to draw strength from that. But now she noticed that the ears were hairy too. A thundering filled her head.

The Captain, immersed in his own troubles, was lost to the spiritual chaos engulfing his assistant.

'That cockroach Grogan!' he fumed now. 'He's responsible for all this. I'll kill him! I'll tear him limb from limb. He's ruined me. I'm a laughing stock.' Suddenly feeling the need for comforting, he raised his fleshy arms. 'Oh, precious.'

But adroitly she slipped off him.

'I need to pee,' she said and scampered to the bathroom. He lay there, arms still extended, astonished at his abandonment.

'Sweetie pie,' he cried, broken-hearted.

Deaf to the cries of her fallen idol, the delicately made Darlene rested her little haunches against the bathroom door.

Unbelievable, she thought.

This was her first taste of hash. And already it was changing her life.

Chapter Twenty-nine

The deck of the *Grainne Mac* tilted steeply in the running sea as the skipper, Muiris Regan, brought the trawler in close. The rusting side of the cargo ship which Craven remembered as so cramped and small during their crossing now seemed to tower above them.

'Go to it!' Regan shouted through the raised windscreen as he swung the wheel. His crewman grabbed one of the dangling lines hanging over the side of the freighter and quickly secured it. The fishing boat, riding in the lee of the bigger vessel, bobbed softly on the waves. Regan wound the window closed and turned to Robbie and Tom Craven, who were crowded into the tiny wheelhouse with them. He winked. 'Hunky dory.'

Squeezing past, he opened the peeling white door. A blast of cold wind swept in. Leaning out into the spray-soaked air, Regan twisted to look up at the captain and his Asian crewmen peering down from the deck of the freighter.

'Ready when you are, lads!'

With the door shut again, the air inside quickly returned to its fuggy state. The smell of fish, diesel oil and dampness was overwhelming. Craven glanced at Robbie. The pallor of his first days at sea had returned. The skipper's face, nut-brown above the ribbed grey Aran sweater, made a striking contrast. He grinned at them now, exuding health, the moisture dripping from his curly black hair.

'We're in the home stretch,' he said.

'How long to get it all aboard?' Robbie asked. He gripped the ledge, his legs bending with the heave of the boat.

'Give it an hour.'

Tom Craven felt him groan inwardly.

A muffled mechanical rumble came from outside. They saw a crane arm appear against the ragged sky above the bigger ship.

'Here.' Regan took Craven's hand and laid it on the wheel. He pointed to the instrument panel. 'Keep it on that point, all right? I'm going to give Liam a hand.'

Through the spray-soaked window, they watched him scramble across the tackle-strewn deck.

'I don't think I can take much more of this, Tom,' Robbie said.

'Sure you can,' Craven said. He looked at the two men pulling the hatch back to expose the hold. 'The Irish Republican Navy,' he said. He turned to see Robbie was lowering his head.

'Why don't you lie down?'

Robbie shook his head.

'Couple of hours, it'll all be over,' Craven said.

'I can't wait.'

The twelve crates filled the hold of the trawler. Regan and his crewman set the clamps to seal them in.

'All done,' he said as he re-entered the wheelhouse. 'They want a last word with you lads.' He took the wheel as Robbie and Craven edged out into the open.

The wind hissed round them and spray flew as they clung to the grips on the rusting white side of the trawler's bridge. Ragged cloud raced above the line of the freighter's deck.

'Hey there!' Francis Renata's square face was silhouetted against the light.

Robbie raised a hand, his body swaying.

'Got a present for you,' Renata shouted.

A silver object gleamed in the air. There was a brief sharp thud. The sharp end of what looked like a spoon lay embedded in the deck.

Renata leaned out from the side of the ship, grinning. He waved a fist.

'Got that the first day,' he shouted. 'I could have stuck you, your friends, anytime.'

Robbie leaned forward now to hold the rusting rail. Craven saw that he was grinning back. He hardly looked sick.

'You think I didn't know?' he shouted as the wind whistled around them. 'It was inside your trousers. Behind your left hip. I knew all the time!'

Renata stared. The crewman cast off the forward line and moved to the stern. Suddenly, the mobster grinned. 'What did I tell you?' he shouted. 'A million bucks you'd make. You ever need a job, Robbie, come see me.' He waved.

The trawler's diesel revved as the last line came away. The deck shuddered as its propellers took grip. It began to heel in the rough seas as they pulled away from the shelter of the bigger ship.

Renata raised a hand in farewell. 'Give the bastards hell!' he shouted.

He stayed watching them for a few moments. Then he turned away.

Robbie moved back towards the bridge door.

'Maybe I will lie down,' he said to Tom.

* * *

The darkness descended quickly. Craven had been watching the cargo ship shrink in the distance. Suddenly the grey-flecked sea began to disappear. In its place a veil of darkness spread. The trawler's navigation lights came on. Soon, only phosphorescence from the vessel's wake was visible in the wind-blown night.

Craven pressed against the rail as the trawler heaved forwards through the blackness. With the parka hood tight around his head and the thick gloves, his body felt warm. But inside, he felt a rising gloom at the thought that it was all coming to an end.

Suddenly, he found himself thinking again of Nan. She was lucky to remain behind with all this, he thought. He wondered if he might have made it with her if he had tried things differently.

Even now, with this affair reaching its climax, he felt no sense of achievement, no sense that his involvement had been worthwhile. He did not want to think of tomorrow. Or beyond. He only knew that the life he had led before he took on this assignment was ending. All changed, changed utterly, he had been taught to chant as a schoolboy in Abbeyleix.

A terrible beauty is born.

He heard a rattling behind him and the door of the wheelhouse opened. Regan poked his head out.

'You're a divil for taking punishment,' he said. He glanced up into the windy night then back to Craven again. 'C'mon. There's a bite and a drop of tea below.'

Inside, the warm stale air quickly enveloped him. He stripped off the dripping parka.

'How long before we reach Gweedore?' he asked.

Muiris looked at him, eyes quizzical for a moment. Then he shrugged. 'Couple of hours.' He gestured to the narrow companionway. 'Down you go.'

Robbie lay on a bunk in the cabin, his face still pale and his eyes closed as if sleeping.

The crewman, a bony man with thin greying hair, sat at the bolted-down table, eating a thick sandwich with ham protruding from its sides. He seemed oblivious to the heave of the boat.

He held up the battered pot. 'Tea?'

Craven nodded and hung up the parka. He sat down, watching as the crewman poured the inky black liquid into a brown-stained mug.

'Want some bread?' the crewman asked, as he poured milk in.

'No thanks.'

The tea was hot but with a bitter taste as if salt water had got into the water tanks. Tom drank and glanced at Robbie. 'How's he been?'

'Suffering, the poor man.' The crewman raised his bulging sandwich and took another bite. 'Takes a bit of getting used to.'

Tom Craven found the complacent champ off-putting. And when he saw him reach for the cream crackers, it was too much. He drank as much of the tea as he could, then rose.

'Think I'll have a nap too.'

He stretched on the mildewed bunk opposite Robbie's. The rocking motion of the boat alternately soothed and disturbed. He drifted slowly into sleep.

He woke suddenly to a change in pitch from the engines. They were humming evenly now, with none of the high whine of earlier. The sea seemed smoother, the movement of the trawler far less violent. He glanced quickly at his watch. Ten past three. He had been out for several hours. He sat up and peered out of the porthole above the bunk. In the darkness, he suddenly saw tiny pinpoints of lights. He leaned closer to make sure. No doubt about it, they were approaching land.

Very quietly, he swung off the bunk.

'Robbie?' he whispered.

Driscoll didn't stir.

Softly, Craven drew over his boots and pulled them on. Rising, he took his parka from the rack and climbed the companionway to the wheelhouse.

Regan looked around as he came up through the door. He smiled. 'Aren't you the early bird?' He pointed ahead through the dried windscreen. 'You're just in time to catch the holy ground. There she is.'

Tom Craven looked ahead and saw the small cluster of lights glowing ahead of them.

'It's going to take another twenty minutes,' Muiris said.

Craven stared at the little port, his jacket on his arm.

'Think I'll take a look from outside.'

Muiris nodded to his jacket. 'You won't need that now. The headland's taking the brunt. It's not nearly as brisk as before.'

It was indeed warmer outside. The sea was calmer too although still a little rough. Craven glanced about and saw the dim outline of the crewman sitting by the stern hatch, smoking his pipe. Climbing down the ladder to the cluttered deck, he made his way to the bow.

From the dark outlines on either side of the trawler, he saw they were running down the centre of a wide inlet. The diesel chugged softly, the soft wash sliding off the bows. Craven reached the raised prow and stood, examining the little port of Gweedore glittering like a tiny set of jewels in the velvet darkness. Squinting hard, he made out the pier area with the faint outline of tiny warehouses.

Scattered lamps rose up the hill showing the steep rise of the village.

Craven felt inside the jacket resting on his arm, searching for the pocket. Slowly, he drew out the long plastic cylinder. He could feel the wind ruffling his hair as the trawler pushed forward in the darkness.

He began working quietly.

Suddenly, a voice spoke behind him.

'Drop it, Tom.'

Craven froze. The deck rose on the gentle swell. He could hear the hiss of spray sweeping by.

'I said drop it,' Robbie Driscoll repeated more harshly.

Slowly, Tom Craven opened his hand. The flashlight dropped to the deck and landed with a clatter on the surface. The beam skewed off at an angle as it rolled to the side. Craven turned.

Robbie Driscoll, his face ghostly pale in the darkness, stood six paces away, the gun pointed at Craven's heart.

There was a long silence.

'So you knew,' Craven said quietly.

Even in the gloom, Robbie looked ghastly.

'It was Renata,' he said. 'People like him have an instinct for spotting informers.' He paused. 'Why did you do it, Tom?'

Craven stared briefly, then shrugged. 'Because it was right,' he said. 'All those people killed. The country turned into a slaughterhouse. That's the biggest reason.'

'We're in a war, Tom.'

Despite the gun facing him, Craven was angered. 'Oh. A fucking war, is it? And what right do you have to declare war? That's for the people to decide, not you and your guttersnipe friends in some Belfast ghetto.' He stared at Robbie, contemptuous now. 'And just look at what your bloody war has done to you. Murdering and

341

kidnapping people who have nothing to do with the battle you're supposed to be fighting. I watched you. It's breaking you up, Robbie. You know what you're doing is wrong.'

But Robbie Driscoll's gun remained steady.

'You shouldn't have interfered,' he said.

Craven's frustration exploded. 'Who the hell do you think you are. Telling me I'm interfering. This is my goddam country! I've got my right to a say, too.'

Robbie said nothing. The gun began to rise.

Craven said quickly: 'You can't get away with this, Robbie. Renata was right about me. I did pass the word. But I did it before we left New York.' He gestured towards the shore. 'The Guards are waiting in Gweedore for you.' He stared at him, suddenly feeling no pleasure at the declaration. 'You're finished, Robbie. It's over.'

Robbie Driscoll gazed at him. A look of terrible sadness crossed his face.

'That's not Gweedore, Tom.'

An awful fear gripped Tom Craven's heart.

'I changed ports.'

The trawler struck a wave and a film of spray swept across them. Mist flickered in the cone of the abandoned flashlight. The gun levelled.

'Don't, Robbie.' Craven's chest was heaving.

'Why, Tom? Why did you have to tell the police?' Robbie whispered, his voice thick.

'You bloody fool!' Craven said, his voice high. 'Don't you understand? I am a policeman!'

He caught the startled face, the sudden hesitation.

In that instant, he charged.

It might have been that Robbie Driscoll was still ill. Or even tired. Or maybe there was something else. Whatever the reason, the gun did not go off.

The momentum carried Craven's larger body into him. As they collided, Driscoll's smaller frame seemed to move sideways under the impact. Craven's full force skidded off his hip and shoulder. Suddenly, with shocked astonishment, he felt himself being heaved. He scrabbled, off-balance, trying to stop himself. But it was too late. His thigh struck the low rail and in an instant he was over the side.

He fell, arms flailing, into the water.

The first sensation was shock. Freezing bolts shooting inwards from the nerve ends, blasting his heart and brain. His body contorted as he went down into the depths. The change, so sudden and so unalterable, could have been final. In those terrible moments, just by opening his mouth, he might have drowned.

But he didn't.

The months spent at Forty Foot saved him. The grey encrusted rocks there forced you to dive rather than slide into murky green water. The impact here after the first shock was almost the same. The sea off Donegal was no colder than it was in Dublin Bay.

Dimly conscious, he fought his way to the surface. By the time he broke water, he knew what he had to do. Not bothering to look, he filled his starving lungs with the dark night air and plunged down again below the surface. With powerful strokes, he swam as far away as he could get from where he had surfaced. Finally, when his lungs could endure no more, he rose again.

This time, he shot a quick look back. For a moment all was black. He trod the swelling waves, the only noise coming from the water swishing around his head. He turned, quartering the sea. Suddenly he saw the faint light receding in the darkness. His relief had barely time to register before it was replaced by anger. The bastard had left him to die.

Damn him. Damn them.

Without waiting, he struck off at right angles to the *Grainne Mac*, his eyes searching for a light, any light, that would tell him where the headland was.

Robbie Driscoll came back to the wheelhouse, his shoulders slumped, the gun loose in his hand.

The diesel engines drummed, making the timber floor shudder as he stepped inside. He put the gun on the panel ledge and wiped the mixture of sweat and spray from his face.

'How much longer?'

'Ten minutes.' Regan threw a quick glance at him. 'I don't want to tell you your business, but was that necessary?'

Robbie didn't reply.

Regan turned back to the wheel. 'I hope you know what you're doing. It's over a mile to shore from where he went in. With a seaward current, it's a safe bet he won't make it.'

Robbie lay back against the vibrating wall.

'What was he? Another fucking informer?'

Robbie didn't answer.

Silently, Regan opened the small compartment alongside the instrument panel. He drew out a flask of brandy.

'Here.' He held it out.

Robbie shook his head.

Regan shrugged, unscrewed it himself and took a swig.

'Tell you, though,' he closed the bottle and shoved it back into the compartment, 'you couldn't pick a better spot to lose a body. The current will take him down the coast. He won't turn up for weeks.'

He turned one of the knobs on the panel. The diesel quietened to a soft rumble.

'Turn back,' Robbie said suddenly. He took out the flashlight he had retrieved from the deck.

'Eh?' Regan looked at him in surprise.

'I said turn back.'

Tom Craven was breasting the swelling sea when he heard the rumble of the *Grainne Mac*'s diesels returning. He rolled over on his back, staring into the darkness.

The noise grew louder. Suddenly he made out the faintly lighted wheelhouse. The trawler was about two hundred yards away. Staying on his back, he continued to pull away as he kept it under observation. The waves broke around his head, the splash of the water mingling with the rattle of the boat. He saw a dim angle of light as someone opened the door of the wheelhouse. It disappeared again as the door closed.

He strained and thought he could see a shape above the bow of the *Grainne Mac*. He pulled away harder.

Suddenly, a thin beam of light shot across the water.

'Tom?'

His heart pumping harder than the physical effort merited, Craven's eyes remained locked on the light. Pulling away, he continued to put distance between himself and the boat.

The beam, filled with smoky mist, moved across the water away from him. Then it slowly returned.

'Tom?' The ghostly voice called again.

Craven watched the probing light come towards him, its shape distorting with the swell. He let it approach, then took a deep breath and sank silently below the surface. His cheeks bulging, with arms and legs moving in a slow ballet, he watched the light pass overhead and disappear.

He stayed down for another twenty seconds then came to the surface in a rush of spray. Bobbing in the water, he searched for the light.

It was closer to the trawler this time. He watched, more sure now that they would not find him. But the sense of triumph was blended with a new rush of anger.

They had not even been content to let him drown. They had to come back to finish him off.

Bastards.

Fuelled by resentment, he turned on his face and began the slow crawl to where he thought the shore must be.

Robbie Driscoll returned to the wheelhouse, turning off the flashlight.

'No sign?'

Driscoll shook his head. He retrieved the gun from the shelf and slipped it into his pocket.

'Let's move in.'

He sat, forcing down the bitter tea, as they entered the grey-stoned harbour. The sea-sickness had faded. But now it was replaced by another sickness that completion of his mission did nothing to assuage.

The seven years of subordinating feeling to ugly deeds was suddenly exacting a price that he never thought he would have to pay.

Accept the deaths of innocents now, the first Provisionals cried, and we'll preserve those in the next generation. Now for the first time, Robbie Driscoll was beginning to wonder if his experiences, from the death of the young Colgan boy in Glenvoy to the killing of Tom Craven, had anything to do with the next generation. Of if they were simply an illustration of how deep his slide had become in this one.

But even as he thought that, he fought against the conclusion. Sitting alone in the cabin, he told himself, because he had to, that the weapons he carried were worth the price. They had the power to allow the movement to return to direct confrontation and the original rules of the game of war. Soldier to soldier, man to man.

He wanted to believe that that was what would happen. But he feared that no cargo of metal, no matter how effective, could provide the solution. Not if the men behind the metal were the problem.

The cabin shook suddenly as the trawler jarred against the pier wall.

'Robbie!' He heard Regan call from the wheelhouse. 'We're home.'

He rose from the bunk

Seven years before he had left home to escape a nightmare and pursue a dream. Now it seemed that the dream he followed had turned to nightmare again. He had mistaken flight for freedom. The real truth was that there was no escape.

Chapter Thirty

Tom Craven heard the rush of water flooding around the distant rocks. The rush of hope that followed almost did him in. But somehow he kept going. He was long past his limit and sinking into despair when he suddenly felt the miracle brush of the rough stone against his hand. Hardly conscious, he dragged himself out of the water and sank soaked and battered on to the rocks.

He lay against the wet stone, seeking oblivion. But his body would not grant him peace. His nerves, aroused to the frantic defence by the attacking cold, set him shivering. His teeth chattered, making his lips graze off the rock beneath. Pain forced its way into his exhausted mind, making him groan.

Struggling to his knees, he beat at his clothes trying to rid them of water. His breath whistled in his lungs as the effort almost toppled him. Only the agonizing pain of blood forcing itself through his frozen limbs made him persevere. The touch of wind too, faint though it was, was piercing. To flee from its torment, he finally staggered to his feet and started forward over the rough rising ground.

He had no idea of time or how long he was moving but suddenly he struck a low stone wall in the inky darkness. It was no more than three feet high, but by then it was too much. He fell against it, tears of frustration in his eyes. In a welter of self-pity, he began to slap, over and over, against the crude stone.

Suddenly, he heard a noise nearby. He raised himself. It was a sheep. A bloody sheep.

Oh God. He began to laugh. With a fresh burst of energy, he heaved himself at the wall and fell across it and then down into what appeared to be a crude sunken lane. He lay on the damp earth for what seemed a long time, gathering strength. Then, panting from the effort, he dragged himself to his feet and stumbled forward again. The ground was soft but now he was sheltered from the wind.

Hardly daring to hope, but feeling he had a chance, he pushed on, heading in the direction of the village which he had thought was Gweedore.

Robbie Driscoll, angry and frustrated, stood inside the warehouse, watching the uncrated weapons being loaded on to the flatbed truck. The place stank mightily of offal. But that was not what upset him.

No true history of subversion can ever ignore the incompetence which plagues its practitioners. For every daring coup there has always been the massive blunder to compensate. Now, after all the effort, that inevitable blunder had appeared in the Setanta mission. Somebody down the chain had forgotten to inform the second trawler involved in the operation that there had been a change of port. It was now sitting in the real Gweedore, twenty-two miles away, with the cargo of fresh fish that was supposed to cover the weapons on their journey into Northern Ireland. It was the kind of error endemic to a movement that was inclined to do much of its planning in whatever pub happened to be convenient.

Since the phone lines in this area were not secure, a fuming Regan had to dispatch a man to Gweedore to reroute the waiting trawler. This journey, along with the return voyage by the vessel and the unloading and repacking of the fish to hide the weapons would take up another three hours. Instead of leaving for the border at 4 A.M., they would be abroad in early light. The only consolation was that the kindly customs officer who took a delivery of personal fish and turned a blind eye as a result would be on duty until 8 A.M.

Standing in the warehouse, Robbie felt a sudden fury at a system that let so much effort balance finally on the shoulders of someone who was clearly not fit to shovel manure.

Regan approached.

'Well?'

'We'll just have to throw a tarpaulin over the stuff and leave it for the present. I'll have two of the lads stay to keep an eye on things.' He glanced at Robbie. 'No point in you hanging on here. Come on up to the house and we'll give you a fry. It'll warm you up.'

But Robbie shook his head. 'I'll wait.'

Regan watched him for a moment, then finally shrugged. 'I'll make sure you get something hot.' He turned to leave, then stopped. 'And don't worry about that Andy Ryan fella making a balls-up of this. I'll knock his head off when they bring him in.'

Fat lot of good that will do, Robbie thought. But he said nothing. What was the point? There was no shortage of fools to take his place. He settled down to wait. And to keep his fingers crossed. As every commander including the cleverest knew, no matter what ingenuity went into an operation and no matter how hard you worked for success, it always came down to a little bit of luck in the end.

* * *

Now, it was Tom Craven's turn to get lucky.

The high ground he was crossing again was exposing him to fresh winds. His sodden clothes were pulling down his body temperature. With increasingly unsteady gait and spreading lassitude, he realized he was losing the battle.

But then he stumbled around a corner in the lane and came face to face with a miracle. That was the only word for it. Because the figure he had muttered a prayer to earlier stood before him in a rosy aureate light.

It was the Virgin Mary.

True, she was not life-size. Or even flesh and blood. And the heavenly light came from electricity. But there she was, a small plaster statue in the window of a thatched cottage facing him across an earthen yard.

He stood, momentarily confirmed in a faith that twenty-four years of diligent dunning by the Catholic Church had failed to infuse. He stared, his body shuddering but his eyes aglow. Vaguely, he tried to cross himself. Then he headed for the door. He almost tripped on the paving stone, but recovered in time to rap on the heavy wood.

He waited in the growing silence. Suddenly, with overwhelming relief, he heard a voice within. He wanted to bang again. But his strength had ebbed and he had to lean against the door for support. A fresh fit of shivering overtook him.

The latch lifted and the door opened, but only by inches. A middle-aged man with a bald head and sunken jaws peered out. He wore a shirt and pyjama bottoms.

'Holy Jesus,' he said.

'What is it, Marny?' a woman's voice said behind him.

The man didn't answer. He stared at Tom.

'I was in the sea.' Tom began to sag. 'The sea . . . swam ashore.' His legs gave way and he fell against the

351

door. It gave under his weight pushing the man backwards. Craven sank to the stone floor at his feet.

'God Almighty.' The stout middle-aged woman in a flannel nightgown who stood inside stared in fright.

The man said: 'Came from the sea, Maura. That's what he said.'

'He's soaking wet.' Tiny rivulets seeped out on to the stone from under Craven's body. She came forward.

'He swam in,' the man said.

The woman suddenly seemed to assert herself. 'Well, are you paralysed? Get him in.'

Gingerly, they raised Craven. The woman slipped his arm over her shoulders, ignoring the wetness that stained her nightdress. 'Help me get him to the couch.' Together they managed to get Craven on the sofa facing the fireplace.

'Better get the fire going,' she said, as she began pulling up Craven's jersey. 'And while you're at it, bring me a few towels.'

Marny raised his eyes, but he was quick. Tossing her the towels he bent to get the fire going as she removed Craven's shirt. She slipped a towel behind his back and knelt beside him.

Cautiously, she touched his chest and felt his coldness again.

'Good God,' she said. 'He's freezing.' Taking the towel, she began to rub him down. At first, Craven barely felt the friction. Then, as the blood began to course through the numbed flesh, his lips contorted in agony. He groaned.

She stopped.

'No. Go on,' he whispered.

Her face reddened as she rubbed and, for the first time, he could smell her milky warmth. He tried to smile.

Encouraged, she worked harder. This time he stifled his groans.

Marny went outside to get more firewood.

She looked down at his wet trousers. 'You'll catch your end if you leave them on.'

'Take them off,' he said.

Nervously, she undressed him, quickly covering him with a towel.

'You'll be right as rain in no time,' she said brightly now, as she continued to dry him.

'Maura's the name, is it?' He touched her hand.

'Yes.'

'Thanks, Maura.'

She flushed. 'No more than a Christian could do,' she said.

Marny entered with an arm full of firewood.

'You're the lucky man it's mild out there. You could just as easy have been whipped away.' He dropped the wood by the fireplace.

'Hurry up and make some tea before the man freezes.' She looked at Craven and smiled.

'Stop fussing, woman, I'm about to,' Marny said. He winked at Craven. 'She's more like a bloody tyrant than a sister.'

The exchange and the warmth of the house were all contributing to reviving him. After the drying ended, he began pulling himself up on the couch. The woman quickly went to help. He felt the warm ample breast press against his shoulder as she raised him.

She glanced across at Marny as she stood up. 'We'll need some dry clothes, Marny.'

'Mother of God, does she ever give up?' Again, though, he grinned and went to an inner room.

'He's not a bad fella really,' she said, smiling. 'Just likes to hear himself talk. Here, let me see to that tea.'

Craven found himself snug, almost sleepy, as he took the steaming mug. The shivering had faded.

'Here we are.' Marny returned with a rough bundle of clothes. 'I'm not sure if they'll fill the bill but at least they'll keep you decent.' He grinned, noticing Craven's recovery. 'You must be as fit as a flea to come round like that.'

'Stop bothering the chap,' Maura said impatiently. She watched Tom Craven drink his tea.

After he finished and while Maura modestly averted her eyes, he dressed in Marny's clothes. Afterwards, he took a second cup. With the fire glowing in the grate, the cosiness was spreading to encompass him. His lids drooped.

'Look at him,' Marny said. 'He'll be fast asleep before we get the story out of him.'

'There'll be no story until he's ready,' Maura said. 'Whenever that might be.' Gently, she eased the cup away from him.

'Well, you won't find me waiting,' Marny said. He looked at Tom. 'I've to be away to the grounds by six. And half the night's gone already.'

'Well, go on then. Go back to bed,' Maura said.

He rose reluctantly. Even before he had left Tom had slipped into a doze.

He woke with a start. The kitchen was quiet. As his eyes focused, he saw the woman in the rocking chair, watching him. She sat up, reddening, when she saw him stare.

'Awake are you?'

He smiled.

'The sleep did you good.'

'What time is it?'

'Half past four.'

He struggled upright.

'Maura, I have to get to a police station,' he said.

She looked at him, a protest on her lips.

'It's important,' he said.

'But you're in no state.'

'I must.'

'Could you not wait a while?' She leaned forward. 'Just an hour or two? I'm sure it would do you a lot of good.'

'I can't.' Stiffly, he got off the sofa. 'It's too important.'

Robbie was resting on the old car seat in the darkened corner of the warehouse when Muiris appeared. He was carrying a flask and a thick brown bag.

'I hope you like brawn.' He handed over the bag.

Robbie took it gratefully.

'Conor is back from Gweedore,' Regan said, watching him unfold the wrapping from the sandwich. 'They put out to sea immediately.'

'How long before they get here?'

'Well, it's a decent boat.' Muiris looked at his watch. 'Another hour and a half, I'd say.' He unscrewed the flask. As Robbie bit into the sandwich, he poured coffee into the plastic cup. He smiled and passed it over. 'I suppose you're used to this after your trip.'

Robbie balanced the sandwich on his knee and drank. It had a hot milky taste. 'What about the roads? Are there patrols?'

'Very few. The army works mostly to the north. And we've only a one-man police station here. Flanagan, the fella who runs it, tends to keep his head down. The Special Branch fellas pop in occasionally. But it's rare. Ask me, I'd say we're fairly safe.'

'Two hours then and we're on our way?'

Regan nodded. 'I'd think that would be about right.'

Tom Craven looked down at the ill-fitting trousers of Marny. A gap had opened between them and the loose brown sweater.

'How do I look?'

She giggled. 'We have scarecrows that look better.' She handed him the thick yellow waterproof jacket. 'At least this will keep you respectable.'

He struggled into it and grinned as he smoothed the hard surface. 'I feel like one of those old tobacco ads.'

She regarded his brightened face. 'Marny had it right without a doubt,' she said. 'You must be fit as a flea to come back like this.'

'But not without you,' he said quickly. 'What would I have done if you hadn't taken me in hand?'

'Go on with you.' She drew the nightgown across her chest and folded her arms. 'You're the man that did it.'

'Maura, I can't thank you enough. You were marvellous.'

'Ah, stop it.' She was enjoying the play. 'I was glad to help.'

They were silent for a moment.

'Well,' he said finally, 'I'd better be on my way.'

'Anything before you go? Another drop of tea, maybe?'

'No,' he said, 'I must go.'

She followed him to the door. He stopped and pointed to the window.

'It was the statue that brought me,' he said.

'I'm glad,' she said. But suddenly she was looking at him and not at the statue.

He opened the door. A faint draught blew in from the darkness outside. As she held the door, he stepped out on to the paving stone. He felt the cold through his still wet sneakers.

'Will you be coming back this way at all?' she asked suddenly. 'You still have to tell me your story, you know.'

'I can't say for sure,' he said. 'But I'll try.'

He looked at her, the stout body framed in the light from the kitchen.

'You're a sweetheart, Maura.' He paused. 'Thanks for everything.'

She let go of the door and came forward. He felt her arms encircle him in a quick hug.

'Maybe you'll try to come back,' she said.

Chapter Thirty-one

The first grey streaks of dawn crossed the sky and a light wind rippled the water as they gathered on the quayside. They could see the trawler from Gweedore passing the headland. They expected it to reach port shortly.

Robbie Driscoll stood apart from the men who would do the unloading. He gazed out at the grey water washing against the stone piers. His face, long since pale, now seemed aged.

In the hours of waiting, the image of Tom Craven vanishing in the wash of the *Grainne Mac* had recurred like a steady pulse beat. In his exhausted state, Robbie Driscoll was beginning to link the loss of Craven with a disintegration in his own spirit.

Along with the death of the child in Glenvoy and the killing of Salvatore Genta, the throwing of Craven overboard was overwhelming him. The belief was hardening that he had travelled far beyond the line behind which he had originally chosen to fight. The question most disturbing him now was not whether he could get back again. It was if he wanted to.

'She's signalling.'

Driscoll came out of his reverie and looked down the inlet to where the raised arm of one of the men was pointing. In the faint grey misted light, he saw the men moving on the trawler's bridge.

Regan, grinning, came towards him. 'Thirty minutes from now and it'll all be done.'

Robbie nodded, his eyes scanning the drifting grey sea

water whose detail was growing in the morning light. He felt anguish again as he thought of Tom Craven, drifting out there somewhere beneath the waves.

One simple movement might have at least spared him that pain. For if he had turned around and looked up at the village behind him, he would have seen a figure in a yellow waterproof entering one of the upper streets.

Tom Craven, close to exhaustion but still very much alive, was approaching the local police station.

If he had arrived fifteen minutes earlier, the darkness would have prolonged his seeking. But as the grey light spread along the craggy lip of mountain above the village, Craven caught sight of the tall radio aerial above a whitewashed house standing in detached grounds at the end of the narrow street. Nearing it, he saw the familiar plaque of the *Garda Siochana* over the door. He had the right place. Even though it was closed now and in darkness.

He went up the path to the massive black door and rang the bell. The buzz sounded hollowly inside the station. He paused to let consciousness strike whoever was inside, then buzzed again.

Still waiting, he turned to inspect the inlet below. The station was marvellously sited for observation. The harbour and the widening sea passage spread out below him. He saw the tiny group clustered under the fading arc lights on the pier. From that distance, he could not make out much detail but it looked very much like a welcoming party. Not at all like the scattering of fishermen one might expect to find in a small harbour like this at such an hour. He felt a tremor of hope. Maybe they were still here. Just beyond the harbour, he saw a small trawler approaching the entrance, but it had no significance for him.

The door rattled. He turned as it opened.

A burly red-faced man in his early forties wearing a dressing-gown stood in the lighted doorway. He had black ruffled hair and the broken nose of a boxer. His close-set eyes looked sleepy. His face appeared displeased.

'What is it?' he growled.

'The name is Craven. Thomas Craven. 802155. I'm with Special Branch.'

'Eh?'

'I'm a member of the force,' Craven said patiently. 'Look, I need to contact the Gweedore detachment. It's urgent.'

The other was suddenly awake, but irritated. As Craven entered the stone hallway, he closed the door harder than necessary behind him. 'Don't you people ever do anything that's not urgent?'

'Pardon me,' Tom Craven said. 'Maybe I'll mention your concern to the subversives who happen to be over-running your fucking village at the moment.'

The man looked at him and then at the door, as if he expected to see a flood of subversives bursting through. It took a moment for his natural scepticism to reassert itself.

'For Christ's sake.'

Grumpily, he led the way into the day room, which had a small counter and a desk behind it. He pointed to the radio in the corner. 'There. You can use that.'

'I don't know how,' Tom said. He saw a gleam of satisfaction in the other's eye. 'You do it. There's an Inspector Edge waiting in Gweedore with a Special Patrol Group.'

They patched in quickly.

Inspector Joe Edge's deep Cork accent echoed in the empty room.

'Craven? What the hell is happening, man? What are you doing in Innishlae?'

'They've changed ports, sir. They got on to me.' He glimpsed the local man straightening his dressing-gown as if the Inspector had him under observation and might suddenly question his dress.

'Are you all right, lad?'

'Yes, sir. But you better get over in a hurry. I think they're still here.'

He heard a quick conference at the other end.

'Tom?'

'Sir?'

'It's going to take forty-five minutes to reach you. You're at the station, are you?'

'Yes, Inspector.'

'Good. You'll have fine observation from there.' He paused. 'Are you armed?'

Craven looked at the local man who shook his head.

'No, sir.'

'Well, keep the door locked and your head down. Don't even think of tackling these bastards. We'll be along presently.'

As Craven switched off, the other man held out a hand sheepishly. 'Tim Flanagan. Sorry for snapping at you.'

'There's an arms shipment coming in,' Craven said. 'Down in the harbour. Can we watch it?'

Flanagan nodded.

'From the bedroom.' He led the way out into the hall. As Craven waited, he locked the front door. On the stairs, he paused. 'I'll have to rouse the wife,' he said apologetically.

'Go ahead. I'll wait. Do you have binoculars?'

'Yes. I keep them upstairs.'

Craven waited on the stairs, resting against the banisters. After a few moments and a *sotto voce* discussion from behind the opened bedroom door, a woman came out on the landing. She was short and thickset, her hair piled in an unwieldy mess around her pale face. She nodded quickly to Craven and hurried into a back room.

'Come ahead,' Flanagan said from the bedroom door.

He was pulling the bedclothes across the bed as Craven entered the large airy room. Craven could see it was not his forte and thoughtfully averted his eyes.

Between them, they manhandled a sofa to the window. Flanagan produced the Zeiss binoculars.

'Have you had much subversive activity in the area?'

'No,' Flanagan said, 'but I've been smelling a rat over the way some of them have been behaving recently. Bringing in arms, are they?'

Craven had the binoculars raised. 'They've done it already.'

'The bastards.'

'See that trawler moored on the left. The *Grainne Mac*?'

Flanagan took the glasses and focused.

'Muiris Regan's boat. That's one of the crowd I've been suspicious of.' He passed the glasses back.

'Well, that's how the stuff came in. Last night . . .' Craven stopped.

Jesus.

His glasses had picked up Robbie Driscoll in the cluster at the pier.

'They're still here,' he said, excited.

'Christ.' Flanagan slapped his thigh. 'If only your lads

hurry.' The thought of a reprieve was clearly in his mind. 'We could collar them all, eh?'

Craven was staring at the gathering below. The fishing boat he had noticed earlier was edging into the pier.

'They've been waiting for that other trawler.' He read the name. '*Sea Sprite*. That a local boat?'

'No. But I can check the register. Most likely it's out of Gweedore.'

Craven lowered the glasses. 'I don't understand. Why would they wait for another boat?'

But Flanagan had no answer.

They watched as the *Sea Sprite* moored and began transferring its catch in long boxes to a flatbed truck alongside. The scene looked depressingly normal. Only the presence of Robbie Driscoll reassured Craven. He was certain that wherever Driscoll was, the weapons would not be far away.

In the brightening dawn, the truck was quickly loaded.

'It has to be something illegal,' Flanagan said as he watched. 'I've never known those bastards to work that hard for ordinary wages.'

They watched the filled truck rumble away to the nearby warehouse. Driscoll and the other men, whom Flanagan was now busy identifying, walked behind.

'They're all co-op men,' Flanagan said. 'So's the warehouse. By Jesus, I'll have their guts for garters.' It was clear he regarded the conspiracy as a personal affront.

'What time are we now?'

'Thirty-nine minutes past five.'

They sat quietly watching the grey metal warehouse as the room lightened around them. Flanagan fetched the fishing register and established that the *Sea Sprite* was from Gweedore. More for the net, he thought grimly. He had the policeman's resentment at seeing people he was

363

acquainted with committing crimes without bothering to tell him. Craven could see he was looking forward to the coming purge.

It was just past six when they were jolted to alertness. The flatbed, still loaded with fish came slowly out of the warehouse and stopped on the apron. As Craven watched, Robbie Driscoll came out of the opened doors with some of the other members of the group. They clustered together by the truck and Driscoll shook hands. Then he opened the door of the cabin and swung up on the running board.

'He's moving out.'

'Christ,' Flanagan said. 'Looks like your lads will miss them.'

Craven lowered the glasses. 'Do you have a car?'

Flanagan nodded.

'I'm going after them,' Craven said.

'Wait a minute. You don't know the area.' Flanagan eased his heavy bulk off the sofa. 'Far better for me to do it.'

'They're armed.'

'Don't worry. I'll keep well back.'

'Take a pad and some tape from the office,' Craven suggested. 'There might be a chance to stick a message up somewhere if they turn off.'

'Clever,' Flanagan said. 'Now listen. They'll either go back towards Gweedore or out by the Bunbeg road. If you watch from the back of the house you'll see which one they take. After that, we're stuck with potluck. There's a fair few unapproved roads crossing the border up here.'

'OK, but be careful. The man in charge tried to do me in last night. I don't imagine he'll be any better tempered today.'

Flanagan nodded. He did not seem alarmed as they hurried down the stairs.

'That bastard, Muiris Regan,' he said, as they reached the bottom. 'I've been looking to upset his apple-cart for a long time.' He looked back at Craven and grinned. 'You might not guess, but I'm an awful man to bear a grudge.'

They took the Bunbeg road.

Flanagan gave them several minutes before he followed. Craven watched the blue Ford Escort pass out of sight beyond the stunted trees at the bottom of the garden.

'Mister.'

He turned. Flanagan's wife stood in the kitchen door. 'Tea,' she said, offering the eternal dark bromide of the Irish countryside.

He went inside and drank it gratefully, but quickly. He did not tell her that her husband was at risk although considering the quiet confidence she clearly had in Flanagan, he wasn't sure if it would arouse much concern. Thanking her, he hurried out to the main road to await the Branch men's arrival.

Standing at the junction, he felt conspicuous in the yellow jacket. Like a bloody crossing guard, he thought. But he knew he would look even more ridiculous in Marny's ill-fitting clothes. And at least they were warm enough to protect him from the faint brush of wind now coming in off the sea.

He was standing on the edge of a wide plateau that overlooked the vast grey stretch of the Atlantic. Inland, the ground unfolded like a slightly faded carpet before it rose into a chain of steep grey hills. The sky above them was now a delicate pink, with the first glint of orange catching the edges of its patchy cloud. To the south, the road from Gweedore lay empty, a thin grey thread in the barren landscape.

He was watching it for more than ten minutes and with growing impatience when he finally saw them coming.

There were three of them, black sedans in convoy, looking like tiny beetles in the vast emptiness. As they came nearer, he saw they were moving at high speed. He began waving when he heard the roar of the engines but it took several minutes before they arrived in a squeal of brakes.

Inspector Edge rolled down the window from the passenger seat. Behind him, the other cars were packed with burly figures.

Craven pointed. 'They've taken the Bunbeg road.'

'Get in.'

The two parka-clad men in the back seat nodded as Craven squeezed in beside them. He saw the dull gleam of metal as one of them shifted the Uzi submachine-gun by his legs. The car groaned under the extra weight. In the Irish security service, vehicles always seemed dwarfed by the men who manned them.

'Get moving,' the Inspector said. They heaved back under the sudden acceleration.

The Inspector turned. A tall lean man, Joe Edge was in his early forties with thin sandy hair and a face that was slightly pockmarked but imposing. He put a clipboard to one side as he leaned back to shake hands.

'Good to have you back, Tom.'

'Thanks, sir.' Without waiting, Craven brought him up to date. Edge listened, oblivious to the heave and bump of the car as the driver tried to keep it in contact with the uneven surface.

'I hope that man Flanagan has his wits about him,'

Edge said when he finished. 'Those boys wouldn't be above putting a slug into him.'

Craven thought of the following cars and the bruisers packed into them. The opposite was true too. Not for nothing were these men called 'the heavy gang'. Above any other, the men of the Irish Republic's Special Branch were the people the IRA feared most. They were pitiless hunters, made more effective by the native psychology they shared with the hunted. In any affray, the uniforms were pulled back and these men were sent in. They were not inclined to count the bullets.

The Inspector looked at him. 'This flatbed truck. Loaded with fish boxes, eh?'

'With the arms underneath I'm guessing,' Craven said.

'I know, I know,' Edge said, 'I was thinking of something else.' He looked at the driver. 'What speed would you give them on a road like this, Larry?'

'If they don't want to pitch their load,' the driver paused, 'forty miles an hour. Forty-five max.'

The Inspector put the clipboard on his knee. 'You say they left ten minutes before we arrived?' He began to write.

'Yes,' Craven said. The Branch man beside him grinned and raised his eyes to heaven.

'And we're doing,' the Inspector continued, glancing at the speedometer, 'around seventy.'

He continued working.

'That's it,' he said, finishing. 'We should catch them within fourteen miles if they stay on this road. Now, let's see what happens if they don't. Where's the bloody map?'

He examined it.

'Ah.' There was a faint smile on his lips. 'Only four unapproved roads running across the border in this stretch. Two of them join up just before the crossing, so

367

that makes it three in all.' He pored over the map. 'I'll give you money they're headed for Enniskillen.'

'Want to pass the word, Inspector?' the driver asked.

'Give it time. Let's see how the uniform does first.'

Tom Craven leaned forward. 'I just hope they don't harm him.'

'That would be very foolish,' the Inspector said. 'These lads have a very short fuse when it comes to anyone mishandling one of their own.' He turned and grinned. 'Right, lads?'

'Right, Inspector,' They chorused.

Craven could see they liked him.

It was Robbie who spotted the car. Flanagan had been keeping well back, but the empty landscape and the bare thread of road made concealment impossible. Robbie watched for a time in the rearview mirror, then opened the window to lean out and make sure.

Muiris Regan, driving, glanced at him.

'Somebody's following us,' Robbie said as he came back in. 'Small blue car. It's about a half-mile back. Been keeping that distance for the last while.'

'Be damn,' Regan said. 'From the sound of it, it's that bastard Flanagan.'

Robbie rewound the window. 'How far to the turn-off?'

'About fifteen minutes.'

Robbie looked at his watch. 'We can't afford to stop.'

Regan said: 'Well, we can't outrun him. Not in this bucket. If it is Flanagan he knows the set-up around here.'

The truck bounced on the narrow road.

Regan glanced at the young man in the centre. 'Jimmy,' he said. 'If I let you off, would you stop him?'

The young man shifted uneasily. 'How would I do that?'

Regan leaned over and opened the glove compartment. He took out a Smith and Wesson .38. 'With this.'

He held it up and waited. 'Well, what do you say?'

The young man continued to fidget. Finally, he cleared his throat.

'All right. I'll try.'

Muiris Regan looked across at Robbie and winked.

They dropped him under the brow of the next hill. Jimmy ran back to the top, the gun awkward in his hand.

Flanagan, approaching at a steady pace, saw the young man appear out of the lonely landscape, standing framed on the hill against the growing orange sky. He had planted himself in the centre of the road. Now he raised his hand. As Flanagan slowed he caught the glint of metal held at the young man's side and knew.

For a moment he thought to accelerate and take the risk but recognizing who it was he decided against it. Young Jimmy Canavan could be a nervous customer on occasion. No telling what he might do if spooked. Groaning to himself, Flanagan slowed down and came to a halt. He wound down the window.

'Hello, Mr Flanagan,' Jimmy said.

'Don't tell me,' Flanagan said, before Jimmy could raise the gun. 'You've had a breakdown and you're looking for a hand.'

The Branch cars continued to streak across the countryside. The Inspector sat silent, tapping a finger on his knee. Finally, he turned.

'This fellow Driscoll.' He rested an elbow on the seat top. 'What's the chances of him coming quietly?'

'You'll have to catch him first,' Craven said. 'Which won't be easy.'

'None of them are,' Edge said. The very thought seemed to amuse him. 'As you'll find out, Tom, now that you're coming back into the fold. It's not because they're clever. It's because every one of them is different. If there was a more annoying crowd of so-called bloody terrorists in this world, I'd like to see them. This mob has as many MOs as there are people.'

'Driscoll is like a chess player,' Craven said, 'he picks up things without saying anything and stores them for use later. He's always thinking a couple of moves ahead.'

'Inspector.' The driver pointed up front without slowing.

They saw the little blue car in the distance, isolated in the bare landscape.

'That has to be Flanagan,' Craven said.

'Just hope he's all right,' Inspector Edge said grimly.

And indeed he was.

He was standing, grinning by the boot of his car as they roared to a stop. The Inspector rolled down the window.

'They're only five minutes ahead. And they'll be taking the Annehely road.'

'How do you know?'

Flanagan opened the boot and reached in. The frightened and bloodied face of Jimmy Canavan appeared in his fist.

'See that, lads?' the Inspector said. 'This man has the makings of a Branch man.' There was muttered approval. Edge leaned out of the window. 'Garda, I'm going to give you two men. I want you to go back in there to Innishlae and clean out the rest of those bastards.'

'Yes, sir!' Flanagan said delightedly.

'Every one, mind you.'

As the Inspector detailed two men from the last car, the grinning Flanagan leaned down and waved through the window at Craven.

Tom smiled. Some people deserved their breaks.

Edge returned to the map as they roared away to continue their pursuit. He located the turn-off to Annehely and reached for the mike.

'Now we'll call Monaghan command post. And let them call the Brits. Even so, I don't think we'll need them. We're nine to two. If we hurry, I think we might bag them on our own.' He grinned at Tom Craven. 'Clever or not, I think we can safely say that your friend has caught his balls in the mangle this time.'

Chapter Thirty-two

Muiris Regan swung the large wheel and brought the flatbed into the narrow Annehely lane. The truck's undercarriage rattled wildly on the rough surface. The lane, neglected and overgrown with wild hawthorn, ran downhill in a winding course towards the border.

Regan glanced in the mirror. 'Let's hope Jimmy did his stuff with Flanagan.'

Robbie Driscoll, silent, held on to the dashboard as the cabin rocked and swayed. Swatches of low hanging branches rushed by the window.

'A right sleeveen, that man is,' Regan said. 'Delighted to sit in Dessie Hagen's pub after hours, telling everybody about his great boxing career. Acting like one of the boys. Until there's any smell of trouble or the brass arrives, then he's out hounding the life out of everybody. He hasn't a decent bone in his body.'

Robbie shifted the gun, which was beginning to dig into his side. He glanced at his watch.

'And the hypocrisy,' Regan went on. 'It's enough to make your stomach curdle. Standing up there at the altar on a Sunday with his wife and son as if they were the Holy Family. When it's common knowledge that he's pronging Maura Gregan up on the headland.'

Robbie felt a stir of interest. 'Eh?'

'I admit he's not alone. Nearly everybody else has too,' Regan said. 'Still, he's a two-faced hypocritical son of a bitch. And that's only the half of it.'

They crossed a narrow stone bridge that looked as if it had seen other centuries.

'Five minutes,' Regan said. 'And we're done.' He glanced at Robbie and smiled. 'You won't be sorry to see the end of this one, I think.'

Robbie nodded. Still, he wasn't about to relax yet. He recalled a phrase he had heard the baseball commentator use in New York. It was apparently famous in America.

It's not over till it's over, was what he said.

Inspector Joe Edge pointed to the battered Annehely sign. 'That's it. Down you go, lad.'

The driver turned into the rough lane.

'Jasus. Look, sir.' He pointed.

A scattering of mackerel lay on the verge.

The Inspector laughed. 'If Agatha Christie put something like that in one of her stories, she'd lose her reputation.'

'She doesn't know her IRA,' a detective said.

The Inspector glanced back at Tom. 'I thought you said your man was smart?'

Tom shrugged. 'Blame his driver,' he said.

'Blame, is it? Let's hope the bugger stays as careless as he is.'

The road snaked downhill, the driver skilfully holding it on the rough pot-holed surface. The Inspector turned. 'Better load up, lads,' he said. He picked up the mike and passed the same order to the cars behind. The two detectives jammed in with Tom Craven brought up their Uzis. Craven watched silently as they loaded magazines.

The Inspector handed a pair of binoculars to Craven. 'You hold on to these, Tom. And keep out of trouble. You've had your ration of excitement for today.' He shifted to look at the others. 'As for the rest of you, remember, we're not hunting Scott medals here. I don't want any heroics.' He lifted his own Uzi. 'And no using these bloody things unless we're fired upon.'

'And if we are?' the detective beside Craven asked quickly.

Inspector Edge shrugged. 'Then blow the arses off them,' he said.

They passed through a sunken copse, the early sunlight mingling with the trees. Engines revving, they mounted the opposite hill. Rolling over the top, they suddenly emerged from the trees on to a broad slope, its long grass dappled with light and shadow.

'There they are!' the driver exclaimed. Tom Craven leaned forward, gripping the seat.

The flatbed, almost toy-like, sat in the bed of the valley at the bottom of the winding road. It faced a small stone bridge that crossed a narrow stream. Two men stood by the bonnet but they were too far away to identify.

'Look,' the Inspector said. 'The bridge is spiked. They can't get across.' He slapped his thigh triumphantly. 'We have the buggers!'

The two men by the truck heard the engines. They turned now to look up.

'That's far enough,' the Inspector snapped when he saw them. 'Pull in.'

The driver thrust a hand out of the window to warn the others. All three cars came to a stop. In a quick scramble, everyone spilled out on to the damp grass.

'Spread out!' the Inspector shouted, as he took his place in the middle. 'No bunching, mind.' Stumbling and cursing, the burly men formed a rough line across the uneven ground. The Uzis glinting dully at their hips, they began advancing down the slope.

'Craven!' the Inspector shouted. 'Get that bloody

jacket off!' Hastily, Tom Craven pulled the bright yellow coat over his head and dropped it to the ground. He felt an icy cold wind on his bared midriff. The detective beside him glanced at his shrunken outfit and grinned.

Below them, the two had taken cover behind the truck. In the silence, they could hear its engine still idling.

They closed to within 300 yards without response. Inspector Edge raised a hand. 'Hold it, lads.'

They halted in a ragged line spread across the heather-sprayed hillside, watching the Inspector expectantly.

Edge cupped his hands to his mouth. 'Driscoll! Robbie Driscoll! Can you hear me?'

The echo rolled across the valley. There was no reply from the men behind the truck.

'Driscoll!' the Inspector called again. 'Listen to me!' In the stillness, Tom Craven could hear the moan of wind in the trees above them. 'It's hopeless, man! You can't get away. So why don't you come out with your hands up?'

Behind the bonnet of the truck, Muiris Regan looked at Robbie crouched beside him.

'Seems like the bastards have us,' he said. He hesitated, his face grey with tension. 'What do we do now?'

Robbie was carefully laying out a handkerchief on the wet grass at his feet. He stopped to glance up at Regan and smiled. 'I think you should do as he says, Muiris.'

'And you?'

'I'll follow later.' He began to take out the spare ammunition clips.

Regan stared at him. 'Don't be stupid, man.'

'I just want to take a little more time,' Robbie said. He laid the clips on the handkerchief.

'There's at least ten of them,' Regan said. 'You can't take on odds like that. You'll get yourself killed.'

'I'll be all right,' Robbie said. 'Just go ahead. Before they get any closer.'

'Robbie.'

'I said go.' Driscoll's voice was sharp. 'I know what I'm doing.'

Regan half rose, his hand resting on the bonnet. 'You're bloody crazy,' he said. 'Like the rest of them. All wanting to be martyrs.'

I'm showing him up, Robbie thought, and he resents it.

He reached across and took Regan's elbow, pressuring him forward. 'Go on, Muiris.'

'Are you sure?' Regan asked after a pause.

'Yes.'

Regan grimaced. 'It's your neck,' he muttered. Rising slowly, he lifted his hands above his head. 'Good luck,' he said, and without looking back, stepped cautiously out into the open.

The Inspector glanced at Tom Craven as Regan came slowly up the hill.

'Is that him?'

Craven shook his head. 'It's the boat skipper, Regan.'

The Inspector stared down at the flatbed. 'So we have a diehard,' he said softly.

Regan approached, his hands still raised above his head. There was a nervous smile on his lips.

'What's this about?' he called as he neared.

Suddenly, he saw Tom Craven beside the Inspector.

'Oh, shite,' he said and froze.

Tom Craven grinned. 'Morning, Muiris.'

Before anybody could move, Regan turned quickly.

'Robbie,' he shouted. 'Craven is alive!'

'Get him!' the Inspector roared, as the sound rolled across the valley. Two of the detectives bounded forward.

Regan half raised his hands as one of the detectives swung his Uzi and whacked him on the head. He slumped to the ground. Grabbing his limp arms, they dragged him up the hill and dropped him, as a pointer might, at the Inspector's feet.

'Good work, lads,' the Inspector said. He turned to Tom Craven. 'What the hell did he mean there?'

Craven shook his head. 'I'm not sure.'

Suddenly, a shot cracked, the sound rippling across the hillside.

'Down!' the Inspector shouted and everybody hit the ground.

Edge scissored rapidly across to Tom Craven. There was a smudge of damp earth on his chin. He looked angry.

'What's the matter with this fellow? Is he mad or what?'

'I told you. He's no easy mark.'

'But ten to one?' The Inspector shook his head, the long grass rubbing his chin. 'The bugger is missing the full shilling, if you ask me.'

Craven stared down at the truck, isolated below them. 'Listen, can I talk to him?'

The Inspector shrugged. 'I'll be surprised if it does any good. But go ahead.'

Craven started to rise, but Edge pulled him back. 'From down here,' he said.

For several minutes, Craven called Robbie's name. But he got no answer.

'Forget it, Tom,' the Inspector said finally. He rose on his elbows.

'You lads on the end,' he shouted. 'Spread out and start moving down. We're going to take him.'

Slowly the line spread into a half circle with the outer men moving more rapidly, tightening the net. Robbie must have seen what was happening. Almost immediately, he started firing. Bursts of machine-gun fire began to intersperse with the single shots as the detectives returned the fire.

'This fellow is worse than Mad Dog McGlinchey,' the Inspector muttered as they edged slowly downwards towards the truck.

'No,' Tom Craven said. 'There has to be a reason for this.'

'Like getting himself killed?'

Maybe that too, Craven thought.

They were barely 150 yards away when Robbie made his move.

Like a ghostly wraith with his blond hair and pale face, he appeared suddenly from behind the truck and sprinted towards the bridge.

He almost died right then.

Two of the detectives had raised their guns when Tom Craven found his voice. 'No! Don't shoot!' he shouted.

Coming from where the Inspector was, the command made them hesitate. In the brief seconds that went by, Driscoll covered the last twenty yards to the bridge. Then he was skipping like a child between the spikes. In another heartstopping interval, he was over.

'Shit!' the Inspector scrambled to his feet.

Tom Craven stared, his heart pumping.

'What in God's name were you doing?' Edge turned to look at Craven. 'Don't you know that was the border?'

Tom shook his head. 'I'm sorry,' he said.

The other detectives were rising, looking oddly at him.

'We didn't have to kill him,' Craven said.

'Look at the bastard,' Edge said. 'He's thumbing his nose at us.'

While that did not quite describe it, Robbie Driscoll

had turned to face them and was indeed smiling, knowing he had sanctuary now in Northern Ireland.

Mockingly, he raised his gun and waved.

'Inspector,' Tom said quickly. 'He won't fire on me. Let me go down and talk to him.'

'Absolutely not,' Edge said. He was staring across the valley now. Slowly, he raised a hand and pointed. 'Anyway, it's too late. They must have got through to the other side from Monaghan.'

Tom Craven followed the pointed finger to the heights on the other side of the valley. A thin line of figures showed against the dawn sky. Fumbling, Craven raised his binoculars and focused.

There were at least thirty of them. Big bony men in camouflage with blackened faces. Wearing the maroon berets of the Parachute Regiment. They were moving down through the softly waving heather now, their rifles extended in front of them.

Robbie faced the river, still smiling, unaware of what was closing on him from behind.

'He doesn't have to die.' Craven lowered the binoculars. He turned to the Inspector. 'Please, sir. Let me talk to him, and try to get him across.'

The Inspector looked at him, then shrugged. 'I don't know why I'm doing this,' he said softly. 'But go on, lad, give it a try.'

Craven began running downhill, stumbling, almost falling in his haste.

'Robbie!' he shouted. 'Wait!'

Driscoll heard him and stood to watch, his chance of escape shrinking with Craven's progress.

'Don't go,' Craven shouted, pointing as he ran, 'they'll get you.'

Suddenly grasping the warning, Robbie turned to look

behind. Craven saw him freeze as he saw the paratroopers. They were coming down the hillside, almost skipping through the heather in their haste to reach him.

'Quick, Robbie! Come across!' Craven shouted. He was almost level with the truck now. 'Hurry!'

Slowly Robbie turned back towards him. The calm slow smile on his face was to remain implanted in Craven's memory. It was like no smile he had seen before or would again.

Robbie Driscoll shook his head.

'No, Robbie!' Craven skidded to a halt before the bridge.

But Driscoll was walking away now. Suddenly, he straightened, more smartly, and began a quick march towards the approaching paratroopers.

They were coming faster over the rough ground now, closing the gap. Someone shouted a command and they slowed, pointing their rifles.

Suddenly, Robbie stopped. As Craven watched, he raised the gun. The paratroopers began dropping to their knees.

'Robbie!' Craven screamed. 'Don't do it!'

But Driscoll had aimed his gun.

'Sorry, Tom!' The words floated back in the grey air.

Then he opened fire.

Through moistening eyes, Tom Craven saw the barrels of the soldiers' rifles swivel. A volley broke out along the line. Robbie seemed to stumble, then recovered and fired again. A second fusillade rang out and he fell, toppling slowly down into the heather.

Craven was in tears now. Anger was mixed with grief as he stood rigid, hating Robbie Driscoll for what he had done to him, but loving another part of him that would never return now.

He hardly felt the Inspector's hand on his arm.

'Easy, lad. It's over.'

As the paratroopers closed in on the prone body, Craven let himself be led away. They reached the truck where two of the detectives were already pulling fish boxes off the flatbed.

'Inspector,' one of them called suddenly. Joe Edge stopped and turned.

'There's nothing here, sir. No arms, nothing.' The detective shook his head, bewildered. 'Looks like the stupid bastard died for nothing.'

The Inspector was still holding Tom's arm. He released it now.

'So it was all a diversion,' he said.

Tom Craven stared silently at the half-bared flatbed, despising himself for the sudden feeling of happiness rising in him.

'You were right, Tom,' the Inspector said softly. 'That was a clever man.' He paused. 'And by his own lights, he didn't die for nothing, did he?'

'No,' Tom Craven said. 'I don't suppose he did.'

The Inspector gazed back towards Northern Ireland and shook his head. 'God knows what damage they're going to do with all that stuff he's given them now.'

At that moment, Tom Craven found he hardly cared.

Paul Raymond McGovern stood on the narrow road outside the white two-storey house in Donegal and watched the removal crew load the furniture into the van for transport to Belfast.

He hardly moved as Liam Ring left his car on the rough verge and approached. They stood, briefly silent, watching as the workers pushed pieces up the ramp.

'You heard?'

McGovern nodded. The wind sweeping down into the valley barely ruffled his short hair.

'He was wrong to go down like that,' he said suddenly. 'Particularly when he achieved his mission. He should have thrown in the towel.'

'He wasn't that kind of man.'

'So it seems.'

Across the valley, the morning sunlight played on the grey hills. A distant bird called, the haunting sound carrying faintly in the clear air.

'We should pay him some honour. He deserves respect,' McGovern said. He glanced at Ring. 'What about a good funeral?'

'I asked him about that in the past. He said no.'

'Well, there's the family then. Can we do something for them?'

'He said he had none.'

They watched the workers finish the loading and start to raise the ramp.

'It doesn't seem right,' McGovern said. 'Letting him disappear into history like this. What he's done is going to change things. We must pay some tribute.'

The engine of the truck started up.

'There's a poem,' Ring said. 'Kuno Meyer called it one of the great epitaphs of history.' He looked towards the ancient sloping hills looming above the valley.

'Where is the great Setanta,
Lord of Ulster in the field?
"All that remains" they said
"Is his shadow under the shield."'

They were both silent. Then McGovern briskly zipped up his jacket.

'Well, we have lots to do,' he said. 'There's plans to prepare, and training too, if we're to use this stuff properly.'

'You want me to see to it?'

McGovern shook his head. 'You've had far too much to do of late, Liam. I think it's time we thought of passing the baton.'

Ring frowned.

'One thing, though,' McGovern said as he took his arm. 'Wherever your friend is, he can rest easy.' He smiled grimly as they began walking. 'Thanks to him, we're going to give them what for now.'